REFUGE
FOR
MASTERMINDS

Also by Kathleen Baldwin

A School for Unusual Girls
Exile for Dreamers

REFUGE FOR MASTERMINDS

A Stranje House Novel

KATHLEEN BALDWIN

TOR TEEN

A TOM DOHERTY ASSOCIATES BOOK

New York

REFUGE FOR MASTERMINDS

Copyright © 2017 by Kathleen Baldwin

A Tor Teen Book
Published by Tom Doherty Associates
175 Fifth Avenue
New York, NY 10010

www.tor-forge.com

Tor® is a registered trademark of Macmillan Publishing Group, LLC.

The Library of Congress Cataloging-in-Publication Data is available upon request.

ISBN 978-0-7653-7604-6 (hardcover)
ISBN 978-1-4668-4929-7 (e-book)

Our books may be purchased in bulk for promotional, educational, or business use. Please contact your local bookseller or the Macmillan Corporate and Premium Sales Department at 1-800-221-7945, extension 5442, or by e-mail at MacmillanSpecialMarkets@macmillan.com.

First Edition: May 2017

Printed in the United States of America

0 9 8 7 6 5 4 3 2 1

My dearest daughter,

I often find you walking in the pages of my books. It delights me to discover your traits hidden inside my characters. Why wouldn't they be, when I admire you so much? You are my very own beloved unusual girl. Thank you for your priceless help and lasting inspiration.

Contents

CONTENTS

One

LADY JANE MOORE

The oil lamp flickers and hisses. It is late, very late. The oil will run out soon. Even though it is long past midnight, I continue working at my desk in the library, listing possibilities, drawing lines from one hypothesis to another, scratching out those lines and mapping new ones, trying to calculate which of the many options our enemy will take next. In my mind, the players line up before me like pieces on a chessboard, and it keeps coming back to this—to Lady Daneska.

Evil queen takes knight.

Checkmate.

We lose.

Except Daneska isn't a queen. She was once one of us, one of Miss Stranje's students. Now she's Napoleon's clever little troublemaker, and paramour to Ghost. Ghost is code name for the British traitor who leads the emperor's secret Order of the Iron Crown. I set down the quill and massage my forehead.

The knight is in danger.

Alexander Sinclair, nephew of the American inventor Rob-ert Fulton, has been hiding at Stranje House. He's slated to leave in three short days. Captain Grey and Lord Wyatt plan to help him sail the prototype of his steam-powered warship to London where they'll demonstrate its capabilities to the British Admi-ralty. Everything hinges on Alexander and his warship arriving unscathed in London.

They shouldn't risk that journey. Not yet, not until we have more safeguards in place, but I've been overruled. They insist there isn't time.

Why can't they see what will happen?

Lady Daneska wants that steamship for Napoleon, and she doesn't care whose throat she has to cut to get it. She proved that when she tried to steal the plans a few days ago and nearly killed Tess and Madame Cho. And if Napoleon gets that warship, England will lose this war.

She'll try to steal it. I know she will and I can predict exactly how it will play out. Their men will attack at sea, pirate the ship, and capture Mr. Sinclair, or send him and the others to graves at the bottom of the ocean.

Mr. Sinclair scoffed at my warning yesterday. "You fret too much, Lady Jane. The *Mary Isabella* is highly maneuverable." He and Georgie are exceedingly proud of their prototype of Fulton's remarkable invention. "That vessel can outrun any other ship because she can sail against the tide and winds."

Their boastful assurances are all well and good, but my mis-givings remain. "Have you forgotten we've been infiltrated?" I protested. "Stranje House has a traitor."

They shrugged off my objections. "The Iron Crown has fake

plans." Georgie tried to placate me. "That buys us the time we need."

We survived Lady Daneska's last attack and sent her away with falsified plans, so now everyone is convinced we finally have the advantage. When in truth, the temporary advantage we may have gained slips away with every deadly tick of the clock.

There must be a way to make them listen to reason.

I slump over my desk, weary and troubled, well aware there is another, less altruistic, thought vexing me. Even if, by some miracle, we succeed in getting Mr. Sinclair and Fulton's remarkable warship safely to London, Mr. Sinclair will then most likely make a hasty departure to the United States.

Of course, he will. Why shouldn't he?

What does it matter?

I sit, ramrod straight, hoping proper posture will alleviate the pinch in my neck. He is nothing to me. *Less than nothing.* To be frank, the golden-haired inventor is the most maddening young man of my acquaintance, and that's saying a great deal considering my two plague-y older brothers and their wastrel friends.

My head begins to throb abominably. I stand, slide my papers beneath the blotter, and extinguish the lamp. Mr. Sinclair is a sharp-tongued fellow with boorish manners, and he is not even an Englishman. The idea of parting with him ought to be a relief.

Ought to be—but it isn't.

The thought of his leaving twists my stomach into a Gordian knot. Some warm milk might ease it out of its misery. Yes, that is exactly the tonic I need, a calming cup of warm milk. I pad silently out of the library and head down the dark hallway toward the kitchen.

Stranje House is an odd place at night when everyone is asleep. It's as if the old Tudor manor is alive the way it creaks and the windows shudder. A young lady given to flights of imagination might feel as if the walls are leaning in as she walks through the unlit hallways. I, however, do not indulge in such far-fetched thoughts. I'm quite certain that moaning sound is nothing more than wind breathing through the secret passages.

I've no need of a candle. Even in the deep of night, I know my way around Stranje House well enough and prefer to forgo the wobbly glare of a flame. Besides, the heavy darkness suits my mood.

The last stairs leading down to the kitchen are wide stone steps with no banister. They can be a trifle thorny to navigate in the dark. Fortunately, thin gray moonlight whiskers up from the downstairs windows and I glide my hand along the wall for added guidance.

Stepping into the spacious room, I breathe deep the smell of baked rye bread and onion soup that still lingers. But something yanks my attention to the window above the baking table.

It might've been a wisp of fog, or an owl soaring by to catch a mouse in the garden, except it had seemed bigger and more human. If I were prone to fanciful ruminations, I might've thought a phantom flitted past, but my suspicions run in an entirely different direction. I rush to the window and lean up on my toes to peer out. In the distance I spot the creature, cloaked in gray, who passed by the window, and she wears a dress.

Most decidedly not a ghost.

Although she may be working for one.

Unless I miss my guess, this particular phantom is going about her duplicitous duties, reporting our plans to Ghost's cohorts. I press closer to the window hoping to see her more clearly. Rubbing the glass, I squint, straining to identify her, watching as the clever minx leads the dogs to their pen and shuts them in.

This has to be our betrayer—our traitor. The person responsible for all our slanted looks and unspoken suspicions. The sneaky girl who is ripping apart the bonds of friendship here at Stranje House. At least, when Lady Daneska betrayed us, we'd known who she was, and she didn't hide the fact that she ran off to join Napoleon's cause.

This traitor moves in secret, slowly stealing away the confidence we have in one another's loyalty. She is a disease, rotting us from the inside out. For what are we without trust? Naught but a group of misfits and outcasts. Trust is the foundation of our strength. Without it, we will surely crumble and leave the path clear for Napoleon to sail in and conquer England.

Which of us would commit such a crime?

I intend to find out.

Pulling my shawl around my shoulders, I hurry to the bench beside the kitchen door and slip on Cook's pattens, the wooden clogs she wears to go out into the muddy garden. Her mud shoes are three sizes too big but they will have to do. I leave the door unlatched so I can return easily, and sneak out to follow our poisonous little turncoat.

Last week I cut holes in the right side pockets of my dresses. I slip my hand through the opening and reach for the dagger strapped in a sheath to my hip. Ever since Tess taught me how to wield a knife in a close fight, I've kept it on my person. I breathe easier once I feel the hilt in my palm. Without a coat and bonnet, I am not properly dressed for an outdoor excursion, especially one in the middle of the night, but at least I'm suitably armed.

I keep to the shadows, as does our traitor. We skirt through the trees alongside the drive, all the way to the towering gates that guard Stranje House. She opens the ancient iron sentinels just wide enough to slip through. They creak. She pulls her hooded cloak tighter and glances over her shoulder, as if she senses she's being watched. I hold back, crouching in the undergrowth, not daring to get any closer lest the culprit see me and pretend she is simply out for a late-night stroll. The misty night hangs over us in a swirling fog, and I am too far away to make out her features.

I wait until she scurries on her little rat feet far enough down the road that she won't see me pass through the open gate behind her. Unlike Tess, I am not skilled at creeping through the woods and undergrowth. Each branch that cracks and every pile of leaves that crunches underfoot causes me to hold my breath, expecting to be discovered.

In truth, I am nothing like the other girls at Stranje House. They all have extraordinary talents and skills. Tess is a warrior who has the advantage of prophetic dreams. Sera takes notice of every detail, no matter how minuscule, and draws conclusions based on the smallest thread of evidence. Georgie is a brilliant scientist, and Maya's voice is magical, she can soothe tempers with a few, well-spoken words.

I have none of those skills.

As my brothers so delicately phrased it, I am an overly opinionated female who refuses to mind her own business. Of course, they would say that, wouldn't they? After our parents died, the two rascals spent all their time in the brothels and gaming rooms of London. They abandoned me, leaving me to manage the servants and our failing estate. By implementing new farming methods, I was able to make the estate profitable, and by investing the extra capital, I tripled our income. My brothers wanted the money to support their habits. I tried to stop them, restricting their access, and scolding them for their excesses. That's why they packed me up and hauled me off to Stranje House, to keep me out of their way. They may be scoundrels, but they are correct, I am stubborn and rarely obedient. I have absolutely no idea why Miss Stranje allows me to stay. She says it is because I am a mastermind.

Stuff and nonsense!

I'm no mastermind. A mastermind is a strategic genius. I'm nothing of the kind. Oh, I admit I am a bit managing, and I have a rather strong bent toward the practical, but only because I easily grasp the facts of a situation, much the way one does when playing chess. It's a simple thing, really, anticipating an opponent's next few moves, and it's only natural to devise and implement a sensible course of action. After all, it's my duty to protect and care for the people I love. That's all there is to it.

Nothing extraordinary.

Well, I suppose I do have a knack for organizing the players in my plans, and I like to think I do so with quiet efficiency. Occasionally, my friends tell me I'm not as subtle about organizing them as I imagine myself to be. They sometimes tease me about that. Tess, in particular, likes to needle me by saying I would've made a splendid governess. Although, when it comes to teasing, none of them holds a candle to Alexander Sinclair.

What would they have me do? Sit back and twiddle my thumbs when trouble is brewing? *Not ruddy likely.* Not when people I care about are in danger. I was born an earl's daughter. It's only natural that when difficulties arise, if no one steps up into the driver's seat, I do what must be done and take the reins in hand.

That is the very reason I'm out here in the middle of the night, slogging through mud and rotting leaves, struggling to keep from knocking Cook's clunky pattens against rocks and fallen branches in the underbrush. I may not excel at this sort of activity, but I'm certainly not going to allow this villainous creature to escape. She is threatening all of us at Stranje House—my friends, England, and even my annoying Mr. Sinclair.

Truth is, I would wade through a snake-filled bog if need be. Stranje House is my refuge, my sanctuary. I'll protect it or die trying. My no-account brothers will never know the favor they did me by bringing me here to Miss Stranje. She allows me to experiment with crop rotation and animal husbandry to my heart's content, and this is the perfect place for me to hide. As long as no one outside of our little circle learns I am here at Stranje House, there is a chance, or the hope of a chance, no one will discover my secret.

For now, though, it is Stranje House's secrets that need protecting, not mine. I tuck my shawl tighter and press forward. The traitor stops up ahead in a small clearing off to the side of the road. She looks around as if expecting to find someone lurking in the trees up ahead.

Where is that blasted moon? Why must it drift behind clouds when I so desperately need its light to see our betrayer. I hide behind a wide oak and hold my breath, hoping she won't see me peering around the edge as I try to catch a glimpse of her face. If only I could see the color of her hair, or the pattern of the dress she wears beneath her cloak, *anything* that might give me a clue as to her identity.

The sound of chirping insects and piping tree frogs fills the night. A shrill whistle cuts through the noise of the woods—a poor mimic of a hawk screech. The traitor answers with a light trill meant to sound less like a predatory bird and more like an innocent sweet songbird. Ha! There is nothing innocent or sweet about our Judas.

At the edge of the trees farthest from me, a man emerges cloaked in a brown greatcoat, wearing a dark hat pulled low over his brow. She approaches him and mumbles a greeting.

I draw my knife and clasp it tight. The weight of it in my fist makes me feel a little stronger, a little braver. I press against the tree, straining to hear. If I can catch a clear snippet of her voice I'll know who it is, but the dead leaves and the foliage seemed to swallow up the sound. "What've you learned?" He speaks low as if he fears being overheard.

Her voice is higher, much softer, making it far more difficult to hear than his. I only catch a word here and there. I think I heard her say, "Ship."

"When?" he demands. "Where?"

Her answer is impossible to distinguish. She speaks rapidly and gestures toward the coast. I cringe when he asks, "To London?"

She nods.

"Two days." He rubs his chin. "Doesn't give us much time."

It's wretchedly dark and I'm too far from the spies. A smaller tree stands directly in front of me, a narrow alder. It is an enticing two yards closer to them. I hunch low, preparing to dart forward unseen.

Someone grabs me from behind. He claps a hand over my mouth. "Don't," he whispers in my ear.

Instinct takes over. Without a second thought, I move into the training I've practiced with Tess and our defensive arts master, Madame Cho. I jab backward with my elbow and strike him squarely in his ribs. Extending my leg, I clamp hold of his arm and heave him over my shoulder. Immediately, I pounce on the villain with my knife at his throat. I blink, unable to believe my eyes.

Alexander Sinclair! It can't be.

It is him. Those are his disorderly blond curls. It's his broad chest I've pinned to the ground, his rumpled shirt and worn coat.

What in heaven's name is he doing here? My breath catches. *He must be in league with the traitor.* I never should have trusted him. Never. I let my guard down and what happens, the blighter turns out to be a common spy. I dig my elbow into his ribs.

"What are you doing?" he says under his breath, as if I am the one making a blunder.

"Me?" I press the knife closer to his treacherous throat. "What are you doing here?"

"Following you," he whispers heatedly.

I don't believe his innocent act. "You grabbed me."

"Yes, because you were about to give yourself away."

I ease up with the knife and glance over at the traitor and her accomplice. *Too late.* I groan. They've seen us.

Her accomplice curses roundly. "Fool! You've been followed." He shoves her away and takes off like a stag crashing through the underbrush. Our sneaky betrayer follows suit, except she bolts in a different direction.

It's my turn to curse, something I never do. "Dash it all! She's getting away."

I scramble up, springing after her, dodging trees and bounding over fallen logs. Behind me, I hear Alexander scramble to his feet. He quickly passes me in pursuit of the traitor.

My heart hammers like a war drum as I follow them blindly through the moonless woods, slapping branches out of the way. My foot lands in a puddle of fetid water and it sloshes across my dress. The stench makes me cringe. Saplings scrape at my face and arms, as if trying to entrap me, but I keep going. We must catch the culprit.

A crescent moon peeks out for a few silvery seconds, only long enough for me to see we are still on her heels. It disappears again behind clouds, and I feel as if I am drowning in ink. I can't see where I'm going, and can scarcely catch my breath. We turn, I've no idea in what direction we're heading now, but it is heavily wooded and a downhill slope. Cook's pattens are not made for running and it is dark, too dark. Straining to make out Alexander's broad form a few yards ahead of me, I stumble over a root and pitch head first over a rise.

The fall startles a cry out of me. I tumble downhill, snapping branches, bashing against rocks and mounds. Finally, I land with a loud crash, startling birds who squawk and fly from their slumber.

"Jane!" Alexander shouts. "Jane! Are you hurt?"

Only my pride. I've landed in a pile of wet muck and leaves. My hair is full of twigs, and judging by the stinging sensation, I've skinned both my elbows and forearms. My shawl is lost. No doubt it will make a dandy addition to some creature's lair, and this work dress will need a long soak before it will ever be wearable again.

"I'm all right," I reassure him. "Keep after her! We've got to catch her."

Too late. I can hear he has stopped running. He's tromping toward me, charging through the underbrush, breathing hard.

I sigh, guessing what he will say before he says it. "It's no good. I've lost her."

I can't help myself. I grab a handful of decaying leaves and crush them in my fist. "No. No. No!"

"Afraid so. Sounded like all hell breaking loose when you fell.

I worried you'd broken your neck." He squats beside me and brushes clumps of mud off my shoulder. "When I turned back, she'd disappeared."

I moan, not because of the bruises I am beginning to feel, but because I can't bear the thought of having lost her. *We were so close.*

"Are you planning to lie there all night, Lady Jane?"

Flippant as ever. If it weren't so dark, I would make the effort to glare at him. "This is your fault, you know. I would've had her if you hadn't interfered."

"Maybe. Maybe not." He pulls several twigs out of my tangled hair. "There's another possibility. The way I saw it, that fellow had a pistol tucked inside that great big coat of his. If there hadn't been two of us, I figure he would've pulled it out and blown your pretty little brains all over the forest floor."

Mr. Sinclair has a point, but I refuse to credit it. "Don't be ridiculous." I cough up something that must've flown in my mouth during the tumble. "My brains aren't little."

"Right." He tugs another twig out of my hair. "So, instead of blaming me for all this trouble, my lady, what do you say you put those *large* devious brains of yours to work finding another way to catch our traitor? Won't she have to pass through the gate to get back to Stranje House? We could try heading her off there. Or we could lock it so she can't come back through."

I sit up, knowing full well I am plastered in mud and debris. Not caring because, after all, it's not Beau Brummell, the dandy of Mayfair, here with me. It's Mr. Alexander Sinclair, and he is accustomed to sloppy dress. I wipe off as much grime from my person as is possible. "No, unfortunately, our weaselly little traitor can easily bypass the gate by going through hedgerows in the back pasture. Or, she could make her way down to the shoreline and come up by way of the bluffs. For that matter there are a hundred ways she can get back to Stranje House without going through the gate."

He tosses the twig away and stands, holding out his hand to help me to my feet. "Not much use then, that big iron gate."

"It stops carriages well enough." I defend my beloved Stranje House, and busily shake a clump of mud off my skirts. "Now that I think on it, there may be another way to catch her." I look up at him with excitement. "Come! We have to hurry back."

No sooner do I say this than I realize I have absolutely no notion which way to go. I glance about the pitch-black woods and scan the clouded sky, struggling to get my bearings.

"Lost, are you, my lady?" Alexander chuckles under his breath.

"Of course not," I huff, wishing desperately for some landmark by which I might set my direction. I see nothing to point the way, *nothing*, not one blessed thing. I begin hiking uphill, having decided to retrace my steps. One of Cook's clogs flew off during my tumble, so I proceed with a rather lopsided gait, doing my best to dodge pointy sticks and other hazards.

"You're certain this is the right direction?" Alexander follows close behind me, and I hear a mocking smile in his Yankee twang, rippling through his innocent question.

I will not allow him to dampen my confidence. "You may thank your lucky stars that I do. Considering I tumbled halfway down this hill, it is a wonder I've any sense of direction left at all."

"A miracle! I shall notify the church."

I ignore his sarcasm. "You may play the skeptic if you wish, but I'm certain if we retrace our steps we will come out very near the clearing in which we began. From there, it will simply be a matter of following the road back to the house."

"Not a bad plan, as plans go. Excepting, the gal we were chasing was clever as a fox. Seemed quite familiar with these woods. Did you happen to notice she didn't run in a straight line? By my reckoning, she led us a merry looping chase."

Looping? I stub the toe of my clog-less slipper against a rock. I'm hard-pressed not to yelp audibly, but I suck in the pain and limp forward as if nothing has happened. "And you noticed this how . . . ?"

"You're hurt." He grabs my shoulders and takes stock of me. "You've lost your shoe."

"Only Cook's patten. I shall make do with my slipper."

"Balderdash." He heaves out a deep breath. "I'll have to carry you."

I back away from him. "You shall do no such thing. That would be highly improper."

"Begging your pardon, my lady, but I don't see how there's any way around it. If you proceed with nothing but that flimsy excuse for a shoe, you're bound to put a thorn through your foot, or worse. That little bit of silk and felt isn't going to stop a sharp stone."

Much as I am loath to admit it, he's right. I stare down at my offending appendage, which is already soaked with muddy water. Any wound I incur will no doubt become infected. "Never mind. I will be fine."

"You're not stubborn in the least are you, Lady Jane?"

I hobble forward, ignoring his latest insult.

He follows on my heels, so close I feel his breath on my neck as he lets out an exasperated sigh. "We can do this one of two ways. I can sling you over my shoulder like a sack of potatoes, or you can ride, as my nephews like to do, piggyback style."

Piggyback! A sound rumbles in my throat, half indignant squawk, half harrumph. "Certainly not! We shall go on as we are."

"Have it your way. It will be easier to carry you over my shoulder anyway."

I whip around. He stops only a few inches from me, and I crane my neck to look up at him, giving him my most ferocious glare. "Mr. Sinclair, we will observe the proprieties. The fact that you and I are out here in the wilderness alone is disastrous enough. If anyone finds out, my reputation will be in tatters. I absolutely refuse to return to Stranje House hanging over your shoulder as if I am a common tavern wench. And may I remind you, I am not above using my knife on you if the need arises." I plant my fists on my hips and do my best to look imperious.

He says nothing to that, and well he shouldn't. I hope I am at least as intimidating as Tess would be in the same situation. Mr. Sinclair is prone to slow, lazy smiles. Moonlight catches on the twitching curve of his lips. He does not seem worried about me running him through with my blade. So I switch tactics, and the subject, hoping to distract him from carrying me. "Now if you will be so kind as to explain your theory on the traitor's circuitous route. How did you notice? More to the point, do you think you know the fastest way back to the road?"

His smirk vanishes and he stares down at me steadily, unnerving me enough that I drop my arms and take a step backward.

"Haven't done much hunting at night, have you, Lady Jane?"

"What has that to do with anything?" I frown. "Do I look the sort of young lady who hunts at night?"

He laughs. "At the moment I wouldn't take a wager on it one way or the other. You're full of surprises. I wouldn't have thought you capable of cutting my throat either, and yet a few minutes ago you seemed ready to do exactly that."

"I didn't know it was you," I mumble. "Not until after . . ."

"Yet here you are threatening me again."

"Mr. Sinclair, am I to gather from this roundaboutation that you cannot actually guide us back to the house? Is all your talk about looping routes and shortest distances merely bragging on your part?"

"I don't brag." He glances up at the clouded sky, as if re-orienting himself. "Provided you don't stand here jawing me dead too much longer, and those clouds don't change shape any faster than they are now, then yes, I will be happy to show you the quickest path home, my lady. Unless, of course, you prefer to take the long way? I know how much you enjoy my company, and I wouldn't want to deprive you, but it seems to me we've a fairly serious matter to attend to this evening."

"Good heavens, Mr. Sinclair! Do you make a study in how to annoy me? For pity's sake, let's be on our way." I roll out my hand indicating he should take the lead.

Instead, he bows, overdoing it on purpose. While I am casting my gaze heavenward in a silent plea for patience, he swoops me up in his arms, cradling me like a helpless infant.

"Put me down this instant!" I slap my hand against his chest.

"We are in a hurry, Lady Jane. I haven't time to humor you." His long legs are covering the hillside in strides that far outpace anything I could do. "First off, there isn't one single solitary soul out here in the black of night to observe your sacred proprieties. Second, if you injure yourself it will slow us down even more. Do you want to catch this traitor or not?"

I say nothing, brooding because he is right again. The wretch. And I cannot believe he is carrying me, holding me against his chest as if he has every right to such an intimate act. What's worse, what is even more inexcusable, is that I do not altogether dislike it. In fact, I begin to feel self-conscious because I stink of rotting leaves and moldy muck. I am about to open my mouth and apologize when he cuts me off.

"Save your lectures, Lady Jane. When we get to the road I will set you on your feet, so no one will think you are a tavern wench." He looks irritated for some reason. "Not that anyone ever would. One look at you puts that idea to rest once and for all. There is nothing about you nearly so comfortable or amiable as a tavern wench."

Normally, his remarks set my teeth on edge. Normally, I have a quick rejoinder. Or, if I am at a loss for words, I sometimes feel an overwhelming urge to pummel him. *Normally.* But the fact that he finds me less amiable than a serving wench wounds me in unexpected places. I find I'm unable to speak. It's as if he slapped me.

He shifts me in his arms as he wends his way sideways across the hill. "It would help if you could lower your standards enough to hang on to my neck," he says rather gruffly, trying to maneuver us between two tall trees.

I wrap my arm up over his shoulder, still keeping mum, wishing I were someone else. Someone sweet and kind, like Sera. Or someone adorable and clever, like Georgie. *Anyone else.* Even a tavern wench.

Two

ℭOLD HARD FAℭTS

Mr. Sinclair marches on without speaking a word, a rare thing for him. The way he is stomping through the underbrush I worry he may startle an adder hunting for mice beneath the bushes. There's no point in alarming him, so I keep it to myself. He stops to adjust his grip on me and glances up at the heavens as if getting his bearings even though there is nary a star to be seen.

Curse this wretched silence between us! I can't stand it another second. "How is it you're able to use the sky as a compass when it is completely overcast?"

It's a perfectly reasonable question, not insulting in the least. I've no idea why his jaw buckles so tight. He pushes through a bank of scrub oak and finally decides to answer. "It's an old woodsman's trick. One I learned from my pa when he took me hunting."

"A trick?" I ask, using my most congenial tavern-wench voice.

Wearing a narrow expression, he glances down at me as if he suspects me of laying a trap for him. I strive to keep my countenance as innocent as possible, as much like a trollop-y innkeeper's daughter as I can manage.

He still looks like he doesn't quite trust me, but explains anyway. "When I first started out on this little adventure of yours, I noticed the wind was blowing east. There were also some distinctive formations in the clouds. I took note of those as well. So long as the wind doesn't send them sailing too fast or switch direction too rapidly, they'll do for a landmark, albeit a moving one. It's a matter of keeping track of the wind direction and speed."

"Clever," I say, and nod, truly meaning the compliment. It is a handy tool. One I catalogue in the back of my mind for the next time I must chase someone on a dark, moonless night. Another, even more important, question needles at me. "What possessed you to follow me in the first place?"

I feel the muscles in his chest stiffen. "If you must know, I couldn't sleep."

Why, I want to demand. My imagination flares up, racing to all sorts of foolishly romantic conclusions. "You couldn't sleep?" I ask, as if it's an insignificant question.

"No. So I stepped out into the garden for some air, thinking it would clear my head. That's when I saw you creeping past. I suppose I was curious as to what sort of mischief you were getting up to at that hour."

"I wasn't *creeping*." I bite my tongue, endeavoring to keep from letting him goad me into another argument. "Ladies do not creep. Didn't you see the traitor stealing out in front of me?"

"Regrettably, no."

My breath comes out in a long tired exhale and I sag against him. "A pity. It would've been handy if you'd seen something to help us identify her."

As we trudge through tall grass, he seems more relaxed, as if he's no longer annoyed, and stares at me, taking my measure.

I swallow, suddenly feeling awkward. I'm normally contented with my appearance. I'm quite ordinary and that suits my purposes. Pretty enough to get by, but not so much that anyone ever stares. I haven't Georgiana's extraordinary red curls, or Sera's silken white-blond hair. I have plain features, brown hair, and nondescript hazel eyes. I suppose I am a little above average in height, but other than that, there is nothing about me to attract attention.

That's why I fidget uncomfortably when Alexander's gaze skims over me. I'm not accustomed to anyone staring at me. I nervously push back a strand of muddied hair stringing across my cheek before holding on to his shoulder again.

With an indecipherable sigh, Alexander looks away and focuses his attention on climbing over a large fallen log. He shifts me in his arms, which by now must surely be aching. Yet he doesn't complain, not even a tiny groan. So much nobility on his part makes me want to apologize for not being a more agreeable person.

"I'm sorry," I start to say, but it catches in my throat and only half of it escapes out into the night air. It does so at the same moment we startle an owl from a branch directly above our heads. Alexander ducks instinctively and I cling to him tighter.

The enormous creature flaps away, shrieking like a cat whose tail has been stepped on. We grin at each other, embarrassed at being surprised. It takes a moment for our heartbeats to settle. His lips curve into that half-cocked teasing grin of his. "You started to say something, didn't you?"

I shake my head.

"You did," he insists. "I would swear I heard you say the word *sorry*. Couldn't believe my ears. Yet, I distinctly heard that very expression pass your lips. *Sorry* for what, my lady?"

"Jane. You may call me Jane."

"I thought you forbade me such informalities." He sounds irked. "Never mind your title, let's get back to this remarkable *sorry-ness* of yours. What are you sorry about, Lady Jane?"

I cannot prevent the indignant swell of my breast. I have just granted him permission to use my given name and he glosses over it as if it's of no consequence.

I am no longer sorry, not in the least.

I sniff. "It was nothing. I'm sorry you have to carry me all this way. That's all." I might've said anything. I could've said I was sorry for smelling like a putrid bog. I wish I had, rather than diminishing the one thing I actually admired him for doing.

"Wasn't your decision, *your highness*, now was it? It was mine. And a great burden it has been, I assure you. Yet, *somehow*, out of sheer force of will, I managed to haul you uphill and across the countryside, back to our starting point. Look about you, *your majesty*. We have arrived in the clearing."

I'm amazed at the speed with which he has gotten us here. The traitor must've indeed run us in an indirect route. Who could have run so fast and so sure? Only one possibility occurs to me. The thought strikes my stomach with the force of a cannonball. I sink against Mr. Sinclair's arms. It can't be Tess. I refuse to think it. She would never do such a thing. It defies logic. She wouldn't.

But if not her . . .

"Who could've run like that?" I don't intend to say it aloud, but it slips out unbidden. "Not Tess. It can't be Tess."

Alexander strides to the road and sets me on my feet, still holding me closer than he ought. I suppose he's simply making certain I'm steady enough to walk. He sympathetically rubs my shoulder with his palm. "If not her, then who?" It unsettles me that he asks this question with such a mournful tone.

"Not her." I bow my head. "Tess has risked her life for us. Several times."

It can't be her.

Mr. Sinclair lends me his arm so I can limp along beside him as he starts walking up the road. "Well then, let us proceed on that assumption." The gravel beneath my slipper still digs into my foot, but I do my best to hide the discomfort.

"Let us sort through your list of possible suspects and eliminate them until we find the culprit." Alexander approaches this predicament like an engineer. As if this problem breaking my heart can be solved as easily as a mathematical equation. If only it was that simple—a tidy column of numbers that only need to be added up in order to arrive at the right answer. In this case, no matter what the answer is, it will hurt like the very devil.

"Who else could it have been?" He jars me from my brooding thoughts. "Miss Fitzwilliam has been practicing her running occasionally with Miss Aubreyson, perhaps she—"

"No! Never," I say, and it flies out too harshly. "I didn't mean to snap at you. It's just that these are my friends. They're the nearest thing to sisters I've ever had. I cannot imagine one of them betraying us in this manner."

"I understand. It's a difficult matter." He pats the hand I am resting on his arm. "Perhaps if we approach the conundrum from a different direction it will be less painful."

"Perhaps." I sincerely doubt it.

"Who among you, at the prospect of getting caught, is capable of running with the speed and agility of a scared rabbit?"

"That's it!" I tug him to a dead stop in the middle of the road, struck by a most compelling realization. "Mr. Sinclair, you're absolutely brilliant."

"Brilliant?" He tilts his head quizzically.

"Yes. When frightened, *anyone* might've run with that kind of speed. Anyone at Stranje House could've done so. Fear produces that added increase of speed and evasiveness."

He ponders this for a moment and we resume walking. "But you've not decreased the number of suspects, my lady, you've increased it."

"Yes. Any of us." My chest heaves. I am relieved it might not be Tess or Georgie. "Just as a frightened rabbit knows better than to run in a straight line, so would a desperate frantic girl. Her life would depend upon it. Treason is a capital offense in Britain, and heaven knows they hang women and children in London for far less grievous offenses."

"Hmm." He scratches his chin. "Isn't there anyone we can rule out?"

"No one. Well, except me, of course."

"Of course. And me." He sounds as if his innocence is a foregone conclusion.

"We must be practical about this, Mr. Sinclair. I'm not altogether certain we should scratch your name from the list. You could've been there in the woods tonight to protect the traitor. Perhaps you were told to watch from behind and tackle anyone spying on their rendezvous. Which is, I might add, exactly what you did."

"You've a point." He kicks a stone and sends it bouncing down the road ahead of us. "Very well, let's not rule me out just yet."

Alexander's back stiffens and he walks on for a few paces, but then he slows and looks down at me with more sincerity in his face than I have ever witnessed there before. "Ask yourself, Lady Jane, what earthly good would it do for me to expose our plans to the Iron Crown? My *plans*, I might add, plans to take *my* prototype steamship to London? Because that is exactly what this traitor has done. You saw her point to the shore. You heard that fellow mention *London*. You know what all this means."

His lips press tight and he stares hard down the black road ahead of us. We continue walking, but more briskly than before.

It's true. His plans are ruined. His odds of leaving Britain and going home are severely reduced. I knew it the minute the trai-tor pointed at the coastline. I have nothing to say for myself. I let my frustration about whoever is betraying us cloud my judg-ment. I ought to apologize, but apologies never seem to go well with Mr. Sinclair.

In a roundabout way of making amends, I ask, "Why couldn't you sleep?" I pose this question in a solemn respectful tone, a tone he may never have heard from me before.

My change in attitude doesn't seem to astonish him as much as I'd thought it would. It's as if he always suspected I might be capable of speaking to him without biting his head off—at least once in a while. His answer, too, is devoid of sarcasm. "I couldn't stop thinking about leaving."

"Oh," I say, wondering whether happiness or sadness about leaving had troubled his sleep. I dare not ask so personal a ques-tion. It would be presumptuous and forward. Instead, before I can stop myself, I tease him. "There! You may have just confessed to a possible motive. You were so distraught at the thought of leav-ing all of us at Stranje House, you sabotaged your own plans."

He does not laugh as I hoped he would. His lips curve up into a wry half smile. I wait for the stinging barb he is sure to fling at me, but Alexander does not parry with a sharp-witted reply. Instead, he lets my teasing words drift on the night breeze, floating along with us like the last savory notes of a violin sonata.

Several moments pass before he breaks our companionable silence. "We're nearing the gates. Kindly explain this scheme of yours to catch the traitor when we get back to the house."

"No scheme, Mr. Sinclair." I lift my chin, pleased with the simplicity of my approach. "It all comes down to a matter of boots and beds. Whose walking boots are clean and whose are not? Who is in bed asleep and who is not?"

A pothole in the road causes me to stumble and I nearly fly out of Cook's remaining clog. Alexander keeps me from landing on my face, but tripping diminishes the confident effect I'd hoped to achieve. I pretend not to have lost my footing and continue to explain. "The traitor will have worn her half boots out on a murky night like this. Those boots will be soiled with the same muck you see crusted on our . . ."

I glance down at my feet. Cook's big wooden patten is a scuffed, mud-caked, mess, and my silk slipper is completely demolished. It will have to be thrown into the fire.

"Yes. That might do." He stares down at my mismatched footwear. His shoes do not seem nearly so badly soiled and I wonder how that can be. Perhaps he is able to avoid the boggy spots better than I. "I hope you are right." He opens the iron gates for me to pass through.

"I am. You'll see."

He latches the gate behind us, and the closer we get to the house the faster I limp along beside him. "We're going to catch her. We have to." We see no sign of movement in the garden or near the pens. "*Drat!* She must've beaten us back to the house."

"Seems likely." He guides us into the house through the side garden door, explaining he left it unlocked. Cook's patten clunks against the wood floors louder than an old man's cane. I take it off and set it by the entrance, but my slippers squish out scum and muddy water as we go. I yank the useless sodden things off and toss them back beside Cook's lone clog.

We climb the stairs, and while we do, I ponder what I should say when I barge into the dormitorium and find the betrayer. I cannot settle on what words to use, but I know this, I must go in alone. "You won't be able to enter the room with me," I whisper to Mr. Sinclair.

"No, of course not. I'll wait outside the door in case you need me."

"I'm afraid you must wait down the hallway a few paces. It is a girls' dormitorium after all, and we must observe the—"

"*Proprieties*. Right. But if you should need me . . ." He brushes his fingers through his unruly hair as if he means to spruce himself up for a momentous occasion such as this.

"I'll shout for you if I do."

He nods grimly. We reach the landing and turn into the upstairs hallway. I indicate where he should wait, and tiptoe on, but he grabs my hand. "I'm sorry," he whispers. "That it should come down to this."

He means it. He is grieved for me, that I must point the finger at one of my dearest friends. His pity unnerves me. If I speak it might let loose the sorrow I am damming up. I give him a curt nod and ease my fingers out of his grasp.

Five paces. I walk five soul-twisting paces to the door. Five paces, and each one presses heavier and heavier upon me until I can scarcely breathe. My hand trembles as I reach for the doorknob. I am terrified to learn which of my friends I will be sending to the gallows. In one burning gasp for air, I grab the handle and turn, wishing I could close my eyes to what I must discover on the other side.

Instead, I keep them open, fixed on one purpose: identify the traitor.

The old oak door is well-oiled, and glides open without a noise. Our room is even darker than the hall. But my eyes have grown accustomed to the absence of light and my ears attuned to every suspicious rustle, every stirring in the sheets. They are all sleeping. All except Tess. She sits hunched on her bed.

"Jane?" She twists to look at me, as if she is not sure whether she's in the middle of a dream or if I am actually here. "What's wrong?"

I strike a flint and light a lamp. *What's wrong, indeed. You are up and I do not want to think what that might mean.*

Except, surely, if she had been the one running away she would pretend to be asleep. For that matter, any of them could be feigning sleep. Heaven knows, we've practiced doing it nearly every night, in order to fool Madame Cho when she comes in to check on us in the evening.

Georgie moans as if she doesn't like her slumber being disturbed. "Wake up." I turn up the lamp, and say it louder. "You must all wake up."

Sera sleeps nearest to the lamp. She pokes her head out from under the covers and swipes back a lock of her white-blond hair, squinting up at me, blinking against the light. "What happened to you?" She sits up fully. "Is that blood? It is. You're hurt!"

"Never mind." I wave away her concern. "All of you get out of bed." I issue this command in my sternest voice, the same tone my governess used to employ to make me jump to her will.

Sera studies me, making assumptions about the night's events by surveying my bare feet, the rips in my dress, the mud, and the disarray of my hair. She piles out of bed and inspects the abrasions on my arm. Sera is my closest friend in the whole world. It was she who helped me fool Lady Daneska and Ghost with the false plans we created for the warship. She couldn't possibly be the traitor. Not Sera. But then, once upon a time Lady Daneska had been Tess's closest friend and look how that turned out.

"You've fallen," she mutters. "Badly. There's mud in these wounds." She frowns at me as if I'm being extremely foolish, but hurries to the pitcher and basin to pour water over a cloth. Whether I like it or not, she begins washing my elbow.

Maya groans and tugs a pillow over her head. I don't see how she could be the traitor. I was wrong, earlier. Maya is the one girl among us who would never be able to run like a frightened rabbit. She's far too graceful. Rather than try to scamper away, I think she would simply turn and allow herself to be captured. I wonder if Maya even knows *how* to run. She rarely participates in our self-defense classes. On several occasions, she has tried to explain her religion to us. She believes in being at peace with everyone, even her enemies. Death, she says, is but a new beginning.

Nevertheless, I must perform my test. Each and every one of them must be cleared of this offense. "Maya and Georgie, get up," I demand louder. "Now!"

"Why? Is something wrong?" Georgie rolls out of bed and stumbles toward me. "Are those leaves in your hair? Have you been outside at this hour?"

"Of course she has. Look at her." Sera untangles a dried ragwort bloom lodged in the lace of my collar. "She's covered in dirt. We must clean these wounds. We'll need warm water." Sera reaches for my other arm so she can dab at it with the cloth, and turns to Georgie. "Run down and put a large kettle on the fire."

I grasp Sera's shoulders. "Not now. Not yet."

Tess stares at me as if I've lost my mind, and maybe I have.

"Everyone, please listen," I stand as tall as I can in my bare feet. "I need to look at your half boots, your walking boots, any shoes you might wear outside. Do it now. And, please, no questions." I add this last command for Georgie in particular. Otherwise, she will pummel me with a thousand inquiries.

They all gape. Even Maya sits up in bed and studies me. They're beginning to understand this is serious.

"Please," I add softly.

Sera tosses the bloodied cloth into the ewer, goes to her wardrobe, fetches her boots, and, without a word, she holds them out to me. I see no sign of fresh mud on them and exhale with relief.

Maya slips out of bed, pads to her closet, hunts for a moment, and pulls out a pair of walking boots that scarcely look worn.

"I don't see what this is all about," Tess crosses her arms.

"You will," I promise.

Grumbling she stalks off to her wardrobe and Georgie follows suit. They both return with their half boots. Tess thrusts hers at me. I swallow hard and pull one of them from her hand. "There's mud on these."

"Of course there is. Have you forgotten it rained this afternoon? I wore them when I went to let the dogs run loose this evening. What difference does it make?"

I test one of the globules of caked mud. It has a thin dry crust and doesn't feel like fresh mud, nothing like the muck on Cook's patten, sitting by the garden door.

Tess grows impatient with my silent inspection. "Why are you fussing about our boots in the middle of the night?" She plants her hands on her hips. "You do know it's three o'clock in the morning, don't you?"

"Yes, but when I came in you were already awake. Why?" I force myself to look at her, to scour her face for deception. I would know it if Tess ever tried to lie. She has many gifts, but the ability to lie effectively is not one of them.

"You know why." She meets my gaze squarely and frowns, fuming that she must answer to me. I am younger than Tess. She dislikes it when I take the lead. So much so that I am surprised when she finally confesses what I have already guessed. "I was awakened by a dream." She exhales and leans close, narrowing her gaze at me as if I was the cause of her latest nightmare.

Without a doubt, Tess has not been outside running this morning. If she had been, the gloom of her nightmare would not still be hanging over her features like a mourner's veil. I hand the boots back to her.

Georgie hides hers behind her back. When I hold out my hand waiting, she hesitates. Finally, she surrenders them to me. My heart sinks. Her boots are caked with mud, and the clumps are still soft and damp.

"Georgie!" I practically sob her name.

Not her. I trusted her. In France, even though I am terrified of heights, I climbed aboard a silk kite with her, a kite we built together, and we flew across the rooftops of Calais. It feels as if my heart will thunder apart.

"Why?" I gasp, and sink to my knees. "How could you do this?"

"Don't tell Miss Stranje. *Please*," she begs. "I know it was wrong. But he's going away again, and I was desperate to see him in private. You've no idea how hard it is to be apart. I don't know how I'll bear it when he leaves. It was my idea, not his. He warned me that we shouldn't meet in secret, but I insisted. You mustn't blame him."

I struggle to follow her disjointed explanation. Even in that poor light, I see she's blushing. Hope slows down my galloping heart.

"Try to understand," she pleads, and reaches for me but I cannot focus on her outstretched hand, not now. I must be certain of her answers. "It was your idea to do *what?*"

"To slip out and meet Lord Wyatt along the cliffs." She backs away, folding her arms as if she's chilled. "I assure you nothing untoward happened. We just talked."

Lord Wyatt. I nearly collapse with relief.

Tess scoffs under her breath. "What, no kisses?"

"And if we did?" Georgie rounds on her. "What matter is it of yours? You've no right to throw stones—"

She would've kept going, but I interrupt. "And you met him out by the cliffs? Nowhere else?"

"Yes, by the cliffs. Isn't that the reason you're asking all these questions? You've caught me out."

I hand back her incriminating boot, and lower my head into my hands, shaking my head. Sera clasps my arm and tugs me to my feet, guiding me to the bed. "I think it's time you told us what's happened."

I look up at them, at the four of them staring back at me so intently. The feeble oil lamp seems to glow a hundred times brighter. I press my hand against my chest and take a deep breath, one that fills my lungs with glorious clean air.

I know now, what I knew in my heart all along—none of my sisters betrayed us.

"Tonight I chased our traitor."

Three

TRAITORS AND FRIENDS

"Traitor? You mean the monster who let Ghost into Stranje House? You went out in the middle of the night, and chased him?" Georgie clasps my shoulders and I can tell she's itching to give me a hard shake. "The person who helped Ghost and Lady Daneska attack Madame Cho and kidnap Tess? *That* traitor? Have you lost your wits? What if someone else from the Iron Crown had been out in those woods?"

"*Her,*" I say. "Our traitor is a *her.* And you're right, she did meet an accomplice."

Tess crosses her arms and nods as if she has already guessed what took place. "I suppose it's safe to assume both the accomplice and the traitor got away?"

"I wouldn't be checking your boots if they hadn't escaped, now would I?" I tell the story as quickly as possible. The instant I stop speaking, they bombard me with questions faster than I can answer. "Wait!" I hold up my hand to slow them down.

"Lady Jane?" Mr. Sinclair pokes his head in the doorway. "Anything amiss?"

They all turn in astonishment and gape at him. Sera spins back to me. "He was out there with you, wasn't he?"

Georgie's spine stiffens with indignation. "You sneak! You made me feel guilty for meeting Lord Wyatt, and here you were gadding about in the middle of the night with *him*." She points a condemning finger at poor unsuspecting Mr. Sinclair.

I am not a sneak. I admit I have secrets, secrets I must keep hidden at all costs, but that is where I draw the line on deception. "I did not sneak."

Georgie wants to argue, but I hold up my hands warding off her anger. "I admit, I may have left a few minor details out of my narrative."

"Minor?" she says with a huff.

Tess lifts her eyebrows sardonically and nods in Mr. Sinclair's direction. "One rather large detail, I should think."

Maya hides a sudden burst of laughter behind her hand.

Sera frowns at Alexander and turns to me. "How could you?"

"It isn't what you think." I grimace and give them a rather abbreviated account of his role in the adventure. When I relate the part where I threw Mr. Sinclair to the ground and pounced upon him with my knife, Tess almost smiles.

It is not easy to win a smile out of her. "At least you did that much correctly."

He edges into the room, and I prickle up at him for intruding. "Mr. Sinclair, I gave you strict instructions to wait down the hall."

He pierces me with that impudent look of his, the irritating expression that always makes me think *he thinks* I'm a slow top. "Yes, *your highness*. You ordered me to stay put, but only until you discovered which of these lovely young ladies is our culprit. You'll have to excuse me for figuring you'd have accomplished the task by now."

I refuse to let him rattle me, and lift my chin to prove it. "I'm delighted to report, none of them are the traitor. Not only that, but I'm quite certain I know exactly who has betrayed us."

At those words, everyone's attention snaps back to me.

"And if I am correct, we must act quickly to circumvent their plans. But in the meantime, Mr. Sinclair, you *really* must wait in the hall. You simply cannot be in a girls' dormitorium. It isn't at all proper."

"It certainly is not!" Miss Stranje marches up and stands directly behind him.

He shuffles to attention as if he is a soldier in the presence of a general.

"What is the meaning of this appalling breach of etiquette, Mr. Sinclair?" She glares at him.

The other four girls snap to perfect posture as rapidly as did Mr. Sinclair. She sweeps in and levels all of us with one of her fiercest stares. "This is disgraceful. I am shocked at you young ladies, entertaining a gentleman at this hour, and in such an appalling state of undress."

They are all cloaked, *every one of them*, head to toe, in heavy nightdresses that cover far more of their person than even the most conservative day gown. I sit calmly on the bed as our headmistress continues to ring a peal over our heads.

"I've a good mind to take Madame Cho's cane to all of you." She marches up and down our ranks. "This is an outrage. Madame Cho, if she were well enough to be here, would be livid. I consider myself a tolerant woman, but this sort of behavior is outside of enough, completely unacceptable—"

Miss Stranje, who is not actually as tolerant as she just claimed, freezes in her tracks and frowns at me.

There is a magnificent ferociousness about our headmistress, a trait I hope to master one day. I'd wager a considerable sum she is able to stop a person's heart from beating simply by applying that cold hard glare of hers. If she can't make a heart stop altogether, she is certainly able to make it skip a few beats.

I want to be just like her someday.

Today, however, I have fallen a wee bit short.

"What in blazes happened to you?" Miss Stranje never curses or uses strong language. She claims it is a device only employed by individuals with minds too weak to command suitably descriptive speech. I excuse her verbal lapse on account of it being such an extraordinary hour of the night, *or morning*, depending upon your perspective.

I smile serenely, as if I have merely been out for a Sunday stroll, and say, "I chased our traitor." I pause, allowing her a moment to digest this intelligence. "I caught said traitor delivering information to a rather unsavory gentleman who I can only presume must be affiliated with the Iron Crown. Well, I didn't actually *catch* her, I *observed* her. More importantly, it is my considered opinion that unless we take action within the next few hours, Mr. Sinclair's steamship will fall into enemy hands."

She sighs and massages her forehead. "I see." She turns to Mr. Sinclair. "Am I to assume you were party to this disturbing turn of events?"

He does his best to smooth down the front of his rumpled shirt. "I'm afraid so."

"In that case, we shall reconvene in the workroom in a half hour's time. Mr. Sinclair, you may be excused to go and tidy yourself up before we meet. You will require clean clothing. Ring for Mr. Greaves and he will see to your needs."

I am filled with positively sinful pride that our headmistress doesn't question my judgment on the matter of our impending disaster. *Not even for a moment.* But poor astonished Mr. Sinclair stands there like a man caught in the path of a cyclone, not certain which way to bolt.

"Run along, young man." Miss Stranje shoos him out and he takes off down the hall. She turns back to us. "Now then, I will send Phillip to the dower house with a note apprising Captain Grey and Lord Wyatt of this turn of events. In the meantime, one of you must fetch warm water so Lady Jane's wounds can be properly cleaned. Maya, come with me to retrieve my medicinal kit. I will leave it to you to tend to those ghastly abrasions, while I see to writing the note." She waves her hand at my scraped arms as if I am an inanimate object rather than her most devoted understudy.

At the last moment before she hurries away, Miss Stranje turns and presses two fingers to her temple as if something pains her. "Lady Jane, I ought to have inquired, are any of your injuries serious?"

I draw in a gratified breath. "Not in the least."

Miss Stranje leaves and Georgie dresses quickly so she can run down to the kitchen to get the warm water. Sera resumes wiping away dirt and plucking thorns and gravel out of my wounds. But Tess wheels on me, bothered by the problem of the boots. "I understand why you thought one of us was the traitor. Given the events of the last few days, we've all been suspects. What I don't understand is this. You thought you'd uncover the traitor by checking our boots, and since it isn't one of us, how can you be so certain you know who it is?"

"The traitor was female." Sera glances up from her work. "After ruling us out, that only leaves the two maids."

Tess paces the floor in front of us. "I don't see how either of them could outrun Mr. Sinclair."

"Fear does remarkable things to one's speed," I explain.

She stops and gallops her fingers on the bedpost. "Do you think it might've been our footman, Phillip, dressed up to look like a girl?"

"Doubtful," I say, trying not to wince, as Sera digs out a tiny stone lodged in my elbow. "I considered that, but Phillip is much taller than the person I followed, and she had a high-pitched voice."

Sera blots blood from a lengthy scratch on my forearm. "Phillip would only have adopted a disguise if he thought he might be followed. At that hour, the traitor would've assumed he or she was free to move about unobserved."

"Just so." I stand and Sera helps untie the tapes in my gown. "We know it can't be Cook. The woman is a veritable mountain, taller than most men and, even though the traitor wore a hooded cloak, even a strand of Cook's white hair slipping loose would have gleamed like silver in the moonlight. As Sera said, that only leaves Alice and Peggy and, of course, Miss Stranje and Madame Cho."

Tess glares at me as if she might draw her knife and come after me for even suggesting either of her beloved mentors might be the perpetrator of such treachery. "Madame Cho is still recovering from the blow Daneska dealt her. She's barely able to conduct our defensive arts lessons. For pity's sake, she still has to take laudanum at night for the pain—"

"I'm well aware of that. It can't be either of them," I snap. "Which explains how we know exactly who it is."

Tess plops down on the bed. "Well, it can't be Peggy. She's been here forever, and she's plump enough you would've recognized . . ." With a groan, Tess sinks back against the pillows. "*Alice*." She exhales loudly. "Has to be Alice."

"Exactly."

Tess slaps the coverlet. "That's why she kept peering over my shoulder when I was working on the maps. And here I had excused her behavior, thinking she was simply nosy."

Sera inhales sharply. "You know what this means." Her arms drop to her sides and her voice lowers to a mournful whisper. "They'll hang her."

"Probably." Tess stares at the quilt as if seeing the gallows. "It'll be up to the courts. We've no say in the matter."

Sera presses her hand over her own throat. "I can't bear the thought of it. We can't turn her in. *We can't.* Poor Alice. Hanging would be too horrible."

"Poor Alice?" Tess sits up suddenly. "I shan't like to see Napoleon come charging up the shore leading an army of Frenchmen with their swords drawn and muskets aimed at us, either. That would be even more horrible." She jumps up, hands on her hips. "Not only for us, but for *all* of England, and that is precisely what will happen if little Miss Double-dealing, Two-faced Alice gives our plans and secrets to Lady Daneska. Think, Sera, it will mean all of our necks." Tess makes the sign for slitting a throat. "Not just Alice's."

I step between them, hoping to stave off Tess's anger. "I don't think it will come down to that. I've an idea—"

"Won't come down to what?" Georgie carries in two kettles of steaming hot water.

"Hanging Alice, or Napoleon's soldiers shooting us." Tess opens her wardrobe and pulls out her running dress.

"We shouldn't make these assumptions without proof. I'm going to find Alice's boots so we can be certain." Sera heads for the door.

"Wait!" I grab her arm. "I've got a plan. Whether it is Alice or not, we mustn't let the traitor know we're on to her. Everything depends upon her believing she has gotten away with it. There is a chance, if this works, she might be spared the hangman's waltz."

Georgiana hefts the two kettles, reminding us that we are in a rush. "We can discuss it later. Miss Stranje won't like it if we're late and your water isn't going to stay hot much longer."

Miss Stranje is not one to let innovations pass her by. Our indoor privy has one of those newfangled water closets, and also a glorious bathing apparatus, called the Feetham machine. This miraculous contraption is one of my favorite things about Stranje House. Many members of the aristocracy are convinced bathing is detrimental to their health. Miss Stranje insists the exact opposite is true, that cleanliness is a healthful practice. I hope she is right, because it is an absolutely heavenly thing to bathe under warm running water.

Georgie climbs a stepstool and pours the kettles of hot water into the basin at the top of the apparatus. She uses the hand pump to circulate the water, while I stand under the fount allowing hot water to sprinkle down atop my head and soothe my bruises. I close my eyes, and droplets trickle over my lashes and cheeks. All too soon, the water raining over my head begins to chill and I know the extravagance of this bath must end.

Maya rustles around outside the bathing tank, and knocks on one of the pipes. "I have prepared a salve for your wounds."

Whatever time providence allotted me is spent. Evil will not stop and wait for me. I step out of the bathing machine and wrap myself in warm linen towels. I dry quickly and slip into the comfort of a fresh chemise and gown.

Sera does her best to towel off my wet hair. I close my eyes as she plaits it into a braid. "You're fretting," she scolds.

"I am not," I lie. Maya chuckles to herself, but it's Sera's gentle silence that makes me confess. "How did you know?"

"You're here, but your mind seems to be elsewhere. You must be thinking about what the Iron Crown will do next and what we ought to do as a countermeasure."

I twist to look up at her. "Aren't you doing the same?"

She shakes her head and tugs my braid back into place. "I can only see what is. Pondering what *might* happen would overwhelm me."

"You would do well to learn this from Sera." Maya wipes something that stings over the cuts on my arm and I blow on them to reduce the burn. "You worry too much. These burdens are not yours alone to carry."

She's right, I tell myself. Miss Stranje and Captain Grey are capable and clever, and far more experienced than I am. Why, then, does it still feel as if a twelve-stone weight is crushing my shoulders?

It's him. I'm worried about Alexander. No, it's more than that. I'm worried about Stranje House, about my friends, about England.

Millstone about my neck or not, I must march forward. She's right, I am not alone. We must march on. We must do what is required. No one will ever know the things we at this school do for England. No one will ever know what we have done to keep our countrymen free from Napoleon's ravages.

Maya daubs a thick soothing paste over my scrapes and binds them with a soft linen cloth. "There. That should heal quite well."

My nose crinkles at the strong smell coming from the bound-up concoction. "It smells like one of Cook's soups."

She smiles. "I am not surprised. The salve has onion, garlic, and wine in it."

Georgie dries her hands after draining the Feetham machine for me. "Are you ready to go down?"

Ready? No.

My ideas are not perfected yet. I can only see a short way ahead. It's so much better when the whole board is visible and I can see more of the possibilities. If only we had more time to make certain of the details.

"Ready." I nod with more confidence than I feel.

Georgie and Sera head out of the bathing room. Maya rests her hand on my shoulder. "You must trust that wisdom will come when you need it. You were made for a time such as this."

Made for a time such as this.

Maya's voice is so unusual, it seems to vibrate from some place deep in her chest, almost like a cat's purr. A cat's purr is perhaps a childish way to describe such an extraordinary gift. All I know is, when Maya speaks, the warmth and depth of her pitch causes something to ease inside me.

"Thank you," I say, and before I realize it, she has walked me halfway down the stairs. We move quiet as monks through the old house, winding through the dark corridors on the main floor leading to the workroom.

Only two oil lamps light the room, and without speaking, the five of us take our seats around the large table and await our headmistress.

Four

PLANS AND PIRATES

One oil lamp sits on the table and another casts its amber glow from the sideboard. Our shadows float like grim gray phantoms against the walls. An 1811 map of Britain and Europe rests in the center of our table. Several sheets of vellum are tacked over it, with new lines marking where Napoleon has altered Europe's many borders.

I lean forward, calculating the time it will take to travel by sea from here to the mouth of the Thames, the river Alexander will need to navigate in order to reach London. A rustle at the door draws my attention.

Mr. Sinclair steps hesitantly into the room and my breath stands still in my lungs.

It is an unbearably early hour of the morning, and yet Greaves has done something extraordinary to our quirky American inventor. I cannot decide whether to call it a miracle or a tragedy. Alexander is wearing a new set of clothes, his shirt is clean and neatly pressed, the cravat articulately tied rather than hanging in a haphazard loop, and even his hair is freshly combed.

He . . . he looks . . . *like a gentleman.*

I find this unsettling in the extreme. He ought to look like our rough, unpolished Mr. Sinclair. Not this pattern-card Adonis. I have a nearly irresistible urge to go and mess him up, to rumple his shirt, to tousle his hair, and to muddle up his cravat.

Georgie's mouth hangs open, as astonished as I am.

"I know." He gestures at his attire. "A bit much, isn't it? I look like a great, galloping gadfly."

"Nothing of the kind." Georgie points him to a chair at the table. "You look quite handsome, very respectable. You shall be a credit to us in London."

He looks to me to confirm this opinion. Despite the room being chilly, heat singes my cheeks, and I look away, finding myself at a loss for words.

Alexander tugs at the sleeves of his coat. "Mr. Greaves said we ought to try it out, seeing as all the ladies would be present. And, as he put it, the maids would need a month of Sundays to get the stains out of my other clothes." Again, he waits for some sort of response from me.

It is impossible to gather my thoughts into a coherent string of words.

His expression transforms into a challenge. "I take it you do not approve?"

"No, it's not that. I . . . I . . ."

Devil take it. I am stuttering like a toddler in leading strings. Ladies do not stutter. I swallow a fur ball of confusion and struggle to master my useless tongue. Agitated in the extreme, I blurt, "It is satisfactory."

The compliment lands on the table like a two-day-old gutted

fish. So, I try again. "Miss Fitzwilliam is right." I wave my hand at his ensemble. "It will do for London."

"I see. *Satisfactory.*" He gives me a curt bow before taking his seat. "High praise coming from *your ladyship.*"

"Oh, for pity's sake, do stop mixing up your forms of address. I'm not a duchess."

"Could've fooled me," he mutters.

"I have excellent hearing, Mr. Sinclair. If you mean to deliver a slight under your breath, you must endeavor to do so more quietly."

He opens his mouth, undoubtedly intending to toss out another insult, but at that very moment Miss Stranje walks in, so he stands as is required of a gentleman.

"You may be seated." She shuts the door and waves him back to his chair. "Good, you are all here. We've no time to waste." Except she stops and squanders two perfectly good seconds appraising Alexander's attire. "Splendid. The new clothing suits you, Mr. Sinclair. Do give Greaves my compliments. He has outdone himself."

Alexander slants a quick gloat in my direction, one bursting with righteous indignation. Then he turns to Miss Stranje and inclines his head, accepting the compliment as if he were born to the role of a London gentleman.

I fiddle with the knot on one of my bandages, fighting some darker part of my nature. Some untamable part of me wishes to vigorously shake the lordly Englishman nonsense out of him. Mr. Sinclair is a rustic, an American, and he ought to have the decency to maintain his proper role.

Miss Stranje taps Tess's shoulder and glances suggestively at the tapestry hanging high up on the far wall. "Secure the room, if you would, please, Miss Aubreyson."

The antiquated needlepoint depicts King Henry hunting deer along with his entourage of lords, ladies, and royal hounds. More importantly, it hides an opening to one of the school's many secret passages. That particular eavesdropping perch is a leftover from the bygone Tudor era when everyone spied on everyone else, and is the only vulnerability in this particular room.

Georgie follows her gaze and pales. She once fell from that very spyhole, but she quickly composes herself. "I don't think the servants are familiar with that passage. I can assure you it is no longer frequented. It's crumbling and covered in spiderwebs and so much debris as to make it nearly impassable. I only stumbled upon it by accident."

"Merely a precaution." Our headmistress takes her seat.

Tess moves silently through the shadows to do our headmistress's bidding; she lifts a measuring stick from one of the drawing tables. Georgie gives her a nod and fixes her eyes on the tapestry. With a quick jab, Tess runs the rod up beneath the heavy cloth and flings the hanging open. A gust of chilled air wafts into the room, but there is no movement from within the black gaping spyhole. Not even a rat's rustle.

Georgie signals the all clear, and Tess closes the tapestry.

"At least for the moment, it appears we have some privacy." Miss Stranje gestures for me to get on with it.

I glance sideways at the tapestry. "I doubt Alice would be so bold. Not after almost getting caught tonight."

Miss Stranje winces at the mention of Alice's name. "You caught her in the act?"

"No. I've no solid proof. But we know who it *isn't* and that leaves little doubt it is one of the maids. We can't very well report her based on mere conjecture. Not to mention the awkward position making such a grave accusation would put us in."

Miss Stranje wears a shrewd *I'd-already-thought-of-that* expression, she drums her fingers waiting for me to say more.

"I believe we would be better served by exploiting her betrayal for our purposes."

"Ah, very good." Miss Stranje relaxes a fraction of an inch. "Now then, Lady Jane, let us hear this proposal of yours for keeping the warship prototype out of the Iron Crown's hands."

I take a deep breath, careful not to even peek in Alexander's direction. "We must assume that by now Lady Daneska and Ghost will have discovered the steamship drawings they stole from us are hoaxes."

"So soon?" Maya seems genuinely taken aback. "It has only been two days."

"I'm afraid so." Mr. Sinclair agrees with me, something he so rarely does. "Any competent engineer, if he were to study those drawings for more than an hour or so, ought to be able to sniff out the deception."

"Thank you." I'm careful to avoid looking at him, while acknowledging his contribution. "Which means we must presume Lady Daneska will have immediately sent a message to alert her cohorts in our region. Why else would the traitor have ventured out this evening, so soon after—"

"They figured it out, and summoned Alice out of the nest." Georgie balls up her fists atop the table. "Lady Daneska saw the *Mary Isabella* the night they kidnapped Tess and fled with the plans. She'll want the prototype."

Tess sits back and crosses her arms. "How much do you think they know?"

"Mr. Sinclair and I saw the traitor point toward the cove. Alice must've told him when we planned to sail the steamship to London. We overheard him complain that two days didn't leave much time."

Sera touches my arm to draw my attention. "What do you suppose they'll do?"

Miss Stranje gives a nod for me to go ahead and share my speculations.

"They only have three choices." I tick the possibilities off on my fingers. "They must either attempt to steal the steamship, waylay it on its voyage, or abduct Mr. Sinclair and beat the actual plans out of him."

Even in the poor light I notice Mr. Sinclair draw in a steadying breath and clamp his jaw tight.

His pallor makes me regret my callous tone. In a feeble attempt to reassure him I say, "You needn't worry, Mr. Sinclair. Abducting you is the least advisable of their choices. Highly impractical. They tried capturing you before and it didn't work. More importantly, doing so would fail to keep the steamship out of Britain's hands. At best, it would only give Napoleon a chance to build one to compete with ours."

Tess grumbles. "Don't underestimate Lady Daneska's vindictive streak. She will be furious at having been tricked."

"Doubly so for also having lost you." Sera glances pointedly at Tess. "You were to be her gift to Napoleon, his own private dreamer."

Georgie clasps her hands even tighter. "Tess is right. We cannot depend upon logic in this case. Lady Daneska may be so angry she'll abandon common sense in favor of revenge."

"That would be true, if it were not for one thing . . ." I tap the table calling us all back from the nightmare we so recently experienced. The trauma of our last encounter with Lady Daneska and Ghost is still too fresh. We almost lost both Tess and Madame Cho.

"One thing?" Georgie is skeptical. "I can't see how any *one* thing would influence Lady Daneska to behave within the boundaries of reason and common sense."

"Time is crucial," I explain. "It is imperative for Napoleon to strike Britain while our armies are pinned down in northern Europe and we're vulnerable. Lady Daneska will do anything to increase her standing with the emperor. We need only ask ourselves which of the alternatives would prove most beneficial for Napoleon? That's the thing she and Ghost will order their men to do."

"She'll send them to steal the ship," Tess says with quiet conviction. I'm impressed. No one here knows Lady Daneska better than Tess.

"When?" Sera leans in beside me and repeats the question, this time loud enough for everyone to hear. "*When* do you think they'll try to steal it?"

"That depends." I pick up the compass and use the point to indicate France, where it is possible Lady Daneska is conferring at this very moment with Emperor Napoleon. "If their spies here in England wait for orders from Ghost or Lady Daneska, I expect it will be tomorrow night. If they act on their own volition, it is my considered opinion they will come for it today, before the sun rises."

"Then what are we doing here?" Mr. Sinclair stands abruptly. "Daybreak is only a few hours away!"

Before anyone can answer, the door swings open and bangs against the wall. The unmistakable silhouette of Lord Ravencross stands in the doorway.

"What the devil is going on?" He strides into the room looming over all of us like the long shadow of a giant.

Tess jumps up from her chair and is halfway to him, but Miss

Stranje blocks her path. "My lord. You should not be out of bed. The doctor gave strict orders—"

"By my reckoning neither should any of you." His voice is more of a low growl than the civil tones of a gentleman. "Now, I won't ask again, why are you all sitting here in the dark like druids at some sort of midnight sacrifice?"

Tess steps around Miss Stranje. Her words are a scold, but her manner is gentle and soothing. "My lord, your house is across the park. When last I checked you are not authorized to issue orders here. If you mean to bark commands we will have you carried home on a litter." She takes his arm and guides him to the settee. "If those stitches in your chest rip out again, I shall be quite cross with you. Shall I summon the doctor? I thought he gave you laudanum to help you sleep." At Tess's touch, he softens, and allows her to situate him on our worn workroom settee.

She props a cushion beneath his head, and he complains to her. "I can't very well sleep with girls and footmen and *everyone* else in the county stomping around as if it is noonday."

"No one has been stomping, my lord." She tucks a crocheted afghan around him.

He refuses to settle in and sits back up, frowning particularly hard at Mr. Sinclair. "Why're you here? How come you're slicked up like a dandy on his way to court?"

"As a matter of fact, I was just leaving." Mr. Sinclair bows curtly to us. "Ladies, if you will excuse me, I must go protect my ship."

"Wait!" I spring to my feet. "You must listen to the plan first."

Mr. Sinclair does not turn back, neither does he answer, because Lord Wyatt and Captain Grey burst into the room. "We came as soon as we got word."

Georgie bolts out of her chair, and I feel the need to scream at all these intrusions. Instead, I sigh loudly. "We have very little time. Please! Everyone stop and think." I stab my finger at the map, right beside the red pin marking the location of Stranje House. "If the Iron Crown isn't able to steal the steamship here in the cove, ask yourselves, what will be their next move?"

Alexander turns and gives me a quizzical sideways frown, considering my question.

Captain Grey, who can always be counted on to keep a level head in a crisis, strides to the map. He stares at it thoughtfully and points to a spot beyond the mouth of the Thames where the river begins to narrow. "If I were them, I'd try to take the *Mary Isabella* here where the current is weakest. I'd chase her up one of these tributaries. Here at Holehaven. Or better yet, here, where the Hadleigh Ray empties into the Thames." He raps the map with his knuckles. "Right here, just as the *Mary Isabella* comes steaming toward Canvey Island."

"You're right." Alexander rakes a hand through his hair and leans over the map. "With two or three boats they might be able to pin me in there, leaving me no room to maneuver except up the waterway, where I'd be trapped."

"Precisely. It is the ideal place to seize the prototype." They have confirmed the worst of my scenarios. I struggle to moderate my voice to a ladylike calm. Drawing in a deep breath, I press forward with the rest of my strategy. "Which is why we must make the Iron Crown think that is *exactly* where you are going."

They all look at me as if I'm daft.

"Alice must be convinced you have fled with the steamship this very night." I try to make them understand. "Everything depends upon it."

"What are you saying?" Mr. Sinclair turns a bleak expression on me. "The ship is still there. If they find it hidden in the cove, there won't be any need for them to lie in wait for me at the Thames. They'll have already captured it."

Lord Wyatt holds open his coat and reveals a sidearm pistol and a sword. "We won't let them take your ship."

"Yes, you could go down to the cove," I say, rather loudly, worried all the gentlemen in the room will gallop off to battle before hearing me out. "You could wait for Ghost's men to arrive and shoot them all dead. I'm quite certain the magistrate and his curious son will be delighted to wrestle with the problem of more dead bodies floating up around our school. It's only been two weeks since the last incident. Even so, it doesn't change the fact that you *still* need to get the steamship to London. Which means, you will *still* face the problem of more men from the Iron Crown pirating it on the Thames. Or for that matter, attacking you at sea."

"If shooting the thieving scoundrels is not the answer, what do you have in mind?" Lord Wyatt crosses his arms, vexed, and Mr. Sinclair follows his lead.

Everyone in the room stares at me expectantly, even Lord Ravencross rises up on his elbow, and that heavy millstone returns to my neck. Except this time, it feels like it weighs thirty stone instead of twelve.

This had better work.

"I propose we go to the cove right now and dismantle the steamship, and hide the parts."

Mr. Sinclair groans and tosses up his hands. "Dismantle it?"

The lamp flickers as I lift my hands pleading with him. "Hear me out."

Before I can say more, Georgie pushes in. "Where could we possibly hide those pontoons and all the mechanisms so the traitor wouldn't discover them?"

It surprises me when Lord Ravencross clears his throat. "You could carry it to my barns and cover the pieces with hay."

Lord Wyatt rubs his chin considering this idea.

"Most generous, my lord." Miss Stranje thanks Lord Ravencross, but whirls back to me. "Have you forgotten? Lord Castlereagh and the Admiralty expect the ship to arrive in London next week."

"We will not disappoint them." I answer with a confidence I wish I felt more deeply.

Captain Grey studies me. "If it's dismantled, how do you propose we get it there?"

I meet his forthright gaze and confirm what he has already deduced. "We'll transport it by road."

"That makes no sense." Mr. Sinclair shakes his head. "The *Mary Isabella* is just as defenseless against attack on the highway as it is at sea. More so—"

"Not if it's disguised," I say, turning a piece of graphite over in my fingers.

"Disguised?" Maya, who rarely speaks up in these meetings, sits forward intrigued. "How do you intend to disguise an entire ship? Those pontoons are longer than this table."

Sera is deep in thought, but she glances up, her eyes alight, and I think she has guessed what I am about to say.

I toss down the graphite and place my hands on the table, leaning forward to explain. "Your tenants have already begun shearing sheep, Captain Grey. They're doing it before summer to prevent flies from laying eggs in their coats, that way the wool will be of higher quality. The upshot is, very soon they'll need to cart the wool to market."

"Ah." He nods approvingly. "You're thinking of hiding the ship and her boilers under the bags of wool fleeces."

"Just so." I smile broadly. "Recalling the measurements, I believe if we angle it, one pontoon will fit at the bottom of a farm wagon. So, we'll require two wagons, and I rather thought we might want to stuff the mechanical parts *inside* the bags with the wool to conceal them better."

"Clever," Captain Grey admits. "We will dress ourselves as farmers and ride along to protect the wagons during the trip."

"It might just work. I'll send word to Mr. Digby and a few of the others to come and help us guard the wagons." Lord Wyatt slaps Alexander on the shoulder. "Chin up, Sinclair. You and your ship will astonish the Admiralty. You'll see. All will be well."

Georgie chafes her hands nervously against her hips. "If all of us work together, we ought to be able to take the *Mary Isabella* apart in an hour or two, but we must hurry and all of us will need to help."

Lord Ravencross is stretched out on the couch and even though his eyes are closed he issues more orders. "Miss Stranje, send that footman of yours to fetch MacDougal. I'll instruct him to lend you two or three of our local lads out of the militia, who are encamped at my house. Men we can trust. They can help carry the pieces of Mr. Sinclair's ship up the bluffs and into my barn."

"Thank you, my lord." She inclines her head. "That will speed things along."

I need their attention for one more point. "The moment Mr. Sinclair finishes overseeing the dismantling, we must also hide him so Alice assumes he has sailed away with his ship."

"Hide him where?" Georgie turns back to me. "I suppose the dungeons might work."

"Can't." Tess shakes her head. "That's the first place Alice would check."

Miss Stranje pushes back from the table and stands. "Indeed.

I suspect Alice may have snuck down to see Lady Daneska when we had her housed there last week."

I twist the thumbscrew on the bow compass. "True, and if she sees us going downstairs with food, she's bound to suspect something."

"There's one place she wouldn't look for him." Georgie exchanges a conspiratorial glance with Sera. Sera catches the corner of her lip, as she does when something alarms her. I know exactly where they are thinking of hiding him, and brighten at the thought.

Miss Stranje sharpens her beak in our direction. "Don't tell me you're thinking of housing Mr. Sinclair in the garret above the dormitorium?"

Alexander looks from our headmistress to me. "What garret?"

Her brow furrows. I have long suspected Miss Stranje is aware of the secret meeting place we girls have in the attic. Now, there is no doubt. "I think not. That would be highly improper. No, absolutely not," she declares with finality. "It stretches the bounds of propriety too far."

Captain Grey reaches for her hand to reassure her. "My dear Miss Stranje, there's no need to trouble yourself. Mr. Sinclair will be our guest at the dower house. We ought to have moved him there last week."

My heart sinks at the thought of Alexander spending his last days in our vicinity hiding a half mile up the road instead of here at Stranje House. I risk an impertinent question. "That is a very kind offer, Captain, but can you be certain none of your servants will gossip with ours?"

Captain Grey straightens the hem of his coat sleeve and grants me, not a smile, but his steady forthright assurance. "They are handpicked for their discretion."

"As were *mine*." Miss Stranje bristles.

"Hmm, yes, so they were." Captain Grey thinks for a moment and brightens. "I have it. I shall arrange for both menservants to remain inside until Mr. Sinclair departs. I'll assign them the onerous task of inventorying the entire contents of the household. That should require their attention the entire day, leaving them no time for venturing to the market, public house, or anywhere else where they might gossip."

That seals it. After tonight, Alexander will be gone from our lives. *Forever.*

I make one last attempt to keep him here with us. "Yes, but what if someone sees him while traveling the road to your home? The traitor's accomplice was hiding in the woods along that very road."

Miss Stranje forestalls him from answering. "Lady Jane, you forget yourself. Captain Grey is very successful at what he does. You need not worry. He and Lord Wyatt are more than capable of concealing Mr. Sinclair while on the road. They do that sort of thing all the time. And now, so they'll have an early start traveling that road, it is time we went and took apart the steamship."

Alexander is leaving.

Nothing I can do to stop it. Indeed, I ought to wish him Godspeed. This is the very thing we set out to accomplish. But I don't. I set the writing instruments in order, make sure the map sits squarely on the table, and place a loose tacking pin in the box. I take a long sad look at Alexander's broad back and his golden hair as he walks away.

Lord Wyatt clasps Alexander's arm, stopping him, and frowns. "Hold on, Sinclair. You'll want a change of clothes. Those new togs are bound to get ruined taking apart the boiler."

Five

A SHIP IN SHEEP'S CLOTHING

I am not given to foolish sentimentality. I turn away not wanting to watch him leave the workroom, meaning to attend to another matter of business. Except, the specter of his shadow drifting across the wall stops me. Instead of the *Mary Isabella*, it feels as if my heart is coming apart.

Which is complete and utter foolishness.

Folly.

Sentimental nonsense.

"Never mind him." My lips move but no sound comes out. I take a deep breath and tell myself to get on with the plan.

Tess and Miss Stranje lag behind to assist Lord Ravencross back to his room. However, there is another crucial element to this scheme. I hesitate to burden Tess with this particular task, but it is vital. I tag her arm. "There's one more thing."

"There always is." Tess leans in and I quickly and quietly

explain another piece of the puzzle. She nods, agreeing, and they head out the door.

Miss Stranje calls to me over her shoulder. "Get some sleep, Lady Jane. We can handle everything else. You look done in."

Done in? I frown at the empty room. *Me? I'm not done in.*

I'm as fit and able as anyone else. Mr. Sinclair needs every available pair of hands to take the *Mary Isabella* apart. It is my right to be there. After all, I helped draw up the plans for his ruddy steamship. They shall not leave me out.

I turn the wick knob, dousing the last lamp, and darkness swallows me up. I fully intend to follow them, but this time before venturing out into the night, I intend to be properly prepared. I tiptoe quietly up the stairs and fetch proper walking boots and a pelisse to keep off the chill.

Getting down the cliffs proves a tad more treacherous than I'd expected. It does seem like I am not as sure-footed as normal. Unwilling to admit Miss Stranje may be right, I blame it on the blackness of the night.

Once I reach the beach I slog through the damp sand behind the rocky shore, wending my way toward the cove. I am nearly upon them before I see that they have limited themselves to one small lantern. *Wise of them.* Otherwise, Daneska's thieving henchmen might spot them working. MacDougal and two farm lads have come to help carry parts up the cliff. They all work in a wordless flurry. It reminds me of chickens pecking at a small pile of grain. I stand off to the side watching until Georgie hands me two connecting rods to lug up the bluffs.

I take a deep breath and sally forth on my assignment. Halfway up the steep path I attempt to bolster myself by muttering stern lectures to myself. "You can do this, Lady Jane. Only see how Tess bounds up this narrow trail ahead, follow her lead." But Tess quickly outpaces me and disappears into the inky night.

Now, except for the heaviness of my breathing, I plod uphill in silence. The tide is coming in, slapping against the shore, lacing the air with a fine misty spray. I slip on a wet patch and catch myself by clinging to a tuft of grass with one hand while hanging on to the rods with the other. It is a near thing. All too easily I imagine myself dashed to bits on the rocks below. "Do not look down," I warn myself sternly, and keep climbing until I reach the top.

Level ground is a mercy, but my task is not yet over. Sera passes me on her way back down, greets me with an encouraging smile, and points out the path I should follow. Just as I begin regretting the very long way it is to Lord Ravencross's barn, a young militiaman greets me. He's there to relieve me of my load and carry it the rest of the way.

MacDougal has set up a brigade. How very foresighted of him. Grateful, I hand the connecting rods to the soldier, and head back down the steep path to the beach. I stand aside when I cross paths with Captain Grey, who has Mr. Sinclair's boiler in his arms.

Upon returning to the cove, I stand awaiting the next bit of the prototype to be ferried to the barn. Alexander stops work and peers at me. "You are near dead on your feet, Lady Jane. Take yourself off to bed. It won't do to have you collapsing in a heap." His voice echoes weirdly in the cove, and just when I think he is expressing genuine concern, he goes and spoils it all. "We've too much to do to be carrying you up the hill, as well."

"That is no hill," I argue.

"Exactly," he mutters.

"He's right, Jane." Of course, Georgie would say that, she always agrees with him. "You've been up all night. The boiler and the steam cylinder are apart now. All that's left is the paddle wheel, the decking, and the pontoons."

"I thought I might sit here and unlash the decking."

Alexander grumbles about my being stubborn, but I refuse to give him any heed. It's easy enough to help dismantle the decking. With so many of us working, the ship comes apart much faster than I'd calculated. The paddle wheel collapses into a stack of lumber, two wheels, and a rod. Suddenly the *Mary Isabella* is no longer a ship. She has decomposed into the sum of her parts, and I find I'm feeling much the same.

When the last plank of the decking is loosened, I settle against a nearby rock and slide down until I am sitting, rather unladylike, on a pile of stones. I ease back and watch him work, noting the way he moves in the dark, so sure and confident.

He truly is brilliant.

It pleases me that he is once again wearing his shabby old clothes. I remember being so appalled at his attire when he first arrived at Stranje House. Funny how quickly his comfortable ways grew on me. The moon comes out and through the thin cloth of his worn cambric shirt I note the muscles flex in his shoulder. His curls catch rare bits of lamplight and glint like buttery silk ribbons. They flop in his eyes and he brushes them back without a thought for the dirt or moisture on his hands. If he were mine, I would relish washing those golden locks until they gleamed.

But he isn't mine, and he never will be.

I'm absurdly tired or I would never have indulged in these reckless thoughts about a foreigner who has no place in my life. I turn away and listen to the lap of the waves as the sea rushes in and flows out again. Miss Stranje and Sera are each carrying up Cook's pickling barrels, our makeshift life preservers, the very ones that helped save Lord Ravencross and Tess from drowning a few days ago. Maya carries the coal scuttle and shovel. Georgie holds the lantern, lighting the way for Captain Grey and Lord Wyatt as they hoist the last pontoon on their shoulders and head up the cliff.

Alexander stands on the shore watching them wind up the bluffs. "That's it then."

"Yes, I suppose it is." I throw a stone out into the sea and it sails into the dark. Waves roll in and splash against the rocks. The stone is lost to me. I'll never hear it plunk into the water. "Give my regards to your uncle, when you see him. Robert Fulton is a man ahead of his time."

"As opposed to his slipshod nephew," Alexander mumbles and digs the toes of his already grimy shoe into the sand. "I shall tell him," he says aloud and with more conviction than he ought, for we both know he won't. Why would he tell his beloved uncle about the annoying English girl who was so outspoken and obnoxious?

Captain Grey signals to us from the cliffs, avoiding calling aloud so as not to alert potential thieves.

"Come along then." Mr. Sinclair offers me a hand up. He doesn't let go even though I am standing next to him, but in the dim light of the waxing moon I see his lips slant into that wicked sly smirk of his. "Admit it, Lady Jane. You'll miss me."

"I will." I sniff and pull my fingers out of his grasp. "As much as a toothache."

"Exactly." He hikes up the shoreline behind the rocks, avoiding the worst of the rising tide. "Who will you practice your insults on? You'll be hard-pressed to find anyone as tolerant and charming as I am."

I *will* miss sparring with him, but I mustn't let him know. "You have a point," I say airily. "I suppose I will simply have to sling insults at Harold, the mannequin in our ballroom."

"*Ballroom*. Ha! You mean your *training* room, and Harold must be that poor fellow stuffed with cotton wadding. The one you kick, punch, and stab with knives."

"We dance with him on occasion. He's quite tolerant of abuse and can be nearly as charming as you."

"*Touché*. See there. You are in fine form, ready to slay any gentleman who comes within a mile of you. You ought to thank me for allowing you to sharpen your sword on me."

"True. But what of you, my dear friend?" As I make my way up the narrow path, I glance over my shoulder at him, attempting to gauge his response. Except, Alexander remains as inscrutable as ever. "I don't think there are very many young ladies who will put up with that barbed pitchfork you call a tongue. Not even in *the colonies*."

"Oh, but that's where you are wrong." He sounds positively cheerful. "There are any number of young ladies lining up to do just that. *Hundreds*."

It is still dark and I take a small misstep. His hands are instantly on my waist helping me regain my balance. "Hundreds?" I ask.

"Did I say hundreds? I meant *thousands*."

I huff, and it is not because of the steepness of the climb. "You may not wish to admit it, Alexander Sinclair, but you will miss me as well."

"I've given that considerable thought." He sounds pensive, and for once I think he might not gibe me.

"*Considerable* thought?" I coax, wondering if that is what had kept him from sleeping earlier.

"Well, perhaps not as much as all that."

The tide is coming in and a particularly big breaker crashes against the rocks and mists us with salt water. Perhaps it is because I've had so little sleep, but I find I am chilled to the bone and shiver. He hands me his coat. "Put this on before you catch pneumonia."

As we balance on the narrow sliver of a path, he helps me slide my arms into his coat, and flips the collar up to keep my neck warm. I am unnerved when he continues to gaze at me, holding my arm to keep me from falling. *Good thing,* because standing this close to him makes me feel as if I might melt and flow straight down this ridiculous cliff. The coat is warm and smells of him, of welded copper, of spilled hot chocolate and pencil shavings, of late-night candle wax and the forest we ran through together, of spice cake and clotted cream.

I do so adore spice cake and clotted cream.

As if the scoundrel has read my thoughts, his eyebrows lift. "You truly are a trial, Lady Jane." He speaks these words the way another man might confess his undying admiration.

"Thank you." I lower my lashes, afraid that even in the dark he'll notice the heat rushing into my cheeks.

He sighs heavily. "I suppose you're aware of the fact that you would try the patience of a saint." I've no idea why that makes me grin, but it does.

"So I've been told. Luckily, you are no saint."

"Well, no, there is that." Suddenly he frowns and clasps my shoulders. "Who? Who else says you try their patience?" He demands this, as if no one else on earth has the right to say such things to me except for him. As if he will call out the blackguard, not because I don't deserve the statement, but because I am his, and his alone, to insult.

KATHLEEN BALDWIN

"Hundreds of men," I say, impishly. "*Thousands.*"

I watch him battle a smile. Finally, he is able to twist it into a smirk. "Jane," he murmurs, correcting himself, shaking his head ever so slightly. "*Lady* Jane."

I confess I have never liked my name so well as I do when it falls from his lips.

He's still holding my arms but he leans closer and his grip lightens. "I've a good mind to kiss you just to teach you some proper manners."

"Oh, no." I feign alarm. "How shall I ever survive such a harsh lesson?"

He grins mischievously and draws me close. My arms naturally reach up and wind around his shoulders, his lips brush mine, feather soft, a tantalizing promise of more, my heart whirls dizzily, I lean into him, and—

"Jane?" Georgie calls to us in a hushed voice from farther up the path. The sound echoes through the night and crashes against us, blasting the moment apart like cold sea spray. My arms fall away.

Regret washes over his features and he says softly, "I expect it will be me who has difficulty surviving this particular lesson."

His whispered words tease against my lips, sending my heart winging unsteadily off the bluff. Or plummeting to the rocks below. I'm not sure which, because his words are confusing, no matter how intimately he delivered them.

Georgie calls for us again. "Lady Jane? Mr. Sinclair? Are you there? We're waiting for you." Her lantern glints off Alexander's face as he pulls away from me and straightens.

"On our way," he says loud enough for Georgie to hear.

Still stunned, I stand, unable to move, softened into a useless pudding by the merest touch of his lips to mine. At the same time, his cryptic remark bewilders me. I try to puzzle it out. Does he mean kissing me would've been an ordeal? *Surely not.* He hadn't come toward my mouth like a man about to suffer pain for the cause. Is it possible he meant our kiss would devastate him more than it did me? Why would he think such a thing? Perhaps it saddens him that this first kiss will also be our last, our *only* kiss. I shake my head, unable to fathom a sentiment like that coming from *him*, the glib Mr. Sinclair—I think not. Not him. More than likely, it was another of his meaningless jests.

I am vexed now. Quite vexed.

And to think I almost let him kiss me. Well, if I am to be perfectly honest, I *did* let him. *Heavens above*, what was I thinking? Instead of observing the proprieties, I practically threw myself into the rascally American's arms.

What a fool I am sometimes.

Alexander turns me around, so I am facing the right direction on the path, and with a steadying hand he guides me upward. It is completely unnecessary. I am quite capable of stomping my way to the summit on my own.

At the top, Miss Stranje meets us carrying a satchel with Alexander's belongings. "Captain Grey will be along shortly to conduct you to the dower house. Lord Wyatt is this very moment scouring the woods to make sure there are no spies watching along the road." She says this last part pointedly to me.

I shrug out of Mr. Sinclair's jacket and hand it back to him. "Thank you for the loan of your coat," I say formally, and extend my hand. I expect, even though I'm not a man, he will give it his vigorous American-style shake. "Good luck to you, Mr. Sinclair. I wish you a pleasant journey."

The scoundrel breaks from his habit and bows over my hand as if we are in a proper English drawing room. He bows low, taking advantage of the darkness of the hour, and dares to press a kiss on my knuckles. He looks up with the most impudent grin in all of Christendom. "Farewell, Lady Jane, until we meet again."

I snatch my hand away. "I doubt we ever shall."

He straightens and manages to appear far more imperious than he ought in those shabby clothes. He stares down at me as if from a great height. "We shall see."

Captain Grey approaches and stops beside our headmistress. "Get some rest, my dear." He leans closer to her ear. "We may be in for some rough days ahead."

She says nothing to that, but looks up at him with her eyes warm and her lips resting in a kinder softer line than she normally wears. I have studied her long enough and well enough to know Captain Grey is the only person who will ever be privy to that side of Miss Emma Stranje. She looks away, uncomfortable with his concern for her. She is, after all, a woman who can look out for herself quite efficiently.

Captain Grey places his hand over hers as it rests on his arm and gives it a gentle pat, before turning his attention to Alexander. "We'd best be off. The sun will rise soon."

He's right, gray is seeping into the black horizon, and early-morning fog is rising up from the sea. Mr. Sinclair and the captain walk toward the road, while Miss Stranje and Georgie head for Stranje House.

Just before Alexander disappears forever, he glances back and tips the brim of his nonexistent hat, sending me a final salute.

Six

THE PLAY'S THE THING

We shall see.

What a preposterous thing for him to say. We shall see *nothing*. That is how this works. *You're going away and I'm staying here. There's an end to it. Finito.* That's what I would say if Mr. Sinclair were still standing here beside me.

Only he isn't. Alexander Sinclair disappears into the gray mist, and a profound sadness steals around me, rolling in as thick as the fog.

Off in the distance, bobbing like a firefly in the wind, Georgie hurries back carrying her small lantern. "Are you coming, Jane?" She loops her arm around mine and tugs me along. "Miss Stranje wants me to remind you, if this plan of yours is to work, we have to hurry back to the house before Alice wakes up and starts lighting the fires."

I nod and let her tow me along. I can't keep from stewing over

Mr. Sinclair's inscrutable comments. "What's wrong?" Georgie raises the lantern examining my face. "You seem troubled."

"It's nothing," I say and force my heavy feet to take longer strides.

"Ah, I see." She chuckles softly. "With men, it never is."

She is acting as if she is the older and wiser of the two of us, when she is younger than me. I nudge her shoulder. "When did you become so all-knowing?"

She keeps pace with me, and responds with far more civility than I deserve. "You're just not used to being on the receiving end of advice."

"I suppose not," I grumble.

"I have a beau. I understand how difficult falling in love can be. You can talk to me."

"It is nothing like that. Mr. Sinclair is not my beau, and I'm certainly not falling in love with him or anyone else."

She laughs.

"I'm quite serious."

"Of course you are." Georgie ignores me and prattles on, spouting romantic nonsense.

There will never be beaus, or sweethearts, or falling in love for me. I can't tell her why, not without revealing my secret. This night is nearly gone and I'm so tired that if Georgie wheedles hard enough, I might accidently confide in her. So I clamp my mouth shut and nod attentively as she advises me on the nature of men, and how to cope with their peculiar behaviors.

While she proses on about love and other equally unhelpful subjects, I think of other things. Of Alexander's feather soft kiss. Of the last vexing grin he saluted me with. Of strong cheekbones that belong on a Greek god. And the laughable sound of his cocksure American twang. These are dangerous musings, when what I ought to be doing is forgetting about him.

Soon, I promise myself, I will forget. But for now, all the way to the house and tiptoeing up the stairs to the dormitorium, I allow thoughts of Alexander Sinclair to haunt me. As I lay my head on the pillow and close my eyes, the last thing I see are his lips right before they brushed against mine. I fall asleep to the sound of him daring fate.

We shall see.

I awaken and sit up in a panic.

Good heavens! It is no longer morning. The curtains are open. The dormitorium is empty. I hear the clock chime twelve times. I've slept all the way through breakfast. The day is half gone, and we still have a critical step in the plan to perform. Tess and Miss Stranje agreed we should carry out this next bit of theatrics at breakfast, but it is too late. Breakfast is over. They'll be wondering what is keeping me.

I rush through my morning ablutions, fling on a workaday dress, and patter down the stairs. Dashing through the entry, I turn into the hallway, nearly colliding with Greaves. The elderly butler winces as if I have actually knocked into him. "Begging your pardon, m'lady," he says, in a nasal tone, obviously annoyed at me for rushing about like a hoyden.

"Terribly sorry, Greaves. I'm running late, you see. Would you be so good as to ask Alice to bring some tea to the workroom for me? Perhaps a morsel or two from breakfast if there is anything left."

"Wouldn't you rather I sent the footman? That is the proper thing, and Phillip is far less likely to spill—"

"Nothing formal. A simple tray." A simple tray and *Alice. It has to be Alice.* "Alice will do. I'm sure Lord Ravencross is keeping Phillip busy fetching and carrying for him."

With a disapproving sniff, he inclines his head. "As you wish, m'lady."

"Thank you, Greaves. And do, please, ask her to hurry. I'm famished."

I continue to the workroom at a much more sedate pace. The door is shut and I lean against it for a few moments, preparing myself and giving Alice time to ready a teapot and tray. Their voices are subdued and I cannot make out what they are discussing. Time for my performance, I turn the knob and open the door wide, leaving it ajar as I glide into the room.

Miss Stranje glances up. "Good afternoon, Lady Jane. How very gracious of you to join us." A mild scold, from a headmistress who normally demands promptness.

I bob a curtsy. No one bothers to inquire after my health. They are all studiously engaged in a code-breaking assignment.

"I am well, *thank you.*" I answer the unasked question, which is rather cheeky of me. Miss Stranje lets it pass with nothing more than a narrowing of her expression, not that one such glare from her isn't enough to make a grown man quake in his boots.

When I lower my proud chin to a respectful level, she relents and gives me a subtle nod indicating we should proceed.

"You look the very devil," Tess carps. "You've gray smudges under your eyes."

The others look up from their work, and a twinge of remorse pinches at me. I wish we had been able to tell all of them about this part of the plan.

"Fine words coming from you." I say, accusation dripping from every syllable. "Seeing as it *is* your fault."

"Tess's fault?" Sera sets down her quill.

"You heard me."

"Yesterday was trying. We shall all sleep much more soundly tonight." Maya tries to make peace even though I have only begun to declare war.

I mimic our headmistress's most imperious glare and level it straight at Tess. "I doubt I shall sleep soundly. I doubt any of us will. Not if *she* is still in the house."

Tess glances up from deciphering one of Miss Stranje's code-breaking tests. "What are you going on about? Have I done something to offend you?"

"Oh don't come all mewling and innocent with me." I cross my arms. "You know exactly what you've done."

"No, I don't." Tess shoves back her chair and rises to her feet. "And for your information, I have never *mewled* in my life." The fearsome way her shoulders square and her fists double makes my knees quaver. But there's no backing down now, the play is under way.

Miss Stranje stands. "Ladies, in my house you will address each other with civility."

"Civil? You expect me to remain civil when we have a criminal in our midst?" I point at Tess. "It's her fault Mr. Sinclair had to flee in the middle of the night."

"What are you talking about?" Georgie rises to Tess's rescue. "You know perfectly well Tess had nothing to do with it. How can you say such things? I would trust Tess with my very life—"

"Trust *her*? I'd sooner trust a stewed prune." I ball up my own fists and press them against the table, leaning forward with as much venom as I can muster to make this performance convincing. "She's the traitor."

Georgie is beside herself. "But that can't be. Last night you said—"

"I was wrong. Blinded, because I couldn't see past the person I thought was our friend." I jab my finger through the air again accusing Tess. "She isn't the first person to betray us."

Sera glances from me, her best friend, and back to Tess, whom she adores as an older sister. The stricken look on her face slays me. Then she squints at me studiously, a split second passes, her face brightens, and I know she has figured it out.

I take a deep breath. "No one but Tess could've run as fast as the traitor did last night. Not only that, but—"

"Lady Jane! That is enough." Miss Stranje puffs up like a cobra about to strike.

"No." I stand my ground. "I don't care if you lock me in the discipline chamber and throw away the key. I'll say my piece. Mark my words, Tess is the traitor."

I notice Alice hesitating in the doorway. She carries in the tea tray sheepishly, obviously she's been standing out in the hallway eavesdropping before deciding to enter the room.

"You've gone mad." Tess stands back brooding.

I huff up and clench my fists until I must surely be red in the face. "Don't bother to deny it. I know it was you."

"No, Jane, think what you're saying. You know better." Georgie pleads with me and I feel genuinely sorry for what I am about to say next.

"I have proof. I saw her put Phobos and Tromos in the pens before she went to meet the spy. That's how I know she's the one who is betraying us." I talk so fast, even Georgie can't interrupt.

"*She's* the reason Mr. Sinclair ran away. *She* forced his hand. He had to save his ship somehow. Now he's gone, and who knows what will happen with him trying to sail the prototype to London by himself."

Georgie tilts her head blinking. I know what she's doing. She's trying to add up what I'm saying and no matter how she tries to calculate it she keeps coming up with a different sum.

"Lady Jane! Sit down this instant." Miss Stranje lifts her chin in Alice's direction, giving us the stern warning frown, the one that means we ought to mind our tongues when the servants are around. It is a brilliant touch and I admire her more than I ever have. But now, I must defy her.

"It has to be Tess." I open my hands pleading with them. "Listen to me. You know no one else can handle the wolf-dogs like she does."

"That is not enough proof to make an accusation." Sera comes to stand next to me, and I'm impressed she would risk it. "I have taken them to their pens. So have you. So have we all. Think this through, it could be anyone."

"Yes, *any of us.*" Georgie agrees too quickly. My heart lurches, uncertain whether she has figured it out, or not. If she hasn't, I worry she might say too much in an attempt to protect Tess. She presses her argument. "You've no proof! *None.* It might've been me. Or Sera." She pauses for a heartbeat. "Or even *Alice.*"

We all turn to the maid. Alice flushes and her hands shake as she sets the tea tray on the side table.

"Don't make me laugh," I say. "Alice could no more have run through those woods in the dead of night than a rooster could lay an egg. Could you, Alice?"

"What?" Our normally loquacious maid stands tongue-tied for a full second before she lands upon a suitable reply. "I don't know what you mean, m'lady." She bobs a curtsy to me and turns to Miss Stranje. "Will that be all, miss?"

"Yes, thank you. You may go, Alice."

I've one more nail to pound into this coffin. The minute the real traitor is barely out of the room, I roar at Tess. "I may not have proof. Not yet. But I *will* get it. And when I do, I'll see you hang for betraying us like this!"

"How dare you! You . . ." Tess rushes around the table as if she is about to strangle me. "You poisonous bunch-back'd toad!"

Bunch-back'd toad? I hope Alice hasn't read Shakespeare because Tess is cursing me with lines straight out of *Richard the Third*.

Miss Stranje rushes to the door, flings it open, and startles Alice. "We need help." She orders the wide-eyed maid to fetch the footman and Mr. Greaves straightaway. "Hurry!" Miss Stranje adds, with a feigned desperation that deserves applause.

She wheels back to us, and shouts. "Jane! Tess! Stop, before you kill one another. For pity's sake, don't just stand there, Georgiana, give me a hand. You too, Sera."

We hear Alice's heavy shoes clattering down the hall as she runs to summon help.

Tess's hands are wrapped around my throat, but she's not applying any pressure. I smirk. "Really Tess, *Richard the Third?*"

She lets go and shrugs. "I couldn't think of anything else."

"You were so late coming down, Lady Jane, we'd nearly given up on you." Miss Stranje starts in on me, her hands on her hips. "At least, you came through in the end. Admirable work, both of you. A little overdramatic for my taste, but it will do."

Georgie gapes at Miss Stranje. "You knew all along?"

"Naturally."

Sera chuckles softly, because she'd figured it out from the start.

Georgie shakes her head. "I didn't realize what you were doing, until you mentioned Mr. Sinclair sailing the prototype." She turns to Maya. "And you, did you guess, too?"

"I was not certain." Maya shrugs. "As far as I'm concerned, you English *all* run mad from time to time. Only look at your poor King George."

"I'm sorry for the deception." I put my arm around Georgie's shoulder. "We had to do it this way. None of us are practiced thespians. We were afraid if we told you, your reactions would not be as genuine. You did splendidly, Georgie. I was quite moved by how nobly you defended Tess."

Tess mumbles her thanks and bestows one of her rare smiles on Georgie.

I plop on the couch. "But, I must say, you scared me senseless when you pointed out Alice—"

"Hush. They're coming," Miss Stranje warns.

Tess and I take our places in chairs across from each other, as if we've been forcibly separated. Tess crosses her arms and broods. I put my chin in the air and glare at the faded wallpaper in the corner near the ceiling.

Phillip gallops into the room, breathing hard, staring at the scene before him like a man who'd expected to find murder and mayhem strewn across the Turkish carpet. When he sees there is no blood on the floor he straightens. "You called for me, miss."

Alice and Greaves arrive hard on his heels and out of breath.

"I do apologize for having troubled you." Miss Stranje hurries forward in an effort to hide her warring students from the servants' view. Her bombazine skirts rustle like autumn leaves and even though she is a slender woman, the black silk seems to widen with every step, the way a raven might puff out its wings. "We had a small mishap earlier, but I am happy to say, it is under control now. Thank you for coming to our aid so quickly, but you may go."

The disbelieving servants stare at her, mouths agape, and peek around her edges at Tess and me.

"All is well now." She claps her hands together as if that marks the end of the matter. "Please don't let us keep you from your work." She shows them to the door.

Phillip departs in a daze, shaking his head. Alice walks out behind him but keeps glancing back over her shoulder as if she expects flames to erupt in the workroom. Greaves is the last to leave. The poor beleaguered butler pinches up his wrinkled brow and glares at us as if five of Satan's spawn have infested his beloved Stranje House.

Seven

BIG FAT FLY IN THE OINTMENT

Your pardon, miss. I nearly forgot." Greaves turns back before leaving the workroom and pulls a formal-looking letter out of his coat pocket. "This arrived for you right before the, uh, *incident*." Disapproval oozes out of his every pore. "In my hurry because of the, er, *mishap*, I neglected to bring a tray on which to present it." He holds the letter on his gloved hand and extends it out to her as if it sits on an invisible silver salver.

Miss Stranje stares at the address and eyes the letter as if it is a serpent about to bite her. After an uncharacteristic hesitation, she takes it from him, turns it over, examines the wax seal, and grimly deposits it in her pocket. "Thank you, Greaves. That will be all."

He leaves, closing the door behind him. Our headmistress consults her timepiece and taps it. "The clock is ticking, ladies. I suggest you return to your deciphering work. In the real world, the swiftness with which you are able to decode a message may be a matter of life or death."

"Surely, you intend to subtract twenty minutes to account for the time when Jane interrupted us?" Georgie tries to bargain, even though I peek over her shoulder and see she is nearly finished puzzling out her code.

"It was only seventeen minutes, Miss Fitzwilliam, and, no, I will not deduct the time. Interruptions are part of life. They are bound to occur, especially when you are in the midst of an actual situation, are they not?" Miss Stranje turns to me and gestures to the tray of food Alice left for us. "Lady Jane, you may be excused from this exercise. I expect you require some nourishment."

My stomach rumbles eagerly at the invitation and I rise to peruse the tray. Our headmistress withdraws to a wingback chair across the room. Out of the corner of my eye, I watch her take out the letter and turn it over and over before breaking the seal.

Admittedly, I am curious, but I'm also ravenous. Cook sent up a generous plate of scones accompanied by a bowl of fresh strawberry jam, another filled with clotted cream, and a steaming pot of tea. It briefly crosses my mind Alice might've poisoned it, although I doubt she's that daring. I inhale the fragrances emanating from the tray, searching for a scent out of place and find nothing but deliciousness. One whiff of the clotted cream and I'm whisked straight back to the warmth of Alexander's coat and those last treasured moments with him.

I break open a scone and spread it with a handsome amount of jam and a dollop of cream. With the first bite, I close my eyes and the aromas bring his face back into bittersweet focus.

When I open my eyes, I notice Miss Stranje sitting rather

limply in the chair, the letter clutched in her fist, and her complexion abnormally pale.

Something is wrong. Very wrong.

I drop the scone on a plate, blot my mouth, and rush to stoop beside her chair. "What is it?"

Instead of answering, she presses her lips tight. She corrects her posture and composes herself. "I've had a letter from Lady Pinswary."

Georgie groans and lifts her head up from solving her code. "Not Lady Daneska's irksome aunt?"

"The very same."

Tess comes out of her chair as if she's been jabbed with a pin. "What does it say?"

Sera scoots back from her work and stares in our direction. Maya calmly keeps writing, and says, "It will not be cause for rejoicing, I can promise you that much. Lady Pinswary is not inclined toward the happiness of others, and certainly not ours." She sets down her pen. "There. I have finished." She proudly holds up her deciphered code. Maya often surprises me. In this case, I had fully expected Sera or Georgie to finish first.

"Well done, Miss Barrington." Miss Stranje grants her a strained smile.

Georgie looks from her paper to Maya's. "How did you finish so quickly?"

Maya shrugs, not being the boastful sort. "I had a minor advantage, that is all."

"What advantage?" Sera takes the paper from Maya and examines her work.

Maya waits until Sera stops studying their assignment and gives her full attention. "When Jane came in and accused Tess of betraying us, I found myself growing tense, and more and more agitated, and confused. Angry, even. I did not want to give in to these distressing feelings. Nor did I want them to muddle my thinking, so I chose to concentrate on breaking the code."

"Well done." Miss Stranje stands and her color returns to normal. "I would like all of you to take a lesson from Miss Barrington's calming technique today. In the middle of an emotional crisis, you might try focusing on a demanding task to aid you in organizing your thoughts."

Tess shifts from one foot to the other during this brief lecture, edging closer to Miss Stranje, leaning to peek at the letter. Curiosity and concern are gnawing at me, too. "Are you going to tell us what Lady Pinswary's letter says? Clearly, it is troubling news."

Miss Stranje nods. We gather closer, like children awaiting a tale of ghosts and goblins. She frowns at Lady Pinswary's scrawl as if she is having difficulty reading it. I know it is a ploy to buy time so that she can find the right way to tell us the bad news written on that piece of foolscap. "Lady Pinswary boasts about her niece's connections to Prince George."

Upsetting, of course, but there must be something else troubling our headmistress. Sera draws the same conclusion. "We knew Lady Daneska was well connected. Why is Lady Pinswary bragging about that?"

"Oh, she has a very good reason." Miss Stranje gazes steadily at us. "She tells me Lady Daneska plans to arrive in London within the week."

"London?" Georgie gasps. "Daneska wouldn't dare show her face there."

Sera comes and stands next to me. "She would if she's up to something."

"She's always up to something," I say. "The question is *what?*"

"It doesn't matter." Georgie bounces up and down on her toes excitedly. "Lord Wyatt and Captain Grey will be there soon. They can have her arrested for being a traitor. Then Lord Castlereagh will order her to be locked away in the Tower of London, and we need never see her again. *Ever.*"

Maya rests her hand on Georgie's arm. "Lady Daneska is not a gentle dove to be easily caught and locked in a cage. She is more like a daring tiger strolling into a village. Hunting. She is in London to *do* the catching, not to be caught. She will have contrived a way to stay safe."

"Exactly right." Miss Stranje inclines her head approvingly at Maya. "She has done so in spades. Lady Daneska received an invitation to Carlton House. She is to be an honored guest of the Prince Regent himself."

"What?" Tess growls. "How did she manage that?"

With a deep sigh, I explain the sad truth. "We know her for the murderous traitor she is, but we cannot forget Lady Daneska was the daughter of a duke. Her standing in European courts is of the highest order. She is young, exotic, and beautiful." Tess grumbles at my words, and Georgie bites her bottom lip, but I press on. "We all know Prince George likes to surround himself with the *crème de la crème* of the *beau monde*, the beautiful people in high society. Daneska is exactly the sort of ornament he likes to have decorating his court."

"Just so." Miss Stranje holds up the letter. "So, you see the problem."

"Of course." I sigh. "Lord Wyatt and Captain Grey can't very well march into Prince George's palace and charge Lady Daneska, *the renowned Countess Valdikauf*, with criminal acts against the crown, acts that for all public purposes have never even occurred.

It was one thing when we held her in custody here at Stranje House and threatened to turn her in. We would've done so quietly through private diplomatic channels. One simply cannot drag a foreign dignitary, a guest of Prince George, out of Carlton House and accuse her of treason."

"Precisely." Miss Stranje acknowledges my analysis, but the situation is too grave to warrant a smile. "Too much of our work is done in the shadows behind the curtain."

"Still, it begs the question. What is she doing in London?" Sera rubs at her chin mulling over possibilities.

Georgie is always quick to leap to a conclusion. "I should think it's fairly obvious. She plans to scuttle Mr. Sinclair's ship or steal it from him. Or worse yet, she'll take it from him and murder poor Mr. Sinclair to keep England from being able to build one."

Sera shakes her head. "Maybe, but I'm not certain that's all of it. She could be up to something even worse. At the Prince Regent's palace she'll be in the company of key members of Parliament and the House of Lords. There's bound to be foreign heads of state, and even Lord Castlereagh—"

"You're right." Tess heaves a sigh. "This is Daneska we're talking about."

"And Ghost," I say with a sinking feeling in my stomach. "Not to mention the Iron Crown."

Tess waits for our speculations to cease before naming the thing which we dared not speak. "She might try to assassinate the Prince Regent."

We all stare at Tess. Her words hover over us like a spike-winged gargoyle with terrifyingly sharp teeth.

Maya, whose voice normally bathes us with joy, tiptoes in solemn tones of mourning. "That would not bode well for England."

Miss Stranje smooths the corner of the letter, waiting for us to tumble to all the same conclusions she did, and now I understand why she paled.

I plunk down in the nearest chair. "Assassinating the Prince is a brilliant strategy. The ensuing chaos would provide the perfect distraction to cover Napoleon's attack on Britain."

"Good heavens! She can't do that. Not the Prince Regent." Georgie shoves back a handful of her coppery curls. "For all intents and purposes he is the king. She wouldn't dare."

"Wouldn't she?" Tess scoffs. "Have you forgotten? The Iron Crown didn't shy away from assassinating Louis the XVIII, and he was about to be crowned king of France."

"There you have it." Miss Stranje tucks the letter back into her pocket.

I sit drooping under the weight of these speculations, but she stands without even the tiniest sag in her shoulders, and addresses us squarely as if she is about to send us into battle. "Ladies, the moment is upon us. I believe it is time for us to take an excursion to London."

London. If I wasn't white before, I'm certain all color has now completely drained from my face. "London?" It comes out as an inaudible squeak. The few bites of scone I'd taken earlier tumble like jagged stones in my stomach, and my palms turn to sweat.

I cannot go to London.

I force a brave smile, because that is what is expected of me. I must be Lady Jane, the girl they have come to rely on. I must not be afraid. Above all, I must not show the concerns warring inside me.

Two main thoughts clash with one another. In London, there is a strong chance I will have the opportunity to see Mr. Sinclair again.

Elation.

On the other hand, if I go to London, and we move in the circles Miss Stranje proposes, it will be impossible to keep my secret. My foolish infatuation with Mr. Sinclair will explode into nothingness. My life here at Stranje House will end—my future will be plucked from my grasp and tossed on the fire like a summer flower.

Devastation.

Eight

LONDON CONUNDRUM

Do you mean *all* of us will go to London?" Maya stands very straight with her hands clasped behind her back. If she weren't so delicate, her stance might be almost soldierly. The reason she asks this question saddens me. She's worried that because of the color of her skin Miss Stranje might not be comfortable presenting her in high society. Maya's English step-mother hid her away as if the girl's Indian heritage was an embarrassment. It's one reason she's here with us, rather than in her father's house.

Miss Stranje responds as if it is an outlandish question. "Why yes, my dear, of course *all* of us will go. And you will all attend various balls and social functions."

"Are you sure that is wise?" Maya bravely asks, willing to accept the humiliation of being left behind rather than cause Miss Stranje discomfort.

"Wise?" Miss Stranje appears to ponder her question for a

moment. "Yes, it is the essence of wisdom, Miss Barrington. Over the years I have discovered wisdom is seldom found on the easy path. *All* of us are going, and that is my final word on the matter."

All of us? Impossible.

Not I. I cannot risk certain people in London seeing me. I sit in the armchair, silently ramming my thoughts against a hundred-foot brick wall, while the others bombard Miss Stranje with questions.

Tess snags my attention with a particularly key question for our headmistress. "How do you expect us to keep the Prince Regent safe from Daneska, given the fact that we move in far less exalted social circles than either of them?"

Miss Stranje's left eyebrow rises just enough to make it appear as if she finds Tess's question amusing. "Are you quite certain you know the circles I run in?"

Tess opens her mouth to ask something else, but before she can Sera poses a different question. "What pretense shall we use to explain our being in London?"

"We don't need a pretense." Miss Stranje strides purposefully across the room to our worktable. "I intend to hold a coming-out ball to present you young ladies to society."

Sera blanches so intensely her skin turns almost as white as her hair. "You needn't do that. Not for me. My mother would never approve, surely, and I don't really want one anyway."

"Nonsense. Most girls your age beg for a proper debut. Your mother and father gave me *carte blanche* to do as I please, and it pleases me to hold a coming-out for all of you."

Sera spirals into a panic. "But it's May. The London Season is nearly over."

Miss Stranje does not give her any quarter. "With all the

trouble mounting in Europe, Parliament has a great many things yet to settle. The Season is bound to last until the end of July, or longer." Miss Stranje sits down, squares up a sheet of paper, and begins a list. "Now let's see, we will need the appropriate gowns, slippers, fans, and fripperies we can buy in town, and . . ."

Poor Sera. She sits down beside Miss Stranje with her head in her hands and even from here, I can see she's shaking.

"I *can't* go," I say flatly, having decided I can't risk being seen in London. They all stare at me with mouths agape.

"Why not?" Georgie marches toward me. "It will be marvelous. We can visit London Tower and Vauxhall Gardens. You *have* to come with us. We need you. Who will order us about and make certain we are doing our part?"

I don't answer. They'll have Miss Stranje for that. I pretend to inspect my fingernails. Tess crosses her arms, leans against the wall, and frowns. "What if we need a lock picked?"

She has a point. Lock picking is something I do exceptionally well, but it is not a good enough reason for me to jeopardize my entire future. "You'll be attending balls, not sneaking into the Iron Crown's fortress. There won't be any locks to pick."

Tess is not appeased. "If anyone is to stay behind, it ought to be me. I need to look after Lord Ravencross."

"Oh, for pity's sake." Miss Stranje plunks down her pen. "Yes, there's a fine idea. Why didn't I think of that? I ought to leave you here, Tess, *unchaperoned*, with a gentleman who only two days ago I caught you *kissing*."

We smother grins at this, even me. It is impossible not to. The word *kissing* sounds so peculiar on Miss Stranje's lips, as if it is an objectionable activity. Amusing, considering I'm quite certain she kisses Captain Grey on occasion.

"You'll come to London with us—both of you." Miss Stranje

waves her hand at Tess. "Oh, do sit down, and stop glowering before you give yourself frown lines. If I know Lord Ravencross, he'll pack up and follow you to London. I daresay, the man would chase after you even if he had to travel to Hades and back."

Tess doesn't sit, she paces. "I don't see how I can leave Phobos and Tromos, not when any day now Tromos is about to have her pups."

"We'll bring them with us." Miss Stranje dismisses Tess's argument with a flip of her hand.

"Wolves don't belong in the city. Neither do I," Tess mumbles, but Miss Stranje merely shakes her head.

"Whether Tess goes or stays, I must remain here." I say this quietly, not in an argumentative way, in a sad *I-wish-I-could-go-but-I-can't* way.

Sera turns in her chair. "How will I bear being around all those high-society people without you?"

I shrug. "I'm sorry. I truly am." More than she could ever know, I want to be there for her, and I would dearly love to see Alexander one last time.

Georgie turns cross. She never gets cross. "Whyever not?"

"I can't tell you. Trust me, though, I have very good reasons."

"If you want us to trust you, you must *trust us* enough to tell us your reasons why." Sera stands, and I'm afraid she will come closer and read too many clues in my face.

"Very well, if you must know. I have *hundreds* of reasons." I spray excuses at them. "Someone must stay and attend to matters here. There is the rest of the sheepshearing to oversee. I've planned a new breeding program to increase our wool yield. This is the only time of year those experiments can be carried out. If I leave, it would be the same as taking money from Captain

Grey's pocket. I have to make certain the fields are furrowed using the new methods to facilitate drainage. Spring is our busiest time." I grab a quick breath. "I simply cannot go."

Miss Stranje pierces me with one of her *I-know-you're-not-telling-me-the-truth* looks. "My dear Lady Jane, I appreciate you lending your expertise to Captain Grey's steward. However, it is Mr. Turner's duty to manage the estate. That's why we pay him. More importantly, I am not training you to be a steward."

I fling my hands open. "I'll be of no use to you in London. I can't possibly stop an assassin. I'm only middling good at close range with a dagger. You have Tess for things like that and now Georgie, too. I can better serve you here." I pull in my wildly gesticulating hands and cross my arms, tucking them tight around me. "Besides, someone must stay and keep an eye on Alice."

"You are coming with us, Lady Jane." Miss Stranje turns back to writing her list. "And so is Alice."

"Alice!?" Georgie practically chokes.

"Of course." Miss Stranje dips her quill and begins writing again. "She's a perfectly adequate housemaid and someone has to carry our misinformation to Lady Daneska. Who better to do it than her own spy?"

There's a scratch at the door. Miss Stranje glances up from writing her list. "Enter."

Greaves carries in his silver tray and on it rests a small calling card. "The younger Mr. Chadwick is in the foyer, miss. He specifically requested the company of Miss Wyndham."

Sera, who is already flustered beyond her ability to cope, groans. "What can he want?"

"I've no idea, miss, beyond the fact that the young man carries a bouquet and would not allow me to relieve him of it."

Greaves turns back to our headmistress. "He also asked me to mention he has information which may be of concern to you, Miss Stranje."

"Thank you, Greaves." Miss Stranje takes the card without reading it and flips it end over end, as she thinks. "Show Mr. Chadwick to the blue drawing room."

"Shouldn't we tell him we are not at home?" Sera pleads.

"No, Miss Wyndham. It's best we listen to what the magistrate's son has to say. I suggest you take the back stairs and make yourself ready for our guest."

Eager to escape the room, I offer to accompany Sera.

"Lady Jane!" Miss Stranje arrests me at the door. "You and I will discuss the trip to London later."

My stomach clenches, she'll want answers, answers that must stay hidden. Sera and I hasten upstairs to the dormitorium. She fusses with her stockings. "Why must Mr. Chadwick pay a visit today of all days?"

I laugh. "Men are rarely convenient. I suspect they pride themselves on being inconvenient." I smile to myself, thinking of how Mr. Sinclair always seemed to do so. With a wistful sigh, I add, "But they can also be rather wonderful in their own way. I thought you liked Mr. Chadwick. Why does it fluster you so much that he should call on you?"

"I have no idea." Sera rifles through her wardrobe. "Oh, for pity's sake, what shall I wear? There's nothing here."

"*Piffle*. You have several very pretty gowns. You'll look lovely in any one of them." Sera has never understood how beautiful she is.

She pulls out a yellow morning gown, and promptly thrusts it back into the closet. "Why is it *you* never fret about what you will wear?"

"Why should I?" I shrug. "I am simply me, plain brown-wren Lady Jane. I strive to look clean and presentable. If I achieve that much, I'm quite pleased."

"How can you think such a thing, Jane? You're anything but ordinary or plain." She frowns at me before turning back to her wardrobe. "By society's standards you are a classic beauty, extremely pretty."

"Only to you, my dear friend, and that's because your vision is colored by affection." I put my arm around her shoulders because she is so kindhearted. "What about this dress, it's one of my favorites." I pull out a dainty aqua-blue morning gown. "The color highlights your porcelain complexion."

While she changes, I go to the window and aim the spyglass across the park at Ravencross Manor. To see all the way to the barns, I must open the window and lean out. I adjust the glass and spot several men working. From here, they look like small figurines moving in a shadow box.

Sera hurries to the window beside me. "Are they loading the prototype yet?"

"Yes. I expect they'll be leaving for London soon, but I don't see Mr. Sinclair. I doubt they would chance having him there." I know this, and yet I lean further out and refocus the telescope in the faint hope of catching a glimpse of him.

Sera adjusts her collar and tucks in a lace fichu. "I'm sure they'll keep him hidden until the wagons reach the road."

She's right, of course, and I'm behaving like a silly besotted schoolgirl. I pull back inside the window and collapse the spyglass. I help tie the ribbons on her back. "You look beautiful, like a fairy-tale princess."

"Now whose vision is colored by affection? I look like a frightened mouse. Mr. Chadwick makes me so very nervous."

"Why? He's your friend, Sera. A young man who genuinely appreciates your extraordinary mind. He understands you."

"He can't. How can he understand?" She shakes her head. "Mr. Chadwick's family has always approved of him. They even hired tutors for him. He's had every advantage. I'm quite certain Mr. Chadwick's family never locked *him* in the attic for drawing a portrait of his dead grandfather. I doubt they accused him of being possessed. Do you think anyone slapped him for noticing details he ought not? Or for asking questions about things he should not have seen?"

Sera sinks onto the bed her hands folded meekly in her lap. "I tried so hard to keep out of trouble. I thought if I kept quiet, if I painted or drew pictures to pass the time, no one would get nervous or upset at me, maybe I wouldn't frighten them so much. I missed my grandfather. He had been fond of me. Granpapa called me his bright little angel. I should've hidden the pictures I drew of him. How was I to know it would upset my mother and my aunts—"

"You have a peculiar family, Sera." I brush her silky white hair and pin it up in a bun. "They're foolish and superstitious. You mustn't judge the rest of the world by them."

Her hands ball into fists. "My mother said she wished I hadn't been born—"

"She didn't mean it. If you hadn't been born, the world would have been robbed of one of the kindest, dearest girls I know." I finish tying a ribbon in her hair. She is fine and delicate, but her mind rivals that of any man in England. I clasp her shoulders and look at her squarely. "Listen to me, Seraphina Wyndham. As beautiful as you are, your brain is your most impressive feature."

She blushes rosy pink, and I feel an overpowering urge to take a horsewhip to the cruel people who made her feel so timid about her intelligence. "Come. We mustn't keep Mr. Chadwick waiting any longer. Admit it. Aren't you the tiniest bit curious to find out what he has to say?"

"No. Well, maybe a little."

At Sera's request, I accompany her and Miss Stranje into the blue drawing room. Tess and Maya are spying on us from behind the Chinese silk painting. We saw them slip into the understairs passage as Sera and I entered.

Mr. Chadwick springs up from his chair. I have to admit there is something cheering about his broad smile, as if his features were specially created for happiness. He hides a rose-colored flush by bowing rather long to us.

Finally, he straightens and thrusts a bouquet at Sera. It's a cheery collection of hyacinths, daffodils, and a few cowslips with charming purple bells. "From my mother's garden." He runs a finger around his high collar and cravat in a vain attempt to loosen his neckwear. "I thought, er, you might enjoy . . . um . . ."

"They're lovely, Mr. Chadwick." Miss Stranje walks into the room and spares him any more stumbling. "Spring flowers are always so heartening."

"Yes. That is to say, I hope Miss Wyndham likes them, too." He risks a direct glance at Sera. She holds the flowers in her arms as if they are as fragile and dear as a newborn infant. He swallows and turns a brilliant shade of red again.

Laughter threatens to bubble up in my throat, so I busy myself by going to Sera's aid. "I'll have Greaves put them in some water for you, shall I?"

She nods, even more tongue-tied than he is. I extract the

flowers from her, plunk them in a nearby Chinese vase, and hand them over to Greaves. Our butler heads for the door holding the vase of blooms away from his person as if it is something repugnant the dogs tracked in. Before he can escape, Miss Stranje stops him. "Greaves, do send Phillip back with a tea tray, if you would, please."

"As you wish, miss." He shuts the door on his way out.

Miss Stranje turns to our guest. "How very kind of you to call, Mr. Chadwick. Have a seat, won't you? Greaves tells me you have information of particular interest to me."

"Yes, I do." Mr. Chadwick waits for Sera to sit, and chooses the chair nearest her.

"I'm intrigued." Miss Stranje smooths out her skirts and laces her fingers in her lap. "Pray, do tell us your news."

His face loses some of its jubilance and turns serious. "I came here by way of the beach. I confess, I had hoped to have another look at that extraordinary steam vessel you have in your possession. Although, given its small size, I suppose one can't really call it a steamship, can one? Is it a steam-powered raft?"

Miss Stranje does not betray even the slightest concern about the direction this conversation is taking. "We call it the *Mary Isabella*," she says brightly.

"Yes, well, I went to have a closer look at the *Mary Isabella*, and you can imagine my surprise at finding it missing."

"Not *missing*, Mr. Chadwick. The ship is on its way to London." I say this quite pleased with myself for offering a completely honest response.

His face twists up as if that is a perplexing piece of news. "Are you quite certain?"

"Yes, of course, I am." *After all, a few minutes ago I saw them loading up the wagons. Any minute now, they'll be on the road to*

London. "In fact, I bid Mr. Sinclair farewell myself." That sounds a wee bit too personal, so I add, "We all did."

Miss Stranje tilts her head, studying the young man. "Why? What is troubling you, Mr. Chadwick?"

He answers her bluntly, as if he is a student confessing difficulty adding up his sums. "When I entered the cove, I noticed a great many footprints along the shore. Since you were all on the beach bidding him farewell, that explains them. However, I also noted impressions of various pieces of equipment, and long flat prints which could only have been made by planks, almost as if the vessel had been taken apart." He searches our faces. "Dismantled, and carried ashore."

"How very peculiar." Miss Stranje stands, goes to the door, and opens it to peer out into the foyer. "I wonder where our tea tray is?"

Miss Stranje isn't concerned about the tea. She's worried Alice might be in the hall eavesdropping. Making certain there is no one outside the drawing room, our headmistress wanders to the wall beside the fireplace and leans down to check the grating, a grating that hides another listening hole. "I assure you, Mr. Chadwick, we were all there this morning to see Mr. Sinclair off as he departed."

"Yes," I rush to corroborate her statement. "It was a sad moment. *Truly.*" I do not have to feign my downcast look.

He shakes his head. "I felt certain there had to be more to it than that." I wish we could tell him the truth. A frown on Mr. Chadwick's countenance looks so terribly out of place. Confusion does not rest easily on his features. He bounces his palm against the arm of his chair as if he can drum answers out of thin air. "You see, not only did I find impressions of gears and machinery in the sand, but I also noticed several men hiding behind the rocks at the top of the bluffs, spying on my movements."

At this, Miss Stranje's attention whips to him. "Men? What sort of men?"

"I cannot believe they were a good sort. When they saw I'd spotted them, they took off as if they'd been caught in the act of doing something criminal. That's the very reason I'm doubly concerned about the missing ship."

"How many men did you see?" Sera's shyness vanishes.

He sits straighter, responding eagerly to her question. "From that distance and angle, at first I only noticed movement. It wasn't until they stood to run away that I had a better look at them. I gave chase, but by the time I ran up the bluffs, they were gone. Their footprints overlaid one another, so I could only clearly identify three distinctive sets of footprints. Given the quantity of prints, though, I suspect there may have been a fourth man. You understand, grass and foliage make it impossible to be sure."

"Of course." Sera nods. "You would only have a clear print if they stepped in mud or dirt."

While they discuss footprints, I worry Daneska's spies will have seen the wagons on the road and add two and two. "How long ago did you see those men, Mr. Chadwick?"

He consults his pocket watch. "Nearly an hour. It took me a half hour to hike back to my horse and ride here. Then, er, I waited here for twenty-three minutes."

An hour. That means the boat thieves fled from Mr. Chadwick while the wagons were still being loaded. Daneska's henchmen will have run straight back to report the steamship has already sailed. I exhale with relief. The wagons won't have been on the road yet.

"This is most upsetting, Mr. Chadwick." Miss Stranje doesn't look very upset. "Thank you for bringing the matter to our attention."

Greaves comes quietly through the door carrying the vase of flowers properly arranged. He places it on the side table so the flowers completely obscure Mr. Chadwick's view of Sera. Phillip comes in behind the butler carrying a tea tray.

Miss Stranje indicates Sera should pour for our guest.

As soon as the servants leave the room, Mr. Chadwick leans forward, warming to his subject. "Given the circumstances, you can understand why I wonder if that unfortunate incident two weeks ago involving Miss Aubreyson and Miss Fitzwilliam might have something to do with the arrival of your American cousin, Mr. Sinclair, and his extraordinary steamship."

Sera very nearly spills the tea.

"My cousin?" Miss Stranje draws his attention away from Sera. "What can his arrival have to do with that horrifying attempt to kidnap one of my students? I thought your father and the coroner settled all that."

"Yes, yes, they did. The matter is officially closed. The problem is, I'm not altogether satisfied with their findings. And now, today, after seeing those men sneaking around the bluffs, spying on the cove where you'd stored Mr. Sinclair's steamship, I have more questions than ever." He accepts the cup and saucer from Sera, and even though words form on his lips, it isn't until he clears his throat that he makes them audible. "Don't *you*?" He directs this last to Sera.

She quickly looks away, as if he hadn't sought her opinion.

"I'm certain there must be a connection." He leans his head nearly sloshing his tea in an attempt to observe her response. When that fails, he sinks back in his chair and studies the ripples in his teacup. "Too many missing pieces."

Sera takes a bite of dry cookie and stares intently at the Chinese painting, behind which she knows Tess and Maya are watching.

"You're an exceptionally clever young man, Mr. Chadwick. I'm sure you will find the answers, if there are any to be found." Miss Stranje waves her hand, the way a magician misdirects his audience, and draws his attention to the flowers. "How is your mother? I see by these lovely flowers that her garden is as spectacular as ever. It must be magnificent with all the spring blooms."

He sets down his cup. "I'm certain she would enjoy showing it to you. You ought to come for a visit. Yes, you should come and bring all the young ladies." He glances sidelong at Sera.

Miss Stranje calmly sips her tea. "Thank you. We would like that, except the young ladies and I are leaving for London in the next few days to attend the remainder of the season."

"London? For the season, I see." Mr. Chadwick looks as if she clobbered him with a pike. In one fell swoop, Miss Stranje has robbed him of a most intriguing puzzle and, in all likelihood, the only young lady in the entire universe to whom he is suited. "Must you?" The words come tumbling out and he turns red.

"Yes." Miss Stranje nods politely, even though she must realize she has just dashed his hopes to pieces. "I'm pleased to say, Miss Wyndham, along with the other young ladies, are to be presented to society. I'm planning a coming-out ball for them."

"A ball. I see." He tugs at his collar again, this time with more force. Poor fellow, he knows what this means. Sera will be on the marriage mart and he will be out of the running. She is as good as gone.

He sets down the cup of tea, and silently taps his finger on the arm of the chair. Suddenly, as if finding a solution, he stands. "Pardon my boldness, Miss Stranje, but if I might impose upon your friendship with my mother, I should very much like an invitation to your ball."

"You would?" Sera's lips part in surprise.

"Yes. Yes, I would. Very much so." He takes a deep breath and straightens his cuffs. "Now, sadly, our fifteen minutes have flown and I must not overstay my welcome. I bid you *adieu* and wish you all a safe journey." He bows to me and Sera and stiffly approaches Miss Stranje. In a quiet voice he adds, "As to the invitation, I'm aware it was presumptuous of me to ask. You must, of course, do as you see fit."

"I shall be delighted to send you an invitation, Mr. Chadwick." Miss Stranje smiles at him warmly. "Thank you for stopping in and alerting us about the intruders on our property."

"As to that, I give you my promise, I shall continue to investigate. Perhaps we might discuss this further, when we are all in London."

"As you wish," our headmistress says with sinking enthusiasm, and gives him a farewell curtsy in return for his bow.

Nine

PREPARING FOR BATTLE

The next few days whirl by in a flurry of activity as we prepare for the journey to London. With all the uproar, anyone would think we were preparing for Armageddon. Like all of the servants, Alice is extremely busy. So far, she hasn't found time to meet with anyone from the Iron Crown. We know, because we've been keeping watch on her movements.

Breakfast is no longer a pleasant conversational hour. It's a beehive, with servants running to and fro, delivering messages, and gathering instructions from the queen of this swarm, Miss Stranje.

This morning the queen bee and Madame Cho are arguing. According to Tess, Madame Cho is actually Miss Stranje's adopted sister, and today they are bickering as if it is true. Madame Cho no longer has a bandage on her head, and she's adamant about making the trip to London with us. "I will not allow you to face Lady Daneska without me." She smacks her hand on the table to emphasize her point.

Personally, I think she wants revenge for the brutal whack on the head Lady Daneska gave her, and the long scar etched on her throat.

Miss Stranje prunes up. "You nearly died. I don't want anything to compromise your health. London is noisy and we are perfectly capable of . . ."

Greaves holds out his silver tray containing several letters.

". . . dealing with Lady Daneska on our own." Miss Stranje glances at the top letter and draws a quick breath. "I'm not certain you're up to the rigors of the journey."

"*Rigors.* Do you think me a cripple?" Madame Cho stands. "Come to the mats today. I will show you rigors. I can best any of these young sprouts." She sweeps a hand at all of us, and crosses her arms imperiously. "*Rigors.* Bah! I'm going."

It surprises me, when Miss Stranje relents so easily. "Very well, it will be a comfort to have you with us." Obviously distracted, she picks up the letter and breaks the seal.

"What is it?" Madame Cho shifts in a flash from annoyance to concern.

Miss Stranje scans the contents. "It's from Captain Grey. The wool wagons arrived safely in London."

A question pops out of my mouth before I can stop it. "And Mr. Sinclair?"

She rubs the bridge of her nose for a moment. "Yes. There's a letter from him enclosed for you, Lady Jane." She hands the sealed note to me with two fingers, as if Mr. Sinclair painted the parchment with rat poison. "This is highly improper. You must not encourage this sort of thing from a gentleman to whom you are not engaged."

She thinks it's a love letter. Heat blazes into my cheeks. "I didn't encourage him. Not in the least. I'm sure he merely has a question about his ship's notes, or some other business matter."

She shakes her head at me, as if I'm responsible for Mr. Sinclair's breach of etiquette, and heaves a sigh. "I suppose one must excuse his manners. Mr. Sinclair is, after all, an American. They can be so very uncivilized." She sends one last frown in my direction. "And brazen."

Miss Stranje never said a word, *nothing at all,* when Georgie received several notes and letters from Lord Wyatt, and they're not engaged, either. I hoist my chin in the air and stuff the *uncivilized* American's letter into my left pocket, the one that doesn't have an opening next to my dagger and sheath. It's difficult pretending the parchment isn't making my fingers itch to tear it open.

"Is there any other news?" Sera leans forward, drawing our attention back to Captain Grey's letter.

"Lady Daneska has not yet arrived in London. Her ship is expected in port tomorrow." Miss Stranje's shoulders stiffen, as if the next sentence makes her uncomfortable.

"What?" I demand. "What's wrong?"

She pinches her lips together before answering. "Captain Grey has heard rumors that Ghost will arrive incognito on the same ship as Lady Daneska."

A monstrous claw reaches up and clutches my stomach. I can hardly breathe as she continues speaking.

She continues reading. "He also mentions that his men observed several fast-moving sloops armed with guns, anchored in the Thames near Canvey Island."

"*Pirates.*" Georgie nearly knocks over her water glass. "You were right, Jane. The Iron Crown sent them to take the *Mary Isabella.*"

Miss Stranje inclines her head in my direction. "Well done, Lady Jane. Your plan kept Mr. Sinclair and his prototype safe thus far."

Thus far.

Small comfort. Ghost is coming.

Possibilities for disaster gnaw my composure to shreds. I can't stand the uncertainty a second longer. "Does he say where they're staying? Are they well hidden? Do they have men standing guard at their quarters?" It is not like me to barrage her with such desperate questions.

"For now they are safe. That's all we know." Miss Stranje folds the letter primly and glances pointedly at me, a silent scold for my outburst. I turn away as she addresses the others. "We will be altering the departure date for our journey. I would like to arrive in London as soon as possible."

"How soon?" Maya's tone is buttery smooth, but I detect a peppery hint of nervousness, highly irregular for her.

"We shall leave in the morning." Miss Stranje claps her hands and rises. "Attend to your sewing today, ladies, and pack your things this evening."

A collective groan rises among Georgie, Sera, and Maya. Changing the schedule means they have hems to finish, lace to add to collars, sleeves to stitch in place, bonnets to trim, ribbons to match, and slippers to dye. Tess and Madame Cho head to the ballroom for morning practice, but the rest hurry off to the yellow parlor.

On the same day Miss Stranje decided we should make this trip to London, she turned her upstairs parlor into a massive sewing room and hired a dozen women from the village as temporary seamstresses. There are more comings and goings from the upstairs parlor than from a field marshal's tent. High-pitched chatter floods the hallways. Barked orders ricochet off the walls. *"Pass the scissors. This seam puckers, tear it out. Hand me the pink thread. Stand still! That hem is crooked."*

Thank goodness my wardrobe is already ample, and I'm spared the aggravation of fittings, pinnings, and hemmings. I dash into the library and close the door, shutting out the clamor and fuss. I want a quiet place where I might read my *brazen* American's letter.

The library is my favorite room at Stranje House. My safe harbor. I relish the smell of oiled leather bindings and lemon-waxed shelves, and the way the books soften the noise of the world. I wander to my private desk beside the window, and run my hand over the smooth oak. Everything on it stands in perfect order, the blotter is squared and everything is in its place.

Grateful for this haven of peace, I sink into one of the overstuffed chairs by the fireplace, and stare at Mr. Sinclair's highly improper letter. Lifting the folded paper to my nose, I expect to find a whiff of something that will remind me of him, perhaps the musty tang of welded copper, machine oil, or *anything*. Except there's nothing, only the scent of paper, ink, and sealing wax.

I break the seal and read:

My dear Lady Jane,

The Mary Isabella arrived in London without incident. Your ingenious idea to hide the smaller parts in bags of wool worked admirably. Now, however, little tufts of sheep's fuzz are stuck to everything. I anticipate hours of cleaning ahead. Wool and grease seem to be attracted to one another despite their drastic differences. Does that remind you of an equally cockeyed relationship?

Enough sentimental drivel—on to more important points.

Drastic differences. He means us. *Cockeyed.* It's another of his absurd American expressions. It conjures the image of a half-blind rooster tilting its head stupidly, which must indicate his opinion of our "relationship."

"*Sentimental drivel,* indeed." I feel a sudden urge to punch something.

I read the paragraph again, and squelch a low growl rising in my throat. Ladies do not growl. It's unbecoming. A small rumble escapes. *His fault.*

And to think, Miss Stranje was worried he might've written me an improper declaration of his affections. "Ha!"

I lower the letter and glare across the room. I don't see the oak paneling or the fireplace. Oh no, *he* stands before me. Alexander Sinclair leans casually against the mantel, his tousled blond hair catches sunlight from the window, his unpredictable eyes spark with mischief, and, of course, there is no escaping his customary smirking grin.

A hallucination sent to mock me.

Or humiliate me.

Or both.

I've half a notion to wad up his ruddy note and throw it through my hallucination into the fire. Instead, I give way to curiosity and continue reading his *cockeyed* note.

You will be delighted to learn I arrived in London without a scratch on my person other than those you left etched in my heart. I passed myself off as a sheep farmer quite easily. The question is—can I pass for a gentleman? Lord Wyatt tells me the Admiralty and the Prince Regent himself intend to inspect the steamship once we get her put back together. Lofty company indeed. I wish you were here to guide me.

My mouth curves into a soft smile and my shoulders relax, melting toward him. Not all the way, mind you, I'm only thawing a bit.

I have a request. Lord Wyatt tells me Miss Stranje is bringing all of you to London for a visit. Might I impose upon you to teach me the steps to one or two of your English dances? Before you roll your eyes and wrinkle up that adorable little nose of yours, allow me to explain.

The Prince Regent requests my attendance at a soirée wherein I'm to be introduced to a number of key naval dignitaries. Naturally, there's to be dancing at this gathering and several young ladies whose fathers are men of influence, and I'm told they are eager to make my acquaintance.

Does he mean their fathers wish to meet him, or their daughters? I believe the rascal left it intentionally vague.

To be perfectly frank, I would rather not dance at all, but Captain Grey says refraining may be considered ungentlemanly. I don't wish to disappoint the Prince or his esteemed guests. Therefore, my dear friend, I'm relying upon you to keep me from making a cake of myself. What do you say, Lady Jane? Will you teach me to dance?

With deepest regards,
Alexander Sinclair

The letter wobbles in my fingers. Mr. Sinclair's apparition still stands across the room, only now he wears a fine set of clothes. His black coat sets off his halo of gleaming curls as he innocently smiles at dancers in the ballroom at Carlton House. He does not see Lady Daneska waltzing toward him. Does not see her concealed dagger until it is plunged into his ribs. She whirls off, carefree and laughing. He crumples to the floor.

I flinch, even though it's only a mirage, a figment of my imagination, a fear.

A perfectly rational fear. Lady Daneska will be at the Prince's soirée.

I pace to the window. Alexander is in danger, and I don't see how we can protect him *and* the Prince? How can we truly protect either of them when Daneska is so stealthy? It seems impossible.

Thinking this way does no good. *There is always a way.* That's what I tell myself in times like these. "There's always a way," I murmur, hoping it's true.

A copy of the London *Times* sits on the side table. Picking it up to distract myself from morbid worries, I smile remembering how Mr. Sinclair spoke to me of using his uncle's ingenious design to create a steam-driven press for newspapers. "Mark my words," he said. "Someday, the London *Times* will be printed using a steam engine."

The world is racing forward, and Alexander Sinclair is precisely the sort of man who will be holding the reins as it gallops into the future. I must make sure he survives to do it.

With a sigh, I scan the news. Several items catch my eye. The Duchess of Oldenberg is staying in London at the Pulteney Hotel, and last Saturday afternoon the Prince Regent introduced her to the Prince of Württemberg.

"How very odd." The Prince of Württemberg is the duchess's cousin, they hardly needed an introduction. The paper reports that the duchess also received a letter from her brother, Tzar Alexander I, who is rumored to be visiting in Paris.

I wonder if the Prince Regent is trying to broker a marriage between the Duchess of Oldenberg and his ally, the Prince of Württemberg? If that's the case, why is the duchess's brother, Emperor of Russia, in Paris visiting Napoleon Bonaparte?

I'll wager it has something to do with Lady Daneska's visit. Plots and possibilities swirl through my mind and send my thoughts spinning. I fold the corner of the page intending to discuss this matter with Miss Stranje later, and scour the rest of the gossip column for clues. Two paragraphs later, one name grabs my attention by the hair and gives it a painful yank.

A name that rings in the destruction of my future.

Lord Harston.

It is the very name I feared. The one man I must avoid at all costs. His name traps the breath in my lungs. Nay, it stops my heart, and squeezes until I am cold and shivery.

It will be impossible to dodge him in London. "He'll find me."

Lord Harston, the paper says, was seen riding in the park this afternoon with the Prince Regent. Later in the evening, the Prince Regent was observed entering White's Gentlemen's Club in the company of Lord Harston, Lord Alvanley, and Sir Lumley Skeffington. According to reliable sources, Lord Harston is currently the Prince's guest at Carlton House.

I drop into a chair. *Can fate be this cruel?*

As if I have not been kicked in the teeth enough, one paragraph below Lord Harston, the paper mentions my two good-for-nothing brothers.

"Blast!" Once again, the wastrels have disgraced me. Breath comes shuddering back in furious heaves. *They*, at least, are *not* guests of the Prince. I ought to be grateful for that one small blessing, instead I groan under the weight of my humiliation.

The report says my eldest brother, the notorious Earl of Camberly, and his younger brother, Bernard Moore, caused a riot at the Royal Theatre in Drury Lane. It began innocently enough, with Francis and Bernard throwing rotten fruit during a performance of *Othello*. In and of itself, throwing fruit at the stage would not have been newsworthy. After all, vendors sell rotten apples and moldy pears in the theater for that very purpose.

The *Times* explains that my brothers, in an extremely drunken state, purchased two entire baskets of moldy oranges. Reeling, as they must've been, their aim was sadly off. Many of their throws missed the stage entirely. Fruit flew every which way, and my siblings began amusing themselves by aiming at several distinguished members of the audience, some of whom were visiting dignitaries from Vienna and Russia. When audience members decided to return fire, disrupting the performance altogether, my ne'er-do-well brothers were forcibly removed and tossed into the street.

The *Times* goes on to comment on the disgraceful behavior of some members of the nobility, and castigates my brothers by name, noting their shameful examples, et cetera, et cetera, et cetera . . .

My attention whips back and forth between my brothers' embarrassing public reprimand and the paragraph about Lord Harston. The tighter my jaw clenches the blurrier the words get. All I can see are names I wish did not exist. The newspaper trembles in my hands, until I give up and crumple it in my lap.

I'm done for.

I cannot go to London.

Mr. Sinclair will need to find a different dance instructor. Miss Stranje can teach him. Yes, and Tess is far more capable of protecting him than I am. It's true. She's ten times the fighter I am. And yet, I dread leaving his care to anyone else.

What choice do I have?

My heart crashes against my chest as if it's a rock tumbling down the cliffs toward the sea. Appropriate, considering it feels heavier than a millstone.

Head in hands, I curl over my knees. I'm tired of these millstones. *Go ahead, toss me in the sea. Let me drown.*

No, that's foolish thinking. I slap my legs and straighten. There's an obvious solution. I won't go to London. That's all there is to it. Tess and Lord Wyatt will protect Mr. Sinclair. They'll do as good a job or better than I could do.

If I go, my brothers will heap shame upon me and everyone connected to me, Mr. Sinclair included, and Miss Stranje. *Everyone.* The scoundrels are bound to be in debt up to their eyeballs. They will undoubtedly try to find some way to bilk money out of my being there. Their rotten problems will become my rotten problems simply by proximity.

Even worse, if they should meet Lord Harston, and discover the truth . . .

No. No. No!

I simply can't go. Not with my money-grubbing brothers prowling about. And especially not with Lord Harston in town and running in the same circles with the Prince Regent and Lady Daneska. The entire trip reeks of disaster.

I can't go.

I won't.

The decision is made. I take a deep breath, smooth out the newspaper, fold it neatly, and set it on the table exactly where I found it. I arrange the blotter on my desk so it is perfectly squared. I close the desk drawer, turn the key, and lock away my emotions.

Ten

TRUTH

Tess broods all during dinner, not silently, as I do, she fumes noisily, huffing and grumbling, and thumping down her glass. When she stabs her roast beef a little too viciously, Sera tries to draw her out. "Are you upset because the doctor gave Lord Ravencross permission to go home today?"

"No. Why should that upset me? I'm not upset, I'm angry. He thinks he is fully recovered. Stubborn man—he insists he's going to go to London, too. 'I've obligations in the House of Lords,' he says. *Folderol.* He's going because he's worried about me. I've tried to make him see reason. Nothing I say will make him change his mind."

"Of course not." Georgie smiles. "Whither thou goest . . ."

"Don't sermonize me." Tess bristles up like one of her beloved wolf-dogs. "It's too dangerous for him in London. With Daneska coming to town, you know perfectly well his brother, Ghost, will be there, too, lurking in the shadows. I want Gabriel to stay home and recuperate where it is safe."

"Yes, but how can he, if he is worried about you?" Georgie makes the mistake of trying to argue with her. "He's a man. It's only natural that he wants to be close by to protect you."

"Don't be absurd." She leans into Georgie holding her fork at a dangerous angle. "I can take care of myself."

Georgie backs away. "Of course you can. Everyone knows that."

"At least." Sera's voice cracks nervously as she tries to disrupt their fuss. "You needn't worry about Punch and Judy. Phillip promised me he would take scraps to them now and then."

Tess's only answer is to shuffle food around her plate, something we are both doing. Maya offers light conversation by asking how many books she might bring. The others spend the rest of the dinner discussing which maps to bring, and how many gowns and bonnets to pack.

Miss Stranje finishes her dessert course, sets down her spoon and turns to me. "You're very quiet this evening, Lady Jane. Are you ill?"

"No." I stab a spoon at my half-eaten custard.

"Are you certain? You don't look yourself."

"Quite sure."

She waits with an unrelenting *hawk-on-the-hunt* stare.

"Very well then." I set my spoon down carefully beside my bowl and face her. "I considered pretending to be sick, but decided it would be better to be frank. I simply cannot go with you to London."

"What!" Georgie springs out of her chair.

Miss Stranje holds up a silencing finger. "You are all excused from the table. I would like a moment alone with Lady Jane."

She gestures for them to leave. Our wily headmistress doesn't say a word until the dining room door closes behind Tess.

I wish there was a way to avoid this conversation. "You know they'll be listening."

"I expect so, but if you speak softly enough they won't be able to hear." She scoots her chair closer to me. "What is troubling you about this trip? Is it the prospect of seeing Mr. Sinclair again?"

I shake my head. "Nothing to do with him." *That's not entirely true. In some respects, it has everything to do with him.* "Suffice it to say if I go to London it will spell disaster for me."

"*Disaster?*" She raises one eyebrow skeptically. "A strong word. How so?"

"For one thing, it will result in my being taken from your school." I evade her scrutinizing gaze, and trace the ornate pattern on the spoon handle. One sympathetic glance, one well-placed word, and she would unravel my composure and I might spill my secret.

"Is it because your brothers haven't paid your tuition this year?"

"They haven't? Good grief! I should've guessed." I shove the spoon handle away and huff loudly. "Those dirty, rotten scoundrels. I'm astounded they would imprison me here and then fail to send money for my upkeep."

"Imprison you?"

"That's not what I meant. My brothers think Stranje House is a prison. Not I. I like it here. You know I do."

"I'm delighted to hear it." My headmistress's shoulders twitch and her mouth quirks up at the corner. Leave it to her to find mirth in this situation. "In that case, you will be pleased to know, I sent a letter to your eldest brother concerning your welfare here. Lord Camberly wrote back and suggested I allow you to stay in exchange for you serving as a tutor or a ladies' maid to one of the other girls."

"How very thoughtful of him." I groan and bury my face in my hands.

"You needn't worry on that score, my dear. I required him to pay quite handsomely when he first brought you to me. I don't require any more tuition from you, if that's the cause of your distress."

"If only it were that simple." Realizing I must give her at least a partial explanation, I take a deep breath. "Let us just say, certain parties in London will remove me from your care if they learn of my whereabouts."

Her mouth purses up. "Let us say a bit more than that, *shall we?*"

"You don't understand. My brothers didn't tell anyone that they sent me here. I've no idea what Banbury tale they spread abroad to explain my absence, but I'm quite certain no one knows I'm here. Which is exactly how I prefer to keep it." This sounds rather snappish of me, so I try to soften my tone. "There is someone in London who absolutely *must not* know my whereabouts."

"Someone, other than your brothers?" She digs for an answer.

I swallow and hold my ground with a curt nod, saying nothing.

Miss Stranje utters an exasperated sigh and I make the mistake of looking up. "If you explain the matter to me," she says. "*In more detail.* Perhaps I can help you. I am not without connections, you know."

Not even you can dissolve a legally binding contract.

"No one can help me." My insides tighten up at the thought of telling her the sour, stinking truth. The familiar sting of my parents' betrayal burns me. Hot tears well up in my eyes. I squeeze them back down where they belong. This is not a crying matter. "There's nothing you can do. It's too late."

"Humph."

I blink. "You don't believe me?"

"I've no idea what to think, Lady Jane. You say *it's too late*. In my opinion, only a thimbleful of situations in life are that dire. Death begins and ends the list. Everything else is simply an obstacle that must be dealt with." She sets her custard bowl to the side and folds her hands. "You are not dead. So, unless you are in the process of dying, I sincerely doubt it is too late."

I exhale with frustration. "It would make things considerably easier if I were dying."

Her eyes narrow disapprovingly.

"There is only one way around this particular obstacle." I cross my arms to hold in my turmoil. "I must remain at Stranje House instead of going to London."

"That won't do, Lady Jane." She lifts her chin. "Stop shilly-shallying and tell me the problem so we can solve it together."

I'm tempted. Heavens above, I would dearly love to confide in her. Trouble is, I know Miss Stranje. If I tell her, she'll make me keep the wretched bargain my parents made. She lectures to us often enough about loyalty, honor, and duty.

Besides, even *thinking* about telling her what happened causes me to hang my head. If I tell her the disgraceful truth, she'll never look at me the same. It's hard enough to admit to myself the ugly thing my parents did.

How can I bring myself to tell her? Shall I say . . .

Allow me to introduce the real *Lady Jane*. Here is the truth behind my noble title, my proud heritage, and my aristocratic parents. I am an earl's daughter, and worth less in this world than a horse at auction.

It's the plain, puking truth.
And I hate it.

My parents traded me to pay their gambling debts. I was thirteen when they paraded me in a scandalously revealing dress in front of Lord Harston. "Lower your eyes," my mother warned at the time, as if at that raw age I could triumph over my red-faced embarrassment. "Do your duty. It's this or we lose everything."

Lord Harston had been drinking when they closed the door to his drawing room and left me alone with him. *Alone.*

The cad lounged on a couch with a tumbler of whiskey in his hand and allowed his gaze to linger rudely over me. "You're a passable filly." He slurred his words and spoke into the crystal cup, swirling the amber liquid. "I s'pose if I must marry, you'll do as well as any of those other whey-faced debs." He lifted his glass in a toast. "What say you, Lady Jane? Want to be my wife?"

I was too angry and shamed to say anything.

He chuckled to himself. "No, I don't suppose you would, would you. How old are you? Twelve? Thirteen? Fresh from the nursery, I'll wager. Still playing with dolls, aren't you?"

That much I could answer. I had never played with dolls. "No."

A mistake. He gave me his full attention then, and I wondered if he was half as drunk as I'd originally thought. He rubbed his chin. "Tell you what, my girl, let's flip a coin to decide. What do you say, heads or tails?"

How dare he ask me to chance my future on the flip of a coin?

I stood as straight and disapproving as I could in that foolhardy dress. "I do not gamble, sir."

"My lord," he corrected angrily. "I am *Lord* Harston. Didn't they even tell you that much?"

"My mistake. But my answer remains the same, my lord. I don't approve of gambling."

"Oh you don't, do you?" He laughed mockingly. "You *are* Camberly's brat, aren't you?" He got to his feet and strolled toward me. "You *do* know your father and mother are famous for betting on everything. *Everything.* From the color of coat the Prince will wear to dinner, to which racehorse will come in dead last." Harston wasn't as ancient as I'd feared he would be, but he was old, at least thirty, and his breath smelled of cigars and whiskey. "There isn't a hazard table in town they haven't played at—" He lifted a lock of my hair as if inspecting the color, comparing it to the whiskey in his glass. *"And lost."*

I backed away, tugging my hair out of his fingers. "I'm well aware of my parents' vices."

He chuckled. "I suppose you would be." He raised his glass to me again. "Thing is, my dear Jane—"

"Lady Jane."

"Yes, well, *Lady* Jane, your brothers don't seem to share your scruples, either. The oldest, what's his name?"

"Francis," I answered, searching for something to hit Harston with if he came one inch closer. I noticed a candlestick on a nearby table, and edged in that direction.

"Aye, that's the lad. I watched young Francis toss away three hundred quid at piquet last Tuesday. The misbegotten whelp didn't bat an eye." Lord Harston tossed back the rest of his drink and slammed the tumbler on the table.

I reached for the candleholder. He grinned mischievously. "What's the matter, Lady Jane, afraid of the dark?"

"No." I hoped there was enough warning in my voice and eyes. My parents would be furious if I struck him. I didn't care. I would do what I needed to do to protect myself. Let them beat me for it later. I hated being alone with this dog of a man. I hated him gawping at me. Most of all I hated them for valuing me so cheaply.

Bartering my future against their debt was mortifying enough, but parading me in front of this stranger like a plucked goose at the butcher shop was more humiliation than I could stomach. I refused to endure one minute more. I gripped Lord Harston's silver candlestick ready to smash it over his head if he took another step closer.

I was no fool, not even at thirteen. I knew what he might try to do. I'd overheard my brothers talking enviously about Harston's exploits with lightskirts and married women. He was an unscrupulous rake. Yet, my parents would saddle me with him for life.

This paragon of depravity had two virtues my parents coveted above all else. *Luck* and *money*. Where Papa and Mama lost at hazard tables, Lord Harston won. If they bet at a cockfight, his rooster lived, and theirs ended up roasting on a spit. If he sat at their card table, he ended the night with a stack of their shillings. It didn't matter if it was baccarat, whist, or piquet, he may not have won every hand, but he won often enough that they offered him vowels to keep playing. Eventually their IOUs mounted so high that to pay him the money they owed, they would have to sell off the better part of our estate.

Or make a bargain with the devil.

The latter suited them best. So they had rushed home from London and ordered the maid to dress me in that indecent frock and stuff cotton wadding into my chemise in certain places. My father, still flushed with gambling fever, inspected the servant's work. "She'll do."

My governess pleaded with my parents to reconsider. She begged them not to do it, saying I was too young to make such a decision. "Don't be daft." My father shoved her aside. "The law says a girl can marry at twelve." When she dissolved into tears, he ordered her to pack her bags and go. "Find another house to plague. We've no money left to pay you with anyway."

"We've no choice." My mother explained without looking me in the eyes. She pinched my cheeks and fussed at the maid about pinning up my hair properly. "We owe Lord Harston a king's ransom."

"In that case, how am I to be payment enough?"

She pinched my arm for mouthing off and whispered heated instructions. "You're to smile at him, and none of your smart talk. Do you hear me, Jane? Keep a civil tongue in your head."

Two hours later, there I stood in Lord Harston's drawing room armed with a candlestick while obediently keeping my tongue in check.

"Calm yourself, Lady Jane. I'm not going to steal your virtue today." Lord Harston grinned at me. "I'll say this though, you've got pluck. I like a girl with pluck. Too skinny by half, but you'll do for a wife. Not today, mind you, but maybe in three or four years, when I can no longer stave off my nagging relatives, and . . ." The cur ran his finger down the sensitive curve of my neck. "After you've filled out."

I flipped the candlestick, so the heavy end was up, and raised it in warning.

He laughed. "And when you're a little less frightened of me." He gently wrested the candlestick from my hand. "And not as eager to bash me over the head with my own silver."

"I'm not afraid of you." I stuck my chin in the air and wished my shaky voice sounded more convincing. If my parents were going to force me to marry this beastly excuse for a man, I needed to establish my ground from the start.

"Yes, you are, Lady Jane. As well you ought to be." Lord Harston set the candlestick down with a plunk, and strolled back to the couch. He flopped down and sprawled out in a lazy ungentlemanly way. My soon-to-be fiancé lounged back and closed his eyes. With a wave of his hand, he shooed me away. "Now run along, and send your parents in to finish negotiating our deal."

Thus, my parents signed promissory marriage agreements with this drunken gambler, bartering me away as if I was nothing more than a goat at a county fair.

I try very hard not to remember the acidic details of that day. Because when I do, they burn a hole in my heart. I find it difficult not to be furious with my mother and father for spending my freedom so cheaply, for tossing my future away on a throw of the dice and the turn of a card.

Too late to be furious with them.

Irony of ironies, my illustrious parents are no longer here to receive my fury. With their debt to Lord Harston settled, they raced back to London, eager to attend Lady Archer's exclusive evening of dining and gaming.

Of course, they did. How can I forget their excitement that night?

The memory makes bile rise in my throat. Free of their debts, the two of them returned home from Lord Harston's bouncing like jubilant children, toasting their good fortune, poring through their invitations. For them, it was a night for celebration. For me it felt like an early grave. Dressed in their finery, they prepared to leave. I sat at the top of the stairs, still wearing that dreadful dress. *Forgotten.* They didn't even wave farewell.

Later that night our household awoke to loud banging on the door. Apparently, in their giddy haste, my parents' carriage overturned. Strangers hauled their battered bodies into the house.

My father had been killed instantly, but Mama was still alive. The doctor came, but shook his head, warning us she was past help. A few days later, she, too, died.

And now, here I am . . .

Sitting in Miss Stranje's dormitorium with a contract hanging over my *unlucky* head. A contract forcing me to fulfill my parents' obligation and wed an equally contemptible gambler. No, that's not true, they're not his equal. Lord Harston is worse than they were. Not only is he a gambler, he's also a *care-for-nothing* womanizer.

What are the odds I will be able to find happiness with him, I wonder?

A thousand to one? A million to one?

No chance at all.

If I *were* the wagering sort—I'm not, but if I were—I'd bet Alice the maid, Alice the traitor, stands a greater chance at happiness than I do. A joyless laugh catches in my throat and nearly strangles me. I clench the tablecloth until my knuckles bulge white.

Miss Stranje covers my tight fist with her hand. "I can see that whatever is worrying you is painful." She's not the demonstrative sort, so I feel this quiet show of compassion more deeply than its face value. Except, I don't deserve it, and pull my hand away.

"Very well. I'll not press you, Lady Jane, but I will say this." She stands. "Troubles that lurk in the darkness of our own thoughts often feel gigantic. It's not until we expose these shadowy monsters to the light, by telling our friends, that they shrivel to a more manageable size. Whatever your problem is, you'll not be free of it by hiding."

She rests her hand on my shoulder. "You may choose to let

me help you or not, but you will come with us to London." Suddenly her hand feels as if it weighs forty stone.

I bite my trembling lip. "You don't know what you are sentencing me to."

"No, and I can't, unless you tell me. Let me be clear, Lady Jane, I have plans for you. Grand plans, and none of them include you hiding yourself away here at Stranje House."

Grand plans?

I can't bring myself to ask her what they are. A more pressing obstacle stands in the way of any plans she might have.

"If I go to London, your plans will come to naught. You won't be able to save me." I glare up at her, powerless to stop a lone tear from leaking out and burning a salty trail down my cheek. "Even if your connections extend all the way to the Prince Regent himself, you cannot keep me from disaster."

She pulls her hand from my shoulder, but the terrible weight remains. "Perhaps not, but in my long life I have found we must face the demons that haunt us. Running and hiding merely staves off the inevitable. Lady Jane, you may count on me to give you whatever assistance is within my power to grant, but I cannot help you if you will not trust me."

"Trust has nothing to do with it," I snap.

She smiles softly and tilts her head, narrowing in on me with birdlike shrewdness. "I believe you'll discover it does."

I shake my head, denying her words, but this burning truth she has spoken singes me.

She's right. I don't trust her.

I'm a hypocrite. I claim to hold loyalty and trust above all other virtues and yet I don't trust her. The most trustworthy person I've ever met. I nearly scream and an even more agonizing realization scorches through my mind. *I don't trust anyone.*

Not a single living soul.

I draw in a quick breath and look up, my cheeks blazing with shame, stinging from a heat far worse than any fever. That errant tear sliding down my cheek, now scalds into ash.

Miss Stranje brushes back a lock of my hair that has straggled across my brow and I risk meeting her gaze.

"When you're ready to confide in me," she says. "I will be ready to listen." There's kindness in her face, and tenderness. If I were *ever* going to trust anyone, it would be her. If only she had been my mother, I wouldn't be in this fix.

Except, it's wrong to think ill of the dead, so I force those thoughts aside. I lower my head, barely able to speak, and mumble, "I'm sorry." Unsure of what I'm apologizing for, it may be a hundred things, or nothing at all.

"Rest well, Lady Jane. We leave for London in the morning."

Thus, she seals my fate.

Eleven

ROAD TO RUIN

Before sunup the next morning, I climb obediently into the coach and head toward the disaster awaiting me in London. I contemplate running away, but that would most likely end in an even bleaker future than a loveless marriage to a scoundrel. So I choose to face the known evil, rather than hazard the unknown.

Our caravan of three coaches and a wagon, packed to the gills, bumps up the rutted road to London. From his perch, the coachman curses the fact that it rained last night. I sit inside, praying another storm will blow in and delay this ruinous trip indefinitely.

Once again, the fates align against me. Morning dawns a rosy pink, with nary a cloud in sight. The sun dries the road and we speed on our way to London. Whenever one wishes a journey to pass quickly, the road is bound to be plagued with detours, mud, and fallen trees. Conversely, when one is galloping toward destruction, the trip seems shorter than it ought, and the road miraculously free of trouble. In our case, there's not even so much as a pothole to break a wheel spoke.

I sleep along the way, having lain awake most of the night, mulling over various ways to avoid Lord Harston, and different disguises I might adopt. Not until we hit the cobblestones and cross Westminster Bridge am I jarred from slumber. We are here.

London.

St. James's Square.

When our coach finally stops, I stare out the window and my mouth falls open. *We are in Mayfair!* The heart of London's most elite addresses.

Never in a thousand years did I dream Miss Stranje could afford a mansion such as this. I'd thought I might be able to hide, to remain outside of Lord Harston's social circles. This is not the address in which to do that. There will be no anonymity here.

How in the world did she land us in Mayfair? I'd assumed Miss Stranje would rent modest lodgings on the outskirts of town. Never this, a mansion in the center of everything that is fashionable.

As if in a bizarre dream, I climb out of the coach and stand on the cobblestones gawking. It's five stories tall, with a sixth level below stairs. "Do close your mouth, Lady Jane." Miss Stranje walks up beside me. "Why are you gaping as if you've never seen a townhouse?"

"Not just any townhouse. This is . . . how did you . . . ?" My mouth works, but I struggle for a complete sentence, until finally I blurt, "The window tax alone must cost a small fortune." I shake my head.

"I suppose we all have our secrets." She smiles to herself.

"Surely, you didn't expect I would hold a coming-out ball for you young ladies in a rustic cottage up in Islington. I have a reputation to uphold."

I continue to stare at the towering facade, and soon realize there is something decidedly off. Unlike the neighboring townhouses, the windows on our house are shuttered tight; and those that aren't, are draped with black curtains.

Sera edges in next to me, and gestures at the second story. "Those shutters haven't been opened for quite some time. Do you see the debris collected on them? This is a house in mourning, and it has been so for a considerable amount of time."

"Nonsense." Miss Stranje sniffs. "Houses can't *mourn*. Whatever tragedy may have occurred here, a year is long enough for idleness. I won't have you spouting superstitious drivel. A house is nothing more than bricks and mortar, a place to hang our hats, a roof over our heads—that's all there is to it." She delivers this unwarranted tirade, fluffing out her black skirts like an annoyed raven. "Do you ladies intend to stand here all day? I, for one, would prefer to unpack."

She marches up the front steps, and turns to frown at us. "Tess, do *please* settle those dogs. And for pity's sake, all of you stop gaping like yokels. You are making an unfavorable impression on the neighbors." She raps the knocker smartly.

Indeed, several neighbors are peering discreetly from their windows, and I note the curtains drawing back across the street and next door. Sera whispers, "Something is amiss."

I agree. But I can't admit it aloud. I must remain stalwart for all of us. Miss Stranje is right, we ought to remove ourselves from the street. "Come along, whatever it is we'll simply have to deal with it." I loop my arm through hers, and tug her forward. Everyone else follows us inside.

The household staff stands in a formal line inside the large foyer awaiting inspection. Miss Stranje's heels click smartly against the black-and-white marble flooring as she marches in. An elegant spiral staircase winds up beside us, and a glass dome in the ceiling provides the only light filtering into the foyer. Despite the opulence, a dark stillness weighs heavily on us as we enter, perhaps because most of the furniture is still under covers and the windows are shuttered.

Tess comes in with our two snarling wolf-dogs in tow, and the butler backs against the wall. "What are those?"

She doesn't stop to explain. "Which way to the gardens?"

He points to the back and signals the first footman to show her the way.

"Our dogs are normally well mannered, Mr. Peterson," Miss Stranje assures him. "As soon as they accustom themselves to their surroundings, they will be as meek as lambs."

Lambs. I choke back a laugh.

Mr. Peterson doesn't look convinced. He adjusts his black coat and solemnly introduces the staff to Miss Stranje. There's a smugness about Mr. Peterson, as if he thinks himself above serving our headmistress. If Greaves were here, he would grab the insolent man by his ear and call him to task.

Mrs. Creevy, the housekeeper, seems pleasant enough, as do the housemaids and footmen. When Mr. Peterson learns we are adding to his staff our maid, Alice, and our cook, Magda, the man acts as if we have kicked him in the shins. "But, madame, we have a cook—"

"*Miss.*" Our headmistress takes a brusque gunshot step toward the butler. "It's *Miss* Stranje. As to the other matter, I am aware of your cook's excellent reputation, and she will, of course, have command of the kitchen. Mrs. Elderberry, isn't it?"

"Yes, miss." The apron-clad woman next to the housekeeper bobs a curtsy.

Miss Stranje smiles at her. "I'm sure Mrs. Elderberry will appreciate the extra hands in the kitchen when she is preparing supper for our upcoming ball."

"Aye, miss, that I would." Mrs. Elderberry stares up at our enormous cook and does her best to smile.

"A *ball?*" Peterson puffs up indignantly, his nose twitching out of joint. "I was not told there would be a gathering of that sort. I'm not certain it is entirely appropriate given the tragic circumstances of—"

"Mr. Peterson, I rented this house intending to hold a coming-out ball for my young ladies, and that is exactly what we shall have." Miss Stranje is not gigantic like Magda, but neither is she a short woman. When she stretches up to her full height and brandishes that stern expression of hers, any man's knees would knock. "Mind you, not just *any* ball. Ours will be a splendid affair, the highlight of the season. You and your staff are to remove these dreary draperies and dust covers immediately, and begin the task of restoring this house to the land of the living. Do we understand one another?"

Mr. Peterson blinks, and blinks again. The changes in his situation seem to settle on him with a painful thump. His countenance sags and his chin loses some of its supercilious height. "As you wish, miss."

Miss Stranje sets the servants to work hauling in our luggage, and the housekeeper leads us upstairs to show us to our rooms. "Six fine bedrooms," she declares as we wind up the staircase. "And that doesn't count the servants' quarters. Haversmythe House was once a grand residence. If I may say so, the grandest on our street, until—"

"It is lovely." Miss Stranje exclaims more exuberantly than normal. "Let's have a look at those rooms, shall we?"

Servants trudge up the stairs behind us, toting stacks of bandboxes and luggage. Before we are able to settle on who is to sleep where, Mr. Peterson arrives on the third floor landing huffing and puffing. He stops to catch his breath, and prunes up as if someone tracked in dog droppings, and announces, "You have *guests*, Miss Stranje."

The corner of our headmistress's mouth quirks to the side. "Thank you, Mr. Peterson. Who are these mysterious guests?"

"*Three gentlemen*," he says, as if this makes his news even more repulsive.

Miss Stranje calmly asks, "Perchance, did these mysterious gentlemen give you their names? Or cards?"

"Yes, miss, they did." She waits patiently as Peterson squares up two cards in his white gloved fingers, and reads, "One Captain Grey, and Lord Wyatt, a viscount. Another young man, a Mr. Sinclair, offered us no card, miss. *No card.*" Peterson hands her the aforementioned calling cards and sniffs disapprovingly. "I'll send them away, shall I? Surely we are not ready to receive guests."

"No, Mr. Peterson, we shall not send them away." She smiles to herself, happiness flaming into her cheeks. She averts her eyes and studies the cards, even though she knows by heart exactly what's written on each of those small ivory rectangles. "These gentlemen are our dear friends. You may seat them in the first-floor drawing room, and tell them we will be along shortly."

Mr. Peterson goes off to do her bidding, looking as if he just swallowed a lemon.

Georgie slips out behind our new butler and follows him as far as the balustrade overlooking the foyer, and I admit, I wander quietly behind her and peek over the railing, too. Servants are still unloading our trunks, the front door stands wide open, spraying sunlight across the marble foyer. There they stand, all three gentlemen, alive and well, still wearing their hats and coats.

As if Lord Wyatt knows Georgie is gazing at him, he glances up. When he sees her, Sebastian whips off his hat and smiles up at her with pure unadulterated adoration. I find it difficult not to sigh with envy.

Mr. Sinclair stands beside Lord Wyatt, and the unruly rogue leaves his hat on and grins broadly at me, waving his hand as if he intends to flag down a cabriolet. I cover my mouth, doing my best not to smile at his odd behavior. But if a small grin accidently slips out it is merely because I cannot resist how charmingly provincial he is. He doesn't care one whit about what is proper, or improper, nor what anyone else thinks of him. Alexander Sinclair is everything I am not.

"Come along." Miss Stranje orders us away from the balustrade and guides us up to the third floor. "Lady Jane, you will share that room with Maya and Sera. Georgie, you'll be with Tess in this bedroom." She sweeps her gaze over our spacious third floor. "Perfect. We will all be here on the third floor together, exactly as we are at home. No need to make the staff run up and down to the fourth floor."

"That's a mercy." Mrs. Creevy unlocks Georgie's bedroom door. "Especially considering the fourth floor is—"

"Exquisite, I'm sure." Miss Stranje aims a warning glance at her, but it is lost on the housekeeper.

"Oh yes, it's quite fine." Mrs. Creevy throws open the door to Tess and Georgie's bedroom. "But what I was about to say is—"

"That it must be a great relief you won't have to run up and down all these stairs?" Miss Stranje is not the sort to interrupt anyone. In fact, she would scold us if one of us did so, but she is certainly doing her share of it today.

Mrs. Creevy pinches up with confusion and shakes her head. The gray curls poking out from her mobcap spring up and down. "No, miss. You needn't worry yourself on that score; we're all quite accustomed to the stairs. What I was about to tell you is the fourth floor is—"

"Off limits." Miss Stranje says sternly, as if it's a command to us.

"No, it's where the murders happened," Mrs. Creevy blurts. "Gives me chills—"

"We will not discuss the . . ." With a slow deliberate inhale, Miss Stranje straightens to her scariest posture. "Your former employers."

Mrs. Creevy rocks back on her heels. "As you wish, miss."

"Good." Miss Stranje nods curtly. "Kindly inform your staff, I'll not have anyone filling my young ladies' heads with tales of what may or may not have occurred."

"Right." Mrs. Creevy ducks out of the room, mumbling under her breath. She strides rapidly down the corridor and unlocks our bedroom, and I hurry beside her in time to catch the very end of her muttered rant. "Tale, my arse. I know what I saw."

I'll coax the story out of the servants soon enough, but I enter the spacious blue bedroom, and the entire matter wafts out of my mind like a scrap of paper tumbling across the cobblestones. No time for that now. I'm far more interested in changing out of my traveling clothes and hurrying down to see Mr. Sinclair . . .

Oh, and the other gentlemen, too.

Of course.

Twelve

Visitors

I tap my foot impatiently. Sera and Maya are still overseeing their unpacking. My things are unpacked and tucked away in under fifteen minutes. No, *where-shall-I-put-this* business for me. I have a simple orderly system. Stockings and underthings in their own little boxes. Gowns are hung as they ought to be, according to type and color, as are my ribbons.

Five more minutes pass and they're still directing maids and putting things away. I have already changed and washed my face, so I excuse myself to go downstairs. I step out into the hall, just as Georgie bursts out of her room and nearly collides with me. I grab her arm and stop her from scampering down the stairs like an unruly child.

"We are not street urchins." I tuck her to my side. "Nor do we want to appear overeager. This is a golden opportunity to practice descending these stairs with the elegance they deserve."

"Phfft." She ruffles air over her lips. "I don't give a fig for elegance. Besides, I don't have your patience. I am not now, nor will I *ever* be elegant. I simply haven't got it in me." Georgie reluctantly matches her steps to mine.

"Elegance is simply a state of mind." I realize I sound like a governess, and she will tease me about it later. "Think of it as a performance anyone can master, like learning the steps of a dance."

She groans. "That isn't much encouragement, considering the fact that I don't dance well, either."

"If you had any interest—"

"There you have the root of the problem. I don't. Mightn't we walk a wee bit faster, Lady Jane? I *do have an interest* in getting to the drawing room sometime before I reach old age."

"If you wish to surrender your dignity and dash your feminine mystique to pieces, go ahead, run after him." I let go of her arm, and Georgie hurries down the stairs ahead of me. I sigh, envying her unabashed affection for Lord Wyatt, and wishing I had her trusting view of the world. On the last flight of stairs, though, I notice Georgie slows down.

When I finally enter the parlor, the gentlemen are hatless and already standing. I'm surprised to find that somehow Miss Stranje preceded us into the room.

"There you are." Alexander strides forward and takes my hand. I stare at his bare hands grasping mine and nearly miss what he is saying. "I was just telling Miss Stranje about our plans for you to teach me how to dance."

Our plans?

Georgie chuckles. "Oh yes, Lady Jane is first-rate at teaching other people how they ought to dance."

She is paying me back for my scold on the stairs. Perturbed, I withdraw my fingers from his grasp. "You must be mistaken, sir. I'm unaware of any such arrangement."

A muddled expression flits across his features and his brow pinches up. "Didn't you get my letter?"

"Yes, but I have not yet replied."

"Oh, well, that's easily remedied." His customary sunny disposition breaks forth. "What do you say, Lady Jane? Will you teach me one or two of your English dances, and perhaps that newfangled waltz everyone is talking about? Bear in mind it is a matter of national importance, no less than your sworn duty to king and country. Governments may topple should you refuse to carry out this grim task."

The wretch has me flustered. I catch my bottom lip in my teeth. I know he's jesting with these ridiculous assertions about it being my obligations to king and country. And yet, it troubles me that Alexander Sinclair has unwittingly stumbled upon the most effective way to coerce me. At least, I think he *stumbled* upon it. Surely, he can't have already figured out that I am helpless to say no in the face of a duty or responsibility.

At my failure to agree, he appeals to Miss Stranje. "You'll tell her to do it, won't you? She must teach me to dance, mustn't she?"

Miss Stranje watches me closely. "If she agrees, Mr. Sinclair, I have no objection. My only concern is that you ought not take time away from your more urgent and important tasks. How is your ship coming along?"

"Quite well." Mr. Sinclair straightens with pride. "Captain Grey secured a dry dock for her in the Woolwich Naval Yards. We should have the *Mary Isabella* back together in a few days."

Georgie tips up on her toes eagerly. "We would be happy to help with the reconstruction."

"Splendid idea." Mr. Sinclair whirls back to me. "We would be glad of your assistance, too, Lady Jane."

"Ahem." Lord Wyatt clears his throat. "The naval yards are no place for—" At a warning glance from Captain Grey, he changes tactics. "Thing is, I'm concerned about how the sailors and ship-wrights will react to young ladies working in the dockyards." He notes Georgie's frown and swallows hard. "You must understand, your presence there would be highly distracting to the men, not to mention the damage it might do to your reputations."

"Lord Wyatt is correct," Miss Stranje says to Georgie with surprising sympathy. "This is London, Miss Fitzwilliam. It is one thing for you to be hammering metal and up to your elbows in grease and grime when we are at home in our secluded country estate. It is quite another to perform such tasks at the naval yards in full view of the dockworkers and sailors. Members of the *beau monde* are bound to hear of it."

"But—"

"I don't like these restrictions any more than you do, my dear. But you must heed my advice on this. If we were not embarked upon such a sensitive and crucial undertaking, I would not mind testing the limits of social strictures. As things are, we cannot take that chance. It rests on us to uncover and stop Lady Danes-ka's deadly scheme. Which means it is essential we guard your reputations." She glances over her shoulder at Tess, Sera, and Maya, who slip quietly into the room. "*All of your reputations.* Otherwise, we risk losing entry into the very gatherings we must be allowed to attend."

That, then, is that.

Georgie's face, ever readable, collapses into a frustrated funk.

Miss Stranje turns a rare approving smile on Captain Grey.

"It's a marvel you were able to secure a berth for the *Mary Isabella* in the naval yards on such short notice. Well done!"

The Captain is handsomely tanned from his hours in the sun. Even so, I detect a slight pinkness blooming on his cheeks as he acknowledges her compliment. "I cannot accept all the credit. The naval yards are excessively busy, and the credit must go to Lord Castlereagh. As Secretary of Foreign Affairs he has excellent connections with the Admiralty; otherwise we would still be waiting."

Mr. Sinclair scuffs at the thick Turkish carpet. "Since ladies are not allowed, I suppose we'll have to muddle along without you. *Somehow.*" He promptly brightens. "If reconstruction goes as well as it has so far, we plan the unveiling and demonstration to be on Thursday." He angles his next comment at Miss Stranje. "Surely, on so momentous an occasion, ladies will be welcome in the naval yard? It's bound to be all right because his majesty, the Prince Regent, and several of his foreign guests plan to attend—"

Sera blurts the thought that snaps into all of our minds. "Lady Daneska will be there."

"I suppose so," Alexander continues undeterred by the fact that our murderous enemy will attend his unveiling, even though she may plan to end *his* life. "Lord and Lady Castlereagh will be there as well—"

"Begging your pardon, miss." Mr. Peterson shuffles in the doorway and stammers, "You have *more* guests. Lady de Lieven, Lady Cas—"

"Yes, yes, my good man." A short plump matron swishes in, dismissing him with a flick of her wrist. "She knows who we are."

Three women glide into the drawing room. I recognize them

immediately. Indeed, all of London's high society knows these women.

The butler extends his leg and bows low as the three ladies parade past him. Leading this procession is Lady Castlereagh, herself. Grayish bronze curls stick out around the edges of her pearl-encrusted plum-satin turban, and bounce gaily with each of her exuberant steps. She has on the most ornate silk pelisse I have ever seen. It's covered in lavish embroidery, has gold frog closures and a standing collar, and she girdled this elaborate ensemble with a diamond-studded sash.

"Who . . . ? Are they, the . . . ?" Georgie's whisper trails off in a gasp.

"Yes," I answer quickly and discreetly. "The Patronesses."

Georgie mouths a silent "Oh," and nervously inches closer to me.

For good reason.

These are the arbiters of London's high society. Young ladies making their debut must petition for an audience with one of these reigning queens of the *beau monde* in order to obtain vouchers for Almack's Assembly Rooms, an exclusive meeting place for the *haut ton*. It is the gathering place for the pinnacle of highly fashionable people. No one is admitted through the hallowed doors of Almack's without a voucher card, and those coveted cards must be signed, sealed, and issued by one of the seven illustrious Patronesses of Almack's.

Keepers of the social gate.

Guardians of the aristocracy's matrimonial mart.

Final judge and jury as to who is up to the mark, and who is not.

A debutante hoping for an advantageous marriage might wait weeks, or even months, for an audience with one of these formidable ladies. Or she may not be granted an audience at all. Yet, here we are, on our very first afternoon in London, and to my utter astonishment, three Patronesses are converging in *our* drawing room.

"Did I hear my name mentioned?" Lady Castlereagh strides toward us, smiling with an impish glint. "Should my ears be burning?"

The gentlemen bow. Tess, Sera, and Maya drop into polite curtsies. I nudge Georgie and we follow suit. Miss Stranje hurries forward holding out both hands. "Lady Castlereagh!" she cries with girlish delight.

I'm stunned. I have never seen such behavior from our headmistress before. I hardly know what to think. Is this artifice of some sort? No, Miss Stranje seems genuinely overjoyed. As are our three guests, who surround her in a tight circle.

"My deeeear girl!" the second lady exclaims, and even though she slowly draws out all her vowels in a most pretentious way she is nearly in tears. "Dearest Emma. It has beean faaar tooo looong." She blots her eyes with a silk handkerchief.

I recognize her instantly, of course. Anyone would. This paragon is the incomparable Lady Jersey, epitome of elegance and fashion. Tall, statuesque, and strikingly beautiful, the lady wears a jaunty velvet hat topped with the longest, most luxurious white ostrich feather I have ever seen. It's so long it curls and drapes down over one shoulder of her ermine-collared coat.

On Emma's other side, standing at graceful attention, is a woman tastefully gowned, but in comparison to her companions reserved in dress and manner. This dark-haired woman is none other than the legendary Lady de Lieven, a Baltic Princess in her own right, and married to a count in line for the Russian throne. Her husband has served for many years as ambassador to Britain.

Rumor has it that this lady is friend and confidante to so many heads of state, that Tsar Alexander considers her a diplomat in skirts and often entrusts her with messages for foreign dignitaries. I can see why. She has the gentle bearing of someone in whom men might confide their secrets.

I wouldn't—and not merely because I don't trust *anyone*, mind you. I sense a craftiness hidden beneath her pretty innocence. She may look soft on the outside, but inside I suspect this woman is sharper and more honed than a corsair's blade. I might not trust her, but I do respect her.

In the presence of these distinguished guests, I struggle to remember to breathe normally.

Lady Jersey turns on her heel, her tears suddenly dry. "Gee-antlemen." She holds out her hand to them. "Captain Grey, a pleasure as always. Aoond Loord Wyatt, I daresay, you grow more dashing every time I see you. The young ladies shall be faalling ooover themselves." She gives him a particularly shrewd smile. "What must we doo to persuade you to attend one of oour little evenings at Almack's?"

"Not much, my lady." Lord Wyatt bows politely over her hand. "A loaded musket at my back ought to do the trick."

"Rascal." She laughs gaily and raps him on the shoulder with her fan. "Very well. I shall have Lord Jersey load one for me next Wednesday."

She moves on to scrutinize Mr. Sinclair, who, as luck would have it, is dressed somewhat better than he normally is, and yet his hair is a tousled mess and not in the artificial windblown style that is so popular with dandies. No, his *actually* is windblown. As Lady Jersey scrutinizes him, he presents her with a broad forthright grin.

She responds with a lift of one brow. "I take it this young man is our American inventor, Fulton's nephew?"

"The very same." He bows. "Pleased to make your acquaintance . . ."

Merciful heavens!

He is supposed to wait for an introduction, and I know, *I just know*, he is going to complete that sentence by calling her *ma'am*. Then he will stick out his big paw so he can vigorously pump her hand up and down the way he always does. Inwardly I am cringing and holding my breath, sending silent pleas to the angels above.

Mr. Sinclair's glance flits from Lady Jersey to me, and back to her again. "My *lady*."

In a ragged gasp, I exhale. Captain Grey performs formal introductions and Lady Jersey studies Mr. Sinclair for a moment. At last, she chuckles and extends her hand. "Judging by that audacious grin, I'll wager you're a proper young rogue, aren't you?"

He bends over her hand with an even more mischievous expression. "Begging to differ, my lady. I've been told there's nothing *proper* about me."

"La." She bestows upon him the same anointing fan rap she delivered to Lord Wyatt. "You'll dooo, young maan, even if you are an American. You'll do."

Lady Jersey bears down upon us wearing a deadly serious expression. Apparently, her examination of us requires a quizzing glass, which she produces and raises to her eye as if we are not clearly visible, even though we stand not more than three feet away from her. "Aoond these must be ooour young ladies."

Our young ladies? Why should these ladies, these pillars of society, lay claim to us? We, who have never belonged to anyone?

How can this be, when even our families are loath to acknowledge us?

Lady de Lieven and Lady Castlereagh leave off reminiscing with Miss Stranje, and cast sharpish gazes in our direction. Advancing upon us like thieves on a mark, they close ranks beside Lady Jersey.

I stand in the center of our line, holding our ground, knocking shoulders with Georgie so she won't back up. I wish I could silently shout a command to my sisters, show them no fear. Tess understands. She stands on the end, tall and straight, shoulders squared, not budging an inch. I have never been prouder of her.

Lady Castlereagh elbows Lady Jersey. "Are they not exactly as I described? I wish you'd met them that dreadful night when Lord Wyatt was nearly lost to us. Speaking of which—" She spins abruptly toward Captain Grey, and the skirt of her ornate pelisse splashes against the furniture. "Gentlemen, would you be so good as to excuse yourselves? We've much to discuss with the young ladies. Private matters. I'm sure you understand."

"As you wish." Captain Grey inclines his head to Miss Stranje. "If it is acceptable to you, we shall return this evening for Mr. Sinclair's lessons."

She agrees and the gentlemen promptly bow in farewell. Who dares argue with the Patronesses? *Heavens*, the gossip columns claim Lady Castlereagh has even turned the famed Lord Wellington, commander of the British army, away from Almack's, and all because he arrived three minutes after the closing of the doors.

Nothing more is said while the gentlemen collect their hats and coats. Not a word. Introductions are not even performed. We stand in grave silence. From the hallway, Mr. Sinclair hangs back and gives me a jaunty salute as the men take their leave. I do so wish I could escape with him.

In the ominous silence, we five girls edge closer together. Georgie reaches anxiously for my hand. I hope she doesn't notice my fingers are trembling, too. "It will be all right," I mouth, not at all certain that it will be.

"Close the door." Lady Castlereagh flicks her wrist as if her hand is a wand that makes things magically happen. "I'll not have the servants peeping in while we do this."

Madame Cho closes the door with a deafening click and stands in front of it, grim as a Roman sentry.

What, exactly, are they planning to do?

I swallow nervously.

Thirteen

THE TEST

It is rumored Lady Castlereagh keeps a small menagerie at her estate. She has an Australian kangaroo, a flying squirrel, and even an African tiger. The Patronesses scrutinize us so intently that I know exactly how Lady Castlereagh's caged animals must feel.

Finally, Miss Stranje attempts introductions. "Allow me to present—"

"No, no, my dear, it will be far more fun if we guess." Lady Jersey waves her off, drops her quizzing glass, which dangles from a chain around her neck. "You've written so much about them I feel as though I know them."

"Yes! Let's make a game of it." Lady Castlereagh claps. "Go on, then." She tugs Lady de Lieven along. "The two of you must try to guess. Only think how vexed Lady Cowper and Lady Sefton will be at having missed meeting Miss Stranje's *notorious*

young ladies." She puckers for a moment. "We shall simply con-
trive another private meeting when they return to town."

Some sort of conspiracy is at work here.

Lady Jersey stares at Georgie. "You must be our clever little
barn-burning chemist. Miss Fitzwilliam, isn't it?"

Georgie winces and blushes all at the same time.

Lady Jersey laughs to her friends. "Lady Sefton will adore her.
Look at those eyes. So lively. So alert." She chucks Georgie under
the chin, and elongates her vowels even more than normal.
"Don't loook so forlorn, my deaar. Your ink is helping oour ef-
foorts considorably. You're to be coommended."

Lady Castlereagh extends her fingers in greeting to Georgie.
"We met at my diplomatic ball, Miss Fitzwilliam. I'm sure you
remember. Not an evening any of us will soon forget."

"Indeed." Georgie holds Lady Castlereagh's fingers and performs a deep curtsy. "Yes, my lady. Thank you for your forbear-
ance that night."

Well done, Georgie. I cannot hide my pleased smile.

Lady Castlereagh's shoulders bunch up in what looks to be a
combination of delight and a carefree shrug. "Nonsense. 'Twas
the least I could do."

"It is we who wish to thank you, Miss Fitzwilliam." Lady de
Lieven inclines her head. "Your ink is pure genius. I have relied
upon it a number of times."

"As have I, and my husband. The dear man is in high alt over
it." Lady Castlereagh fans herself with a handkerchief and turns
to Miss Stranje. "Speaking of that terrible night. You've heard,
of course, Lady Daneska arrived and she is ensconced at Carlton House."

Miss Stranje stiffens, gone is her girlish relaxed posture. "Yes,
Captain Grey told me."

"Daneska is no lady. She does not deserve the title." Lady Jersey purses her lips and her haughty accent disappears. "That spiteful little cat had better not try to assassinate our prince."

Miss Stranje tilts her head acknowledging the sentiment. "We intend to do everything within our power to prevent such a calamity."

"What of Ghost?" Lady de Lieven asks quietly. "Do we know his whereabouts?"

Miss Stranje shakes her head. "Captain Grey's men haven't spotted him yet. He may have stayed aboard rather than risk being seen. Or he may have adopted a disguise. He was seen boarding the ship in France. Which means he's on our side of the Channel, but we've no clue as to where he is, or his intentions."

"Whatever his intentions are, it cannot be good for England," Lady Castlereagh says somberly.

Lady de Lieven places an arm around our headmistress's shoulders. "This is a difficult task set before you, Miss Stranje. You have our full support. If we can be of assistance, you need only send word."

"Frankly, I don't see how it can be done at all." Lady Castlereagh fusses from side to side, much the way a hen does after laying an egg. "We've warned Prince George about the rackety crowd he surrounds himself with at Carlton. I swear, Lady Daneska could strangle him in broad daylight and there wouldn't be a sober head in the bunch to stop her."

"You mustn't say such things." Lady Jersey clucks her tongue.

"Well, it's true and you know it." Lady Castlereagh sniffs with annoyance, but swiftly regains her jovial countenance and pats Miss Stranje's arm. "After your letter arrived, Lord Castlereagh requested an increase in the Prince's guards and added some, *er*, less obvious protection. But I ask you, what defense does a man have against the wiles of a cunning young woman like your Lady Daneska?"

Miss Stranje tightens up and sucks in a loud breath. "Lady Daneska is not *my* anything—student or otherwise. She never truly was."

"Hmm, I suppose that's true enough." Lady Castlereagh waves her hand, sweeping away Miss Stranje's objections and paces down the line, studying the rest of us. "But *these* young ladies are a different matter."

The formidable Patronesses of Almack's inspect the five of us as if we are recruits for the King's army and they are generals. Lady Jersey stops squarely in front of Maya. "Ah! And here is Lord Barrington's half-English daughter."

Maya's eyes widen.

"Don't be rude, Sally." Lady de Lieven nudges Lady Jersey aside, and focuses in on Maya. "I've heard about you. You're Indian nobility as well. Your mother was a maharaja's daughter, was she not?"

"Yes, my lady, she was." Maya presses her lips together, but does not meet Lady de Lieven's gaze. I've never seen her this disconcerted.

"Faaascinating." Lady Jersey prods Lady de Lieven aside and resumes her position interrogating Maya. "Tell us about your childhood. What was it like growing up in the wilds of India? Were you educated here or in India?" I sense she contrived this list of questions with some ulterior purpose in mind. All three women stare intently, awaiting Maya's response.

Maya's eyes close briefly. I know what she is doing. She's pretending they're not standing so close. Her tranquility returns, and no princess has ever had as much grace as our Maya. She takes a cooling breath and her calm seems to fall upon all of us, too.

She begins. "My earliest memories are of living with my mother and father in the governor's house in Calcutta . . ." We cannot keep from leaning in to listen. Even Madame Cho takes a small step forward from where she is guarding the door.

It is impossible to describe Maya's voice adequately. It begins as a soft low hum, a vibration from somewhere deep inside her, and flows out as a velvety river of sound, wafting gently against our ears, plucking at our emotions as if our hearts are her harp strings. Hers is unlike any other voice I've ever heard.

Spellbound, we listen as Maya weaves the story of her youth. "One summer, a terrible sickness came to Calcutta . . ."

We all draw back. Not because of her words alone. Something in her tone arouses a sense of foreboding that circles round us like wailing wraiths from the underworld sent to drag us down to their dark realm.

"Many died." Maya shakes her head warding off the dismal spirits suffocating us. "My mother, too, contracted the fever. They would not let me near her. Two days later she died."

She draws in a deep breath. "It may have been cholera, I am not certain. Father will not speak of it. He fell ill, you see, of the same plague that ravaged her. His attaché sent me to stay with my mother's family, far away from the spreading sickness. I lived in a farming village with my grandmother, and my aunts and cousins. Those were happy days with *naanii*, my grand-mother. She and the women of the village trained me in the ways of my people."

Maya's lips rest for a moment in the gentlest of smiles, hon-oring those women of her former life.

We all feel it. Even me. With fondness I remember my governess, to whom I owe my education, but I cannot help but think of my mother, too. Of spooning broth into her mouth during her final days, of hearing her mumbled regrets, and the expression in her eyes as she lay dying. Not until then had I realized I mattered to her. My mother felt something for me, after all. That fragile ember of her affection still flickers in a place deep inside me, locked away, where it can never be extinguished. Not even by me.

I press my lips tight, struggling to put aside these thoughts. When I glance up, I see a similar melancholy mirrored on Tess's face, and on Miss Stranje's, and on . . .

All of us.

Even the Patronesses are not immune. It is more than Maya's magic wringing out our hearts.

Can it be that all mothers possess the power to both break and mend the souls of their children?

I swallow hard against the tightness rising in my throat.

Maya plucks another note, this one higher, less mournful, more strident. Instantly, we are back with her in India. "War broke out a few years later. Father did not send for me, not yet. Perhaps he felt it was safer for me with my mother's people. I remained in our village, until his governorship in India ended, eight years later."

Here, she pauses and I see pain bite into Maya's features. "All those years we had not seen each other. When he returned to England, he brought me with him." She doesn't have to tell us that he ripped her away from the warmth of her homeland and carried her away to a cold damp land, to live among unwelcoming strangers. Her cadence says it all for her. "I had no formal education in your English ways until he sent me to live at Stranje House."

She stops, this is all she will tell us, even though we would have listened the rest of the day and long into the night. It takes us a moment to break free of her mesmerizing spell.

Lady Jersey turns to Miss Stranje. "Your letters did not do her justice. She is divine—and that voice." She whirls back to Maya. "You sing, don't you? Yes, of course you do. That's it! Prinny has asked me to serve as his hostess for a soirée at Carlton House tomorrow night. I have devised a musical to entertain his guests after supper. Miss Barrington, you shall be our surprise performance."

Maya shakes her head vigorously. "I have never sung in public, my lady. I have played the flute and the hand harp for my village, but this is . . ." She shakes her head. "I am a foreigner, they are an *English* audience, and *singing . . . singing* is a different matter entirely—"

Lady Jersey takes no notice. "Nonsense. I have ears. Your tongue is so melodic you're practically singing now. Aside from that, this is a perfectly splendid way to introduce you into society. Think of it, child. If *I* have invited you to sing for the Prince Regent, the *beau monde* will have no choice but to accept you into the fold."

"Ah, yes, that will work." Lady de Lieven nods her approval. "Make her stand out, instead of trying to slip her in unnoticed. A brilliant strategy, my lady."

"There, you see?" Lady Jersey sweeps her palms wide, her gloved fingers sparkling with rubies and diamonds. "I'm certain your headmistress agrees with me, too. Don't you, Emma, dear?"

Maya turns to Miss Stranje hoping for a reprieve. But Miss Stranje inclines her head to Lady Jersey. "Yes, of course. Thank you, my lady. Miss Barrington will be delighted to sing for our prince if you can secure invitations for us in time for his gathering."

"Secure them?" Lady Jersey chuckles. "Why of course, my dear, he put me in charge of the guest list. Consider it done."

Maya practically dissolves into the Turkish carpet.

Lady Castlereagh pats Maya's arm. "It will be all right, Miss Barrington. You'll do quite well, I'm sure of it." She leans closer. "By the by, I met that stepmother of yours. Didn't care for the woman at all. Not one little bit. You may be interested to know, we denied her entry to Almack's."

While Lady Castlereagh whispers to Maya, Lady Jersey is sizing up Tess. The look on Tess's face makes me nervous. I know that expression, it's the one she gets right before she tosses me down on the mats in our practice room.

"You're the young lady from Wales, aren't you?" Lady Jersey raps Tess's shoulder with that darned fan of hers. She's lucky Tess doesn't snatch it away.

"I was born in Tidenham," Tess corrects.

"Close enough." Lady Jersey tilts her head to the side, and her ostrich plume scoots forward almost touching Tess's cheek. Tess doesn't flinch. Lady Jersey stares as if she's a magistrate about to pronounce sentence. "I've heard stories about you. They say you're the young lady who finally lured Lord Ravencross out of his cave."

Tess stands toe to toe with Lady Jersey, saying nothing for far too long. Miss Stranje presses her lips together apprehensively. Finally, Tess answers. "I should think Ravencross manor is a trifle more accommodating than a cave."

"Ha." Lady Jersey grants her a wry smirk. "I suppose it is. I can see why the young man likes you. A pretty thing, aren't you?" She says this with authority, both of them possessing the coveted dark hair and porcelain skin. She leans closer, searing Tess with a warning glare. "Mark my words, young lady. It takes more than looks to survive. You'll need wits, too, if you're to swim in these waters."

"*Careful*, my lady. Miss Aubreyson has wits enough." Lady de Lieven calmly urges her friend to step back. "I've heard this one is capable of climbing in through your bedroom window and cutting your throat."

Tess's attention whips to Miss Stranje, who stands nonchalantly behind the Patronesses.

"Can she really?" Lady Jersey's face lights up with newfound respect. "I must say, that would be handy. What else can you do?"

Lady Castlereagh answers for Tess. "She dances very prettily. I daresay she had all the young men at my diplomatic ball eating out of her palm. Quite the lion tamer, our Miss Aubreyson."

"Very well . . ." Lady Jersey steps back, knocking into a side table. She quickly recovers and casts a speculative gaze from me on one end of the line, back to Sera on the other. Tapping her chin with one finger, she approaches Sera. "Only two left. You are either Lady Jane Moore or Miss Wyndham."

Sera sinks into a curtsy. "Miss Wyndham, my lady. Though I think you already guessed as much."

"So I did. Very good, Miss Wyndham. Now then, tell me, what do I have behind my back?"

Lady de Lieven and Lady Castlereagh close in on each side of Lady Jersey.

"Begging your pardon, my lady?" Sera blinks rapidly. Her shyness causes her shoulders to curl inward. I feel a nearly irrepressible urge to rush to her side and protect her from this inquisition. Unable to stand it another second, I step forward, but Miss Stranje sends me a silent warning to stand down.

Lady Jersey does not relent. "Humor me, child. I've been told you're rather clever at observation. Can you tell me what I have behind my back, or not?"

A test.

This is all a test!

My hands ball into fists. It's cruel of them to put Sera on the spot like this. Not just her, it is wrong of them to quiz all of us as if we're children in the schoolroom.

"Think of it as a parlor game," Lady Castlereagh coaxes Sera.

Sera stares down at the carpet, a shock of her white-blond hair falls across her cheek. I worry she's going to freeze up and refuse to answer. I take another step forward, but Sera beats me to it and bravely speaks up. "I cannot see through blood and bone, my lady, but I will do my best to give you an answer."

Remarkable. Sera actually seems to be enjoying their inquisition. The reason dawns on me—finally someone outside of Stranje House is interested in her uncanny abilities. Instead of condemning her, as her family did, these highborn ladies are eager for Sera to demonstrate her talents.

"There are many things behind you." Sera's voice lifts, growing stronger, more certain. "The ermine head from your fur collar dangles down your back near your waist. I suspect you have a fondness for a large gray-haired dog, because your pet rubbed up against you before you set out today. A number of his hairs remain on the back of your skirts where you did not brush them away. And I'm fairly certain you're holding your fan behind your back, along with the small Grecian urn you snatched up from our side table."

Lady Jersey extends her closed fan to Sera. Looped over the end, dangling by its handle, is a small decorative Grecian urn.

"Well done." Lady de Lieven pats her gloved hands together

in muffled applause. "Admit it, Lady Jersey. She even guessed about that hairy monster you call a dog."

"Fredricko is not a monster, he's a dear." Lady Jersey twists to brush stray dog's hairs off her satin skirts. "Do another," she demands, still brushing away hairs. "Tell us what Lady Castlereagh has in her reticule?"

"Yes, do." Lady Castlereagh quickly whisks her purse behind her back.

Sera plays along with their game. "As I said, I'm no soothsayer. Lady Castlereagh's bag is thick velvet and well lined, which means I cannot possibly see through it. However, I noticed square corners protruding on each side. Which leads me to believe that, among other things, Lady Castlereagh carries a book with her." Sera glances at Lady Castlereagh and attempts a hesitant smile.

"Brava!" Lady Castlereagh triumphantly exclaims. She opens her reticule and pulls out a small polished leather journal. "It's our record book for Almack's. A list of who we've sent vouchers to this year, who we've declined, those we've banned, and, of course, the rules." She flips it open and reads. "No alcohol, except for weak ratafia. No gentleman admitted unless properly attired in knee breeches, white neckcloth, a dark long-tailed coat, so on and so forth. You are a marvel, Miss Wyndham." She pats Sera's shoulder. "Naturally, we shall send Almack's vouchers for all of you, straightaway."

Miss Stranje breathes a deep sigh of relief. "Thank you, my lady. That is most generous."

"*Generous?*" Lady de Lieven stands directly in front of me, staring at me with undisguised shrewdness. "I should think it is rather *necessary* for the work we do. Isn't that right, Lady Jane?"

The work we do.

Then it is true, we are part of a larger sisterhood of spies.

Political intriguers. Or, as Miss Stranje prefers to phrase it, diplomatic *aides.*

"So it would seem, my lady." I curtsy and return Lady de Lieven's intent gaze.

It makes sense now, all the rumors about these women. Lady Jersey holding political discussions in her drawing room. Princess de Lieven with her deep connections to so many heads of state in Europe. Lady Castlereagh married to one of the most powerful men in England. The other two Patronesses they mentioned, Lady Cowper and Lady Sefton, are both from powerful families.

A slow smile twists the corners of Lady de Lieven's mouth. "So, you're the one."

The one?

My face must've given me away. Lady de Lieven glances over her shoulder to Miss Stranje. "You haven't told her." Her tone is accusatory.

"Not yet," my headmistress replies.

Lady Castlereagh laces her hands across her broad middle and taps one finger. "I suppose you think it is a trifle too soon?"

"I thought it best you meet her first." Miss Stranje joins them as they close ranks around me, speaking of me as if I am not staring straight into their faces.

Lady Jersey slaps her fan against her palm. "If you're right about her, she'll put two and two together. Daresay, she already has. Haven't you, Lady Jane?"

I lower my eyes. *What should I say? That I believe you influence England's politics. That you are puppet masters, pulling strings from behind the throne?*

"See there. She's already tumbled to what we're about. Question is, does she know the part she's to play?" Lady Jersey chuckles softly. "Oooh, look how coolly she plays her hand. Not a flinch. Not even so much as a maidenly blush rising up her neck. You'd be a formidable card player, my dear. Usually win, don't you?"

"I've no idea, my lady. I *never* gamble." I say this, because it's what I always say. I hate gambling.

"Nonsense. I knew your mother and father. You have gambling in your blood. I see it in you."

No! It isn't true. I am nothing like my parents. "I abhor cards and dice."

"*Cards. Dice.* Bah! What do they matter?" She pokes my shoulder with her dratted fan. "Life is a gamble. And this business *we're* engaged in . . . this is the ultimate venture."

Lady Castlereagh nods gravely. "She's right, my dear."

"Of course, I'm right." Lady Jersey leans in close. Too close. Her rose water is suffocating me, and her blue eyes shimmer with disturbing intensity. "Never forget it, my girl. We don't stand to lose a few coins in this game. Oh, no, it's our lives, our hearts, and our country on the table. *We* are risking everything."

She steps back. Her chin elevated higher than ever.

"*Everything.*"

Fourteen

WOLVES AND MEN

Very unorthodox.

The Patronesses do not take their leave of us in the expected manner. No, Madame Cho opens the door and, without so much as a by-your-leave, they all stroll out of the room, heads still bent in conversation with Miss Stranje. I'm determined to hear what they're saying. All this business about what I do know and what I *don't* know has me willing to risk being rude. So I follow close behind, eavesdropping. Sera tries to tiptoe behind me, but I wave her back.

"You'll need to explain the rest to her soon," Lady Castlereagh counsels Miss Stranje.

Lady de Lieven glances over her shoulder and sees me spying on them. But she only lifts her eyebrow mischievously, as if the two of us are in on a grand secret. They stand in the foyer and their conversation echoes quite readily to where I'm hiding behind the door, peering through the gap by the hinges. Miss Stranje rubs at her temple. "Yes, but I cannot tell her until I am certain she is fully committed to the work."

Lady Jersey's ostrich feather bobs up and down. "Ah, so there's the real reason. Does she have entanglements?"

"I suspect so. She hasn't confided in me. Either way, it is a lot to ask of a young woman. She must be willing to give up so much, and as you say, risk everything."

"The sacrifices are many." Lady Castlereagh sighs heavily.

Madame Cho glances sideways at our headmistress. "Many."

Lady Jersey loops her arm through Miss Stranje's. "Speaking of sacrifices, isn't it time you put poor Captain Grey out of his misery, and give him his long-awaited answer?"

Miss Stranje rubs her temple. "I can't. Not yet, not until he retires from the war office."

Madame Cho nods gravely, as if she agrees with this plan.

Lady Jersey stops abruptly in the middle of the foyer. "But my dear, that is putting it off dangerously long. By then you may be too old for children."

"Listen to her, Emma." Lady de Lieven moves to Miss Stranje's side. "You know I'm devoted to our work. And I love the thrill of running errands for the Tsar and Prince George, but I must confess, I love nothing so well or dearly as my children."

"Stop pressuring her." Lady Castlereagh pats Miss Stranje's arm. "She knows the costs. Some of us are called upon to make these grave sacrifices." At her stern glance, the other two look away.

"I have my girls." Miss Stranje swings her hand back, indicating us still in the drawing room. I flatten against the wall out of her view. Tess and Georgie crouch behind the other door, and

Maya and Sera are sitting on chairs nearest the foyer pretending to read books.

Miss Stranje protests against the Patronesses' pitying expressions. "It is enough."

"Is it, Emma? I do hope so." Lady Jersey's tone is kind; even so, one cannot help but hear notes of skepticism and concern. "You look more drawn than I have ever seen you."

"It's this latest ploy of Lady Daneska's." Miss Stranje lowers her head and I can hardly hear her. "As soon as we get to the bottom of it, I shall feel greatly relieved."

"As will we all." Lady de Lieven sighs.

The four of them seem lost in their own thoughts for a moment, until Lady Jersey glances up at the fourth-floor balcony and points. "This is where it happened, you know." She draws her finger down to the marble near her feet. "Lady Haversmythe landed right here. I fancy there's still some of her blood curdled between the stones."

"What a grotesque thought." Lady de Lieven wrinkles her nose. "I'm sure the poor woman's blood was scrubbed away long ago. But Emma, darling, why didn't you encamp with one of us?"

"Yes." Lady Castlereagh sounds genuinely wounded. "I would've adored the company."

"I doubt it. There are seven of us." Miss Stranje laughs. "Not to mention the servants and our dogs."

Lady Jersey perks up. "Do you still have your father's wolves?"

Miss Stranje glances around to see if any servants are nearby. "Any day now Tromos will have pups."

"Wolf puppies!" Lady Castlereagh squeaks with delight. "I could've kept them in my menagerie."

"Phfft." Lady de Lieven waves away this suggestion. "They'd

be miserable. My dear Lady Castlereagh, one does not cage wolves. Tigers perhaps, but not wolves. They'd never survive the captivity. Wolves are like men. They must, at least, be allowed the illusion of freedom."

"Enough of wolves and men." Lady Jersey shrugs off their discussion. "I suppose it is for the best you rented a house. We ought to keep our connections somewhat ambiguous. The less anyone understands about us the better."

"You are too kind—all of you. Thank you. I appreciate your offers."

"Of course." Lady Jersey bats away the compliment. "But *this* place—why this place?"

In answer, Madame Cho chuckles. It is a rare sound. If a cat could snicker, that is what it would sound like.

"Owing to the house's history I was able to rent it at a significantly reduced rate. And—" Miss Stranje adopts the same tone she uses when challenging us to draw a deeper conclusion. "Can you think of a more suitable situation?"

"Oh, but of course! Now I see." Lady de Lieven joins Cho in snickering. "How very clever. Curiosity will make them attend your ball. There isn't a soul in the *beau monde* who wouldn't come, simply because they are curious about the grisly crime that took place here."

"Morbid curiosity." Lady Castlereagh shivers. "I don't suppose you've seen—"

"Nothing out of place." Miss Stranje does not allow her to go on. "We'd only been here an hour before you arrived, my lady. You know as much as I do."

"In that case, we ought to leave you to your unpacking." Lady Jersey bestows a kiss on Emma's cheek. "The girls are remarkable. You're doing a splendid job."

"They're so young." Lady Castlereagh tilts her head and glances back at the drawing room. "They remind me of us not so many years ago."

"Ah, yes." Lady de Lieven grins and prods Lady Castlereagh. "Do you remember that night in Hamburg? It's a wonder any of us survived."

"Who can forget?" Lady Jersey laughs and clutches Miss Stranje's arm. "I was afraid your father would find out and be furious at us."

Miss Stranje shakes her head and a smile escapes. "Looking back, I can't believe we dared such a thing."

"You and your ideas." Lady Castlereagh nudges Lady Jersey and clucks her tongue. "It was a terrible risk. You were as reckless then as you are now. Think what might have happened if we'd failed?"

"But we didn't." Lady Jersey waves away her scold. "Life is full of risks."

"Not risks that could topple governments." Lady Castlereagh brushes out her skirts even though they are perfectly fine.

"Fiddle-faddle," Lady Jersey snaps. "You know perfectly well, we had to do *something* that night."

"And so we did." Lady de Lieven urges her friends toward the front door. "Let us hope Emma's young ladies never face waters as troubled as those."

Lady Castlereagh bobs along in front of her. "I daresay, from what Emma told us about what happened in Calais they already have."

I slip out of the shadows to watch them go. Lady de Lieven glances over her shoulder, and grants me a swift wink.

Fifteen

CLOCKS AND COBRAS

We gather in the second-floor library to work. It is no surprise when Alice comes peeking in and offers to bring us a tea tray. Miss Stranje doesn't look up from the letter she is composing. "No, thank you, Alice. We shall wait for dinner."

She peeps nonchalantly at the table. I fold the map, obscuring her view. "Very well, miss," she says. "If you change your mind, I'll be just down the hall." Alice glances around the room as if simply passing the time.

"When do they intend to serve dinner?" Georgie glances at the clock. "It's already five and I'm famished. I shall never get used to these town hours."

"Me, neither, miss. Torture, they is." Alice sways nearer to our worktable. "My stomach is always a-rumblin'. Mr. Peterson tells me they don't usually serve dinner until seven o'clock. I says to him that you all will be wishing it earlier rather than later. I expect he'll be along any minute to announce the hour."

"Alice, you are not to advise Mr. Peterson as to our wishes." Miss Stranje addresses her in a stern tone. "Mr. Peterson is head of the household staff. Remember, you answer to him and to Mrs. Creevy while we are in residence here."

Alice's face pinches up. "Yes, miss. Begging your pardon, miss. Thank you, I'll do my best to remember." She says this in an irritating singsong *I'm-a-good-girl* manner and turns to go, but not before an ugly splash of resentment dashes across her features. "I were only makin' a suggestion."

We return to studying maps, until Mr. Peterson steps into the library to hand Miss Stranje a letter from Lady Jersey. "A word, miss, if I may?"

Miss Stranje looks up from her correspondence. "What is it, Mr. Peterson?"

"It's about your *dogs*." He aims a prickly glare in Tess's direction. "They appear to be digging up the garden."

"Oh! That means Tromos is making her den." Tess shoves a map of London rookeries at me and scoots back from the table. "She must be going to whelp soon." She dashes out of the room.

"A den?" Mr. Peterson does not look happy. "But, miss, what about the shrubberies?"

"Nature, Mr. Peterson." Miss Stranje smiles at him pleasantly. "It is a force beyond our control. Unless you would prefer to lend Tromos your bedroom so she can have her pups in privacy, I'm afraid nature must take its course."

He draws back so indignantly, anyone might think she'd told him to go hang himself.

"Rest assured, Mr. Peterson, we shall have the damage repaired before we vacate the house."

This seems to mollify him somewhat. "Very good, miss. Do you wish me to serve dinner at half past six?"

"That will be fine." She opens Lady Jersey's letter. As Mr. Peterson leaves the room my stomach growls in protest. *Half past?*

"The sooner we accustom ourselves to life in London, the better." Miss Stranje instructs as if I have complained aloud. "Our invitations for the Prince Regent's soirée arrived." She holds them up. "And Lady Castlereagh will send our vouchers for Almack's tomorrow."

We dine on a light supper of roast chicken and vegetables. It is a silent affair as most of us are quite hungry. Only Tess drags her fork around her plate, probably because she's missing Lord Ravencross or worried about Tromos.

"Finish your dinner, ladies. The gentlemen sent a note saying they will call at eight to proceed with Mr. Sinclair's dancing lessons." Miss Stranje drops these tidings into our plateful of silence. A fork loaded with chicken, potato, and carrot arrests halfway to my mouth. "They're really going to take time for *dance lessons?*"

Miss Stranje looks directly at me. "Do not underestimate the usefulness of proper dancing skills, Lady Jane." She takes a bite of carrots and green beans. "Miss Wyndham, I noticed a pianoforte in the Grand Salon, perhaps you and Miss Barrington would be so kind as to provide the music for this endeavor. I would offer to do it, but this evening Captain Grey and I will have much to discuss regarding the Prince's protection at the upcoming functions."

I ought to be there for those *discussions*, except I can't very well teach Mr. Sinclair to dance at the same time. "Perhaps given the circumstances, we might postpone lessons for tonight—"

"No, the soirée is tomorrow. He needs instruction. Moreover,

I believe it is just the tonic we need." She spreads butter on a roll and tips her knife subtly in Tess's direction, pointing my attention to the fact that Tess is still dragging her fork half-heartedly around her plate. "Despite the seriousness of the situation, it is important we keep up our spirits and go on as if nothing is amiss. To that end, I have invited Lord Ravencross to join us for dancing this evening."

"He agreed to come?" Tess looks up and blinks with disbelief. "He hates dancing."

"That may be, but he sent a note of acceptance." Miss Stranje's mouth curves up on one side. "He is settled in at his townhouse, and says he's looking forward to your company."

Tess flushes and makes quick work of her chicken.

After dinner, I make the rounds to each of the clocks, checking to see if they're wound correctly and are actually ticking. *They are.* Can a second actually be that slow? Finally, eight o'clock arrives. Thanks to me, all the clocks in the house chime in perfect unison.

"Do sit down, Lady Jane. Your pacing makes my head spin." Miss Stranje is sitting with us in the Grand Salon, which serves as a ballroom. I sit, as ordered, but my leg jiggles up and down.

Three minutes after the hour, Mr. Peterson ushers Lord Ravencross into the ballroom. He stands in the doorway running a finger around his collar, looking like a man trapped in a dress shop. Tess laughs, and strolls to him. "You're the first one here."

"So it would seem. I can go and come back later if you wish."

"Courage, my lord. It is only dancing." She holds out her hands to him.

He takes one of them and bows over it. "I would trade it for a battlefield any day of the week."

"I don't doubt that." She smiles. "Since we are making confessions, I'll admit I would trade everything I own for an empty field to run in."

"I wasn't aware you owned anything."

"Didn't you know? I'm heiress to a large estate in Tiddenham."

He stops mid-floor. "Are you?"

She draws back with a grin. "I'm jesting. Poor as a church mouse. Not a farthing to call my own."

"Well then, at least there's that." He seems relieved. "If you want a field to run in, it looks as though you'll have to marry me after all. Now, does this ballroom have a balcony? I confess I'd like some air."

The candles in the chandelier sputter when they open the balcony doors and step out into the night. A few minutes later, they return and Tess is blushing.

At quarter past the appointed hour, Miss Stranje sets down her sewing and rises to greet the rest of our guests. Mr. Peterson announces Captain Grey, Lord Wyatt, and finally, *Mr. Sinclair.*

The Grand Salon at Haversmythe House is painted an elegant soft blue with lavish white moldings. Queen Anne chairs, upholstered in a matching blue velvet, are arranged along the walls. Two enormous chandeliers hang from the ceiling. One is lit for this evening, and it glitters with fifteen brightly glowing candles. The floor is smooth and waxed to a brilliant shine. But the most notable feature is how perfectly this room sets off Mr. Sinclair's features.

He is clad in his new Corinthian black coat and navy blue breeches. I will not remark on how his hair glows in the candlelight, nor how the blue walls are a perfect foil for his angelic features. The effect is somewhat marred by the fact that he is smiling at me like a roguish pickpocket.

He bows over my hand and one might almost think him a gentleman. I run through all the things I should like him to say.

I'm yours to command, Lady Jane.

You look perfectly stunning in that gown, my lady.

My dearest Jane, I've been counting each torturous minute until this moment.

To all these compliments, I plan to offer a ladylike laugh, and playfully scold him the way Lady Jersey would. I will say, *mind your tongue, Alexander Sinclair,* and then smile coyly.

He rises from his bow, and I perform a slow languid curtsy.

"All right, Lady Jane, what are you up to?" He stares down his nose at me. Which, by the way, looks as if it was broken at one time or another. There is a decided knot in the fine lines of the bone. "I see cogs turning in that dangerous little head of yours."

Dangerous. Not pretty. Of all the things he could've called my head, lovely, or even clever, he chooses to say *dangerous.* What's worse, I am completely innocent of plotting at the moment. I was merely enjoying looking at him.

"I'm not up to anything." I cross my arms. "Why should I be?"

"Because you always are." He says this with a modicum of respect, as if it is not entirely an insult, even though it is. "Craftier than a mongoose chasing a cobra, you are. I never know what to expect."

A mongoose?

Suddenly, I want to punch him. My fists are balled and I have half a mind to actually do the deed, except that would not be ladylike, and fortunately for him Captain Grey and Miss Stranje are approaching, otherwise I might fling caution to the wind and smack him properly, right there on his angelic cheek.

Mongoose, indeed.

Miss Stranje greets Mr. Sinclair, and says, "Lady Jane, we will leave you and the others to instruct Mr. Sinclair on the finer points of our English country dances. Mind you, the gentlemen have an early morning tomorrow. So, you only have an hour and a half before they must take their leave."

Mr. Sinclair bows to her and holds out his arm to me. "I am ready for your instruction, my lady."

"I'm surprised you would trust a mongoose."

"With my life, *your majesty*." He adds a jaunty smile. But his flippant remark, *with my life,* jolts me back to the cold cruel fact that his life may indeed rely on whether or not I can catch the cobra.

My fists uncurl.

Sixteen

WALTZING WITH DANGER

Maya plays the flute beautifully and Sera's fingers dance over the pianoforte keys with admirable determination, considering it is in dire need of tuning. Meanwhile, Georgiana and Lord Wyatt, Tess and Lord Ravencross, and I, are doing our utmost to teach Mr. Sinclair, *the most obstinate man on earth*, steps to a simple country dance called *La Boulangère*. After cajoling and prodding, we managed to teach him how to weave in and out among the other couples. At least we did our best, considering there are only six of us, and it really requires at least eight.

"No, no! That is not it at all." I stop and gesture vehemently at Mr. Sinclair's long lanky legs. "Your knees must rise higher. Like this."

"What do you mean?" He waves his hands at my gown. "I can't see a thing. Your skirts are in the way."

I raise them, so he can see how to do a proper twirl and hop.

He shakes his head. "Still can't see it. Do it again."

I repeat the step, but this time Lord Wyatt sputters into a guffaw. I whirl around and see Alexander, *the scoundrel*, grinning and indicating I should lift my skirts even higher.

"Wretch." I drop my skirts. "You've seen more than enough. Now, you try."

"I can't believe you expect me to hop." He crosses his arms. "Lord Ravencross doesn't prance around like a giant flapping goose."

"Well, but . . ." I sputter, not sure how to answer appropriately. "He was wounded in the war, which excuses him from such exertions."

Lord Ravencross grumbles something I can't quite hear over the music.

Alexander remains unmoved. "And what's Lord Wyatt's excuse?"

Lord Wyatt waves away this line of defense. "Oh no, you cannot lay blame on me, my friend. I'm only doing this for your sake. I usually avoid dancing at all costs. I'm not about to leap around the ballroom like a ruddy gazelle."

Georgie laughs at Lord Wyatt's quip, which does not assist me in teaching Mr. Sinclair the proper forms of skipping and leaping. "It is *meant* to be danced enthusiastically." Annoyed, I wave my hands to explain. "With *vigor*. The higher a gentleman jumps the more impressive he is thought."

He remains skeptical.

"Very well, I'm done cosseting you, Mr. Sinclair." I cross my arms and lift my chin. "Do you wish to learn the steps, or not?"

The piano and flute fade to a stop.

"*Cosseting?*" His mouth falls open as if I have shocked him.

"My dear Lady Jane, *that* is not cosseting. Wolverines have more patience than you do."

"How very flattering. First, you liken me to a mongoose, and now I'm a wolverine. I'm not sure if you have elevated me or demoted me in the animal kingdom."

"Oh, it's a step up to be sure." Alexander may not be willing to gallop around the ballroom floor, but mischief is always doing a spirited jig in his eyes. "Speaking of high stepping," he says. "I find it hard to believe that a civilized country such as yours requires gentlemen to hop and skip around like a bunch of silly schoolboys." He squints hard at me as if there is a smudge on my face.

I brush the bridge of my nose. "What are you looking at?"

"You. You're playing a joke on me, aren't you? I'll look like a right fool in front of everyone at the soirée, and you'll have a good laugh over it. That's what you're up to, isn't it?" He appeals to the other gentlemen. "She's jesting about this hopping and leaping business, isn't she?"

Lord Ravencross shrugs. "Dunno. I do my utmost to avoid balls."

No help at all.

Lord Wyatt glances sideways at Georgie, and the two of them grin as if they are sharing some private joke.

I press my hands against my hips to keep from flinging them in the air with exasperation. "How can you think I would play such a mean trick on you? Although, now that you mention it, I wish I had thought of it. Tell him, Sera. Tell him I'm not making this up."

Sera plunks the out-of-tune G on the pianoforte. "She's telling you the truth, Mr. Sinclair. English gentlemen jump, and twirl, and prance across the ballroom floor. It is the nature of our country dances." She leans back over the pianoforte and ripples her fingers over the keys. "Perhaps we should try a waltz. It might be more to his liking."

"No." I stomp my slipper against the floorboards. "Not until he's proficient with *La Boulangère*."

Sera shakes her head. "He knows the steps. He simply doesn't want to do them." She plays the opening strains of a waltz with as much volume as the old instrument will allow.

I purse my lips at Sera. "I thought you were my friend."

"I am." She smiles to herself and continues playing. Maya joins in the one-two-three, one-two-three, flowing tempo of a waltz.

I am outnumbered.

Overruled.

Mr. Sinclair holds out his hand. "Come, Lady Jane. Complete my education." He uses a rakishly seductive tone.

"Don't be impertinent." I refuse to look at him. "I'm not at all certain this is proper. Young ladies aren't supposed to participate in a waltz until one of the Patronesses has granted permission." I glance around the room, and without regard for the rules, the others are already waltzing.

He moves closer. "From what I saw in the parlor yesterday, my lady, those high-and-mighty Patronesses would do more than grant you permission. They would command you to dance with me immediately. So, if you want to do what is right and proper—"

"Oh *you!* You heedless American. What do you know about what is proper?"

"Heedless? Me? You wound me. I'm a very considerate fellow. Not heedless at all." He leans close and whispers, "Didn't I carry you when you lost your shoe . . ." He straightens. "Oh, now I see.

You didn't mean heedless, you meant to call me a *heathen*." The wretch stretches out his hand, awaiting mine.

"No doubt, you really *are* a heathen." I study the ceiling briefly, then glance to the floor, anywhere but at his eyes. I know what I'll find there, and I know how it will dissolve whatever is left of my resistance. I exhale loudly. "I daresay, you are the most persistent gentleman I have ever met."

"Persistent, yes. But a *gentleman?* I'm surprised to hear you say so." His melt-butter grin renders me helpless to resist. His hand still awaits mine, open and inviting. If he were not six feet tall and golden-haired, I might think him a devilish imp sent to lure me into misbehaving. I place my hand in his palm. Glove to glove. And yet, the heat of his hand warms me through.

I make the mistake of looking up to see if he feels it. Alexander is staring at my fingers clasped in his hand, his lips part gently as if it surprises him, too. I forget how much I crave the inviting lines of his mouth.

A litany of warnings spring to mind.

This is too great a risk. I'm contracted to marry someone else.

You will leave soon. You'll sail off to America and forget all about me.

And break my heart—what little there is left of it.

I ought to run from the room.

But I don't. Instead, I watch as he swallows, and savor the slow uneasy bob of his Adam's apple. "Now what?" he asks, in far too husky a voice.

"Now . . ." *I don't care if you are leaving soon, I want you to kiss me.* I gulp down a hot blast of bashfulness that singes my cheeks. "*Now*, you must pay careful attention."

Not that you aren't already paying too close attention, studying me as if you wish we were alone.

I nervously place my other hand on his shoulder, and do my best to play teacher. "Your right hand is supposed to rest lightly on my upper back, just beneath my shoulder."

His palm slides into place and my breath catches.

"Like so?"

I can only nod as the touch of his gloved hand on my back makes prickles of excitement race down my arms.

A blotchy scarlet flush crawls up the inside of his neck and floods his cheeks. "And, *um* . . . what do we do now?" He inhales deeply, squares his jaw, and tugs me closer.

I cannot look up at him, afraid of what I might do. I glance down at our feet and struggle to breathe evenly. "It's a box step. You step forward, one. Two, to the side, and three, backward."

"One. Two. Three. Like this?" He takes over from there, with none of the hesitancy he'd shown on *La Boulangère*.

"Exactly. If you would like to do a more sweeping turn, we simply take a wider step like—" I make the mistake of trying to guide him. We tangle and nearly stumble. He clutches me tighter and corrects our misstep.

I glance up. Which proves an even graver error. Our mouths are perilously close. My lips part, and suddenly it is as if the ocean is roaring in my ears, and I smell the tang of salt in the air. Memories of that night wash over me. It feels as if we are back on the cliffs, when we . . .

He leans nearer, and I know he, too, is remembering that night and the softness of our lips touching.

Except we are not on the cliffs of Stranje House. We are in Mayfair. In a room surrounded by onlookers. We cannot—we *must not*—kiss here.

There is a scandalously narrow distance between us. As we move into the next step, I ease further away from him. "The Patronesses have rules about the waltz. There must be two feet between us."

"Two feet," he mutters, as if it grieves him. "And will these Patronesses bring a measuring rod to the ball?" He does that thing again, twists his features into such overdone earnestness, that I can scarcely keep from laughing.

I press my lips together to keep from bursting into a very unladylike laugh, and pretend not to notice. "I cannot say, Mr. Sinclair. I learned the steps with the other girls, of course, but until now I have never actually danced the waltz with a gentleman in public."

"Never?" A slow smile spreads across his wretchedly enticing lips. "I'm glad to hear it."

Not until this moment do I realize Alexander has waltzed us around the perimeter of the room without so much as one single blunder or any other difficulty. He spins us in a surprisingly competent whirl. There can be only one conclusion: he's not nearly as unpracticed in the art of dance as he pretended earlier.

I thump his shoulder. "You, Mr. Sinclair, are a charlatan."

"A *charlatan?*" His steps falter ever so slightly. "I am a great many things, Lady Jane, but never that. I'm baffled. What can you mean?"

"That you know perfectly well how to dance. You have been pretending ignorance. To what end, I cannot presume to know."

"Oh that." He shrugs and performs another proficient whirl. "I'm a quick study."

"Do not try to gammon me. No one learns the waltz this well in one short lesson."

"Hmm. I suppose you have a point." He does a reverse turn and now I have no doubt he has been pulling the *not-so-innocent* sheep's wool over my eyes.

I say nothing. I've a mind to step on the rascal's toes, except he's wearing great big shoes and I have on these flimsy silk slippers.

"Come, my lady, there's no point in brooding." He tries to pull me closer, but I keep my distance.

"I'm not brooding. I never brood."

He smirks as always. "You do realize this particular dance is extremely popular in France, don't you?"

"Of course." I sound cavalier, but I'm not. I see where he's going and I don't like it. *I don't like it at all.* Too easily, I envision Alexander holding some coquettish French girl in his arms the way he is holding me now. We dip into another turn and my stomach sinks low. So low, it feels as if I'm dragging the darned thing behind me along the ballroom floor.

He clears his throat to get my attention. "So naturally, I—"

"I do not want to hear about your exploits in France." I intentionally look away from him as we go into the next turn.

"*Exploits?* You make it sound sordid."

"It is," I snap. Doesn't he know he is supposed to be my fair-haired innocent American boy? I cannot bear the thought of his arms around anyone else. "I've heard all about those forward French girls."

He laughs. "Why, Lady Jane. I do believe you're jealous."

"Never." I lift my chin as if I'm giving him the cut direct.

"You are."

I refuse to say anything. It is time for this infernal waltz to end. I try to snatch my hand out of his. He wraps his big fingers around mine trapping them.

Trapping me.

I level my sternest stare at the scoundrel. "Need I remind you, I have a dagger and I will not hesitate to use it?"

"I should think I know it better than anyone." He does a quick turn which forces me to hold on to him. "Reckon you'll stab me with that toothpick sooner or later, my lady. Before you do, let me explain. I was a lad of fourteen, when my uncle's lady friends taught me to waltz. Ladies, I might add, who were old enough to be my mother."

I stop trying to tug free.

The rogue ought to keep his tongue still now that I am mollified, but of course, he can't leave well enough alone. "Mind you," he says, "they were very pretty ladies."

I flick his shoulder with my upper hand, the hand which had been free to escape all along.

Finally, he stops talking. I see by his smirk he is still laughing inwardly at my expense, but at least he's quiet. We float around the ballroom in companionable silence. This is pleasant, almost heavenly, with his arm firmly around me, and our tongues not at war with one another. I confess I feel quite contented. Almost happy.

Almost.

Until he tears apart our peace. "I suppose you heard about the fellow from the Iron Crown prowling around the docks today?"

It is as if the music screeches to a halt. It didn't, but it may as well have because my feet stop suddenly. "What!?" My arms jerk away from him.

"Forget I mentioned it." He tries to scoop me back into his embrace. "I shouldn't have said anything."

"Well, *someone* should've said something. Why wasn't I told?" I grip his shoulder, my fingers trembling with both fear and anger, and fight my way back into the rhythm of the waltz.

"I suppose because they were afraid you'd react like this. It's nothing to trouble yourself about."

Nothing?

"It is not *nothing*. It is a very dangerous *something*. A life or death something. You must be careful, Alexander. It's your life as well as others' hanging in the balance." I'm so shaken I accidently used his given name. I don't care. He's *my* Alexander, annoying or not, and I mean to keep him alive. "You must tell me exactly what happened, every last detail."

He takes a deep breath. "I shouldn't have mentioned it. There've been so many messengers between the captain and Miss Stranje today, I thought you already knew."

"Well, I didn't. And now, you're going to tell me."

"All right, but only if you promise not to make more of it than it is." His jaw flexes. It's not like him to tense up. He's normally so relaxed and carefree.

I nod my assent.

"Lord Wyatt noticed some fellow poking about the yards while we were working on the *Mary Isabella*. He wasn't one of the regular men from the dock, so Captain Grey had him followed. Sure enough, after he left Woolwich he headed straight along the Thames, past the London Bridge, and then he turned north and went into the Drowning Sow tavern."

My heart sinks a little, guessing what he will say next. "And?" I ask impatiently.

Alexander shrugs. "He went in and disappeared. Near as we can figure, he must've snuck out a back way."

"You must be careful. Stay alert at all times."

"Stop fretting. Trust me, I can take care of myself."

Can you?

"I don't fret." *That is a bold-faced lie. I wish I didn't, but I do.* Desperate to change the subject, I say, "Speaking of trust, why did you pretend you didn't know how to waltz?"

"For this." He caresses my back with his hand, holding me

much closer than the regulation two feet. "For this, my lady." He leans close to my ear and whispers. "And may I say, it was worth it."

The music finishes, but he doesn't release me for a moment. When he smiles at me the way he is doing now, I am helpless. Captivated. I would be quite content to gaze at him all night.

He bows because that is what one does at the end of a waltz. I take a quick breath and remember to curtsy. He offers his arm so that he might guide me back to the others. "Admit it, Lady Jane. You find me handsome and charming."

His audacity is boundless.

"In our country, Mr. Sinclair, it is customary for the gentlemen to bestow compliments upon ladies, rather than the other way around." I plaster on a smile because Miss Stranje and Captain Grey are standing beside the pianoforte clapping, and watching us closely.

"Exactly what I aimed to do. Give you a chance to show your good judgment, so I might compliment you on it."

Nonplussed, my mouth falls open. I close it and shake my head. "Words fail me."

"High praise indeed, my darling wolverine."

Seventeen

MISLEADING ALICE

That night, as we prepare for bed, Alice carries a tray into our bedroom. Sera frowns at the three glasses of creamy liquid. "What is this? It doesn't smell like milk."

"No, miss. These here are warm brandies an' cream. Miss Stranje sent me with 'em, sayin' as how these'll help you sleep, what wi' this being your first night in London an' all."

We each take a tumbler from her tray. Before we left Stranje House, Madame Cho gave us a lesson on detecting poisons. In case the little traitor laced our drinks with a sleeping draught or something worse, I sniff the brandy and cream before taking a small sip. Not detecting any bitterness, I take a deeper swallow and the smooth mixture warms my throat. Maya and Sera watch me closely and follow my lead.

Alice helps us out of our gowns, while Maya, Sera, and I talk among ourselves as we normally would. Except tonight is differ-ent. Acting on orders from Miss Stranje, we make certain Alice overhears us discussing Lady Daneska. We speak low enough she ought to recognize it is a private conversation, but with enough volume she's bound to hear a word or phrase here and there.

Georgie pretends to argue and raises her voice. "If you ask me Lady Daneska is here to kill Mr. Sinclair, or at the very least recapture him."

Alice edges closer and takes an inordinately long time hanging my day gown in the nearest wardrobe.

Maya shakes her head. "Perhaps not. She is staying with the Prince Regent. Surely, he is her target."

"She wouldn't dare!" Georgie flings down her petticoat. "She would never take such a chance. Too many people watch over the Prince. If Lady Daneska tries to harm him, she'll be caught in the act, and they'll hang her for it. *Or worse.*" Georgie shudders quite convincingly.

"Oh, but she is that daring." I don't need to pretend the anger I feel. "Have you forgotten what she did to Madame Cho, and how she took Tess captive? Her recklessness is precisely what Miss Stranje is counting on. We're one step ahead of her, and this time she'll fall into our trap." I slam my fist into my palm. "This time, she won't get away with it."

Alice is easier to read than a nursery rhyme. She gives off telling clues when she is eavesdropping. She stands there folding Maya's long silk, but at the mention of Lady Daneska's name, she pauses overlong and catches her bottom lip.

"You may go now, Alice." Maya thanks her for folding her sari. "And you must make one of those wonderful brandy-and-cream concoctions for yourself. They are very soothing and it has been a very long day for you, too." It sounds as if she is genuinely concerned for our traitorous maid. Knowing Maya, she probably is hoping the girl will change course.

Alice has never liked Maya. She refuses to look at her directly and her curtsy is only halfhearted. "Thank you, miss. I will."

She won't change. People don't. My parents didn't. My brothers won't.

Late that night, we gather, the way the five of us normally do in the attic back home at Stranje House. Only tonight, Miss Stranje and Madame Cho stand with us in the bedroom Georgie and Tess share. The window provides enough light that we can forgo a candle.

Tess checks the door, making sure we're alone, and makes her way to our circle. Sera scoots sideways. "Alice left the house, didn't she?"

Tess squeezes in next to her and whispers, "Yes, I heard Phobos and Tromos yip. She must've sneaked out the back way, past them."

Georgie pulls her dressing gown tighter. "It might've been anybody disturbing them, another servant, or a passerby."

"No. Had to be Alice," Tess says flatly. "If it was a stranger, or one of the other servants, Phobos would've raised a bigger alarm."

"It was her." Sera turns to me with her earnest, *you-believe-me-don't-you* expression. "I heard her sneaking down the stairs a few minutes ago." Our servants are assigned bunks in the attic, because the Haversmythe staff requires all the rooms in the basement below stairs.

"How can you be sure?" Georgie shivers as if she's chilled. "I'm surprised you can hear anything at all. Even at this hour of the night there are so many blasted carriages rattling through the street, I doubt I shall ever be able to sleep."

"London is smelly and loud," Madame Cho grumbles in agreement.

Sera shrugs. "There are noises, and then there are noises. I know what I heard. It was Alice sneaking out."

Georgie turns her attention to our traitor. "Has Captain Grey assigned someone to follow Alice?"

After Miss Stranje nods, Georgie poses another question. "What do you think she'll tell Lady Daneska's men?"

Tess crosses her arms and answers for our headmistress. "She can only tell them what she knows, which isn't much." She turns to Miss Stranje frowning. "I thought you said we were keeping Alice on so we could mislead Daneska?" She flicks her hand at me, Maya, and Georgie. "Nothing they let her overhear will trick her. It was only the truth."

"Isn't that what I've always taught you to use? The truth." Miss Stranje does not scold Tess for her irritable tone, but she does veil her features with a stern mask. "Alice will serve us in several ways. First, and most importantly, she may help us ferret out Ghost if her contact reports directly back to him. At the very least, we should discover where their London quarters are located. We already have an idea of their general direction."

"Past London Bridge. They think it's somewhere in Spitalfields." I relate what Alexander told me about the man they followed.

"Yes," Miss Stranje continues. "Secondly, Alice will tell Lady Daneska that we have guessed what she is up to, and that we are laying a trap to catch her. This should force Lady Daneska to proceed cautiously. It might even force her to delay her plans."

"Or hasten her into action." I sigh, wishing I needn't make this observation, but it had to be said. Sera glances sideways at me and nods in agreement.

"You're right, of course." Miss Stranje presses her palms together. "That is the risk. However, I think because Lady Daneska's schemes went so badly awry last time, this time she will act with more prudence, to avoid rushing into another failure."

A low rumble in Tess's throat turns all of our heads in her direction. "When has Daneska ever acted prudently?"

Madame Cho grunts—a short terse thing, that sounds like an uncomfortable blend of a chuckle and choking growl.

"We all know the answer to that." Miss Stranje peers down her nose at Tess and Madame Cho. "But we also know something else—Lady Daneska *always* acts in her own self-interest, and this time her neck is in a noose if she fails."

"I have a suggestion . . ." I divert them from the bottomless pit of analyzing Lady Daneska's character. "Since we are to be guests at Carlton House, what if I were to slip into Lady Daneska's bedroom while Maya distracts everyone with her musical performance? I could bring lock picks in my reticule. She's bound to have some sort of correspondence, a letter, or perhaps a note from Ghost, sketches, or maps—*something* must be hidden in her room that will help us figure out exactly what she's planning."

Miss Stranje tilts her head and I am privy to one of her seldom-seen smiles of approval.

"Hmm." She crosses her arms contemplating my suggestion. "Yes, it might work. But it's a grave risk. You do understand, don't you? You will have to work alone. If more than one of us disappears from among the guests, Lady Daneska will guess what we are doing, and you'll be caught."

"Yes."

"And if you are caught. We cannot rush to your aid. You will be labeled a thief and we will have to distance ourselves from you. It grieves me to say, but you will be on your own."

It's a risk I must take.

Eighteen

CARLTON HOUSE

Everyone's nerves teeter on edge as we prepare for the soirée at Carlton House.

Maya won't stop meditating even though it is time to leave. Miss Stranje keeps popping into our room with last-minute instructions. Sera sits on the bed, staring blankly. A ring of tiny white rosebuds decorates her hair—a perfect complement to her blue silk gown and nearly transparent overdress. She wears an angelic ensemble, and yet she seems to be staring into a dark unseen chasm.

"Stop worrying, Sera. Everything will be all right. You'll see." I finish hiding my lock picks inside the hollow quills of two ostrich feathers. "Come help me arrange these in my hair. I can't very well ask Alice to do it."

Miss Stranje ordered me to devise some way, other than my reticule, for transporting the lock picks into Carlton House. "You won't want to be weighed down by your purse all night. And if the picks slip out of their pouch, the clinking might arouse suspicion. We don't want people to think you're absconding with the silver."

"I have a bad feeling about all this." Sera sighs, and rouses herself to come help me. "What if Alice told them something that tips Daneska to tonight's plan?"

Last night, Captain Grey had Alice followed, and they saw her talking with an agent of the Iron Crown. Captain Grey's men followed her contact past London Bridge north of the river. Unfortunately, the fellow entered a tavern and they lost sight of him, surmising that, like the other fellow, he exited through a rear door and vanished into the dark narrow streets of Spitalfields.

"Alice can't have overheard our plans. She wasn't here." I sit in a chair and hand my disguised picks to Sera.

"I know. But no one can predict how Daneska will react to hearing we intend to trap her." Sera studies the feathers. "That's not the only problem with this dreadful evening. Think of it, Jane, there will be dozens and dozens of guests at the palace, and I won't know anyone—"

"You know all of us." I twist in the chair and smile up at her. She isn't convinced. "Hold still."

"Tonight will turn out fine, you'll see. Besides, Tess hasn't had a bad dream about it." I secretly cross my fingers, hoping that's true. "It's going to be a lovely evening. How often do we get to dine with the Prince?"

"I would be perfectly contented to never have that honor." Sera secures the last feather in my hair and arranges the curls falling over my shoulder. "There. Your picks are tucked in and no one will guess what they are."

I hug her. "It's time for us to go down."

Gently tugging Maya back to the real world, I hand her the flute case. "You will amaze everyone."

"May I offer you a trade? You sing, and I will break into Lady Daneska's rooms."

I laugh nervously. "It would be unkind of me to torture the Prince's guests."

"I think you mean you would rather face Daneska's ire than sing for these strangers."

Daneska will do more than show me her ire if she catches me going through her papers. I swallow hard, and the three of us descend the stairs silently, to join the others in the carriage.

Carlton House is magnificent, every room is a masterpiece. Here in the grand conservatory, gilded columns and arches span the length of the glass walls. Ornate golden fretwork on the ceiling dazzles the eye, making it a sumptuous feast of gold and red satin. The Prince Regent's soirée is a maddening crush. There are so many people here I can scarcely turn around. Which, of course, means this evening is a raging success.

Lady Jersey greets everyone with her lavish high-pitched elongated vowels. While the Prince himself is a gracious and welcoming host, friendly to all. He even greets Miss Stranje as if they're dear friends. He seems to have invited every Lord and Lady who ranks above a viscount, and we are surrounded by royalty from Russia and Austria and several other countries. Around every corner, I hear yet another language being spoken.

"He's here." Sera presses up behind one of the golden columns.

"Do you mean Mr. Sinclair? Yes, I think I see him."

"No. Mr. Chadwick. What's *he* doing here?"

"I have no idea." I look around, but for the life of me, can't see Mr. Chadwick. "His family must've been invited."

"I'm going to find some place to hide until dinner. You stay here and distract him."

"How am I to do that, when I can't even see him?" I turn back to ask Sera where he is, but she is gone. When she disappears there's no finding Sera unless she chooses.

I'm adrift in a sea of brightly colored satin gowns, black-coated gentlemen, and distinguished military men. Indeed, there are more admirals floating through Carlton House than there were at the battle of Trafalgar. Nearly two hundred people fill these rooms, but only one face grips my attention.

He draws me as if we are tethered by an invisible cord. I drift without thinking in his direction. We meet in the center of the swarm. When he takes my hand, the shuffle and push of the crowd disappears. For a moment, I forget the risks I must take tonight. The plots and counterplots whirling around us seem unimportant. For one blessed moment there is only Alexander Sinclair holding my hand to his lips.

"Lady Jane," he says.

His greeting is not decorated with compliments, or gushing praise. He does not compare my beauty to that of the stars, or the moon, or some rose that will one day wilt. It's only my name, but the way he says it floods my cheeks with warmth. As if mine is the one name he has waited all night to say.

"Mr. Sinclair." I curtsy.

He places my hand on his arm. "There are generals here tonight, and kings of countries I didn't even know existed. Shall I introduce you to Admiral Elphinstone? He is Commander-in-

Chief of the English Channel. Perhaps you know his daughter, Lady Margaret?"

"I haven't had the honor."

"Charming young lady."

"I'm sure."

"There you are!" Lady Castlereagh rushes up and greets me as if we are dear friends. She presses a piece of paper into my palm as I rise from my curtsy. "My dear girl." She leans forward to kiss my cheek and whispers. "It's from Lady Jersey. Directions to a certain room. You'll have fifteen minutes. No more."

"Delighted to see you again, young man." She smiles broadly at Mr. Sinclair. "That reminds me. Lady Jane, you must come with me. There's a gentleman I wish to introduce to you. Oh there he is."

When I see who she's waving at, my heart thrashes around my chest in a hopeless effort to find a place to hide. I take a step backward, knocking into Alexander.

"Come along, child. Don't be shy." Lady Castlereagh tugs me forward, steering us toward the one man in all of London I most want to avoid. "You really must meet him. He's the one, you know . . ." She leans into my ear again. "The one we trusted to watch over Prince George."

Good Heavens!

"You can't mean Lord Harston?" My feet stop cold, frozen solid. Mr. Sinclair bumps into me, and Lady Castlereagh nearly stumbles.

She catches herself on my arm. "Why yes, my dear. Do you know him?"

Before I can answer Lord Harston strides to us.

"Lady Jane? It that really you?"

I stand, too panicked to answer, wondering briefly if I might deny knowing myself. Except that seems a rather futile exercise, since Lady Castlereagh intends to introduce us.

"Lord Harston," I mutter, and remember to dip in a curtsy.

"It is you." He seems as startled to see me as I am to meet him. He bows and I stare at his reddish-brown hair. When I was a child, he seemed so very old. Now . . .

I see he is actually not much more than thirty and fairly handsome. He is clean-shaven, not overly tall, but exceptionally well proportioned, and his cravat is tied to perfection, and he has an easy athletic manner that bespeaks a natural confidence.

Lady Castlereagh smiles as if she finds this all highly amusing. "How very intriguing. Am I to assume you two already know one another?"

"Yes. We, uh—" *Egad.* What am I to say?

Alexander clears his throat, and I remember my manners. "Lord Harston, may I present Mr. Sinclair from the Coloni—from the United States."

Lord Harston extends his hand. "So you're the American inventor. I've heard a great deal about you. The Prince Regent is looking forward with great anticipation to the demonstration of your steamship."

Mr. Sinclair gives him a firm handshake. "Thank you, but it is my uncle, Robert Fulton, who is the inventor. I'm merely his apprentice."

Lord Harston smiles. "Your humility is commendable. But I've been told you constructed this prototype of Fulton's warship entirely on your own. Obviously, you paid close attention while working with your uncle."

"Thank you, but I didn't do it entirely on my own. I had help." Alexander glances sideways to me. I think he is about to credit me and Georgie for helping, but his expression twists to consternation. He stands straighter, rising to his full height, which forces Lord Harston to look up. "May I ask how you are acquainted with Lady Jane?" Mr. Sinclair asks this brash question the way a father might charge a young man for overstepping his bounds with his daughter.

"Oh my." Lady Castlereagh fans herself, and remains riveted to our conversation.

I take a deep steadying breath, dreading the answer.

Lord Harston tugs at his high-pointed collar and coughs. "She and I . . . we are . . ." He adjusts his coat sleeves. "What I mean to say is, I was acquainted with her parents."

Acquainted. Ha! That is one way to put it.

Mr. Sinclair looks to me for a further explanation. I can't very well say, yes, meet Lord Harston. He owns me. Mum and Dad owed him a rather large gambling debt so naturally they traded me off in payment.

Instead, I stand there mashing the toe of my slipper into the Prince Regent's marble floor, ashamed and terrified Lord Harston will tell Alexander the humiliating truth. Silently, I scream—nay, I shriek and plead—*Please, don't tell him.*

Please, please, please, don't say it.

"I see." Alexander nods sagely. "So, you are *acquainted.*" His intonation makes my association with Lord Harston sound positively scandalous. Alexander squints at me and I know that look. It means he knows we are hiding something.

"*Somewhat* acquainted," I mumble.

I'm surprised to look up and see a crimson blush streaking up Lord Harston's cheeks. Or maybe the candlelight is playing tricks. Two seconds later a hard coolness washes over his features, and he rises to Mr. Sinclair's stance. His chest puffs out and I know,

I just know, what he is going to do. He intends to put this impertinent American pup in his place and tell him we have a marriage contract.

More than anything, I want to drag Alexander away, or cover his ears with my hands, or tell him to look over there, *one of the Four Horsemen of the Apocalypse has just trotted into Carlton House.*

Except there is no horseman. Only an apocalypse. The kind that ruins my life.

I have to say something—*anything.* I need to keep Lord Harston from telling him the truth. "Lovely to see you again, Lord Harston." I tug on Mr. Sinclair's arm, all but dragging him away, but he doesn't budge. "Come along, Mr. Sinclair." I order. "Oh look, I see Miss Barrington waving at us. We must go and greet her at once." I pretend to wave back.

Lady Castlereagh turns to look. "I don't see her."

"*We?*" Lord Harston squints at my hands wrapped possessively around Mr. Sinclair's arm, challenging my familiarity with the American. My legs turn to sand. He takes a frightening step closer to us, almost nose to nose with Alexander. "And how are *you* acquainted with Lady Jane, Mr. Sinclair?"

"Oh dear," I murmur.

Equally terrified as to what Alexander might say. The two men stand there, neither of them backing down, each of them taking the other's measure.

Lady Castlereagh watches this interchange with all the delight of a child at a puppet show.

Mr. Sinclair stands his ground. "Lady Jane is my *particular* friend. She assisted me on the steamship project. As a matter of fact, she drew up all the notes for the *Mary Isabella.*"

My heart stops trying to waddle up my throat. His answer sounds fairly reasonable, not too terribly out of bounds. There's no mention of kissing on the cliffs by Stranje House, or carrying me through the woods in the middle of the night. I feel it is safe to take a breath.

"Your *particular* friend?" Lord Harston tilts his head, narrowing his expression to a sharp point, the end of which is aimed straight at Alexander.

"Yes, sir. *Very* particular."

I cringe. *So many gaffes in those four words.* I briefly consider diving through the glass window to escape the red-hot burn of embarrassment.

"My lord," Harston corrects sternly. "I am a baron. In this country you're to address me as *my lord.*"

"Your pardon, *my lord.*" Alexander acquiesces, but he uses *that tone,* the one which borders on the razor's edge of insolence.

"*Very particular,* eh?" Lord Harston no longer appears to be on the verge of running Mr. Sinclair through with his dress sword. Instead, he turns to me with a great deal of warmth and a surprisingly fond smile. "Ah, yes, I think I understand. As I recall Lady Jane was *exceedingly particular.* Even as a child."

Lady Castlereagh gurgles with barely contained laughter.

I swallow and glance at the floor-to-ceiling windows again. *Truly,* if shattering the glass wouldn't hurt innocent bystanders, I would throw myself out that window, truly I would.

Oddly enough, Lord Harston's comment seems to appease Mr. Sinclair. "Oh, you knew her as a child. You're a family friend, then?"

Lord Harston laughs. As well he should. At least he doesn't say, *Lord Camberly and his wife, my friends? Heavens, no. I merely swapped their stack of IOUs for their daughter.* Instead, he bows slightly to me. "I certainly hope the lady considers me a friend. After all, we are—"

Oh no! He's going to say it after all.

Except there's no time.

"There you are, Lord Harston! I wondered where you'd disappeared to, and who is this you're with?"

I'm spared humiliation by a most unlikely source. In a flash, things go from mortifying to dangerous.

"Lady Daneska." I growl, and reach through my pocket to clutch the hilt of my dagger. She sidles up beside Lord Harston, but her eyes remain fixed on Mr. Sinclair. I wedge myself between her and him. Unfortunately, this also closes the distance between Lord Harston and me. The bounder lets his gaze drift lazily down to the neckline of my gown. Appraising, I'm sure, whether I have filled out adequately.

Lady Castlereagh puts her nose in the air and walks away, snubbing Lady Daneska with an obvious direct cut.

Lady Daneska doesn't seem bothered in the least.

"Lady Jane." She and I both dip in short perfunctory curtsies. Never mind that she may plan to murder Alexander on the spot. Never mind that I am wedged between my fiancé and the man I love most in the world. We perform these social niceties, she and I, without thinking, because we must, because centuries of breeding make it an instinct.

Like breathing.

I glance up and see Lord Harston is still staring where he ought not. Mr. Sinclair tugs my elbow possessively and we both step back.

Lady Daneska smiles charmingly. "Lord Harston, I see you have met our extraordinary American engineer." She fans herself and I find myself wondering if she has laced the sharp tips of her fan spindles with a deadly poison. She claps it together and instead of piercing Alexander with a deadly barb, she tosses him a compliment. "Your little steamship is the talk of the town. I daresay everyone is vying for an invitation to the unveiling." She says all this as if she is completely unaware that only a few weeks ago the Iron Crown tortured Mr. Sinclair in the hope of forcing him to build a similar craft for Napoleon.

"What brings you to England?" I ask without the least degree of friendliness.

She laughs, a high-pitched titter that threatens to break the window glass without my jumping through it. "*Ma chère*, I am here for the season, of course. What else? To attend all the festivities, soirées like this, and to enjoy your fine English weather."

She's lying. I'm not sure what she's up to, but she has no interest in English festivities, and London weather is far from fine. She's probably hoping for an opportunity to shove one of her beloved daggers into Mr. Sinclair spleen, or the Prince's.

Alexander says nothing, but I feel his grip on my arm tighten. I can almost taste the hot tang of anger flowing from his fingertips.

Lady Daneska is unable to say anything more, because trumpets blare and announce dinner. The Prince has a flare for the dramatic.

Lady Daneska takes Lord Harston's arm. "You'll escort me in to dinner, won't you, my lord."

"But of course, I would be honored." Lord Harston bows to me. "I look forward to conversing with you later, Lady Jane."

Mr. Sinclair tilts his head. "Later?"

I try to urge Alexander forward, and say in a hurried whisper, "It was a formality. He won't actually—"

"At dinner." Lord Harston raises his hand in salute. "I strolled through the dining room earlier and was surprised to see your name on the place card next to mine. I thought it must be a mistake until I saw you with Lady Castlereagh."

"Oh *snake's eggs*." I moan inwardly.

Alexander's jaw is working harder than a coal miner, as he grabs my hand, claps it on his arm, and tows me toward the dining room. "What is that fellow to you?"

"What? Do you mean who is he? He is the second Baron of Harston, a close friend of—"

"Don't dodge the question."

"What is it you would like to know?"

"There's something . . . I see it in your face when you look at him. Something you aren't telling me."

"I don't see how it's any concern of yours. You'll be sailing off to America in a week or two, if Lady Daneska doesn't kill you first."

"There's a happy thought."

The line to the tables is getting shorter by the minute, and I don't want him to leave with such a sour thing having fallen off my tongue. "I didn't mean it like that."

"You never do."

"Alexander—" I turn to him genuinely sorry.

"Mr. Sinclair," he corrects, and hands his newly printed card to the footman, who directs us to opposite sides of the table.

Nineteen

ⅅINNER AND ⅅISASTER

Lady Jersey devised the most perverse seating chart in the history of mankind.

Sera is seated beside Mr. Chadwick and the two of them are blushing in turns and looking perfectly awkward. She knocks her fork off and he swoops to catch it for her. On Sera's left sits Mr. Chadwick senior, our magistrate from back home who is boisterously trying to engage her in conversation. If I know Sera, she is considering crawling under the table and curling up in a tight ball. I smile encouragingly at her.

I am seated next to Lord Harston. To avoid discourse with him I turn to a very talkative naval lieutenant by the name of Baker, seated on my left.

The officer takes my hand in greeting and inclines his head graciously. "Ah, the fair Lady Jane. I had hoped to make your acquaintance. You have been highly praised by several of my acquaintances. How fortuitous that we should be seated next to one another." *Blah, blah, blah, and so on and so forth.* I nod dutifully as he dithers on.

Directly across from me sits Mr. Sinclair. When I say directly across, I do not mean it is a short distance. No, it's not an arm's length or even a meter. The Prince's table is enormous. It is well beyond the width by which anyone with good manners may talk across the table.

To make matters even more maddening, on either side of him are two young ladies of dubious intellect. Proof is in the fact that he glazes over whenever the young lady on his right chatters at him. It is only when she giggles monstrously loud that his eyes open with pure attention.

The other lady does not seem to bore him nearly as much. Nevertheless, I question her intellect because she relies upon the low-cut neckline of her dress to engage him, rather than employing actual words. She is full of coy looks and suggestive batting of the eyes. I've half a notion to pelt her with peas. My brothers taught me how to fire peas from a spoon and look the other way afterward so no one would be the wiser. Perhaps, given the circumstances, it might be more prudent to simply lend the little trollop my shawl.

Curse this misbegotten seating plan.

If Lady Jersey were anywhere near my end of the table, I should very much like to run her through with my fork. My meat fork, mind you. Not the dainty dessert fork.

As soon as the partridge course is served, Lieutenant *jabbermouth* Baker occupies himself gobbling down his bird. Lord Harston leans in and speaks quietly. "I am glad we have this opportunity to speak."

I'm not. "You are?"

"I wish to discuss our arrangement."

The peas and fish soup begin to spin in my stomach. "You do?"

Just when I fear the fish will leap back up my throat, a happy thought occurs. Maybe he wants out of the arrangement because of my brothers' appalling behavior at the theater the other night. I would, if I were him. *Anyone* would. But if he does want out, wouldn't I be obliged to pay back the money my parents owed him?

I cover my mouth and earnestly whisper, "I don't have the money to pay you back. I may never have the money to pay you back."

He looks positively mystified. "What in heaven's name are you talking about?"

"I assume you don't want me for a wife. Can't blame you for that, but—"

He draws back as if he's affronted. "No, that's not it."

Oh horse feathers.

"I would never go back on my word. A gentleman cannot. It simply isn't done. I merely want you to know why the arrangement was made in the first place."

Because my parents owed you wheelbarrows full of cash. "I know why."

"Do you?" He stares at his curried partridge. "Your parents came to me with that harebrained scheme to contract you for marriage in exchange for their IOUs. I knew if I didn't agree to it, they'd find someone who would. I decided to meet you before determining whether I should leave you to your fate or not. Thing is, I expected you'd be as foolhardy as they were. In that case, my conscience would be clear. I'd let them move on to the highest bidder. A silly-minded girl would do just as well with a rummy old goat as long as he had bags of money. Trouble was, I met *you*."

I remember that night well.

He cuts apart the partridge and doesn't take a bite. "You were not what I expected. You were fine and good and I couldn't bear the thought of . . . well, you know." He finally takes a bite.

"*Oh.*" I'm astonished. All these years I'd thought the worst of him. When in truth, he'd agreed to the whole arrangement to spare me a worse fate. I set my fork down having suddenly lost my appetite. "But all that money—"

"IOUs. Not money." He shrugs. "I wasn't out anything except my time."

Accounting sheets stack up in my mind's eye. "And now I suppose my idiot brothers have ticked up additional debts to you."

He nods, and my insides still. Every pulse feels intentional. Every breath a labor. I owe this man too much to default on my contract with him.

"I'll let them out of it, if that's what you would like."

"No. You mustn't. I want them to learn to be responsible and make better decisions. If you forgive their debt, they'll only run up more. Besides, why should you let them out of it on my account?"

"It doesn't seem right to make my brothers-in-law pay. Since we're to marry, that is."

The minute he mentions our marriage, I can't help it, my gaze snaps to Alexander.

To golden hair and irresistible lips, lips which are not smiling. To hazel eyes, which normally flash with mischief, but tonight stare at me with fire.

Is he angry? Or worried? His beautiful jaw buckles and unbuckles, and even though the giggling debutante on his right tugs on his arm, he remains fixed on me. He only pauses now and then to glare daggers at Lord Harston.

"Oohh. I see." Lord Harston sets his wineglass down with a plunk. I'm still watching Alexander, but I hear a smile in Harston's voice when he says, "You're in love with the American inventor."

"No." My attention whips back to him. "No, that isn't true."

"Lady Jane, I'm not blind."

"I'm not. I can't be." The words ring false even to my own ears.

"Lie to me, my lady. But don't lie to yourself." He lifts his glass again in a mock toast.

Love is an overbearing word. I can't bring myself to think it. "I pride myself on being practical, Lord Harston. I never lie to myself."

Pride. My pride keeps getting in the way of the truth.

I pick up my knife and fork and saw violently on my partridge. *Poor thing.* I stop and shake my head, humbled by this entire conversation. "But, I find I am mistaken from time to time. Oh, fiddlesticks! The truth is, I don't know. I suppose you might be right. I might be foolish enough to be smitten with him." I turn back to the inventor in question. He is brushing the debutante's fingers off his arm and scowling at Lord Harston and me. "Not that it matters whether I am or not. Nothing can come of it. I'm promised to you, and he plans to return to America as soon as possible."

"He's going to leave? Are you certain? He doesn't look like a man who would easily surrender you to the competition."

"I'm sure of it. He'll return to his home in America. Why wouldn't he? It's where he belongs. It's the safest place for him." I stare at my plate and stab a piece of carrot and a parsnip.

"I can think of a very good reason why he might stay." Lord Harston sits back swirling his goblet of wine. "I know you don't like to gamble, Lady Jane. But I'm willing to bet that young man will be staying in England." He lifts his cup to me. "Care to lay odds?"

"I told you before—"

"Yes, I know. You don't gamble. Tell you what, my lady, I'll make it easy for you, a one-sided wager. If he stays here in Britain, you don't have to marry me. If he goes, I'll hold you to our original bargain."

"But he *is* going. I'll lose."

Lord Harston shakes his head, laughing, and stabs a forkful of partridge and parsnips. "Haven't you noticed by now, my lady? I'm not in the habit of losing. Especially to anyone in your family."

He has a point there.

Lord Harston washes down his bite with another generous gulp of wine. "I should have mentioned I never place a bet unless I'm certain of winning." He taps his finger on the table between us. "You can tell what cards are in someone's hand by reading your opponent's face, my lady. The answers are right there if you know how to read them."

He takes another drink and raises his glass in a mock toast to Mr. Sinclair. "My dear Lady Jane, I haven't felt this happy since the day I signed that confounded agreement. I'm free. Do you know what that means? You ought to—it means you're free, too."

I frown at him. "I'm delighted you're so pleased to be rid of me. But you haven't won your bet yet, my lord."

To which he laughs out loud, exceptionally loud.

Rude as horse snot.

"Shouldn't you be sitting next to the Prince," I ask. "Tasting his food in case it's been poisoned, or something?"

The wretch laughs again. "A Trojan, Lady Jane. You're a regular Trojan."

"I have no idea what that means."

He picks up his fork and cheerfully surveys his food. "A beautiful amazing woman with the backbone of a warrior."

"I suppose that's all right then."

"I'm so happy I could kiss you." He loads his fork with a gingered parsnip and a bite of meat.

"Yes, I can tell. You're elated because you think you're finally free of me. I'm flattered."

"I would do it, too, if I didn't think Sinclair over there would jump across the table and beat me senseless."

I glance across at my intrepid inventor and see he is indeed beginning to seethe. I don't believe I've ever seen Mr. Sinclair's nostrils flare before.

"Nonsense!" I say, even though Lord Harston spoke the truth. "My lord, I believe you've had too much wine." I lift my shoulder, as if I'm annoyed with him, and turn to Lieutenant Baker, having neglected him long enough.

Lieutenant Baker drones on and on about how thrilled he is to have been invited to assist Admiral Gambier at the unveiling Saturday of Mr. Sinclair's steamship. I point out we are fortunate to have the steamship engineer himself seated across from us. Lieutenant Baker squints hard at Mr. Sinclair. "That's him? Odd-looking fellow."

"I don't think he's odd at all. Quite handsome, in fact." I have no more use for the pompous lieutenant.

Maya sits across the table and several seats down. The young man next to her speaks to her with great animation. He makes her laugh, which is no small feat. I instantly like him for putting her at ease. Something about him looks very familiar. I study him while taking a bite of a stuffed pastry. It dawns on me he looks so much like Lord Harston they must be brothers.

"I didn't realize you had a younger brother."

"I don't." Lord Harston sets down his knife and fork. "Oh, you mean Ben." He smiles in Maya's direction. "Lord Kinsworth. He's my nephew." Pain briefly crumples his features, but he quickly recovers. "And my ward as well. Last year my sister passed. He's a good lad. Lady Jersey is a gem to seat him next to that particular young lady. He's fascinated with India. Wants to sign on to the East India Company as soon as he's of age, but I have other plans for him."

"They seem to be enjoying each other's company."

"Yes, I will step in later and put an end to it. I saw the young lady with Miss Stranje. Which means she's one of *those* girls."

"*Those* girls?" I ask, ready to stab him with my fork.

"I've heard Miss Stranje runs a school. Not just any finishing school, one for troublemakers." He fills his mouth with apple and pork pastry.

"Yes, I'm well aware of her school. I'm one of her students. And Miss Barrington is one of my dearest friends."

Lord Harston's eyes open wide and his lips part until he remembers to continue chewing. I smile pleasantly and turn away.

The dessert course arrives, and we eat in relative silence. At the end of apples and cheese, Egyptian dates and nuts, custards, creams, tarts, and an endless array of sweet delicacies, the Prince Regent rises at the head of the table. He lifts his cup to us and we all raise ours. A shout goes up. "Long live the Prince Regent! Long live the Prince. Huzzah!"

After several more huzzahs and a hearty round of applause, the Prince announces that we shall retire to the Grand Blue Salon for an evening of music, after which there shall be dancing in the ballroom. Another cheer echoes round the dining chamber.

My stomach begins to quiver with excitement and nerves. The ostrich feathers are making me itch where the picks stick out and rub against my scalp.

I bob a farewell curtsy to Lieutenant Baker. "I shall look for you at the steamship demonstration."

Lord Harston offers me his arm to promenade to the salon where Maya and a number of others are to sing. As we pass out of the dining room, Alexander brushes against us and turns as if surprised to have collided with someone he knows. "There you are, Lady Jane. I see you enjoyed dinner." He bows his head with only scant civility to Lord Harston.

Lord Harston answers him. "We had a splendid time. Didn't we, my lady? An illuminating conversation. I wonder, Mr. Sinclair, if I might impose upon you to escort Lady Jane to the music. I'm afraid my duties to the Prince require me to be elsewhere this evening."

Alexander looks from Lord Harston to me, suspicion tightening his features. He holds out his arm. "It would be my pleasure."

Alexander guides us toward the middle row of chairs. Lady Daneska is sitting toward the front, not far from the Prince Regent. She glances over her shoulder at us, and for one fleeting second I feel her cold-blooded hatred. Like lightning, her expression shifts, and she smiles as if she is pleased to see me. Lady Castlereagh brushes past me, and furtively reminds me, "Fifteen minutes. No more." She and Lord Castlereagh take seats toward the front.

I glance around the room, worried Ghost might be here among the crowd, disguised. Watching all of us. Except, all I see are the faces of the Prince's guests, the *beau monde*, the beautiful people.

I tug softly on Alexander's arm and whisper, "I need to sit toward the back of the room, near the side door." *The door I plan to slip through later.*

He frowns. "You're up to something?"

"A small task I must attend to for Miss Stranje." I edge him backward to the seat I need to occupy. "Might we sit here?"

He allows me to take the chair of my choice and grumbles as he sits down. "You're not planning to sneak out and meet *him* are you?"

"*Him?* You mean Lord Harston? Heavens no! What do you take me for?"

"A complicated woman." He crosses his arms.

Lord and Lady Dunbar sit down next to us, which puts an end to the vehement whispering going on between us. I cross my arms and sit back frowning, exactly as he's doing. Darned ostrich feathers are itching my head again. Alexander brooding beside me doesn't make my task tonight any easier.

I go over the plan in my head, as I've done a hundred times this evening. I remain in my seat throughout the first singer's performance, waiting until Maya has the audience properly transfixed before slipping out to go to Daneska's rooms.

The first performer is Miss Dorothea Twilling, a broad-chested young lady with a head full of bright blond curls, and a prominent nose that certainly allows for a great deal of resonance. The young lady chooses a song which repeatedly hits high C and displays her tonsils at their warbling best. Suffice it to say, Miss Twilling could shatter crystal at forty paces. I fear for the chandeliers.

The minute she begins singing I comprehend Lady Jersey's ingenious plan. This high-pitched soprano will sound like a shrieking barn owl when compared to Maya. At last, Miss Twilling's operatic showpiece comes to an extraordinarily loud conclusion.

When she takes her curtsy, I wonder if some of the clapping is to thank her for relinquishing the floor. Lady Jersey continues to applaud Miss Twilling as she rises to introduce Miss Barrington.

Maya glides out and stands before us with her head down, half-hidden by a veil draped elegantly across her thick black hair. As she slowly lifts her head and faces the audience, I see several heads tilt quizzically. *"Who is this?"* they say behind their hands.

Maya's dress is a brilliant combination of the French Empire style, except one shoulder is draped with a long flowing length of saffron silk that matches her veil. It is embroidered along the edge in a pattern harkening back to her homeland. *Perfect.* The gown itself bespeaks her origins and yet conveys her nobility in both lands.

Maya lifts her flute. She plays a short, melodic piece that leads us on a merry dance. It fills the air with joyous passages that reminds us of Bach, and yet she blends in stanzas that make us think of the exotic spices of India.

How clever of Lady Jersey to have included a curried partridge in her supper. When Maya stops playing, it takes a moment or two before her listeners are able to abandon the dream she has led us on. Maya lowers her flute and moves hesitantly beside the piano where she sits down in a chair on the raised platform. She lifts a small flat harp into her lap, plucks the strings, and begins to sing. Her voice is so low and round and rich, that I hear gasps. She is a singing a ballad we all know, and yet it has never sounded like this. She falters at the sound of their gasps.

I cannot leave yet. What if Maya cannot distract them. I wish there was a way to spare her their indignities. I mouth the lyrics. If I had a pleasant voice, I would rise and sing it with her. She regains a little of her confidence, not as strong and sure as when she started, but nevertheless it is sweet and beguiling.

Despite the allure, some callous listeners lean toward each other and whisper behind their hands. *Critical louts.* How can they dare whisper, when every note she utters is exquisite. I am on the point of abandoning my task for the evening by standing up to sing with her, when I see him, walking up from the back of the room, Lord Harston's nephew. As Maya breaks into the chorus, he joins in, his rich baritone blends magically with her contralto. When her notes rise, his follow, like a musical chase. Their voices waltz through the air around us.

Whispers from the audience change into gasps of awe. This is a feast for the ears. Their voices twirl around one another, melding at the exact right moments, until they both lift in a glorious crescendo as the song ends. The room falls deathly silent for a split second, and then erupts in joyous clapping, and cries of "*more, more.*"

I've stayed far too long. Time for me to go.

I slip out of the side door and sneak down the staircase to Lady Daneska's rooms. From the grand staircase, I hear them start another song together. No one will be leaving that room anytime soon, not even Lady Daneska.

I scurry down to the section of the palace where Lady Daneska's apartments are. The light here is dim, but I pull out Lady Jersey's sketch, and count seven doors and test the handle on the eighth. It opens, but I find the inner chamber locked. Listening for the sound of servant's footsteps and hearing none, I pull out my lock picks.

I need only scoot them halfway out of the feathers in order to use them. I squat down to the lock checking for traps she might have left. A ribbon or a thread left to warn her if the room has been breached.

"Ah." There it is, a short scarlet thread draped over the catch.

Easy enough to replace on my way out. I drape it over the handle and set to work on the lock. I love picking locks. It feels as if I possess a magic key to unlocking anyone's secrets. I push the spring aside with one pick, and use the other to turn the latch. *Voilà!* The lock clicks and the door opens.

I smile, shove the picks back to their hiding places, and stick the feathers in my hair. "That's done," I whisper. In the distance, I still hear the faint strains of music. In my head, I count each remaining second. *Each and every pesky tick.* Twelve minutes left. Now, to find where Lady Daneska hides her important papers. I close the door and light a small oil lamp.

Daneska's room is a disorderly mess. She must've dismissed the housemaids. Of course, she would. She knows how traitorous servants can be. The chaotic clutter of bandboxes and clothing strewn everywhere may also be part of her evil genius. It certainly makes it difficult for me to locate pertinent papers. In search of something that explains what she and Ghost are planning, I head straight for the wardrobe.

Earlier today, Miss Stranje suggested Daneska might roll up her papers and hide them inside a boot. That's the first place I check. Nothing but empty shoes. I run my arm beneath her mattress, and look inside every vase in the room. She has a large portmanteau. It makes me nervous to tap the sides, but I must check for secret compartments. I find one, but it holds a sapphire necklace and a jewel-handled dagger. No papers.

I check under the liner on the wardrobe shelf, behind the curtains, beneath the washstand. I hunt for false bottoms in every drawer and bandbox in the room. There's a small pistol hidden in one drawer, but that's all. I remove the sear spring, rendering the pistol useless. *Where would she hide her sensitive papers?*

The ticking in my head won't stop. Only eight minutes left. I sit down to think. A small escritoire stands against the wall. It can't be that easy. Lady Daneska would never leave important correspondence in a desk. Not in a palace like this, where everybody is inclined to spy on everybody else.

Or would she?

Is she so clever that she would hide her secrets in plain sight? I open the lid. There, innocent as lambs, sit a half-dozen letters. I grab the stack and quickly thumb through them, carrying them with me as I go to listen at the door, making sure I still hear the faint sound of music. Sorting through them, I stop by the lamp. One letter in particular draws my interest. It bears the royal seal. I do not need to decipher a code to read what's in it. The words in the short letter knot my stomach into a monkey's fist.

I flip over a second parchment, holding it above the heat of the lamp to see if they've used one of the old methods of invisible ink. When it looks clean, I move on to a third letter. The sentences are contrived and stilted, which means this one is definitely employing a code. I try counting the fourth word in every sentence. No good. The capitals in every sentence. Still no luck. The third letter of every fifth word. Closer. It's a sentence code. I can almost see it. My heart drums. I hear the music upstairs has stopped, and the crowds are shuffling. I hurry to the door and listen. No footsteps outside, but my time is running out. One more minute and maybe I can crack this wretched code. I hold it closer to the lamp, struggling to concentrate while still staying alert for footsteps.

The door flies open.

"Lady Daneska!"

"*Bonne chance*, Lady Jane. I'm surprised to find you here."

"Are you?"

"Of course I am, *ma chère*. In my experience, the mouse seldom prowls through the cat's lair."

"There's your mistake. You think *me* the mouse." I toss the letters onto her bed and reach for my dagger. She already has hers out.

She kicks the door shut behind her and laughs. "You are full of bravado today, aren't you?"

I ignore her false compliment and we circle one another. Not as growling wild dogs might do, but as two wary lions. Slowly. Calmly. Calculating when to strike, or *if* to strike.

"What is your game, Lady Daneska? We both know you intend to assassinate the Prince Regent. The only question is when and how."

"This is what you truly think?" She chuckles, her posture appears relaxed and languid, but I sense alertness prickling beneath the surface. One wrong move and she will spring. "You malign me, Lady Jane. I would never do such a terrible thing."

"Why else would you be here, instead of in France with your beloved Napoleon?"

Lady Daneska's smile is as coy and false as a harlequin's mask. "Perhaps I missed your company."

It's my turn to smirk at such an absurdity. "Oh come now, we both know you've always disliked me."

"Yes, well, I may have underestimated you. Turns out you're a tiny bit more entertaining than I'd thought."

"I doubt that. I'm still just plain Lady Jane. It doesn't take a genius to figure out what you're up to."

"*Plain?* Ah yes, I see what you mean, physically the dull hen."

"As poisonous as ever, I see."

Her nostrils flare and I expect her to lunge at me. Except she doesn't. She buttons down her hatred and presses her lips into a conniving curve. "Why this pretense of humility?" she demands. "Do you think I haven't heard what they whisper about you?"

Whisper?

She anticipates my question. "You are Miss Stranje's pet. Her protégée. Her young *mastermind* in training."

"No one says anything like that." I raise my blade and point it at her. Except they had. I'd heard the Patronesses suggesting it, but I hadn't believed my ears. *How could I?* Miss Stranje is my beacon, my hero. I want to be like her. I hope to be like her. But the idea that it might ever actually happen is . . .

Impossible.

Daneska blinks. She draws back in surprise. "You did not know?" She laughs, breaking up my thoughts with the grating sound. She snaps into form again. "How very amusing."

"Lies. You're making it up." I accuse her of this, knowing that even though she's telling the truth, she's baiting me. Trying to make me lose focus. I can't think about my future. Not right now. My mouth turns dry. I lick my lips and ready my knife. She'll attack if I show weakness.

"Fah!" She dismisses me with a flick of her wrist. "Miss Stranje is wasting her time with you. In my country, we have a name for fools like you. What is it you call such a person here?"

I block out her words.

They mean nothing.

Deadly games.

Diversions.

"Ah yes, now I remember, *a cabbage head*." She sneers at me and points her dagger at my skull. "Thick."

"Stone." I aim my silver point at her black heart. "Isn't that what it takes to be an assassin?"

"*Mon Dieu.* You truly think this? An assassin? *Moi?* You give me too much credit. You miss the boat for the trees."

"Forest," I correct.

"*Forests. Boats.* What does it matter? You have misjudged me. I am not like you and your sneaky Miss Stranje, I have no hidden purpose. No secret plot."

"Ha!" I force a laugh. "You always have a scheme."

"Think what you will." She juts her chin. "I am here by the invitation of his Royal Roly-Poly-ness. I can show you the letter. Or did you already find it?"

I had, but I'm not about to admit it to her. "How you tricked him into that, I'd like to know."

"Silly girl." She waggles her knife at me with a scolding frown. "*I* did not have to trick him. If you read the letter you will know I am here as an emissary of his highness, the Emperor of France."

"Emperor *of the world,* if Napoleon has his way."

"*Mais oui.* Ask yourself, would that be such a bad thing? Think on it, Lady Jane. There would be peace. No more war. No more bloodshed." She says this while shifting the dagger to a dangerous angle, the perfect angle for cutting my throat.

"You're wrong." I edge out of her reach. "There would still be war. One man cannot rule the world. It is impossible."

She draws back, as if she doesn't intend to slit my throat after all. "Oh but, *ma chère,* that is where *we* come in. Don't you see? Emperor Napoleon will do what he always does. He will place his loyal subjects in positions of power."

"You? He'll put *you* in power?" My blood churns at the thought. "It sickens me to think of you ruling over us, or men like Ghost. *Tyrants,* who have no love for the people they govern. That is precisely why Napoleon must be stopped. We already have a king. We don't need you, or your emperor."

"That's where you are wrong, my dear cabbage head. You *don't* have a king." She sneers, and I know she is once again gauging how best to carve my throat. "Have you forgotten? Poor King George is out in the pasture chewing grass and running mad. One wonders if he even knows his own name. And now? Who sits on the throne of England? His son. A spotty fat man with more gout than brains."

I hope she comes at me. I would like nothing more than to put a stop to her wicked tongue. "Be that as it may, Prince George is our sovereign, and we mean to protect him."

"Protect your royal dumpling all you want. I told you, I didn't come here to kill Georgie-Porgie. Why should I? When he is so very receptive to Napoleon's invitations."

Invitations. Suddenly the code for the second letter snaps into place.

"Enticements, you mean?" My stomach does an unsuccessful somersault and lands in a twisted worried mess. It can't be what I think it is. Surely not. Prince George would never ally with Napoleon. *Would he?*

"Enticements. Offers. *C'est la vie.* It is all the same." She spreads her arms wide, daring me to make a move.

"Bribes." I forgo her open stance. It is a tempting gambit, but I resist, even though I need this dance to end. Every fiber of my being wants to turn and run to find Prince George, and give him a violent shake and shout at him, *whatever Lady Daneska is telling you to do—don't!*

For mercy's sake, don't do it.

"Either way . . . his fat goose is cooked." Lady Daneska moves into attack position again. "Mark me, *plain* Lady Jane. If I wanted your pudding-headed prince dead, he would already be laid out in his funeral clothes."

There! That is the Lady Daneska I know—cold, beautiful, and threatening. Hell-bent on murder and destruction. If he doesn't agree to parley with Napoleon she will kill him. My world tips back into balance, and I see a way to stop her.

Or, at the very least, a way I can slow her down.

The cost is minimal. What is my one life against the thousands of lives in an entire nation? I straighten to my most dignified posture and slip my dagger back into its hidden sheath. "If you intend to kill me, do get on with it."

Her gaze narrows. "What game are you playing?"

Game? How ironic that she should say that. I sigh, remembering Lady Jersey's prediction. The Patroness is right. I do gamble. Except these stakes are much higher than anything my parents ever wagered.

Here are the cards in my hand.

If Lady Daneska kills me in her bedroom, she will come under heavy scrutiny. True, she might claim I was thieving, but who would believe her? She may be a guest of the Prince, but she is also a foreigner. I am the daughter of an earl and a guest of Lady Jersey. It will be difficult to explain my death. At minimum, Daneska will be detained for questioning. My murder will throw a smelly blanket of scandal over her visit. The upshot is, the charming Lady Daneska will be kept away from Prince George, and her overtures from Napoleon will be received with considerably less cordiality.

I lace my fingers and await my fate. "Do you intend to stand there all day gaping like a slow-witted baboon, or are you going to get to work and stick me with that hat pin you call a knife?"

She hates me now more than ever. Lady Daneska doesn't even bother to disguise her vicious expression. With a bark of anger, she throws the dagger.

Daneska's blade is fast. Too fast. I'm unable to dodge even an inch before it cuts through the sleeve of my dress, slices the edge of my arm, and plunges into the door. The quivering *thwang* of the blade as it sticks in the wood, rings in my ear.

Stunned. I slump back against the door. "You missed," I whisper.

"I never miss." Daneska sneers. "Do you think I can't see what you're doing? *Playing the martyr.* You little fool."

I'm surprised she hasn't thrown another knife. She already has it drawn. She would *like* to cut me again, I see it in her. But not kill me. That would be too inconvenient.

"As if I would be stupid enough to kill you here. I'll do it, mind you, and with pleasure, but not here."

A shadow moves over her left shoulder. Suddenly the air freezes in my lungs.

"What took you so long?" Daneska asks without turning. "Did you not see my signal?"

Ghost steps into the light and I suck in my breath. I'd seen him once before, in Calais. But now he seems so much bigger than I'd remembered.

He is even taller than Lord Ravencross, same dark hair and broad shoulders but that is where the resemblance ends. This man is as cold as a grave. His shrewd eyes are like those of an adder, dark and pitiless. Yet there's something spellbinding about him. I cannot look away.

He doesn't respond to her question. Clearly, he is a man who never answers unless he chooses.

Daneska yammers away, but his presence is so commanding I can scarcely hear what she's babbling about. "You see, my cabbage-witted mouse. We were expecting you. The minute you snuck out of the musical, I knew you had taken the cheese."

A *trap*.

I slowly reach into my pocket for my knife.

"Lucien, are you going to do it or not?" She offhandedly points her dagger at me. "Oh, and mind her right hand, dearest. Lady Jane carries a blade these days."

The corner of Ghost's mouth curls. He's hoping for a fight, and I intend to give him one. I whirl away from the door, knife drawn. But before I can complete my turn, he grabs my throat.

Fast. He's blazing fast.

I thrust my blade backward, aiming for his thigh. But he clamps hold of my knife hand and holds my wrist in place with a grip like an iron vise. In one powerful movement he yanks me against his chest. His hand on my throat presses the tender place at the base of my jaw. My knife clatters to the floor.

"Careful, my dear, mustn't kill her. Not yet." Daneska cautions him, but he doesn't let up on my throat.

I tug frantically at his arm. He presses harder. Blood throbs in my ears. *Slow. Too slow.* I feel the need to vomit. The room spins. Still he squeezes.

"Sleep well, Lady Jane." His rough rumbling whisper frightens me more than a knife ever could.

Daneska's annoying titter fades. I can no longer hold on to my thoughts. The world darkens to a deep suffocating black.

Twenty

TRAPPED

I awaken, bound and gagged, lying in the back of a small horse-drawn wagon.

When faced with a crisis, you must rely upon your training. Miss Stranje's refrain echoes through my rattled mind. I quiet my frantic thoughts and recite our training. *If captured, first, determine where you are. Second, assess the best way to free yourself.*

I try to orient myself, but there is a tarp thrown across the bed of the wagon blocking my view. I hear hooves and wheels clacking. We're still on cobblestones, but seem to be angling downhill. I envision the maps we studied, but they don't help me figure out if we are going east or west, only that we must be heading south, toward the river. The smell is unmistakable.

There's a slender gap at the corner of the wagon bed, and I wriggle sideways so I might see something through it. Occasionally we pass a streetlamp or a lighted window; otherwise, it is wretchedly dark. There's still traffic on the road. I hear the clip-clop of carriages drawn by teams, and the fast trot of high-perch phaetons whipping past us. The farther we go, the fewer conveyances I hear. We meet a large vehicle, and the drayman shouts at the driver of my wagon to move aside.

Maybe he will hear me if I make enough noise. I wedge myself sideways so I can try to kick the side of the wagon. Roaring as loudly as I can through my gag, I slam my feet against the sideboard. Our wagon bolts forward and we take a sudden turn. I slam my feet against the side again, hoping someone will notice, but there are no longer sounds from other vehicles. The wind is blocked and I feel the closeness of buildings. We've turned down a narrow street or alley.

The wagon stops. It creaks as my driver climbs down. He throws the cover back.

Am I to be let go?

Or killed?

I lift my head, struggling to adjust my eyes to the dark. Ghost's broad shape blocks out the weak light of the London night. His fist slams into my jaw. The blow sends me sprawling against the floor of the wagon.

Whatever indignities I may have suffered in my life, I've never been punched in the face. I hate him for it. My jaw throbs, but pain isn't what makes these tears. Fury and indignation burn through my veins. That's what makes me cry. I do not want to. I want to be like Tess, brave and tough. But I'm not. At least no one will see my wretched sobs. I clamp my lips around the gag, so he won't hear. I don't want him to know he brought me to this weak place.

Shameful angry tears soak my cheeks. They seep into the gag and make me want to spit.

Then they dry.

I will not cry again.

The faraway sound of laughter and music seeps under the tarpaulin. We must've passed a tavern and now the way grows steeper. We leave the cobblestones, and his wagon tilts and sways over an uneven rutted road until we come to a small, stone bridge. It might be a canal or sewer crossing.

I wish I'd studied those maps harder. The wagon soon levels off and we hit the hollow sound of wooden slats. A pier. We're on a pier.

When the wagon comes to a halt, terror chokes me worse than this wretched sodden gag. If he throws me into the Thames bound and gagged like this, I will drown. Never mind that even untied, I would still drown because I don't know how to swim. Count that as one more thing I wish I'd done—learned to swim when Tess was teaching Georgie. I'd foolishly thought I'd never have any use for it.

Ghost yanks the tarp back and slings me over his shoulder as if I'm nothing more than a sack of rice. He carries me up a gangplank onto a ship. At least I'm not going to drown. *Small comfort.* If we set sail, my friends will never find me. I try to fight him, but with my arms and feet bound, all I can do is thrash about uselessly on his shoulder and bang my head on the hatch as he climbs down into the ship's hold.

Ghost wordlessly dumps me on the floor. It is pitch dark down here. Even so, there's no mistaking Ghost's presence. He sucks away the light and drains hope from the air around him. I strive to recapture the anger I'd felt at him earlier, anything is better than the racking fear chomping away at the marrow of my bones.

Except I can no longer summon anger. I shiver mindlessly. My lips turn dry as dust, and all I can remember is how to be afraid.

He lights an oil lamp and hangs it on the center beam. The

light helps me gather my wits. This must be his lair. He stayed aboard ship. Wise of him. Less likely to be found that way. I do battle with my fear by studying the contents of his room. He's more orderly than Daneska. His cot is made, his washstand is organized with a towel and shaving equipment, and the slops have been changed. Papers sit in neat piles on the table, chests and boxes are stacked against the walls, as well as several coils of rope, a barrel of black powder, three metal canisters, and a box of tools.

I leave off cataloging when another man climbs down the steps, a burly sailor. Not a man who bathes regularly, judging by the smell. Ghost kicks a chair into the center of the room. "Tie her to it."

"Aye." The man jams his rough leathery hands under my arms, and lifts me to my feet, dragging me toward the chair. I sweep my feet out to the side knocking it over.

Ghost rears like a wild stallion. Before I know what's happened, he rights the chair, jerks me out of the other man's hands, and slams me onto the wooden seat. He leans near to my face, giving me no choice but to stare wide-eyed at my captor. "One more stunt like that and I'll leave the room. Meaning I'll let Jack do whatever he wants to you. Understand me, girl?"

I nod, and sit meek as a little lamb while Jack wraps cord around my middle, cinching it tighter than he needs to. When he kneels down to tie my ankles, each to a leg of the chair, I make not a peep. Even though his grimy hands linger too long on my legs, I say nothing. Maybe he won't notice I've locked my heels down directly in front of the chair legs, so that later I can shift my feet back beside the legs and the bindings will loosen. *Soon*, he will finish tying me and leave. *Soon*, I tell myself, ticking the seconds in my head.

Ghost is sharpening a knife.

It will all be over soon.

"I could hold 'er for you." Jack stands and runs his fingers around my neck. I can't repress a shudder. His mocking snigger brings back to life my anger. Anger that demands I escape. *I will kill you on my way out,* I think. Jack snatches his hand away as if my furious thoughts scorch his fingers.

"Go." Ghost orders.

"Aye, m'lord." Jack sulks out as if he has been robbed of a prize. He would've enjoyed watching me die.

"Close the hatch."

It bangs, with the startling finality of a coffin lid slamming shut.

"Idiotic feathers." It surprises me when Ghost yanks one of the ostrich plumes out of my hair. Perhaps he finds it difficult to murder a woman wearing something so absurdly innocent as white feathers.

At the plume's unexpected weight, he carries it to the light and discovers the lock pick lodged inside. His gaze snaps back to me, and something akin to respect flits through his eyes. An instant later, whatever appreciation he felt vanishes. He jerks the other feather and isn't surprised to find the second pick. He tosses both on the table, and comes at me with his knife.

It will all be over soon. I turn my head and close my eyes not wanting to see him cut my throat. I feel a swift and unexpected tug on my hair. It's over in a blink.

I'm still alive.

I open my eyes. My curls dangle from his fist. Those are my ringlets, the ones Sera had so lovingly draped over my shoulder. He slaps my hair down on the table beside the feathers, and returns with his knife.

"Make one move, and I'll cut you deeper."

I bite down on the gag, preparing for the worst. He grabs up my skirts, and I suck in my breath, holding in a whimper. His knife rips through the cloth, slicing away a section of my ball-gown and a sizeable hunk of my petticoat including the lace.

He only cut my gown and underdress. Why? What is he doing? What does it matter?

I'm still alive.

Air trapped in my lungs whooshes out, and I close my eyes in relief. An instant later, they open wide. I gasp, feeling the hot burn of his knife slashing through the flesh of my leg. The gag only muffles part of my scream.

Ghost watches my face as if my pain fascinates him. I clamp my lips tight, struggling to deny him my moans of pain. He presses closer, so close his breath fills my nostrils, suffocating me with spent air and the smell of brandy.

Then I realize what he is doing. He's sopping up my blood with the rag he made of my underdress.

Finally, he backs away and holds my petticoat up to the light.

Intriguing, in a way—the spreading pattern of all that bright red blood set against the white fabric and delicate lace. Almost beautiful. *Almost.* It's unbalanced. Too little white. Too much red. Too much blood. *My blood.* Suddenly the sight sickens me. My neck tightens and the corners of my vision explode with fireworks.

Not good.

As the spots whirl faster, I chastise myself. *You're not going to let a little blood make you woozy, are you? Keep your wits, Jane!*

Too late.

No matter how hard I try to cling to consciousness, the light dims, and the room spins away.

Twenty-one

INTERROGATION

I wander in and out of a murky consciousness, struggling to find my way to the surface. When at last I awaken, it is to the terrifying sound of Ghost's voice. "You shouldn't have come."

"You worry too much, *mon ami.*" Lady Daneska sounds flippant and not at all shaken by his tone. "I made certain everyone saw me at the ball. I danced with Prinny himself. The fat prince and I made *le grand spectacle.*"

He slams his hand against the table. "Stop pretending you're French. It annoys me. You could've been followed."

"No, I was not followed, *sweeting.*" The way she drawls out "sweeting" nauseates me. No doubt, she says it that way to annoy Ghost further. "I would never be that careless. I'm never followed, unless I wish to be." She trails her fingers over the front of his shirt.

He brushes off her flirtation. "Do they know she's missing?"

"Poor lovesick Mr. Sinclair tried to tell them." She laughs. "Did you send him the package yet?"

Package. I cringe. My *hair and that darned bloody petticoat.* I picture them in a parcel tied up with brown paper and string. Arriving on Alexander's doorstep.

"He should've gotten it an hour ago. What happened when he raised the alarm?"

"They lied to him, of course. Miss Stranje and her brood insisted Lady Jane went home with a headache. They couldn't very well say she disappeared while pilfering through my rooms. Oh, my dear, I wish you could've been there. It was delicious. You should've seen Miss Stranje on the hunt. She even snuck back into my rooms in search of her precious Lady Jane. Gratifying to watch the high-and-mighty Emma Stranje stoop so low as to pick a lock herself. I left the lamp burning so she could see the blood."

"All the more reason you shouldn't have come."

Lady Daneska pouts. "I want to interrogate our prisoner. Why should you have all the fun?"

"For pity's sake, Daneska. Take something seriously for once in your life. This is England we're playing for."

"Oh look, our little cabbage head is awake." She clasps her palms together. "Isn't it nearing the time you and Jack ought to go and retrieve our wayward American?"

Ghost stomps away from her and climbs up to the hatch. "Don't make a mess."

"I'm not the one who left that pool of blood beneath her chair."

The minute the hatch closes behind Ghost, I try to talk around the gag. "Mr. Sinclair isn't going to give you those plans."

"What makes you think I only want his plans? I want more than that. I want everything. Him. His boat. Everything."

I hear banging on the upper deck, and the rattle of chains, as if they're lowering a rowboat. *A rowboat?* Why isn't he taking the horse and wagon? I remember Jack's putrid stench and the puzzle pieces slide into place. They're rowing up the sewer.

She digs through Ghost's open tool chest. "You saw those plans, didn't you?"

"May have." The gag muffles my answer. "Once or twice." It's then that I notice the tool case is sitting in a different spot. Ghost has been tinkering with something at his worktable. The powder keg is moved, too, and one of the metal cylinders sits atop the table.

"A pity." She pulls out a hammer and rubs her thumb over its head and grimaces. "I think he already used this on someone." She flips it back into the box and pulls out a huge hunting knife. "Ah, now this is promising. You say you only saw the plans once or twice? We both know that is not true. Your handwriting is on the list of materials." She hefts the knife in her palm and slides it between my cheek and the gag, slicing through the cloth.

The gag falls away and I open and close my stiff jaw. "Yes, all right. I helped with the list."

"Good. Start there. Give me the correct list of materials. Not that phony one you embarrassed me with." She runs a whetstone over the blade. "Is this the knife he used on you? Not like him to leave a dull blade."

"No. A different one." *The sight of which, I will never forget.* "You expect me to remember the entire list?"

She continues to sharpen the blade, running the whetstone over the edge with expert strokes. "The mind is an amazing thing, Lady Jane. It will recall almost anything given the right stimulus."

"*Folderol.* We both know that isn't true. Panic makes people forget. What is it you really want?"

"I told you. Everything. Starting with Mr. Sinclair, and you're going to deliver him to me." She flips the knife. "One way or another. Question is, how much fun are we going to have in the meantime?"

I've lost patience with her subtle threats. "Don't pretend to be a sadist, Daneska. We both know you're not a killer."

She turns on me, furious. And here I thought I'd given her a compliment.

"You don't know anything about me!" she screams. "Not one thing. How could you? You never cared two farthings for me."

"True enough." I meet her furious gaze with anger of my own. "But Tess did. She's the one who insists you're not a murderer— that you have a soul after all."

Daneska slaps me. Her face is a raging storm. She walloped me on the same cheek he punched, but I press my lips together and pretend it doesn't hurt.

"Don't lie to me," she snarls.

It's all I can do to speak without groaning. "I'm not."

But now I do lie. I lie to her employing every ounce of deception I can summon. My life depends upon it. Alexander's life depends on it. "Tess has a contingency plan if I turn up missing. She's going to sneak back into your rooms at Carlton House in the small hours of the morning and ask you where you've taken me."

"That is a stupid plan. Why would she do something so foolish?"

"She has some demented idea that because you care about her, you would tell her the truth. I tried to talk her out of it—"

"But I don't! I *don't* care about her. I tried to kill her."

"She doesn't think so. According to her, if you'd aimed to kill her that night at sea, you would have. She says, *Daneska is a better shot than that.*"

"That much is true. I usually hit my mark."

"You mean to say you really *did* let her go? I didn't believe it, but if you say so—"

"I didn't say that." She brandishes the knife at me.

I shake my head as if Daneska disgusts me. That part isn't fake. "You cut Madame Cho. I didn't think Tess would ever get over that."

"There! See? That shows you must be lying. Tess knows if I would hurt Cho, I would not hesitate to kill you, because I hate you."

"Except you didn't kill Madame Cho. You could've, but you didn't." I temper my disgust with a hint of optimism.

"An oversight."

"That's what I thought. But Tess insists it was intentional."

Lady Daneska huffs resentfully. "She loves that old woman."

I mirror her same indignant tone. "Apparently she still cares about you, too. Foolish. We all warned her. Miss Stranje is the only one who urged her to forgive you."

"You're lying. Emma Stranje would never do that."

"You're wrong. She did. Ask any of the other girls. We all sat at breakfast and heard them talk about it." *That's the absolute truth.* "And Tess later told us she forgave you. I couldn't believe it, but she did. For some stupid reason she still cares about you. That's why she has this idiotic idea she can persuade you to let me go."

Lady Daneska shakes her head and paces up and down. "I hate you, Jane. You know that, don't you?"

I almost laugh. "I'd be a fool to think otherwise. So get it over with—kill me and prove Tess wrong."

She draws her knife and holds it next to my face. "Maybe I'll just make you ugly. Then everyone will stop loving you."

She presses the blade against my cheek. "Don't be ridiculous. No one loves me because I'm pretty. I'm plain."

"Yes. Yes you are. Plain, with those no-color eyes—"

"Hazel."

"What kind of color is hazel? Boring. Just like your hair. And your thin-lipped mouth."

"My lips aren't thin."

"Plain." She draws back the knife. "Why *do* they love you?" It is the most sincere question I've ever heard her ask. Then she has to go and ruin it all. "Tell me what it is they love about you. I'll carve it out, and send it to them in a teeny tiny box." She looks down at me with disgust.

"Where did he cut you?" She pulls up my dress and stares. Then she yanks it aside so I can see. "Look! He bandaged you. He does not do that. Lucien does not *bandage people*." She presses on my wound and makes it ooze afresh. "Does it hurt?" She pokes it again just to see me wince. "That's going to leave an ugly scar."

Her gaze shifts to his cot. "That is *his* blanket around your shoulders. *Mein Gott*, he tucked you in—*Ghost* did this!"

"I wouldn't know. I was unconscious."

She flings down my skirts, snatches his blanket away and throws it in a wad onto his cot, stomps back, and kicks my chair. She points the tip of the knife straight at my nose. "What is it you have over people?"

Careful not to move or even breathe, I say, "Nothing. I suspect he was just keeping me alive so you can force Mr. Sinclair to do your bidding."

"Maybe." She backs away an inch or two. "He said he wants you alive." She mocks his commanding tone. "*We will get more out of Sinclair if the girl is still breathing.*" She waves her arm, encompassing the whole room. "Still, he didn't have to cover you with his blanket. Tell me, what is it they all love about you? This Mr. Sinclair. Miss Stranje. All of them. Why do they care about you?"

"I don't know." *That is the pure truth.*

"What is it you give them?"

I try to shrug, as much as possible with my ribs tied to a chair. That's when I notice Ghost must've loosened the ropes Jack tied so tight around my midsection, probably so I could breathe properly. "I have no idea. Perhaps they feel gratitude because I do my best to take care of them. I organize their plans and advise—"

"What? Are you mad? No, no, no. This is not the answer." She waggles the knife at me as if it is her finger. "No one above the age of seven wants a nanny. And no one likes their governess."

"I did."

"Well, no one else does. Take my word on it."

A nanny? A governess? Is that what I am to them? I blink. "If that's not it, I have no idea why they would care about me. Maybe it's simply because I love them."

"Maybe." She sulks at me, hands on her hips. "Is Tess really going to come and plead for your life? I can't believe it." She bends close, the point of Ghost's knife digging in under my chin. "Swear on your mother's grave."

"I swear." Through clenched teeth, and with a clear conscience, I make the vow. Tess and I didn't actually make a plan. At first, I was lying to Daneska, buying time, trying to distract her. But after saying it aloud, I realize it is true. I know Tess well enough that I can predict exactly what she will do. If I don't show up in the next few hours, she and the others will hunt for me first. Then, she'll use the wolf-dogs to try to track me. When that fails, she will go to Lady Daneska and plead for my life.

"You're telling the truth." She growls and gives what is left of my hair a vicious yank as punishment. "That little fool! That *is* exactly what she will do." Daneska paces across the room, roaring with frustration. "Ach!" She stops, and hurls the knife at me.

Instinctively, I try to duck. Not that it would've done any good. The knife lodges in the center post right beside my head. "It's a good thing you never miss," I mutter.

"Tess will be too late. Sinclair will already be ours. Lord Wyatt and Captain Grey, they will try to stop him, but he will sneak out, and give himself over to us to save you." Daneska stops pacing and leans in to scold me. "This is what happens when people make the mistake of loving someone. It turns them weak and makes them vulnerable. I tried to tell this to Tess, but she would not listen. You understand though, don't you?"

"Yes." *Sadly, I do.* "It's true, love leaves us vulnerable. But no, I don't believe it makes us weaker. Love makes us stronger inside. Braver. It gives us something to live for." *And the strength to face death, if we must.*

"Not stronger—foolish. You will see. Your lovesick American, he will come straight to us like a mindless little puppy lost without his master. We will have him then. He will do anything we want to keep you alive."

"One small problem with your theory—Mr. Sinclair doesn't love me. Not really. Not that much. He likes me, yes. But love? I think not."

She laughs. "Liar. I watched him during dinner. He looked so jealous I thought he might leap across the table and rip Harston's heart out. He will come. You will see."

I say nothing, sinking into my ropes, dreading the fact that she may be right.

"So will Tess." She curses in her native language. "Which means, I must go back to the palace and pretend to be sleeping. The picture of innocence. This is your fault. I hate you, Lady Jane."

Twenty-two

ᴅᴀʀɪɴɢ ᴅᴇᴠɪᴄᴇꜱ

Y ou won't need this." Daneska turns out the oil lamp, and snickers because she's leaving me in the dark. She stubs her toe on the ladder and curses me roundly.

I won't miss that lamp, or the stink of the cheap burning oil. Darkness is not my enemy. I memorized Ghost's hold, the position of every pole, every beam, every box and barrel, and more importantly, I know exactly where she left that knife stuck in the center post.

I set straight to work, wriggling my ankles toward the inside of the chair legs. Immediately my ankle bindings loosen. I tip the chair to the left side, leaning against the post to keep from falling over, and shake the ropes on my right ankle until they slide off the bottom of the chair leg. My right foot is free, but I can't risk tipping the chair the other way because there's no pole to brace against. Only one thing to do. I inch my left foot up through the loops, twisting and pointing my toes, but remembering to relax the muscles. Rigid muscles do not pull through ropes as easily as soft relaxed ones. I use the toes of my right foot to help move the ropes, shifting them one by one over the heel until my left foot is free.

It's easy now, to scoot the chair until it faces the center beam and the knife. While Daneska lectured me on the pitfalls of love, I managed to loosen only one of the knots binding my hands. Ghost tied a double sheepshank with a secondary complex double constrictor knot around my wrists. I can't get out of it, and I'm more frustrated than a plucked hornet.

Obviously, he must know Miss Stranje requires us to learn how to untie ourselves. I managed to undo the sheepshank, but that secondary cinch is brutal. He shrewdly employed a smaller rope, which makes it even more difficult. With the sheepshank out of the way, at least I have a two-inch gap between my hands. *Not very helpful.* With my hands still incapacitated, and my ribs strapped to the chair back, I need that knife.

I position myself squarely beneath it. Because my feet are free, I'm able to tip the chair up just enough to get my mouth over the handle. I bite down, trying not to think of how it tastes like years of filth. There's no time for squeamishness. I quickly work the knife free of the post.

Now comes the tricky part. Pressing my chin against my chest, I lean forward pushing the tip of the knife into the ropes around my midsection. I try to isolate one of the cords. This is difficult to do in the dark. As soon as I can tell I've wedged the blade between two cords, I twist so the cutting edge is out, and saw up and down. Jack only tied one knot in the back. If I can cut through one cord all the bands will uncoil. I work the knife as fast as I can.

The whisper-soft pop as each small strand gives way is a victory. I keep my teeth clamped tight around the hilt, even though my jaw is aching, and the wretched thing tastes like greasy palms, fishy salt water, oakum, and ship's tar. I suppress a tremor of disgust.

With a snap, the band finally springs apart. All I need to do now is shift from side to side until the whole pile loosens. I stand up, finally free of that dratted chair! I continue holding the knife in my mouth and I lower my arms so I can step over the ropes binding my wrists. I slice the ropes apart over the blade. My hands are free at last!

I take the knife from my mouth, spit out the disgusting residue, and with cords still dangling from each wrist, climb the ladder. I lift the hatch and peek out, expecting Jack or some other sailor to send up the alarm, but the ship is quiet. It's still dark outside. Not as deep black as midnight, it looks closer to four in the morning. Still, it's dark enough to provide some cover. I slip out through the hatch, careful to close it silently.

I stoop low and skitter across the upper deck, staying close to the railing, aware I'm leaving a trail of bloody footprints on the deck. The gangplank has been drawn up, leaving me no easy way down. I lean over the gunwales judging the distance to the dock. We sit ten or twelve feet above it and about two feet away. If my leg wasn't injured, I might consider jumping. As it is, I would either land in the river or knock myself out crashing against the deck on the pier.

"Oye! Who's there?" It's a sailor or one of Ghost's men. I've no idea which. It's not Jack or I would throw the knife. I spot the heavy rope off the bow tying the ship to the pier and dash for it. I grab what's left of my skirts, toss a length of the silk over the thick rope, and jump over the side. Hanging onto the cloth, I slide down the line, landing with a thud against the docking post.

I find my footing and run up the pier. The man shouts obscenities at me from the upper deck, where he's setting down a gangway to give chase.

Ghost and Jack took the ship's rowboat, and unless my nose misled me, Jack must've rowed him up and down a sewer more than once. I'm willing to bet that sewer leads directly beneath the Drowning Sow Tavern.

I'm guessing it's the same tavern we passed on the way here. There isn't a tunnel leading to Spitalfields as we'd imagined. It's a simple trapdoor to the sewer canals, which run underground throughout parts of the city. The closer to the river, the bigger the sewers are. What better route for smugglers to transport in French wines, brandies, and cognac. And it's an ingenious way for spies to move in and out of the city without being seen. Clever man, our Ghost, and he'll be dropping Mr. Sinclair down that trapdoor any minute if I don't get there in time.

I dash up the pier, praying for darkness and fog to stay with me an hour or two more. Ghost's horse and wagon must be tied nearby. He or one of his men must surely have used it to deliver the gruesome package containing my hair and blood. I reach the end of the dock and scurry up the embankment.

There! The horse and wagon stand under a tree. The harness and rigging are still on the poor creature. He should've been brushed and properly tended. I had expected to find him unhitched, and anticipated I'd have to ride bareback. Faster that way, but this will have to do.

I release the brake and back the gelding up. The sailor from the boat is thundering down the pier toward me. I clamber up onto the driver's seat and startle the poor horse with a rattling shake of the reins. "Go horse! Go!"

He takes a plodding step forward. I give the reins a harder shake. "I know you can trot, darn you. You trotted last night when I was stuck in the back." I grab the whip and smack him good. The ornery horse rears and bolts forward at a full run, bouncing up the road so fast we're bound to break a wheel. I don't care. Ghost's man is running after us, shouting for me to stop. *As if I would.* What kind of fool does he take me for?

I wrap the reins around my palms as I'd been taught as a girl. Except that had been a little buggy and a smallish pony. This horse, who I decide must be named Harold for numerous reasons, is not smallish, he's full size. And even though the wagon is not very big, it's not nearly as agile as a buggy. The blasted thing rebounds over a bump and nearly throws me off.

I am hanging on to my seat with one hand, and praying the horse has some idea where we're going. This fog makes it nearly impossible to gauge what's up ahead more than a few yards. Fortunately, the hill is steep, and Ghost's man only has two legs—he's slowing, whereas my trusty Harold has four, and gallops up the slope as if a demon is driving his wagon.

I look back and see the man throw his hat onto the road as I disappear into the mist. Harold stops running quite so fast and I steer us toward a small bridge that crosses the sewer and angle up the road to Lower Thames Street. We're finally on cobblestones and I allow my poor horse to slow to a trot. "Good boy, Harold," I croon, wishing I had Tess's way with animals. "Keep going," I add quietly. The street is empty at this hour. Each clack of Harold's shoes against the stones startles me with its loudness, but the fog swallows the sound as surely as a snake gulping down a mouse.

The world is silent and asleep except for us, and I wonder if Ghost has already captured Mr. Sinclair.

Concentrate.

Timing is the key.

Unlock the scenario, Jane. Hurry.

It all tumbles out before me—the players in the game, a map of possibilities, and probable options.

They will have been looking for me, *all of them*, including Alexander, Captain Grey, and Lord Wyatt. At the end of the first hour and a half, they'll have subtly scoured all of Carlton House. They'll have found clues that make them think it is a lost cause. Miss Stranje will tell Georgie and the others about the blood she saw in Lady Daneska's room.

They'll think the worst. I'm dead.

Ghost made his move. The package arrived and they will have realized I'm alive. They'll figure out it's Mr. Sinclair the Iron Crown is after, not me. I'm just the bait.

What will they do?

They won't give in. They'll expand their search, broadening it to the streets around Carlton House, hunting for a clue, any clue leading to my whereabouts. Tess will have Phobos out with her; she'll set him on my scent. They may find something that leads them to the docks or they might not. Tess won't give up. Not yet.

Captain Grey will order Mr. Sinclair back to their rooms and send him with an armed guard to keep him safe. They'll tell him he's in too great a danger to be out on the streets. "Lady Jane is all right," they'll tell him. "They won't hurt her. It's you they want."

Alexander won't listen to them. He saw all that blood, and my hair. He won't believe I'm all right. He'll be frantic knowing they're hurting me on his account. His heart will tell him he *must* do something.

My eyes begin to water. I dash away the tears.

Think, Jane, think.

When will he make his move? *How* will he make his move?

Of course! When everyone else was at the soirée, Ghost had someone slip a note into Mr. Sinclair's room, beside his pillow, on his washstand, somewhere only he would find it. That means Alexander will sneak out as soon as the guard they have placed to protect him falls asleep.

I tick the minutes and hours since this game has been in play. My jaw tightens.

It's now.

Now!

Any minute Mr. Sinclair will find his way to the meeting place. I urge Harold into a faster trot, studying the street for movement. Up ahead on the corner, I see the dim flicker of a light in a window. It's the only light on this street.

I slow the wagon, wishing Harold's shoes didn't echo like gunshots. Dangling from the signpost is a carving of an ugly boar with tusks. The Drowning Sow. I pull up not daring to drive the cart past the window. If Ghost is inside, I don't want him to come out to check the street. I turn into the narrow alley next to the crumbling brick building and climb down. There's nothing to tie Harold to, so I pull on the brake. The squeak against the wheels nearly makes me jump out of my skin.

I climb down and pet Harold's nose. "Hush," I say when he nickers. "Wait here and be a good lad."

I tiptoe around to the front window and peek in through the corner. Ghost and Jack are right there, sitting at an otherwise empty table. I jump back and flatten myself against the wall.

They're still waiting. Alexander isn't here yet. I press against the crumbling bricks, my hand clapped over my chest, and close my eyes trying to catch my breath.

Blast this dratted fog.

That's why I didn't see him. *The darkness of the night. The rudeness of the oil lamp flaring from the dirty tavern window.* These are excuses. How did I not see someone on the street? He blends with the night, clad entirely in black, except for his hair—a shock of gold peeking out from under his hat. He's here! Alexander Sinclair reaches for the tavern door.

"No!" I cry out to stop him. On the empty street the sound of my voice echoes louder than I'd expected.

"Jane?"

One quick glance through the window and I see Ghost is out of his seat. I lunge for Alexander's arm and tug him toward the wagon. "Run!"

I scramble up into the driver's seat and struggle with the jammed brake. I give it a vicious shove, and the blasted brake finally disengages. I snap the reins. "Go, horse! Run, Harold. Go, lad."

Harold moseys nonchalantly forward.

"I see you've done this before." Alexander smirks.

Ghost dashes around the corner behind us and roars my name. Jack skids out beside him.

Alexander stops smiling. He grabs the reins from me, clucks his tongue and flicks the whip against Harold's backside. "Get up!"

Harold's ears twitch and he lurches into a trot. Another flick of the whip and Harold flies into a canter. I look back and see Ghost aiming a gun. First, he points it at me. Then he shifts it to Mr. Sinclair. It must've occurred to him that he might not want to kill the one person he needs alive, so he aims the barrel back at me. I duck. The shot skims past my shoulder. If I hadn't anticipated it and dodged—*Ruddy hell!* Ghost meant to put me in the ground with that shot.

"Know how to use one of these?" Alexander hands me a pistol out of his coat.

Loaded. Impressive.

"I'm a quick study." I turn and take aim. Seeing Ghost tamping down for another shot, I fire. A nasty fluff of smoke obscures my vision for a second. I wave it away, and see I've merely grazed Ghost's arm, but the bullet struck Jack square in the shoulder. Ghost looks up from the blood dripping down his sleeve to me. Angrier than ever, he takes aim and this time he won't miss.

"Turn," I scream to Alexander. "Turn!"

Mr. Sinclair seems to be rather adept at handling the obstinate horse. He swerves left onto a street. Ghost's bullet splatters bricks on the corner of a building, instead of my skull. With a flick of the whip, we are galloping east. Racing toward Haversmythe House. Toward safety.

Twenty-three

UNLOCKED

"T urn right at the next street, Mr. Sinclair. If you would,
please."

He complies without saying a word. He's still breathing in
hard heaves.

"And up there, turn left onto Fleet Street." I point. "You may
rest easy, Mr. Sinclair. They won't catch us now. Perhaps you
might want to slow Harold to a trot. He's had a rather exhausting night."

I realize I am giving orders. That's what I do when my nerves
are stretched beyond their limit. *Oh, pig swallup.* That's not true.
It's what I always do. *Do this—don't do that.* I daresay I am probably the bossiest female in all of England.

A streetlamp flickers up ahead, and Alexander swerves toward
it. "Whoa." That is the first word he has said in ten blocks, and
I'm not certain if he's giving a command to Harold or ordering
me to be quiet.

He must've meant Harold, because the horse is the only one of us who obeys. "What are you doing?" I demand. "You must stay on Fleet Street until we come to the Strand, and—"

"You're a mess." He pulls on the brake and tucks the reins under his leg.

"I'm well aware I look a fright, thank you. Delightful of you to notice." I stare at him indignantly. "Although if you had followed Captain Grey's instructions, this race for our lives would've been completely unnecessary."

"How do you know I disobeyed Captain Grey's orders?"

"A bit obvious. You're here, aren't you?"

Alexander is staring at me assessing the bruise on my jaw. "He hurt you."

"Nothing worth mentioning." I wave away his attention. "We really should be going—"

"He hit you." He cups my cheek in his palm. "The brute hit you."

"I was being rather noisy and uncooperative, you see."

"I can imagine." He strokes my cheek so softly it actually begins to hurt less. "I am sorry." His fingers tremble.

"You've nothing to apologize for."

"And your hair—your beautiful curls."

"It wasn't beautiful." I want to hear him say it again, and I don't mind at all that he's threading his fingers through what's left of my hair. "I've been meaning to whack it off. It's the new style, you know. All the rage. Caroline Lamb bobbed hers. It's called: à la Titus."

His gaze drifts down to my lap and the bloodstains all over my skirts. Even in the dim light I see him suddenly turn pale. Judging by his grimace, I think he might be sick any minute.

"It's not as bad as it looks." Now it's me, reaching for him, patting his shoulder reassuringly. "Really, it's not."

"Where did he . . ." He swallows. "Where did he stab you?"

"He didn't. Not a stab really, more of a nick or a cut."

Mr. Sinclair grows impatient with my half-explanations. "Where?" He's reaching for my skirts and I think he might pull them up in search of the wound himself.

I clap my hand over his. "He cut my leg."

He takes a shuddering breath. "How bad?" He glances around the street as if he's searching for something. "There must be a doctor or a surgeon somewhere near here. How bad is it, Jane?"

"I don't need a doctor."

"Are you telling me the truth?" He clamps both of my shoulders in his hands.

I nod and look down. Ashamed I have lied to him so often that he doesn't trust me. "I'm all right. Truly."

He still holds me as if I might slip out of his grasp at any moment. "You could've been killed. Don't you see? And if you had—"

"I'm not dead, Alexander, and I'm not dying. I simply look a little ragged, that's all." I flick my rough, shorn hair and muster up my best smile.

"Thank God." He takes in a breath and clasps my face in his hands. "So help me, Jane, if anything had happened to you, I—"

I have no idea what he was about to say, because I stopped him with a kiss. Or maybe he kissed me. I'm not sure which. It doesn't matter. It was pure heaven and I almost cried. I pressed my lips against his, and the next thing I knew both his arms were wrapped around me. His divine lips are not nearly so gentle as they had been on the cliffs of Stranje House.

I am not complaining.

They are warm and good, and the tender way they work against mine fills me with wonder. I wind my arms around his neck and kiss him back, hiding nothing, opening my heart to him. The sweetness of his mouth makes me forget the gash on my leg, and even Ghost and Lady Daneska. His kiss is pure and good, and it melts away all the evil in the world.

I don't want him to stop.

Except he does.

He draws back and peers at me with soul-melting eyes. That is the exact moment I know—I have picked the locks of his heart. The latch clicked open. His secrets are poured out before me.

"Oh my goodness." I blink up at him, amazed. "You *love* me."

He laughs. "My lady, it's supposed to be the gentleman who declares his sentiments. Not you."

"Yes." I try to sound suitably chastised. "It's just that I'm so surprised to discover it."

"You mean to tell me, even with that giant-sized brain of yours, you're only now tumbling to that fact?" He releases the brake and pulls the reins out. With a cluck of his tongue, the horse obediently takes to the road.

I dive into a lecture on the subject. "Perhaps you failed to notice, I'm not the lovable type. You do realize, I'm managing. I order everybody about whether they wish to be or not. I'm also stubborn, and according to my brothers, my tongue is sharp enough to split a man's skull at thirty paces."

He has the decency to laugh. "Aye, my lady. I know all those things."

"Yet you still love me. I'm astonished. A pity you're going back to America after the Admiralty signs the papers for the warship design."

He has no retort. Only a swallow. An uncomfortable jog of his Adam's apple.

Nothing.

Suddenly, all the lightness and joy I felt vanished into the darkness of the night. Silence is sometimes as killing as knife blades.

As we pass Drury Lane headed for St. James's I ask him to slow down. "No." He objects. "We need to take you to Haversmythe House and care for your injuries."

"But we have to find Miss Stranje and the others first, and they're not at the house. Not yet." *Especially Tess. If we wait too long she'll go to Lady Daneska.* "They're still out looking for me. They'll be in pairs or threesomes. Tess and Georgie will be with Phobos. They'll have gotten this far, and if Phobos picked up any scent at all, they'll be concentrating their search near the river."

We drive slowly down toward the Thames and then up again, and down the next street. It's still so blasted dark. I strain to see into the shadow and past the fog rolling up from the water.

"This is no use, Jane. It's like trying to find a needle in a haystack."

"There!" I point. "Stop. Stop!" I scramble down from the wagon. "Tess!"

She runs for me, Phobos on a lead gallops beside her. It's not Georgie, it's Sera running behind her. In seconds, Tess's arms are around me. She lets go and grabs my head, pressing her forehead against mine. "You're alive. I'd almost given up. I was about to go back to Carlton House and—"

"I know. I know. Thank you." Finally, it's okay to let some of the water welling up behind my eyes leak out.

Sera throws her arms around both of us, clinging to me as if

I'd returned from the dead. "I can't believe you're walking. All that blood. I thought for certain he must've cut you so badly you'd be too weak to move."

I wish she hadn't mentioned it. The darn thing is burning like the very fires of hell and it feels as if it's starting to ooze again. "Where's Miss Stranje? Or Captain Grey? There're things I must tell them immediately."

Phobos yips and sniffs my palms. Sera points. "The next street over. We have a signal if we find something."

Tess puts two fingers in her mouth and issues a shrill whistle. Phobos adds his high-pitched howl to it, and sniffs the blood near my bare feet.

"You're bleeding." Sera stoops down to inspect. "Mr. Sinclair, we need to get Jane home. Quickly."

"That's what I've been telling her." He puts on the brake, and climbs down to lift me into the back of the wagon and help Sera up beside me.

Tess waves us on. "Go! I'll meet Miss Stranje and Captain Grey at the top of the street. I have Phobos with me. I'll be fine."

Sera sits beside me, holding my hand. "How did *he* find you?" She tilts her head in Mr. Sinclair's direction. She means, how could he have found me, Mr. Sinclair, an engineer, not trained in this sort of thing, when she and Miss Stranje could not.

"He didn't. I found him."

"Ah." She nods, as if this is a perfectly logical answer, and begins to figure out exactly what I've been through tonight by observing every mark, bruise, missing shoes, rip and tear on my person. She is too kind to mention any of that. "I think short hair will look quite charming on you."

Twenty-four

REPORTS AND ALTERATIONS

Mr. Sinclair carries me upstairs at Haversmythe House. Our frantic butler, Mr. Peterson in his nightcap and wrapper, follows him carrying an oil lamp, stopping to mop up droplets of blood and complain. "I don't see how this could've happened at Carlton House. Most unusual."

Mr. Sinclair is always honest, so what he says is true, incomplete, but true. "The young lady was set upon by criminals. Hold that light steady, Peterson, otherwise we'll all go tumbling down the stairs."

He orders Peterson to get the maids out of bed to help. "And send for a doctor. Are you deaf? Don't stand there gawking, man. Go."

Two minutes later Mrs. Creevy and Alice rush into our bedroom. "Dear heavens! You poor child." Mrs. Creevy claps her hand over her throat. "We'll take it from here." She dismisses Mr. Sinclair. He stands by the door looking dreadfully worried.

"Shoo, young man. We've got to undress her." She pushes him out of the door.

"If you need me, I'll just be downstairs, waiting for Captain Grey and Miss Stranje."

"Run along," I say as if he is a nuisance, rather than the one person whose arms I wish were still holding me. "These soiled clothes make it look worse than it is. I'll be right as rain in no time."

"Never have understood what's so right about rain," he mutters, as Mrs. Creevy closes the door.

Sera and Mrs. Creevy do a splendid job of cleaning up my wound and dressing me for bed. Alice helps peel off my destroyed undergarments. "*Oye*, m'lady, that's a horrid-looking cut."

I can tell Sera wants to rip into Alice for having sided with our enemy, an enemy who would do this to her dearest friend, but at my warning glance she resists. By the time Miss Stranje arrives I am sponged off and tucked up in bed with a towel around my leg.

Our headmistress looks drawn when she comes and sits beside me on the bed. "I was afraid we'd lost you." She smooths her hand over my brow even though Sera has already brushed my hair back from my face.

I lean up on my elbow. "I've urgent news to report."

"I'm sure you do." She takes a deep breath. "However, you must rest. Sera told me your injuries are quite severe. You need sleep—"

"If you bring me a map I can show you where Ghost's ship is docked. He's not hiding in Spitalfields. He's staying aboard an old galleon anchored about a mile past London Bridge."

"That's all well and good, but *think*, Lady Jane. By now he will have moved the ship or gone to ground somewhere else."

I sigh and sink back into the pillows. "You're right, of course. I suppose it was wishful thinking on my part. I'd hoped if we got there fast enough . . ."

"He is called *Ghost* for good reason. He is a master at hiding and vanishing."

"And he always has secondary plans." I say this, wishing our enemy was not so brilliant.

"Yes, and sometimes he lays in more than a secondary contingency. In any case, he always has an escape plan. The man's a genius. If only he hadn't turned for Napoleon." She shakes her head.

"I believe he may be building a bomb of some kind. At least I *think* he's making a bomb. He had black powder and some odd-shaped canisters."

"Good heavens—"

Mrs. Creevy scratches on the door and peeks in. "The doctor's arrived, miss. Shall you be needin' me, do you think?"

Miss Stranje stands. "No, I'll assist him, Mrs. Creevy, thank you."

Dr. Meredith is his name, and the man is a sadist. "Needs stitching," he grumbles, as if he's irritated with me.

It isn't my fault Ghost decided to make such a deep cut.

"I've dosed her with laudanum, but it'll still take two strong footmen to hold her down. Legs are the worst. Even young ladies can kick like mules when I'm doing the stitching."

"I am not a mule," I say groggily. Something sneaks into the corner of my mind, tiptoeing just beyond my reach. *What is that?* Oh yes, the letter! The letter I saw in Daneska's room. "Miss Stranje, there's something else I needed to tell you. It's important."

Miss Stranje presses me back against the pillow. "Later, my lady. Later. Close your eyes. There's a good girl." She turns and speaks to the grumpy doctor who thinks I'm a mule. "No, Dr. Meredith. I will not allow footmen to view any part of this young lady's anatomy. I'll get the other girls to help me hold her steady."

"It's only her thigh, Miss Stranje, not—"

"No! Absolutely not."

I drift into a distorted nightmare. Hands. Hundreds of hands hold me down while Dr. Meredith sews me up. I scream. I think I'm screaming, but it echoes oddly. Suddenly it isn't Miss Stranje and the doctor, it's Ghost and that awful Jack jabbing me with needles. *Go away. Go away.* But it's me who goes away.

Trapped in a dark malignant forest, I wander aimlessly. Any minute Jack will spring out from behind one of these misshapen trees.

A heavenly light awakens me.

Either I am dead or it is day. I blink. My eyes feel dry as hearthstones. My tongue is so sticky I wonder if that sadist, Dr. Meredith, coated it with glue to keep me from screaming. My leg is tender but I can move it without causing undue pain.

Someone is lifting my head to help me take a drink. It's Maya. Her hands are soft and soothing as she lifts me toward the glass. I swallow greedily.

"How looong has she been uncooonscious?"

Galloping Goats. That sounds like Lady Jersey. I tug the covers up and struggle to focus. My vision clears. It is her! Either that or I'm hallucinating. And it looks as if Lady Castlereagh is standing behind her.

"Ten and a half hours," Miss Stranje answers.

"Well, I muuust say, young lady. You certainly added some excitement to the evening." Lady Jersey has on purple gloves, and she sweeps them in my general direction. "You'll have to do something about that hair."

"What time is it?" I manage to ask. Since my mouth is open Maya spoons broth into it.

Sera leans down and whispers, "Three in the afternoon."

"Where's Mr. Sinclair?" I rasp.

"He's all right." Georgie stands back by Tess, who looks like she didn't sleep all night. "Went home with Captain Grey after the doctor assured them you'd be all right."

Miss Stranje stands by the bedpost. "Do you feel well enough now, to tell us what you found?"

"Yes." I cough trying to clear the dryness in my throat. "But I would thank you to never give me laudanum again."

At Miss Stranje's signal, Madame Cho goes out to check the hall and stand sentry. She closes the bedroom door. The room feels crowded with the other girls and the two Patronesses.

Maya fortifies me with another spoonful of broth.

Lady Castlereagh practically vibrates with curiosity. "You found Lady Daneska's letters, didn't you?"

"Yes. It's not good news. One of you must speak to the Prince as soon as possible."

"What did you find?" Miss Stranje sits on the foot of the bed.

"Lady Daneska isn't here to kill the Prince. Not yet anyway. Napoleon sent her to persuade Prince George to parley with him. She is supposed to tell him Napoleon desires peace and wants to present Prince George with an offer to appoint him Supreme Ruler over England. *Supreme.* Better than being king. No more meddlesome Parliament."

"Good gracious!" Lady Jersey fans herself with a lace handkerchief. "Judging by the way Prinny was talking about Napoleon at dinner, he's well on his way to agreeing to it. Here I thought he'd simply had too much wine again."

I reach out to her. "Then you'll speak to him?"

She draws back. "Is that how you think it's done?" Lady Jersey gapes at me as if I've just sprouted a second nose.

Lady Castlereagh clicks her tongue in a wordless scold, and shakes her head. Anyone would think I had suggested we give the Prince a spanking.

"No, no, my dear child. Never." Lady Jersey stuffs the kerchief back down her sleeve. "One does not simply march in to a king, or a prince who's playing at being king, and say, *begging your pardon, Your Royal Highness, but you mustn't listen to Lady Daneska. She's filling your ear full of poisonous twaddle. And whatever you do, don't meet with Napoleon privately to negotiate peace. The Emperor is a bad fellow and you simply can't trust him.*" She says this in a mocking little girl's voice.

Lady Castlereagh chuckles silently.

Lady Jersey directs my attention to her friend. "See. Lady Castlereagh understands. She wouldn't dream of approaching her husband so bluntly, and he adores her. You simply cannot handle men that way. It takes kid gloves, my deaaar. *Kid gloves.* And you most certainly do not handle a ruler in that manner." She smacks the bed to emphasize her point. "If Prince George hasn't come to that rational conclusion on his own, nor listened to his trusted advisers, he certainly isn't going to come around on *your* say-so. Or mine. No, my dear, it must be handled with more finesse than that." She exchanges a pointed grimace with Miss Stranje.

Duly chastised, I fiddle with the sheets, preferring not to look into her disappointed face. "There was another letter from Napoleon written in code. I didn't have time to decipher the entire thing, but he authorized her to offer Prince George a bribe. A *monetary prize*, he called it."

"How much?" Lady Jersey's accent disappears.

"I was trying to figure that out when Lady Daneska caught me." I don't tell her I noticed Mr. Sinclair's warship mentioned and was frantically trying to decode that part first. "The sum looked substantial."

Lady Castlereagh laces and unlaces her fingers. "Dear me, the money will sorely tempt him. Never mind that Parliament paid his debts to get him to marry Caroline, now that he's regent, he's draining the coffers. His expenditures at Brighton and Carlton are outrageous. Despite all that, I think Napoleon's offer to rid Prinny of the House of Commons will hold the greatest allure. Come, Lady Jersey, I must go home and warn Lord Castlereagh. Poor man, as if his hands aren't full enough."

The Patronesses leave and Miss Stranje accompanies them out.

Maya raises another spoonful of broth to my lips. "You must eat to regain your strength."

"Thank you. You've been very kind, but I am feeling well enough to finish it myself."

"Very well." She hands me the bowl and spoon. I wobble one spilling spoonful to my mouth and give up. The darned laudanum has played havoc with my coordination. I set the spoon on the side table and gulp down the rest of the broth straight from the bowl.

"Lady Jane!" Georgie scolds laughingly and takes the bowl from me. "Where's all that elegance you're so fond of?"

"I suppose I had it beaten out of me." I meant it as a joke, but her face falls.

Sera bites her lip and turns away. Tess paces and finally flings the door open. She doesn't look back at me, but stops in the doorway. "I need to check on Tromos. She's going to whelp any day now."

Silence hangs in the room like a rotting carcass until Georgie asks the question they all wonder. "Was it bad?"

"No." I reach for her hand. "I'm sorry. I shouldn't have tried to joke about it. It was unpleasant and frightening, but nothing like what happened to Lord Wyatt or Mr. Sinclair." She doesn't look convinced. None of them do. "I'm fine! In fact, I would dearly love to get out of this bed, and if one of you thinks you can improve upon this hairstyle Ghost gave me I would be much obliged."

It's as if the sun suddenly beamed straight into the room. Their faces flush with enthusiasm. Maya tilts her head this way and that, viewing me from different angles. "I have long wished to change your hair. You always pull it back too tight."

Georgie is fairly jumping up and down. "Oh yes, you'll look adorable with short hair."

Uh-oh. Their eagerness worries me. I laugh tensely. I've given them *carte blanche* to do as they please and that may be a mistake. "Adorable?" I question their objectives. "That's setting the mark a bit high, don't you think? I shall be delighted if you achieve *passable*."

Sera's eyes glitter with excitement. "Oh, we'll do much better than passable." She holds up the scissors and gives them an unnerving snap. She has an idea and I feel uneasy as I take the chair. Maya grins and wraps a sheet around my shoulders.

For the next thirty minutes, my hair is the center of much

discussion and scrutiny. "Cut that piece shorter." "Oh look how this wave swoops beneath her jawline." "If we cut it shorter here, these locks will fall in charming little curls around her face."

"Not shorter," I plead, but they ignore me. I am no longer master of my own hair.

They argue about what should be done with the back. There is far too much snipping and evaluating to suit me. Must they stand back to check the results of each clip?

Sera surveys their handiwork. "Imagine it without that purple bruise on her cheek."

Maya nods sagely. "Perhaps if we contrast it with a yellow ribbon."

"No. White, I think." Sera pulls one out of my drawer. She ties it around my head and stands back. All three of them smile. *I'm beginning to feel like a one-eyed toad.* "Have done with it! Am I presentable or not?"

"Presentable?" Georgie laughs.

"Oh, for pity's sake." I stand and head for the mirror.

"Wait." Maya pulls my hand. "First let us help you dress. So you can see the full effect." She selects a sprigged muslin morning dress from my closet. I pull it on, noting that the bandages on my leg look dry and clean, which means the wound is knitting properly. There's even a bandage around my arm where Daneska nicked it with her knife.

"Now, close your eyes," Georgie orders and I limp blindly beside her to the mirror. "All right. Look!"

It takes me a minute to recognize the girl in the mirror. She looks younger somehow, sweeter, less austere, far more innocent. When the exact opposite is true. I changed last night. Aged beyond my years. I feel centuries older and far more knowing. I have been knifed, shot at, and thoroughly kissed.

Yet the girl in the mirror really is me. Even with that ugly bruise, there's something there I like. "Pretty." I say it without thinking. It isn't quite the right word, so I turn away from the new Lady Jane, to my friends. My friends, who have the uncanny ability to find something in me that I would never have found on my own.

More than passable. "Thank you."

Tess and Miss Stranje come in the room talking in hushed tones. Miss Stranje looks up and stops. Her mouth opens for a moment before she speaks. "What's this?"

"I think you mean *who* is this," Tess says, with a broad grin. I think she might have even laughed, except a loud disturbance downstairs sends all of us hurrying out into the hall.

Twenty-five

ᴵNTRUDERS

We peer over the railing and see Mr. Peterson down below. "Keep your socks on. I'm coming." Someone is pounding on the door as if they are striking it with a battering ram. Mr. Peterson opens and gruffly says, "State your business." Two gentlemen push their way into the hall. "Sirs! Step back." Mr. Peterson scolds and tries to push the interlopers out. "What is the meaning of this?"

"Intruders." Tess draws her knife.

"No." I whirl away from the railing and press up against the wall. "I know those gentlemen." I hesitate to call the intruders *gentlemen*. I know better. From the look of them anyone might mistake them for scoundrels or dandies. It's worse, *far worse*. "They're my brothers." I peek around the wall and cringe.

My eldest sibling flips a card in our poor butler's face. "That's *Lord* Camberly to you."

"Stay here," Miss Stranje hisses to me. "Don't come down till I send for you." She marches down the stairs. "Lord Camberly, you will mind your manners when in my home. Or I shall personally take you by the ear and toss you out." *She could do it, too.* "You have no right to barge in and bully my servants."

Francis, the *slightly less than honorable* Earl of Camberly, is sufficiently cowed by her tone and takes a step back, remembering to remove his hat when speaking to a lady indoors. His chin lifts proudly, and I know he is remembering he is a tough fellow and a rebel to boot. I can almost hear him thinking; *I am an earl, by George, and I answer to no one except the king and debt collectors.*

"We are here to see our sister," he states flatly. "We've a perfect right to do that."

It isn't a question.

Miss Stranje doesn't seem moved by his plea. "I'm pleased to see you are finally taking a familial interest. However, I'm afraid that due to your lack of payment, your dear sister must first attend to her duties as lady's maid before she is at liberty to visit with you. Perhaps you would care to wait for her in the drawing room. Mr. Peterson will show you the way."

Miss Stranje flounces back up the stairs leaving my brothers gaping in the foyer. She bustles the lot of us into our bedroom and shuts the door. "We will make them wait a good long time, and then I shall go down with you."

"They'll want money," I confess with a dismal sigh. "I don't know how they suppose they will get it from me, but they will have some scheme wherein they think they can pick whatever I have in my pockets. Or perhaps even yours."

She does not seem troubled by this in the least. "You may rest easy on that score. They shan't be picking anyone's pockets today."

I feel bad for them. I shouldn't, because they are the ones who abandoned me to my fate with Miss Stranje. Granted, it turned out to be the best thing that ever happened to me, but had she been another sort of woman it might have been a perfectly horrid situation.

"Are you listening?" Miss Stranje taps me on the shoulder. "Put on your worst frock, something you might wear working in the garden. Your hair is so lovely and it grieves me to ask it of you, but muss up your hair.

Georgie groans. "But it looks so perfect."

"It's charming." Miss Stranje smiles at Sera and Maya, guessing whose handiwork it is. "Too charming for this situation. Smudge your unbruised cheek. A little coal dust here and there ought to do."

"Why?" Sera frowns. "She's not supposed to be a charwoman. Ladies' maids don't look like that. They're usually quite tidy."

"Yes, but her brothers don't know that, do they?" Miss Stranje's eyebrows arch. She doesn't like to be questioned. "Lady Jane must appear as downtrodden as possible."

"I'll change into the frock I wore the night I chased Alice through the woods. The hem is still frayed and I haven't been able to entirely remove the stains."

"Perfect." She checks a small watch she keeps in her pocket. "We will make them wait forty minutes before going down."

As soon as our headmistress leaves the room, Georgie starts teasing. "If you're to be a lady's maid, you ought to have some practice. I need help unlacing my walking boots."

"Oh, very funny." I smirk back at her.

Sera grins. "You must wait your turn, Miss Fitzwilliam. I need our maid to plait my hair first." It is not like Sera to tease, but I'm happy to see her give it a try.

I sit down on the bed. "What about you, Maya. How may I serve you?"

"You appear to be quite loaded down with tasks. I shan't trouble you. But when you get a chance you might tell me what you know about Lord Harston—"

"Oh, *him*. You don't want to know him." His comment about *"those girls"* rings in my ears. I wave my hands through the air banishing him. "Lord Harston is a first-rate rascal."

Maya's bright expression dims.

Daneska is right, I *am* a *cabbage head*. "His nephew, though, seems to be cut from an entirely different cloth. What did you think of Lord Kinsworth? He seemed quite taken with you."

She edges back toward me hiding a shy smile. "I found him . . . intriguing. Except I cannot find his, his, oh what is the English word for this? The vibrations around a person, the sounds from someone's soul?"

Sera perks up and leans forward intently. "Do you mean his aura? Light? Colors?"

"Not colors . . ." Maya holds out her hands trying to describe a moving shape. "I don't know what you English call it. It means something like a voice, but it is more than that. Essence, perhaps? No." She shakes her head and gives up. "Whatever it is called, his hides from me. Just when I think I am on the verge of finding it—poof! It runs ahead of me, just out of reach. Elusive."

Baffled, I struggle to comprehend what she is saying. I don't see or feel vibrations around my friends. Maya must have some mysterious skill I don't possess. "Did you keep trying?"

"I did. That part of him seems to laugh at me and dash away."

I squint, struggling to see anything surrounding her, or Sera, or Georgie. *Nothing.* I'm perplexed. We live in the very same world and yet obviously Maya sees things in it that I cannot. "When he sang with you—"

"Yes." Her attention snaps in my direction, afire with delight. "You heard it, too?"

Now I feel even more lost, but I don't want her to know. I want to learn more about what she's saying. "I heard an astonishing duet. The music, the sound of your voices together, it was magical. Divine."

Her shoulders slump. "You did not hear it, then? The notes."

I puzzle out what she's trying to say. "What do you mean? Did you sing notes I didn't hear?"

She catches her lip for a minute, and I know she must be struggling with the language differences again. "The notes in between. His voice touched them when he sang."

I sit back astonished, wondering what our world must sound like to Maya. I turn to Sera. "Did you hear notes in between?"

She shakes her head, as mystified as I am.

Maya laughs softly, easing away our confusion. She backs away, no longer willing to speak of her world. "It's nothing. Think no more about it. I'm sure I will never see Lord Kinsworth again."

There's grief in her voice and it makes me sad. Maybe I can persuade Lord Harston to be more accepting of her. Suddenly I need them to smile, to laugh. After my nightmarish ordeal the night before, I cannot bear any more heaviness. "I declare, this ladies' maid business is exhausting. You are working me to the bone."

They laugh and I pick up a hairbrush. "Sera, if you would like, I'll be happy to braid your hair for you."

"I wasn't serious, but if you are *truly* offering." She hands me a ribbon. Sera has the softest, most silken hair imaginable. It is as if the strands are spun from gleaming white pearl dust. I take my time brushing it and weaving it into a thick plait, finishing the braid off with a blue ribbon. "I wish I had hair like yours." I sigh, and hand back the brush.

"You only say that because it isn't yours. Mine is straight and unmanageable, it never stays in the pins. Even the hot iron can't coax it into behaving. Whereas your hair curls simply because you coil it around your finger."

"Yes, but mine is plain *brown*."

"Be grateful." Georgie sits by our window reading. She looks up from the book she has her nose in. "Brown is exactly the color every debutante in London wishes she had."

"Not me. I'd rather have something exotic, red like yours, gleaming black like Maya's, or white like Sera's."

She scoffs at me and goes back to reading.

I check the clock. It's time for me to dampen and flatten out my curls, and smear coal dust on my face.

I limp down the stairs with Miss Stranje, and we enter the drawing room to find Francis pacing in front of the fireplace, and Bernard milling about the room investigating the decorations, probably looking for something small enough to slip into his pocket.

Francis whirls toward us. "About bloody time."

Miss Stranje huffs up in her best impression of a raven about to peck out his eyes. "Lord Camberly, I will thank you to watch your language. You may talk like that when you are gadding about with dandies, but there are ladies present here, and you will conduct yourself accordingly."

Francis has the good grace to look at least somewhat chastised. "Here now. Mustn't start out on the wrong foot. Not my intention." He approaches me, gives my shoulders a quick pat, and greets me with a Judas kiss on the cheek. Bernard does exactly the same thing because that's what Bernard always does, *whatever Francis does.*

My elder brother appraises me, while elegantly propping up his chin with his finger, even though his enormous collar should've done the trick. "Must say, Jane, you look a fright."

"Lovely to see you, too, Francis."

He is wearing an exquisitely tailored coat, a shiny gold brocade vest, and a pair of buckskin trousers that must have cost him more than my first year's tuition.

"Do be seated, gentlemen." Miss Stranje takes the largest most comfortable chair.

"Yes, do be seated," I say, intentionally taking the other armchair so that they are forced to sit together on the divan or else pull chairs from the wall. They brush their tails aside and plop on the divan together, sitting there like a pair of schoolboys called in to see the headmaster.

"What brings you to Mayfair?" Miss Stranje comes straight to the point.

"Wanted to see how our sister is getting along. What else? Imagine our surprise to read via the newspaper that you were in town. You were seen at Carlton. They reported it in *The Times*, Jane. For shame. You didn't have a moment to pen a letter to your own brothers? And here we are, ever so worried about you. Aren't we, Bernard."

"Oh yes, ever so," Bernard pipes, but at least his grin is genuine. "Think about you now and again, Janey. How've you been?"

Miss Stranje answers for me. "She is an outstanding lady's maid. Thank you for asking. We are quite satisfied with her service."

"Thank you, miss," I say earnestly, and all but pull on my non-existent forelock to emphasize the pretense that I have been forced into servitude by my brothers' neglect.

"I say, Miss Stranje, I rather thought you'd let her earn her keep as a tutor." The Earl of Camberly looks down his thrice-broken nose at her. "You know, put her in a more respectable position, a teacher, or some such."

"Yes, I see your point." Miss Stranje turns her wrist indicating me on her left. "You wished me to put her to work doing something suitable for the daughter of an earl. Or in this case, the *sister* of an earl." Miss Stranje clucks her tongue. "Unfortunately, I have no need for a teacher or a tutor, and you did mention lady's maid in your letter."

I press my hand over my heart. "Yes, Francis. I will admit I was wounded when you decided to put me into service. I supposed you had fallen on hard times. But, bless my soul, isn't that coat you're wearing tailored by Mr. Weston himself? It is very fine."

His nose juts into the air. "You don't understand these matters, Jane. After you left, I'm sorry to say, Mr. Applegate, the steward—you remember him don't you?—the dastardly fellow ran our estate into the ground." Francis makes a fist and thumps it on the arm of the divan. "Into the ruddy ground."

Bernard cocks his head sideways, as if he's trying to sort the lies from the facts. He combs his fingers through his side-whiskers trying to figure out exactly what Francis is saying. But I know how to get the truth out of my sneaky older brother. "Didn't Mr. Applegate keep to the schedules I left? I was very clear about when the sheep ought to be sheared and—"

Francis waves away my question. "No, no, we sold off all the sheep ages ago. Too expensive to feed them in the winter, you see." He taps his temple. "Have to economize, you know. We men understand these things."

"That's right." Bernard nods sagely. "Haven't had any sheep for two years."

"Hmm." I purse my lips and clamp my jaw tight to keep from screaming at the dunderheads. If my leg weren't throbbing like the very devil, I'd like to run over there and kick him in the shins. "How very odd. There should've been plenty of fodder and hay if the fields were tended properly."

Francis doesn't look at me. He draws circles with his forefinger on the arm of the sofa, and I get a sinking sick feeling in my belly. He finally answers, "I'm afraid the fields had to go, too. Sold 'em off."

Bernard pipes up. "Had to, Janey. Otherwise, how would we pay—"

"Your gambling debts," I all but growl. "Yes, I can guess how that went. So, you've nothing left except the house and the grounds, then?"

Bernard shakes his head. "We let the house. We get a tidy sum from the rents each quarter day, too."

Francis gives Bernard a stern *shut your big mouth* warning.

"Let me see if I understand this clearly. You've lost everything. Does that about sum it up?"

"Not everything," Francis says defensively. "Still have our horses, and the house is *let* not sold."

"No, but only because the house is entailed and you can't sell it."

Francis sits forward, and I remember how he would try to bully me when we were younger. "I *can* sell it. I'll find a way," he says.

"We're going to see our man of business about that tomorrow." He clamps his mouth as if he has said too much. My brother takes a breath and lowers his voice. "But now that you mention it, we've had an idea. An idea that will remove you from this awful school. You should be happy about that."

"Fascinating." I stifle a groan. "This should be a rare treat. Tell me about this brilliant plan you've concocted."

"Just this. If we were to put a pretty enough dress on you, you might do for some merchant fellow, or a banker."

Bernard nods eagerly, as if this is a splendid solution to all our problems. "Oh, yes, a banker, that would be a fine match."

Francis waves him to silence. "That is not to say a duke might not take an interest." He looks me over and wrinkles his nose. "Maybe if he's old enough. Or a marquis. Well, *really,* anyone will do, so long as they have enough money."

A duke.

Or a marquis.

No, an *old* duke. A doddering old rich marquis. *Marvelous plan.* My brothers have truly run mad. It's a lucky thing they don't know about Mum and Dad's agreement with Lord Harston.

I am speechless.

Miss Stranje is not, she manages to bristle even while sitting. "I'm afraid, gentlemen, your proposal is completely out of the question. As you know, Lady Jane is deeply indebted to me for her board and tuition. Consequently, she is obliged to continue serving as a lady's maid. Unless you can afford to pay for her past two years with me, she must remain in service to me for the foreseeable future."

The Earl of Camberly leaps to his feet. "You can't do that."

She remains calmly seated. "Oh, but I can."

"Take heart, Francis," I say in my most calming voice. "I do believe you have stumbled upon a solution to all your money troubles."

He turns to me, his face screwed up tighter than an old lady with a bad case of the vapors. "And what is that, pray tell?"

"My dear Francis, you still have a title. And while you may not have a feather to fly with, titles are still very much in demand." I pause and scratch at my mussed-up hair. "So, you see, rather than marrying me off, which sadly seems to be out of your reach, I suggest you find a wealthy young lady who would like to pay for the privilege of being an earl's wife."

"By George! Capital idea." Bernard smacks his hands against his thighs. "Well done, Janey. What do you say, Francis? Make some young thing your countess and bail us out of the River Tick all at the same time."

"What?" Francis turns a sickly shade of white. "Marry? Me?"

"Yes, my darling brother." I smile pleasantly, emulating my unflappable headmistress. "I suggest you find a rich merchant's daughter, or a banker's daughter. Well, *anyone will do*, really, so long as she has pots and pots of money and is willing to put you on a leash."

Francis turns decidedly sour. "You think this is funny, don't you? I'd nearly forgotten what a wretchedly sharp tongue you have." He stands and tugs down his waistcoat. "Well, my girl, I hope you enjoy being in service, because even if I do find a way out of this mess I have half a mind to leave you working as a maid. See if I don't."

"My dear brother, I've no idea how you'll acquire half a mind."

"Lady Jane!" Miss Stranje scolds me for being rude.

Francis marches out of the drawing room and snatches his hat from Peterson. Bernard hops up from the divan and gives me a quick kiss goodbye. "He don't mean it, Janey. *Really*. We've just had a run of bad luck, that's all. Creditors buzzing around us like bees."

Suddenly, I'm truly sorry for my *wretchedly sharp* tongue. "Oh Bernard." I grab my brother and hug him. "Be good, Bernie, my dear. Do try to stay away from the tables."

He grins broadly. "No need for that. Any day now our luck's bound to turn around. You'll see. Tell you what, if I marry a rich gel, I'll come and get you. I promise."

He accepts his hat from Peterson and gives Miss Stranje a parting nod. "Be kind to our Janey, Miss Stranje. Never mind that wicked tongue of hers. She's a good-hearted girl underneath."

I stand, watching Francis and Bernard bluster out of the door and feel every inch a wretched heel. And so sad, I feel like mopping the floor with my soul.

"I do love them, you know. They're . . ."

Foolish.

Ridiculous.

And even though they're completely useless,

"They're my brothers."

"Of course, you love them. I wouldn't expect anything less from you." She puts her arm around me. "But they're grown men, Lady Jane. It is a difficult thing, but there comes a time when we must let those we love fend for themselves."

Twenty-six

PUPPIES AND DREAMS

Nighttime.

Every time I turn in bed, I bump my leg and the pain jars me awake. I'm drifting in and out of sleep when a mournful howling awakens me. A second loud howl catapults me out of bed, but Maya and Sera are still sound asleep. I pull on my dressing gown and hear Tess scurrying down the hall. The yellow glint of a lantern flashes beneath our door as she goes past. I put on my shoes and quietly slip out after her. "Do you think Tromos is whelping?"

"I don't know." She frowns at me. "You shouldn't be out of bed."

"She howled."

"I heard. I don't understand why she would howl even if she's whelping. Usually they keep quiet when they're giving birth."

We were wrong.

Tromos had already whelped an hour ago, maybe longer. The

mess was gone and her pups were licked clean. Two black pup-pies no bigger than my hand cling to her teats, suckling.

"Oooh," I gasp. "They're so tiny." I notice Phobos nudging a third pup toward Tromos, this one is a tiny silver ball of fur.

"Oh no," Tess laments softly. "It's crippled."

Tromos lets out another plaintive howl, this one softer and obviously directed at Tess. Tess kneels down beside the make-shift den and utters a string of ancient Welsh I can't begin to understand, but I hear the strains of comfort in the old words.

And sadness.

"How can you tell it's crippled? What's wrong with it?"

Tess holds the lantern closer to the silver cub as it squirms helplessly.

Phobos picks it up and dangles the third pup in his mouth. I see one of its little paws is shriveled and misshapen. Phobos drops it closer to its mother. The poor thing wriggles but then flops sideways, its little sides heaving.

Tess explains, "Cubs are all born blind and deaf, but they can smell their mother. It should be crawling toward Tromos."

I scarcely listen. The helpless little waif sprawled in the dirt captures my heart. Except I do hear the next cruel words Tess says, "If the cub doesn't latch on soon, Phobos will have to put it out of its misery."

"No!" My heart pounds in protest.

Tromos lifts her head at my cry and bares her teeth.

I don't care if Tromos is angry at me. I kneel beside Tess. "Do something. Push it closer."

Tess sits back and stares at me as if I've run mad. "Won't help. This is the way of things. It's how they know which cubs will be able to fend for themselves in the wild."

I grab her shoulder. "Look around you. We aren't in the wild." I swing my arm out indicating the garden and walls around us.

I see that silver lump of mewling fur and my heart refuses to let it go. I growl almost as threateningly as Tromos did. "Push that cub closer."

"I'm as sad as you are." Tess frowns and comes at me with a heated whisper. "Why do you think Tromos is howling? It's breaking her heart, too. After she lost her last litter, she grieved so hard she wouldn't eat for days. Neither of them did. Wolves grieve whenever one of their pack dies. Even if it's a lame cub. But this is how it is in nature. We can't interfere."

"*Nature,*" I grumble, staring at the tired hungry helpless puppy. "I don't care. This one is not going to die. I'm not going to let it."

I start to reach in and Tess grabs my arm. "Reach in and you'll lose a hand, or worse. Tromos won't let you touch one of her puppies."

We stare at one another, both of us breathing hard. Both of us sad. She's probably right. Both of us have seen enough death to understand. Except, this is different. This tiny sliver of moonlight made flesh, this little lost girl cub, I simply can't bear it.

I can't sit here and watch it die without doing something. I can't.

We are sisters, Tess and I. Not always friends, but always sisters. I know her heart. I know she aches for that baby wolf as much as I do. "She won't let me." I pause waiting for her to follow my meaning. "But Tromos would let *you* help her. You're one of her pack."

Tess lets go of my arm, and she pulls the lantern back so the wolves' den rests in dim shadows. "I'm not sure. She might. On the other hand, she might take a bite out of my throat if I dare do such a thing."

Tess does not accept closeness easily. Neither do I, for that matter. Nevertheless, there in the faint amber of the oil lamp, it seemed right to put my arm around her shoulders. There is a language every sister knows, a language tender beyond words and rarely spoken. It runs like a string between two hearts, and we only pluck that string in times of trouble. This night, even though I do not know ancient Welsh, we speak as sisters.

"Tess, she called you here. Tromos howled for her pack, and we came. We're here because she needs us. She needs *you*." We stare at one another heart to heart. I hug her tight and let her go. "Now, either you must do something to save that little dog or I will. I don't care whether Tromos bites my hand off, or not."

Tess's shoulders heave. "All right, but you need to stay back. If either of them attacks me, don't run. Don't do anything except back slowly away. Do you understand?"

I nod.

"I mean it. Don't do anything. They might bite me, but I don't think they'd kill me. You, on the other hand . . ."

"They *would* kill me. I understand."

Tess scoots closer to Tromos, murmuring. I've listened to her speak to them in ancient Welsh before, but never like this. The strange language is full of grief and empathy. With a plaintive whimper, Phobos moans and lies down beside Tess's knee. They are mourning, the three of them. Tess reaches for Tromos and softly strokes her fur.

I watch from the shadows, in awe of the compassion in Tess's voice, as she slowly lifts the dying cub to one of Tromos's swollen nipples.

I watch in amazement as Tromos lowers her head and closes her eyes. Hope floods the garden. Hope as palpable as a mist rising in the morning. A mother's last desperate hope. And if wolves can pray, I swear, I hear the prayer of the wolf mother lifting around us.

"Live," I urge the baby wolf, and turn my plea to the stars above us.

Tess edges back, and I ignore the pain in my leg and kneel up, to look over her shoulder. There in the moonlight I see the tiny silver cub has latched on to her mother, and is feeding.

We return to our beds, and sometime before morning, I fall into a fitful sleep. A scream startles me awake. I know that scream. I've awakened to the sound nearly a hundred times in the past few years.

Tess!

I bolt out of bed. Maya and Sera barely stir. I hurry barefoot down the hall and burst into the next room. Georgie stands beside Tess, trying to console her. Tess, wild-eyed and shuddering, pushes her away.

"What is it?" I demand, half expecting the answer to be that Tess had a dream about Ghost or that beastly Jack. "What did you see?"

Georgie shakes her head, warning me not to press the question.

"Who cares what I saw?" Tess moans and tugs at her disheveled hair. "It's the same thing I always see. *Death. Mayhem. Meaningless destruction.* None of it makes any sense." She glares at me, her chest rising and falling in ragged heaves.

"What happened?" Madame Cho and Miss Stranje rush in behind me. "Was it a dream?"

I nod. Madame Cho closes the door and lights an oil lamp. Tess presses her hands against both sides of her head as if she might squeeze away the horrors of her nightmare. When that fails, her arms fall limp and she drops onto the bed.

Defeated.

"How can I run away from it, here in London?" Her voice shifts to a question for us. "Where can I go? I need to run."

I hate seeing Tess like this. She, who is the goddess of strength, slumped and reduced to beaten shivers.

"Be brave," Madame Cho orders.

I lean against the bedpost, my leg aching. "Maybe it will help make sense of it, if you tell us what you dreamed."

She doesn't look at me. Instead, she fidgets with her fingernail. "I'd rather not."

We don't press her. We wait.

Finally, she slams her fists against the bedding. "Very well. If you must know, it was an explosion. I saw half the Admiralty blown to bits, and . . ." She winces and glances hesitantly toward me. ". . . and Mr. Sinclair."

Blood rushes from my head. I clutch the bedpost. I must hold tight or my knees will collapse under me. "Not *Alexander?*" I say, hoping she misspoke. I must've said it too softly for anyone to hear.

Not him.

Miss Stranje presses a bolstering hand on my shoulder and we exchange glances. I shake my head subtly, indicating I hadn't told Tess my suspicions about Ghost making a bomb.

"It's just a dream," Georgie says, as much to me as to Tess. She sits on the bed and puts her arm around Tess's shoulders. "Dreams are just dreams. You said so yourself."

"True." Miss Stranje pulls her dressing gown tighter. "However, I think perhaps you had better tell us a bit more about this one."

"Yes. Speak it aloud, and it will not have as much power to hurt you." Madame Cho says this, even though she is the most tight-lipped of any of us.

"There's nothing to tell. The whole thing is useless. One minute I see Mr. Sinclair on the *Mary Isabella*. Then . . ." She covers her ears. "My ears are still ringing. That sound—it was horrible. A thunderous crack. Deafening. As if the whole sky broke in two. The dock shook. Everything shook. A ball of fire swallowed us, and rushed everywhere. Smoke so thick it hurt to breathe."

I cough. She relates her nightmare so vividly I can almost feel the smoke burning my nostrils.

"Splintered wood. Body parts." Tess hides her face from us, burying it in her hands, shaking her head. "This isn't helping. There's no point in telling you."

"There is." I urge her forward, desperate for more details, searching for anything we might use to keep this massacre from actually happening. "Where were you in the dream?"

"Where was I?" Tess looks up, and her brows pinch together in puzzlement. "Oh, I see what you mean. I didn't die in this one. How did you know?"

"A guess." I grip the bedpost still trying to steady myself. I don't have horrifying dreams like she does, but there is that darned game board in my head. I can't help but see the players moving into position, knocking key pieces off the board. Pieces we need to keep in play if we're to win this war, people we must not lose. One player in particular, one man, one piece of my heart that I refuse to surrender. "Can you remember where you were standing? *Anything?*"

Tess shuts her eyes. "In front of the blast. Heat from the explosion scorched my face. It knocked me down. I remember falling backward. Ugh. And the smell of burnt flesh." She stands up, shaking her head. "No, no more. It's too much. I don't want to remember any more. I can't. I need to run. Where can I run?"

Georgie stands. "What about the garden, if you jog next to the stables and make a circuit—"

"Too small." Tess paces. "I can't run hard enough there, or fast enough."

Georgie turns to Miss Stranje and me. "We have to think of somewhere she can run off the fright."

"I have an idea." Miss Stranje rubs her chin. "Tess, what if you were to ride in the park? This early in the morning, you can even gallop. Would that be vigorous enough?"

Tess stops pacing and blinks. "Might work. Except how can I? You only have carriage horses."

Miss Stranje heads for the hallway. "Lord Ravencross brought his mounts. Get dressed, I'll send word to him right now."

Madame Cho follows Tess into the dressing room to help her change, and Georgie plops down hard on the bed. "If half the Admiralty gets blown up, you know what her dream means, don't you? The explosion is probably at—"

"The naval yards. Yes." I sit beside her. "At the unveiling of the *Mary Isabella*."

"Exactly." Georgie gnaws on her bottom lip for a moment. "Might not happen, though. Her dreams don't always end up the way we expect. It could be symbolic."

True enough. Tess's dreams are enigmatic at best, and often figurative. "I suppose." But I saw Ghost with black powder and canisters. This time it's real.

"She said the sky cracked open. That might symbolize something." Georgie takes a deep breath and purses her lips. "Maybe it's a warning from beyond that the boiler isn't stable."

"Maybe." Except I see what a perfect move this is for the Iron Crown. *Too perfect.* "Tell me, Georgie, can a boiler like the one on Mr. Sinclair's ship explode arbitrarily?"

"Not arbitrarily, no. There's always a reason." Georgie rubs the soft flannel of her nightgown between her thumb and forefinger, thinking.

"What reasons?"

"Too much pressure builds up in the boiler. A blocked steam pipe. Impure coal. Any number of causes. Only . . ." She turns to me, her eyes wide with alarm. "None of those reasons explain a blast as large as the one Tess described."

"That's what I was afraid of." I sigh, and lean forward, head in my hands.

"*A bomb.*" Georgie barely says the word aloud.

"I believe so." I lace my fingers through the hair at my throbbing temple. "It's a horrifyingly logical strategy. Lady Daneska and Ghost would rid themselves of key players in the war, important members of the Admiralty, and they'll have their revenge on us all at the same time."

"*Players?*" she snaps. "They're not players, Jane. These are men. Yes, they're soldiers and sailors, but they're also fathers. *Brothers. Husbands.* And . . ." She says all this as if I'm not painfully aware of who they are. Her voice drops. "Our friends."

People we love.

"They'll be murdered." She clutches my arm and gives it a rough shake. "We have to warn Lord Wyatt and Captain Grey. They must call off the unveiling."

"We will. We will warn them. But calling off the unveiling won't keep it from happening." I clamp my hand over hers, not just to stop her from squeezing my arm, but to reassure her. "First, we have to figure out where Ghost intends to hide that bomb."

She eases her grip.

"Georgie, you know Mr. Sinclair's steamship as well as anyone. If you wanted to place a bomb, where would you—"

"That's easy." She sits straighter, and without realizing it, her hands describe the shape of the boiler. "If Ghost is clever, and we know he is, he'll have his men lodge it into the boiler stack. A large metal cylinder the size of the stack, if packed with black powder . . . a bomb that size would create an explosion as devastating as the one Tess dreamed about."

The canisters on Ghost's worktable would be the exact right shape.

She tugs at the flannel of her nightdress again, working it furiously between her fingers. "That's not the only advantage of hiding it there. If they put it in the smokestack it won't explode until Mr. Sinclair fires up the boiler and the tank gets hot enough. All they have to do is hide it. The heat would ignite the fuse for them, and that would happen right about the same time he begins his demonstration of how the *Mary Isabella* operates."

I close my eyes for a moment, trying to banish the thought of Alexander grinning and talking excitedly to his guests on the dock, and seconds later, his innocent face blown to bits. I try not to think of it, but I can't keep from seeing him swallowed up in a burst of flames. There is no escaping that cruel image, no stopping it from making my heart trip and fall, no way to keep it from suffocating me.

No way, except by focusing on the strategy, the stakes, the game. I gasp for air, forcing myself to draw in enough to allow rational thought.

If this happens,
This will come next, and then this . . .

Sometimes seeing the possibilities makes everything worse.

It's worse than I realized. I slump against her shoulder, my leg aches, I'm exhausted, but if I had an ounce of strength left, I'd go hunt down Ghost and shoot him between the eyes—if I could find him. "You see what will happen, don't you? If they succeed. Not only will there be all those tragic deaths, everyone will blame Mr. Sinclair's steam engine for the catastrophe."

"Oh no!" She straightens, dislodging me from her shoulder. "It's not his fault, but they might think so."

"The navy is already skeptical about using fire to propel a ship. Aside from us, I doubt whether anyone else would believe the explosion to be Ghost's handiwork rather than the fault of the steam engine. Britain will lose the advantage the warship might've won for us. And if Napoleon's engineers are able to construct their own steam-powered ships, we will most certainly lose this war."

Then the rest of Europe will crumble.

It's only a matter of time.

For a moment, the room fades and I see the rest of the world falling from their positions, knocked into a defeated heap; bishops, queens, and rooks, swept from the board after our British king is taken, and the game is lost.

"Jane?" Georgie nudges me. "Lady Jane."

She stops when Tess emerges from the dressing room wearing a new riding habit, a long skirt with a flowing train to drape over the sidesaddle, and matching jacket. I blink, returning to the here and now.

"Tess!" Georgie covers her mouth. "You look beautiful."

Madame Cho looks on with pride, as if Tess is more of a daughter than her student.

A diamond of the first water.

I do my utmost to smile despite the throbbing in my leg and

the cruel chess match playing in my head. "That wine-colored velvet looks stunning on you."

Tess waves away our compliments. "It doesn't matter. Ravencross won't notice. I could dress like a scullery maid and he wouldn't take any heed."

Georgie scoffs. "Lord Ravencross would have to be blind not to notice you in *that*."

"That's not what I meant." Tess almost smiles. "He'll notice *me*, just not the finery. The man doesn't give a fig about velvet versus wool, and frankly neither do I. Miss Stranje needn't have gone to all this expense."

I feel quite certain our headmistress didn't give Tess a proper wardrobe for Lord Ravencross's sake. She intended for us to blend into high society, so we might do our job.

None of us fit in well in society, not really. We are all oddities, each in our own respect. Nevertheless, we can learn to play the part. After all, a good spy must hide in plain sight.

Urgent banging on the front door knocker echoes throughout the house and at the same time the clocks in the house chime five. "Can that be him so soon?" Tess's face already looks less drawn and, at his insistent knock, it infuses with more color.

"Of course, it's him," I chuckle. "He would race here in his bedclothes if he thought you needed him."

Madame Cho clucks her tongue at me, in a wordless scold.

"Don't be silly." Tess pulls aside the curtain and stares down into the street. "See there, he's completely dressed." Tess scoops up her train and hurries out.

After seeing Tess and Lord Ravencross off, Miss Stranje returns to the bedroom. "What did you think of her dream?"

Georgie and I explain our theory. She listens attentively. "And what do you suggest ought to be done?" She asks this pointedly at me.

"We lay a trap. Proceed as if we have no idea of their plan. We'll have someone watching for when the bomb is placed in the stack. At that juncture, we have several alternatives. We could capture the henchman sent to do the dirty work. Interrogated properly, we may be able to ascertain the location of Ghost's lair, although I doubt Ghost would risk revealing his hideout to any of his men. If his man doesn't report back, Ghost will resort to placing the bomb another way, and we will know nothing about it."

Miss Stranje watches me as I explain, her eyes gleaming with something I dare think might be respect.

I gulp down a sudden shyness. "Which is why I think we should let the henchman go, but follow him to see where and to whom he reports. This may lead us to Ghost or it may not."

"We could kidnap *her.*" Madame Cho grumbles, and I know she means Lady Daneska. But we all know that is out of the question. She's under the Prince's protection.

"If we secretly remove the bomb and proceed with the unveiling, Ghost may sneak into the ceremony so he can be there to witness his handiwork. We may be able to capture him there. Failing that, at least if we remove the bomb, the Admiralty will see the ship, proceed with plans to build it, and no one will get killed."

Miss Stranje considers my strategy for a moment without speaking. Finally, she takes a deep breath and nods. She stands and peers down her nose at me with an expression I can't quite interpret. She seems pleased, I think. I see respect. Pride maybe. But there is also a distinct hint of sadness.

Why is she sad for me?

Does she think it will fail? That Alexander will die?

"You don't think it will work?"

Her lips press into a thin flat line resembling a smile, but still edged with inexplicable sadness. "Quite the contrary, Lady Jane. I believe it is our very best hope for a good outcome."

Madame Cho rises to stand beside our headmistress. No sadness or pity in *her* eyes, only fire. Madame Cho is a volcano and, even in this dim light, her black pearl eyes flash with danger. I generally expect her to erupt at any time, but this morning she grants me a grudging nod and pats me on the shoulder.

Miss Stranje brings her hands together in a soft clap, a habit she has that usually signifies the end of a discussion. "Wake the others. Make certain Alice isn't lurking nearby when you tell them what has happened. I know it is early, but it is time we all dressed. The unveiling will be in a few days. We've much to accomplish before then." She turns and both women leave.

Georgie and I stare at each other for a moment. "What do you make of her response?" I ask.

Georgie shakes her head. "I can never quite tell what she is thinking."

Exactly, and I want to be just like her.

Twenty-seven

SECRETS EXPOSED

I start fading at breakfast. When I catch myself falling asleep over my plate of kippers, Miss Stranje orders me back to bed.

Doctor grumpy-bones-Meredith wakes me up late that afternoon to check on my stitches. "No sign of festering. Good. Keep it clean and dry. If you follow my orders, you should be fit as a fiddle in a day or two. I'll pull out the stitches next week." He folds up his spectacles and closes his kit. "I will tell you this much. It's going to leave a nasty scar."

"So I've been told." I don't appreciate him quoting Lady Daneska.

The following day Lord Wyatt, Captain Grey, and Mr. Sinclair join us for dinner. I'm not allowed even two minutes alone with Mr. Sinclair. It is agony. All I want to do is stand close to him and hold his hand and, well, maybe a bit more than that.

They report that the *Mary Isabella* is completely reconstructed and ready for the unveiling on Thursday. Captain Grey has been apprised of Ghost's plan to place a bomb in the boiler stack. His men are watching around the clock, waiting for Ghost to make his move.

That night I sneak out to see the puppies.

Tess is already there and hand-feeding Tromos some scraps of meat Cook salvaged for her from the kitchen. The pups are snuggled against Tromos, their little tummies bulging because they've just finished nursing. Even the silver cub, whom I've named Moonlight, must've eaten because her belly is round, too.

Tess talks quietly, not so much to me, just talking to pass the time. "In the wild, Tromos would go without eating for days. Until she felt she could safely leave the cubs in Phobos's care and go hunt."

"How is she supposed to feed her young if her own belly is empty?"

Tess shrugs. "I don't know."

Tromos stops eating and licks Moonlight, bathing the silver pup with her tongue. She looks up at me and nudges the baby in my direction.

Tess's brows arch up in surprise. "Look. She's acknowledging you. She remembers you helped save the lame cub." Tess turns a curious expression on me, one mixed with amazement and respect. "I think she wants . . ." Tess stares at the way Tromos is nudging the cub. "See if she'll let you pet the gray one."

"Moonlight," I say. "Her name is Moonlight. What if Tromos won't let me?"

Tess shrugs. "Then she'll bite you."

The helpless ball of fuzz mews softly when her mother's nose tickles her. I lean closer, and Tromos doesn't growl. Slowly, I reach out and lightly brush my fingers over Moonlight's downy fur.

Tromos licks the baby where I have touched it. She may only be washing off my scent, but her tongue continues to flick against my fingers as I stroke the cub's fur and I'm awed she's allowing me to share her love for the little one.

I draw back and dash away a tear that has escaped. "She loves Moonlight even though she's lame, doesn't she?"

"Of course she does, it's her pup." Tess frowns at me.

"But Moonlight won't be useful. To the pack, I mean."

"Why should that matter," she says sharply and Phobos growls. Tess's mouth twists in a teasing smile. "You're lame, and yet we still love you."

I blink. I hear Lady Daneska echoing in my head, *why do they love you?*

"I'm not lame," I mumble. Except maybe Tess thinks I am. She said, *we love you.* I didn't think she did, not me, not really. "I'm useful," I protest.

"Phfft." She snorts and turns away.

I don't know why Tess said that. I don't know if it is a mean thing to say, or sweet, or completely upside down. I clench my teeth. "Sometimes I just don't understand you."

I know the reason they keep me around.

I'm useful, that's why. I'm collateral for debts. I can repair dilapidated estates and turn them into productive ones.

I solve problems.

I organize.

I plan.

The tiny crippled sliver of moonlight wriggles closer to Tromos, to sleep cuddled by her mother.

I'm . . . *useful.*

Surely, this is the reason they love me, isn't it?

The next morning Miss Stranje orders me to remain at home resting while everyone else gets to go shopping. I could've gone. I'm able to walk now without significant pain. "I should like to see that it remains so," Miss Stranje says, restricting me to the house.

They return home with various treasures. Tess found gloves roomy enough to hide an extra dagger. Maya purchased a packet of herbs from India, which if ground finely and placed in a glass of wine will induce instantaneous sleep. The exact dosage is apparently critical. Too much and the victim will never awaken. This inspires Miss Stranje to march us all up to the library for a lecture on various antidotes for poisons.

The quiz afterward is blindingly difficult. "Knowing these antidotes could mean the difference between life or death," our headmistress warns.

In the middle of the test, Mr. Peterson scratches on the door. "Lady Jersey and Lady Castlereagh are here to see you, miss."

The Patronesses march into our inner sanctum as if they belong there. Lady Jersey picks up Tess's paper and snorts. "Poisons? Dreary business poisons." She plunks the paper down and taps her finger on one of the answers. "That one is wrong, m'dear. Your toes will curl up and fall off if you try that remedy."

She makes a shooing motion with her fingers which means we are to go away. Miss Stranje excuses us from the room and posts Madame Cho in the hallway as a sentry. "We're not to be disturbed."

She shuts the door and we turn to leave, but a second later, she pokes her head out in the hallway again. "Lady Jane, your presence is required. Gather your notes and join us, if you please."

The other girls look at me as if I am in grave trouble. I hurry to the bedroom to retrieve my notebook out of the false bottom in my hatbox and Georgie quizzes me. "What do you think they want?"

"I have no idea." *That's not true.* I have a hundred ideas. They've found Ghost. Something happened to Mr. Sinclair. Maybe they've found a way to imprison Lady Daneska. The possibilities are endless. "I'll tell you as soon as I find out."

"Be careful," Sera warns. "I think Lady Jersey is hiding something."

"Wouldn't surprise me." I imagine they're all hiding things. Miss Stranje certainly has her secrets. *And me.* Aren't we all hiding something? That is what spies do. But I fancy myself the unlocker of secrets. I will find out theirs and only mine will remain.

I open the door to the Library with my note papers tucked under my arm. They're speaking in hushed voices. "Speaking of innocents." Lady Castlereagh smiles at me. "There you are, my dear." She and Lady Jersey are wearing curious smiles to hide the fact that they are studying me as if I'm to be tested. *Again.*

"We've a few questions." Miss Stranje invites me to sit. "We're interested in your opinion as to when you think the bomb will be planted. Captain Grey's men have seen no movement thus far."

An easy enough question. "I should think it will be Wednesday night, or before dawn Thursday morning."

They glance at one another as if this is exactly what they had surmised.

I explain my reasoning. "Ghost won't want it exploding prematurely. He'll want to do as much damage as he can with one blow. To do that, it must detonate when the Admiralty and government dignitaries, such as Lord Castlereagh and Prince George, are present. It will serve two purposes, killing key officials, and demonstrating Napoleon's reach into Britain."

"Sounds about right," Lady Jersey says dryly.

"Egad." Lady Castlereagh bows her head in her hand. "I do wish I could convince my husband not to go."

Lady Jersey sits back scrutinizing me. "How are you feeling after your ordeal?"

"Well enough, thank you. Grateful to be alive."

"And do you still have a taste for this business?" She drops her accent altogether. "This life?" There's no artifice in her question.

"Truthfully, my lady, I don't think I'm very good at being a spy. I'm probably better suited for the life of a country steward."

Lady Castlereagh chuckles. "Sounds like me, doesn't she? I would've liked living in the country—being a simple farm wife."

"Don't be ridiculous, Amelia." Lady Jersey waves this sentiment away. "You'd have been miserable rusticating on a farm."

"You don't know that." Lady Castlereagh bristles momentarily, but stops and turns to tap the table in front of me. "But my dear child, you do know girls can't be stewards."

I'm astonished to hear that sentiment from her. "You mean to say, we can dash around in the middle of the night, break into a foreign dignitary's rooms in the royal palace, slide down a ship's dock line to escape capture, and shoot at spies who are chasing us, but we're not qualified to raise sheep?"

"Exactly." Lady Castlereagh's smile is angelic in the extreme.

Lady Jersey breaks into a guffaw. "Lady Jane, the point of all this is that we think you did a perfectly marvelous job at Carlton House. We would like to discuss your future."

There's scratching at the door. Madame Cho opens it to find Mr. Peterson bringing us a message, but signals him to stay back. "You." She points at me. "Lord Harston is here to see you."

"Tell his lordship I am indispos—"

"Wait!" Lady Castlereagh holds up her hand to stop me from finishing. "What in the world is *he* doing *here*? Why would he be calling on you, I wonder?"

I'm inclined to say, he's merely my future husband. Thank you for your interest in my private affairs. Instead, I say, "He was acquainted with my parents."

Madame Cho hushes the butler. "One moment."

"How very intriguing." Lady Jersey hides a curious twist to her lips with the corner of her fan. "Tell Lord Harston we will all be down in a few moments."

Drat!

"Run along and change." Lady Jersey shoos me off. "Put on something prettier. Something green." She holds a finger against her cheek, looking me up and down. "Yeeas, greeean will set off your complexion quite well."

I sigh. Madame Cho closes the door, and shakes her head at me. "You are in trouble now."

How does she know?

She fusses at me, hurrying me down the hall. "You have too many secrets."

"Me? I don't have half as many as you do."

She smacks the floor an inch from my foot with her bamboo cane, sending me dashing on my way.

I do own a rather lovely green morning gown. I almost put on the blue silk just to prove to Lady Jersey I cannot be bullied on every decision. In the end though, I reach for the green damask gown, because Lady Jersey is right. Green is my best color.

Though why I should try to look my best for Lord Harston is beyond me.

Descending the stairs a few minutes later, we discover Maya and Sera are already entertaining our guest and his nephew. Maya's laughter rises up the stairwell, a breathy sound as fresh and sweet as wind rippling through the trees. It never fails to make me smile. I'm amazed to see Lord Kinsworth has succeeded in making both girls laugh. Even Sera.

The four of them look up at our arrival and the broad smiles on their faces shrivel at the sight of the Patronesses flanking me on either side.

Lady Castlereagh takes a surprisingly firm tone. "Lord Harston, I'm surprised to see you here. How fares the Prince?"

"Sleeping, my lady. Fast asleep, safe in his bed until three or four in the afternoon, as he is most days of late. My nephew was anxious to call on Miss Barrington, and I thought I might spare an hour to call on Lady Jane. We have, um, a small personal matter to discuss."

Egad. He's not going to tell everyone, is he?

I clear my throat. "Nothing of consequence, I assure you."

"Nonsense. We are all friends here." Lady Jersey holds out her hand to Lord Harston and allows him to bow over it. "What can possibly be so very private between two of our most trusted young people."

"*Most trusted?*" I accidently ask aloud.

Lady Castlereagh spreads her fan and whispers to me. "Remember, I told you we have tasked Lord Harston with keeping a close watch over our dear Prince."

It is a decision I question. I don't see how we can entrust the Prince's safety to an inveterate gambler and rake such as Lord Harston. "I notice he is often in Lady Daneska's company."

Lady Castlereagh brushes one of the ribbons from her enormous Turkish turban over her shoulder and collapses her fan. "Sometimes, my dear, one must run with the foxes in order to keep the chickens safe."

Chickens? I gape at her. Is she likening the Prince Regent, head of our government, to a chicken?

She rattles me further when she says, "I don't see how anything can be so urgent that you would risk leaving him alone?"

I squint at Lord Harston, remembering the debt I owe him, and feel I ought to try to rescue him from the Patronesses' criticism. I extend my hand in greeting. "Lord Harston, how very kind of you to come. You mustn't trouble yourself over that other matter. It's of no consequence."

It's only my future and yours.

I curtsy. "There's no hurry. We can discuss it another day." *Let's say in, perhaps, twenty or thirty years?* "Surely it can wait for a time when you are not needed so urgently by the Prince Regent."

He opens his mouth to answer, but there is such a racket out in the foyer that everyone in the drawing room turns to see who or what can be raising such a fuss. We don't have long to wait. One strident voice I instantly recognize as it crescendos above that of poor Mr. Peterson.

"Swindlers! Crooks, I say! No, sir, you will not keep me standing here with my hat in my hand. I demand to see my sister. Show her to me this instant." Thus, my dear sweet brother charges into the drawing room waving a fist full of papers, and Mr. Peterson tugging on his arm. "Ah! Now I see how it is." He gesticulates wildly at Miss Stranje. "You mean to marry her off behind my back."

I glance sideways, alarmed to see that behind her fan Lady Castlereagh has a small lady's pistol aimed at my brother's heart. Turning to my other side, I note Lady Jersey has slipped a small dagger into her palm. Lord Harston has his hand on the hilt of his sword, and Maya seems to be sprinkling some kind of powder into a glass of port. Sera, bless her, is edging toward the poker on the fireplace.

My brother is about to be murdered in five different ways if I don't do something immediately.

Miss Stranje steps forward, unarmed, thank goodness. "Lord Camberly, how lovely to see you again." She extends her hand. "So soon."

Francis rudely bypasses her greeting. "I see Jane does own something besides those rags you had her wearing the other day."

I find it ludicrous that my brother chooses this inauspicious moment to comment on my wardrobe of all things. I would laugh if it weren't so humiliating. "What do you want?" I snap and regret it the moment those words slip out.

Toad garters. I have sunk to his level of rudeness, which is a testament to how very out of sorts I am.

"Sneak thief!" My brother accuses me and waves his sheaf of papers in my face. "I've been to our man of business, and when I mentioned our plan to marry you off, you'll never guess what document he produced."

If I haven't already turned pale, I'm fairly certain I'm a rather spongy color now. My bad leg weakens and I must drop into the nearest chair or I will fall down.

Francis leans down still forcing the papers at me. "Can't do it, says old man Stanton. She's already taken."

"Taken?" Lady Jersey slides her dagger back up her sleeve. "Fascinating."

"Yes, and by none other than that man, right there." He points at Lord Harston. *Of course, he points.* There is no ruder oaf in all of Christendom than my oldest brother. I slump against the chair. Madame Cho is right. I'm in trouble now.

"It's all right here." He swings his pointy finger to my signature on the incriminating evidence. "Signed a note, along with our parents. They're betrothed, all right. Lock, stock, and barrel."

"I think you'll find there wasn't actually much stock in that barrel," I mutter.

Francis is not finished fuming. Indeed, he's practically foaming at the mouth. I turn to my friends. "Maya, perhaps you'd like to offer my brother some of your special port?"

She looks down at the poisoned cup in her hand, purses her lips, tosses it into a potted plant, and fills it with fresh undrugged port.

"Don't want any." My brother waves the cup away and hunches over me, so we are face to face. Judging by his breath, he's obviously had enough port for one day. "You knew all along, didn't you? And you weren't going to tell us, were you? You, *my very own sister*, and you were willing to let us float all the way down the River Tick while you set yourself up with a rich baronet."

"Baron," says Lord Harston.

"Hear that, Jane? A baron! And a rich baron according to old man Stanton."

"Not *that* rich." Harston clears his throat. "Pardon me, but it seems to me you boys have been doing a pretty good job of paddling down River Tick all by yourselves without any help from your sister."

"You're engaged?" Sera, who is usually mum as a church mouse, squeaks into this quagmire. "And you didn't tell us."

Didn't tell a soul.

Now the whole world knows.

At this point, I can do nothing else but slump all the way over and bury my face in my hands.

Bernard, bless him, pats my shoulder. "It's all right, Janey. Chin up. I forgive you. In fact, I think it's fine news. Better than fine. First off, now you won't have to be a lady's maid the rest of your life. And second, me and Francis won't end up in the poorhouse. Turns out your betrothed owns half of our vowels."

He says this so cheerily, I just want to shake him.

"Personally, I think it's a splendid match." Lady Castlereagh puts away her pistol. "I wish you happy."

She and Lady Jersey kiss Miss Stranje on the cheek. "We shall leave you to deal with this . . . this . . ." Lady Jersey waves a circle with her hand indicating all of us. "Well, I dooon't actually know what to call all of this. But I trust you will be ready for Thursday?"

"Of course." Miss Stranje kisses her friend's cheek in return.

In the doorway, Lady Castlereagh turns back. "Lord Harston, you mustn't leave the Prince for too long. Sleeping or not—every minute is a risk."

Lord Harston stares at my brothers, like a man facing the axe but having no intention of going willingly to the chopping block. He swallows hard and says, in a voice that startles me into sitting to attention, "Gentlemen, the terms of my contract do not designate a date for the nuptials. Your sister and I will discuss this and any other potential arrangements at our convenience. It may be three months, or three years from now. But mark my words, if you impose upon either of us in the meantime, those IOUs you mentioned will become due and payable immediately. Do I make myself clear?"

Bernard nods mutely. Francis raises his wretched finger. "But—"

Lard Harston makes a low warning growl and puts his hand on the hilt of his sword. His nephew steps up beside him and does the same. The two of them are a matched pair of warriors that make me tremble. Whatever argument Francis might've ventured, withers on the vine. He backs away with the contract still clutched in his hand.

Bloodbath in the parlor averted, Miss Stranje moves into the fray. "Thank you for calling, gentlemen." She gestures toward the door. "Peterson, their hats, if you please."

She adeptly maneuvers all of the men out to the foyer, and as soon as they're gone she returns to us in the parlor.

Maya stands beside the window covertly watching them depart. Miss Stranje joins her.

I silently pray Francis keeps his big mouth under control. "They're not knocking swords in the street, are they?"

"Going their separate ways." Miss Stranje smiles at me as if I've done something marvelous. "Well, my dear, I must say that was a perfectly exhilarating afternoon."

Georgie strides into the room with Tess right behind her. "Everyone was so loud, we couldn't help but overhear—"

Tess plops on the sofa. "I can't believe you're engaged and didn't tell us."

I groan. "I knew I shouldn't have come to London. Now my life is ruined."

"Not ruined." Miss Stranje crosses her arms. "Altered."

"Too many secrets. I warned you." Madame Cho leans in the doorway.

They are all staring at me. Sera looks hurt. "I don't see why you couldn't have at least told me."

"You still haven't heard the worst of it."

"There's more?" Maya looks surprised.

"It's a wretched ugly story. One I'd hoped to take to my grave."

"Apparently, you failed to die young enough." Tess crosses her arms and leans back against the sofa.

I laugh cheerlessly. "So it would seem."

Georgie sits beside Tess. "We've three hours until dinner. You may as well tell us."

"Very well. I don't suppose you will dislike me any more than you already do."

Sera takes the chair next to mine. Her blue eyes stab directly into my soul. "I could never dislike you, Jane. You, Tess, Georgie, Maya, you're like sisters to me. That's why I don't understand why you felt you had to hide this from us."

"You hide things," I say softly, toying with the lace on my dress.

"Not secrets. Not exactly." A shadow falls across Sera's face. "Sometimes I can't find words to explain what I'm thinking. That's different."

I pat her hand. "I don't know what that means. But I believe you." Late-afternoon sun glints through the window, washing golden light over all of them, their faces turned to me with nothing but kindness. Now I see that believing is very like trusting.

Trust.

So, I tell them the whole shameful story, every last disgraceful detail.

Afterward, they don't look at me as if I'm a creature to be pitied. They don't pull away from me in disgust. They sit quietly beside me, silently mourning with me.

Finally, Sera catches my chin in her hand. "They didn't know you, Jane. Your parents, I mean. They didn't see you. They couldn't have. If they had seen how truly remarkable you are, they would never have traded you. *Not for anything.*"

Sera holds me while I cry, and the others circle around us.

Twenty-eight

PLANS INSIDE PLANS

By now, *Alexander knows I am engaged.*
Someone will have told Captain Grey. Captain Grey will tell Lord Wyatt, and he will tell Mr. Sinclair. Which explains why I have not heard a single word from him.

Not one single word.

Wednesday dawns and I hide under the covers wishing the sun would go away. Not that there *is* any sun today. There isn't. Nothing but rain and gloom out the window. I throw back the covers. "The puppies!" They'll be cold and miserable. "They could die."

We throw on our clothes and all of us head down to the garden. Tess is already out there, drenched. Water pools in Tromos's makeshift den and Tess has the pups cradled in her skirts. "We have to move them."

So much for her letting nature take its course.

I thought to bring an umbrella out and we all huddle under it. "The gardener's shed," I shout over the clatter of the rain. "It'll have to be the shed." Tess nods and we run for the small out-building but find the door locked. "I need lock picks." Georgie dashes back to the house for the tools and towels.

The shed door has a very loose old lock. Easy as pie to pick. We pry open the squeaky door and Tromos trots in beside Tess, who still carries the babies. Immediately the mother wolf shakes the rain out of her fur, sending a shower over the rest of us. When she's done, her ruff stands out, thick and almost dry.

There's scarcely room in the shed for both dogs and the five of us. I start drying Moonlight first. Tromos circles around our legs growling and uneasy. Phobos roots through the shed, agitated, chasing something scurrying through the shovels and buckets. As soon as the cubs are dry, we fold an old vegetable cover for Tromos to lie on and set the puppies next to her tucked inside the towel. Except for Moonlight. I hold her for a few minutes longer.

Sera strokes her little tummy. "She's so sweet. Georgie, maybe you could build something to help with her missing leg?"

"You mean like a peg leg for a dog?" Georgie asks. Her mind is already churning with ideas. I love that about her.

She inspects the pup's hip. "It can be done. We'll have to wait a month or two till she's fully grown. In the meantime, maybe I can rig a small wheel that straps to her hip. We could call her Peg, or Willa, you know, because it sounds like wheel."

"We most certainly will not." I continue chaffing the cub until it stops shivering and set her next to Tromos to nurse. "Her name is Moonlight."

Sera nudges me. "Who said you could name them?"

"I only named this one. You can name the rest."

Maya kneels next to them. "It's hard to believe they start out so small and grow into such magnificent creatures."

"They almost didn't." Tess looks up at me, and both of us remember Moonlight's rough start. "And this morning, they nearly drowned."

"It looks like you nearly did, too. You're soaked through. We'd better get you inside by the fire." I hold the umbrella over Tess as we leave the shed and run back to the house. "How long have you been out here with them?"

She shrugs. "I should've been out here sooner."

"You need some hot tea straightaway."

After warming Tess in the kitchen, all of us climb the stairs to change into dry clothes. Miss Stranje asks us to gather in the library, where she spreads a sketch of the Woolwich Naval Yards on the worktable for us to study. Tess sneezes and Miss Stranje sentences her to spend the rest of the day in bed. "You're chilled, and I will not have you getting sick. We need you at the unveiling ceremony tomorrow."

"I'm not sick. I never get sick." Tess sneezes again.

"Of course not. Nevertheless, we shall keep you warm and tucked up in bed as a precaution."

"I can't stay in bed all day. Who'll feed the dogs?"

"I will," I volunteer. "Tromos trusts me."

Tess glares at me as if I have said something wrong.

"Well, she does."

Tess shivers and Miss Stranje pulls out the finger of doom and points. "That's it. To your room this instant. Into bed. We will bring you a tray."

This is the warm, sunshiny way our day begins.

We spend the afternoon studying the layout of the grounds, determining where our most vulnerable positions are, going over various scenarios, and deciding the best course of action if an explosion occurs here or there. We discuss how best to protect the Prince, the admirals, and the ship.

Late that night, after the household has gone to bed, a messenger arrives with a note from Captain Grey. I slip on my wrapper and follow Miss Stranje to the foyer. The note informs us that they spotted a man climbing over the naval yard wall and saw him plant a bomb on the *Mary Isabella*. So far events are going according to our plan. Captain Grey and Mr. Sinclair were able to successfully remove the explosive. Lord Wyatt and his men followed the perpetrator at a safe distance. But unfortunately, they could not follow him into Spitalfields without being detected.

Tomorrow is the unveiling, and I cannot get Tess's nightmare of the *Mary Isabella* exploding out of my head. I find it difficult to fall asleep that night.

The morning of the unveiling dawns fair and clear as a jewel. Today, we will either succeed in outplaying Lady Daneska and Ghost, or we will all be blown to bits.

Lady Jersey is right, I *am* a gambler. I hate that I am, and I hate that the stakes are life and death. We at Stranje House are all gamblers, and whether I deserve them or not, the other girls here are my friends. Friends who, for whatever reason, care about me as much as I do them.

I sit in the garden in the early dawn, contemplating the task ahead. Tromos allows me to hold Moonlight. She's stronger now and scoots about quite well despite the fact that she has only three paws. The black cubs are adorable and growing bigger every day. I rub my cheek against Moonlight's soft silver coat. She will always be different from her brother and sister, different like me. *Unusual. Peculiar.* Luckily, she's a brave little lass. "Aren't you, Moonlight?"

She mews at me, and attempts the tiniest of yips. I laugh. "Today I need to be brave, too. And I must trust the others, just as you must trust your pack." Her fur is unfathomably soft, and she curls against my chest sleeping and squiggling. I know she's getting hungry. The others are inching down from where they nest on Tromos's side, making their way to nurse.

"Courage, little one," I say as much to her, as to myself, and place her back with her brother and sister, watching as she scoots three-legged to her mama. Tromos lifts her head to me in farewell. "If it goes badly at the ceremony," I tell her. "You and Phobos must take your children and race to the woods. Run as far from London as you can." Phobos stares at me, tilting his big head, almost as if he understands. "It's what everyone should do, if we fail today. Run. Hide. Because Napoleon will be invading."

The shed door creaks open and I know it is Tess. "Have you been coddling her again?" she scolds, as if she doesn't do the very same thing.

"Of course I have. Are you ready for today?"

"I am never ready for days like this."

"Did you dream anything new?"

"No." She tosses scraps to Phobos and scratches him behind the ears."

"They found the bomb, you know."

"Georgie told me." Tess kneels beside Tromos handing her strips of ham and mutton.

"It's because of you and your dream. You saved all those people."

"Let us hope so."

We arrange for an early breakfast, even so it is a two-and-a-half-hour carriage ride to Woolwich Naval Yards. We spend another twenty minutes passing through the gates. It is well after one o'clock when we arrive at the unveiling.

Tess, Sera, and I quietly stroll about the viewing area looking for anything suspicious. A raised platform has been specially set up on the pier for the Admiralty and other royal guests. The remainder of the spectators will be seated in chairs, which sailors are arranging for us atop the long stone tiers overlooking the inlet. The gates are open and river water is flooding the docking bay in preparation for the launch.

By two o'clock, the Admiralty begins arriving. Lieutenant Baker acknowledges me with a sociable nod as he tromps down the massive stone abutments behind Admiral Gambier. Georgie waits down near the *Mary Isabella* with Lord Wyatt, who plans to help Mr. Sinclair with the demonstration.

Two-thirty, and most of the government officials have arrived. Lord and Lady Castlereagh make their way down the stone risers, greeting other dignitaries. Sera leans over to me and whispers, "Did you notice the bulge in the lady's reticule? It must be the pistol we saw the day your brothers barged in."

I watch with admiration as Lady Castlereagh strides down the steep steps close beside her husband. She wears a fierce protective expression on her normally jovial face. No soldier could guard the Foreign Secretary more zealously.

So many lives hang in the balance today. The perverse sun

continues to shine, not a drop of rain, not even a cloud in the sky. It's England, for pity's sake. There is always rain, or at least a drizzle. I'd hoped for rain. *Just in case.*

Rain would extinguish a fire.

If there is a fire.

If.

I mustn't think that way. There's to be no hedging my bets, not today. Not when all these lives are at stake. We simply will not allow an explosion. That's all there is to it.

The momentous occasion was supposed to start some time ago. We must wait, of course, for the Prince Regent and his guests to arrive. The seats on the platform are nearly full, four admirals, two captains, including the famed Captain Maitland, and three lieutenants, including Lieutenant Baker.

A trumpet blasts from the guard of the gate, announcing the Prince Regent has finally arrived. Three-fifteen. He is only three quarters of an hour behind schedule. This is better than expected.

I mark his labored progress from his carriage. He is a large man. The heat must surely be playing havoc with his gout, but this is the sort of occasion he loves. A military excursion. He is decked out in full military regalia including sash and cape. If he were not so rotund, he would be quite a heroic figure. Lord Harston walks beside him, along with the Prince's entourage of foreign dignitaries, including Lady Daneska.

She draws the Prince's attention. "It is so very warm today. Wouldn't your majesty be more comfortable here in the shade?" Lady Daneska fans herself. Anyone would think the poor girl is positively baking. I know better. She runs as cool as one of Mr. Gunter's ices. She points to the overhang casting a shadow over the top of the seating area. "The view from up here is quite splendid. I'm certain Mr. Sinclair would be honored to give you a ride aboard his marvelous little craft after the demonstration."

Prince George looks from the coveted shade to the glory of sitting on the platform with the admirals. "Stay here, my lady. Be comfortable." He waves his bejeweled fingers in the air, pointing over his shoulder at the shade, and takes a labored breath. "*We*," he says, referring to himself in the royal plural. "Came all this way across town. *We* will jolly well sit with our admirals down below."

The gentlemen in the audience all bow down as the Prince passes and we ladies drop into low curtsies. This makes it particularly challenging for the footmen, who are striving to place small wooden boxes under the Prince's feet to help him descend the enormous stone steps. He generously waves his hand. "Up, up," he commands to those bowing. "We are all friends here."

He is in good humor, especially considering how early in the day it is for him. Lord Harston keeps him from tumbling several times before our Regent stops to greet Lord and Lady Castlereagh. He accepts the hands of Admiral Elphinstone and Admiral Gambier and takes his seat.

"Now then." He claps his palms together. "Let us see this marvel our young American has created for us."

Captain Grey bows, and indicates everyone should be seated. I cannot sit. I couldn't bear to sit. My nerves couldn't take it. Questions keep whirling through my head.

What if I was wrong?

What if they've hidden another bomb somewhere else?

Sera, Tess, and I stand off to one side watching for any false movement. Miss Stranje, Maya, and Georgie are on the other side. I note Lord Harston sitting directly behind the Prince. Lady Daneska remains seated at the top of the risers in the shade. "Of course she sits there," Tess growls. "She knows she'll be clear of the blast."

Lady Daneska is looking around *too* expectantly, and that makes me nervous.

Sera turns and whispers to me. "Do you see how she sits? So impatient. She's eager to witness the bloodbath she's planned."

I'm not certain that's the only reason, but Captain Grey is beginning the unveiling.

"Ladies and gentlemen, allow me to present the *Mary Isabella*." Captain Grey and Lord Wyatt whisk the sailcloth off, revealing the little steamship.

There are no *oohs* or *aahs*. The audience applauds politely. They've all seen more impressive ships, spectacular schooners with tall dramatic sails. I'm sure they are wondering why we're making such a fuss over this small sail-less contraption. Captain Grey continues by introducing my beloved engineer. "Mr. Alexander Sinclair."

Mr. Sinclair doffs his hat with a jaunty grin, bows with a flourish, and jumps aboard the *Mary Isabella*, where he waves from the wheel of the ship. Lord Wyatt follows him aboard and shows everyone how easy it is to throw a shovel full of coal into the already fired up boiler.

"I can't watch." Tess turns and leans into my shoulder. "This is exactly what I saw in the dream."

I note the smug leer on Lady Daneska's face. Captain Grey points out the various pieces of equipment, and touches on how the ship operates. "Put it in gear, Mr. Sinclair."

With a clank, Alexander engages the wheel and the first

paddle slaps the water. "Oooh!" Murmurs hum through the on-lookers as the ship begins to move. A puff of smoke bursts from the copper smokestack.

Lady Daneska sits up straighter in her seat. She leans forward and frowns.

Another puff of smoke escapes the stack

I watch her face, reading it as Lord Harston taught me. *It should've blown up by now*, she's thinking. Her fist presses against the crest of the chair in front of her. Her jaw clenches. Any min-ute she expects it to blow up. *Now. Now. Now.*

She stares forward with poker-hot intensity and I see the ex-act moment when she realizes we have escaped her snare. Her head whips around. Not to us, as I'd expected her to do, to mete out her fury at having been beaten, to spit angry bile at me or Tess. Instead, she scans the guard wall of Woolwich yard.

A sick feeling rushes into my stomach. I follow her gaze. We both see it at the same instant, a glint of sunlight on a mus-ket barrel.

Ghost.

Or it may only be the sentry on the wall. Except it isn't. Both sentries are exactly where they are supposed to be. One stands atop the armory watching the demonstration and the other is making his rounds on the clock tower.

The *Mary Isabella* moves out from the dry dock, making an impressive sharp turn. From there, it paddles straight toward the Admiralty's stand.

Sera grabs my arm. "That lieutenant—something isn't right." She points to Lieutenant Baker. He casts a worried glance over his shoulder in my direction.

Why, I wonder. He turns full around in his chair and now he's looking, *not at me*, but directly at Lady Daneska. She gives him a nod. In a lung-crushing instant, I comprehend. *I've made a horrible mistake.* My hands turn to fists. There's a secondary play. Ghost always has a backup plan. And an escape strategy. *Always.*

"Tess!" I shout. "There's a man with a gun." I point to the far wall.

"Ghost," she curses and starts running, but Ghost, or whoever it is, is a furlong away. Near enough for a musket shot, too far for her to stop him in time.

Lieutenant Baker reaches into his satchel. I can guess what comes next. "Bomb!" I scream, and point at him.

It has to be Baker.

Only I didn't think my counterplay through. *No finesse.* Instead of running for cover, the admirals, *every last one of them,* turn in their seats to see what crazed lunatic female is screaming about a bomb.

Baker stands. It's in his hand—a thick iron canister. But everyone is looking at me. Everyone except Lord Harston. He is dragging His Majesty backward in a most undignified way.

"There!" I scream. Sera and I are both pointing.

Too late. Baker strikes the fuse, raises it in a split second toast to Lady Daneska, and tosses it onto the *Mary Isabella,* which is paddling right beside the Admiralty stand. The bomb rolls onto the deck next to Alexander.

"Alex!" I take a running leap down those monstrous big stone blocks. "Jump!" I scream at him. "Dive!" I command.

He doesn't jump. I do, though. I run, and jump. Flinging myself down those stone steps, ignoring stabs of pain shooting up my leg. I leap past Lord Harston who has pushed the Prince down and covered him with his own body. Lady Castlereagh and Miss Stranje have similarly buried Lord Castlereagh.

Lieutenant Baker shouts, "Viva La—"

A gunshot cuts short his victory cry. One sharp clap. Lieutenant Baker's chest splatters apart with bright red blood. Ghost just killed the one man who could confess Daneska's involvement. That gunshot sends them all to the deck.

"Bomb!" I scream at Alexander.

He sees it.

"Dive!" I shout. "Jump in the water."

Does he do that? No!

Lord Wyatt has the good sense to leap off the ship onto the platform. He dashes up the steps toward Georgie. I know what Alexander is thinking. He's not about to abandon his beloved *Mary Isabella.*

What does he do? He kicks the ruddy bomb. It launches skyward—spins and arcs up into the air. At that exact moment, I take a running leap from the bottom stone step and launch myself at Alexander. I smash into him, sending both of us tumbling into the water.

The bomb blast shakes the earth. Everything quakes. Even in the river, the vibrations ripple through my bones. Tess was right. It's as if the sky split in two. The canister exploded in the air over the bow and blooms like a fiery orange chrysanthemum above the Thames. Shards of fire and metal flecks whistle and spiral toward the onlookers.

My ears ringing, I bob up and down, in the current, splashing, gulping for air. "Alexander!"

He bursts up through the surface beside me, sputtering, and grabs hold of my collar. "I take it you don't swim."

"Course not." I spit out the putrid river water. "Ladies don't—" he lets me bob under for a second, "—swim."

"That's for ruining a perfectly good suit of clothes." He shoves me up onto the deck of the *Mary Isabella*, and pulls himself up onto the deck beside me.

"Had to do it." I wipe debris off my face. "You could've been killed."

He brushes a long strand of river moss out of my hair. "When are you going to figure out I can take care of myself?"

"Probably never." I flick some indescribable piece of garbage back into the smelly river.

He dumps water out of the pocket of his ruined new coat. "I expect that's true enough."

"Anyway, I don't see that it matters." I wring muddy water out of the bottom of my skirts, and use them to swat out a burning cinder scorching the deck next to us. "The Admiralty is impressed with your prototype. At least, I *think* they are. Hard to tell since most of them are hiding right now." I glance over. Some are still ducking behind their chairs. Others are nursing wounds and beating out fires that have started on their clothing, chairs, and decking. The canopy over the ceremonial platform is in flames. "Considering you saved their lives when you kicked that bomb into the air, I imagine they'll be more than happy to send your uncle Robert payment to use his patent and grant you safe passage home." I pull a half-dead dragonfly out of my hair and set it on the deck to dry out. The poor thing flops from side to side, its sodden wings making frail attempts to fly. Fragile things, dragonflies.

And humans.

In the distance, I see Tess coming back empty-handed. *Drat!* "Ghost got away."

"In all this chaos—of course, he did." Alexander points to the drooping bandage on my leg that is now brown with slimy river water. "That's going to get infected."

I flop my wet skirts over the ugly stitches, and give him a trollopy tavern girl smile, the kind he once said he preferred. "Perhaps you ought to stay in England and nurse me back to health."

"Hmm." He frowns as he pulls me to my feet. "Speaking of nursemaids. Isn't that your fiancé over there, brushing off His Royal Highness? I think it would be a grand idea for him to have a whiff of his future wife now, while you're in your finest hour."

"You'd like that, wouldn't you? For your information, Mr. Sinclair, I'm not the only one who smells like a sewer rat."

He climbs to his feet and takes a step toward the wheel, but falters. "Blast!"

"What is it?" I rush to support him around the middle.

"Unless I miss my guess—" He grimaces and limps again. "I broke a toe or two kicking that bomb. What do you say, *Princess*, help me over to the wheel, and I'll see about sailing this rig back to the dock."

As he leans on me, I smile. "See. You do need me after all."

Twenty-nine

FAREWELL

Several days later Mr. Sinclair does, indeed, receive a reward for saving the Admiralty. Not only are they are grateful he saved their lives, Admiral Elphinstone and Captain Maitland assure him the navy intends to build several full-size steamships for use against a Napoleonic invasion force.

Lucky for Mr. Sinclair, peace talks are stirring between Britain and the United States. Admiral Gambier secures a berth for him on a ship set to sail for the United States in five days.

Five measly days.

Three of which, I must spend stuck in bed, unable to see him, because my leg is infected. Miss Stranje summons Doctor Meredith who puts leeches on the wound.

I hate leeches.

They are slimy, despicable creatures and they make me feel weaker than watered-down soup. By the third day, I hurl one of the vicious little bloodsuckers at Dr. Meredith, and he refuses to ever come back and attend me. According to him, I am obstinate and uncooperative.

"If you die, Lady Jane, it will be your own fault." Miss Stranje huffs at me and jerks my pillow out, fluffs it up, and stuffs it back under my head.

"I won't die." *I'm determined to see Alexander again before he leaves.* "I'll be perfectly fine if you will put one of those plasters on it, the kind you and Maya are so fond of concocting. I'd rather smell like garlic stew than allow those vile creatures to suck the life out of me."

She and Maya apply several plasters, each more pungent than the last. My leg improves rapidly. By the fourth day I am up and walking, as if Ghost had never carved me up. Perfectly able to receive visitors, especially one visitor in particular.

See, I was right.

About the plasters.

Not so much about a slew of other things.

Mr. Sinclair comes to visit this evening so I might show him the wolf puppies. Moonlight knows my scent now. I show Alexander how she wriggles toward my hand. "Isn't she the most beautiful thing you have ever seen?" I ask, cuddling the puppy.

"Without a doubt." He smiles at me and strokes Moonlight's fur, which now pokes out all over like a frightened cat.

"What is it you want, Lady Jane?" he murmurs.

I want to kiss you. But I mustn't say that.

"I want a great many things. None of them have any bearing on what's going on in the world." I purse my lips for a moment. "I don't know how I should answer your question."

"No, I don't suppose you do." His lips press together and he looks away for a minute. When he turns back, I'm surprised at what I see. It isn't like him to look so downcast.

"Aren't you happy to be going home?" I ask. "Surely you must miss your family."

"I do." He smooths a finger over the cub's soft fur.

She wriggles up against my neck as if she is hunting for a place to suckle. I laugh softly, but something about her tiny kisses hurts my heart. Or maybe it is Mr. Sinclair looking so melancholy and asking me uncomfortable questions about what I want. All I know is I don't want either of us to be sad. "It's the same as with a wolf cub. Moonlight belongs with her pack. You belong with yours. You'll be safe at home in Pennsylvania. Happy. Away from all this business with Napoleon."

He stands nearer and I think *maybe* he will kiss me after all. Except he doesn't. He asks me another unnerving question, and he does it in a voice so low and tender it nearly makes me crumble. "What about you? Will you be happy?"

I shrug, gathering my strength. I must remain strong. I hide from him, rubbing my cheek against Moonlight's fur. If he looks too deep, he'll know the truth. "I have work to do. After the explosion, Lady Daneska and Ghost disappeared." I talk faster. "No one knows where. And Lady Jersey came by yesterday. She says, even though the bomb could've killed him, Prince George is still considering Napoleon's offer of peace."

"There won't be peace." Alexander's chest fills with evening air and he steps back. "Can't be. As long as there are tyrants who love money and power more than life, and men who want to be free of them."

Free.

I remember how overjoyed Lord Harston was when he thought he was rid of me.

I watch the way the setting sun turns Alexander's hair a burnished gold. "You're *free*."

"Am I?"

"Yes. Of course." I turn away because it hurts to see how beautiful he is, and it hurts even more to see that expression in his eyes, as if I've failed him somehow. "You can do anything you want. You're going home. You have a family who loves you and a bright future. Most importantly, you'll be safe from this wretched war."

"*Safety is overrated.*" He sighs. "I think you ought to figure out what you want, Lady Jane."

I turn away from him, it's time for me to place Moonlight back with her mother.

"Do you want to marry Lord Harston?" His tender tone is gone. The question is hard and unyielding. It doesn't leave me any quarter.

Why must he bring that up? My answer comes out too harsh. "What we *want* has nothing to do with it. I don't think he *wants* to marry me any more than I do him. We will both do what must be done."

He pauses. His jaw works back and forth. He paces and I am afraid he will walk away but he comes back. "Jane, one word from you, and I won't go."

I don't say anything. How can I ask him to give up everything for me? That would be the height of selfishness. I stare at his new boots, remembering the hideous ill-fitting pair he wore that first day I met him at Stranje House. Boots he stole, because his captors had kept him barefoot. The thought of his poor feet in those wretched old things chokes me up. I can't answer.

"My ship sails for New York in the morning. Will you come to bid me farewell?"

"Yes, of course." I catch my bottom lip, because something is shattering inside me.

He's leaving.

The next morning, I stand on the pier watching him walk away. Sea birds wheel and call to one another in the early-morning air. A frigate waits. A ship that will take him away forever.

I wave. Doing my best to smile.

What is this feeling?

What cruel fist is this, that reaches in, grabs my heart, and squeezes? All that is left is the feeble grudging drip of blood in my veins. No, this feeling is not some cruel fist. It is a hot desert wind. One that curls around the stone in my chest and hollows it out, leaving me with an aching emptiness that makes my eyes water.

I'm not sad.

How can I be? He never belonged to me.

What right do I have to grieve? I sent him on his way. He's leaving—that's all. We knew this day must come. It had to arrive sooner or later. I would've preferred later. But, of course, it would come. He must go to his home in America, where he belongs, where his family and friends await him.

And I . . .

Beat, heart. Beat.

Or stop if you like. What's the use in beating?

Life stretches before me, a gaping pit of emptiness. Years of this hollow thudding. No, that is not true. I have my work. I have the school. I'm supposed to take over one day. Miss Stranje claims it is enough. It has been enough for her. Or so she says. Therefore, it will be enough for me. It has to be.

In time, I may grow to believe that.

In time.

Except every limping footstep Alexander Sinclair takes toward that ship echoes like a slamming dungeon door. Locking me away, where there is no golden-haired light, no impish irritating grins.

No Alexander.

Suddenly, my own footsteps are pulsing against the pier. My soles drum a full-on charge. A rush of new fire burns in the former hollow of my chest.

I'm shouting.

Calling his name.

Throwing open my prison doors.

"Wait!" I thunder up the pier. "Wait! Alexander. Wait! Come back. Don't . . ."

He turns. His face, a burst of hopeful sunlight against the endless gray clouds. "Don't what?"

In a ragged gasp, I know the answer. "Don't leave me."

Stay. Please.

I didn't know I had those words in me—words to ask for what I so desperately want. To selfishly beg. To plead for something for myself. Something for me alone.

No, not *something.*

Someone. Someone for me.

Alexander drops his satchel and waits, arms open. He is as astonished as I am when I hurl myself into his embrace.

Thirty

ꞆHE ꞆOMING-OUT ꞄALL

~Two weeks later~

All of us are out in the garden. Mr. Sinclair holds up a lamp, and although we are dressed in our finery, we've snuck out of the house to watch Moonlight take her first steps. The puppies opened their eyes last week, and Georgie has constructed a small wheel to help Moonlight walk. We've strapped it to the wolf cub's hip and placed her on the ground. She looks up at us with big wary blue eyes. I can almost hear her asking us, *what have you done to me?*

I urge her forward. "Try it, Moonlight. Walk."

The cub takes one tentative step, but promptly flips to her side and gnaws on the wheel and straps.

"I thought that might happen." Tess steps back and crosses her arms. "It's not going to work. She'll never be able to resist chewing on that leather."

"I should've thought of that." Georgie's shoulders sag. "Maybe if I wrap the straps with tin . . ."

"No, she's just trying to figure it out. It's a brilliant contraption." Lord Wyatt puts his arm around her shoulders. "Besides, the pup is growing so fast you'll need to make a bigger harness in a week anyway."

"I agree, Georgie. It's a marvel." I reach down and set Moonlight back on her feet, giving her bum a little scoot. The pup yips as the wheel propels her forward. A moment later, she figures it out and gallops around my feet. "See! Look at her go."

I clap, but my glee is short-lived. Moonlight twists sideways, snapping and growling at the leather straps. She rolls onto her back and wrestles with the device.

"There you are!" Miss Stranje calls to us from the garden door. "Time to greet our guests. There's a line of carriages stretching around the block. Mr. Peterson is about to open the doors."

Georgie quickly unbuckles the wheel and sets it on a shelf in the gardening shed. Sera kicks a pebble in the pathway. "I'd much rather stay out here."

I loop my arm through hers. "Nonsense. You'll have friends who've come to see you. Mr. Chadwick plans to come, and the Patronesses."

She groans. "Too many people."

I try to reassure her. "It's going to be a wonderful evening, you'll see."

"That's what you said the night of the soirée at Carlton House and that did not turn out wonderful at all."

Mr. Sinclair chuckles as he opens the door for us. "Our Lady Jane is not much of a prophetess, is she?"

Sera laughs.

"I'm just trying to encourage her." I sulk.

"Obviously, but she is more than capable of taking care of herself without any Banbury tales from you. Isn't that so, Miss Wyndham?"

"Yes." Sera answers with more force than I expected. "I believe so. Thank you, Mr. Sinclair."

I squint at her. My mouth opens but nothing comes out. *Great walloping dewberries!* He's done something I have tried to do for years. Sera looks positively radiant, simply because he expressed confidence in her.

I've no time to digest this alteration, because Miss Stranje is busy positioning us in her formal receiving line. She adjusts the ring of flowers in my hair. "You stand here." She shoos Mr. Sinclair off with instructions for the musicians to begin playing.

The doors open and Peterson announces the first set of guests. Before long, Haversmythe House overflows with people, with admirals, dignitaries, other debutantes and their parents. Lady de Lieven is the first of the Patronesses to make an appearance. I curtsy to her and she pats my hand wearing a mischievous little smile. "Welcome to our world, Lady Jane. I daresay you are already setting a new trend with those short curls of yours."

"I did not come by them intentionally, my lady."

"So I heard." With a merry chuckle, Lady de Lieven moves on to greet Maya on my left. "I understand you and Lord Kinsworth intend to sing for us after supper. Your first performance was so memorable, I'm thrilled we'll have the opportunity to hear the two of you again."

Maya acknowledges the compliment, but I notice a fleeting pinch of consternation that wafts across her brow. Their practices have been pure heaven for those of us listening, but after each session, Maya is left more agitated and puzzled by him than before. She no longer complains of not understanding Lord

Kinsworth. She now insists the young man intentionally eludes her. "How does he escape me?" she demanded of me one after-noon.

"I have no idea what you mean. Perhaps Sera might be of more assist—"

Maya huffed at me. *Maya*, who is the kindest gentlest person in the world, whirled away in a huff.

Prince George sent a courier to Miss Stranje yesterday, an-nouncing his plans to attend our ball. I understand the Prince and members of the Admiralty are attending our ball because they remember that we are the young ladies who first noticed Lieutenant Baker's bomb that fateful day at Woolwich. However, considering the dark reputation of Miss Stranje's school, it astounds me that so many other members of high society are willing to grace us with their presence. I suppose there is no accounting for curiosity.

Lord Harston comes down the receiving line. I greet him as formally as if we are strangers, but he holds my hand a moment longer than necessary. Bowing over it, he looks up with a wry grin. "My dear Lady Jane. I see your young inventor did not board a ship and sail away to America after all." His eyes glitter with humor. "Does this mean I have won my wager?"

I cannot stop the corners of my mouth from twisting up with mirth. "Yes, my lord. You won. Mr. Sinclair intends to remain in England. I have followed the pattern of the rest of my family and lost my wager with you."

He presses a hand over his heart, and drops his chin to his chest feigning sadness. "Then, as we agreed in our wager, you are no longer obligated by our contract."

"Oh, pray, do not pretend to be wounded. Not when I can

see that you're barely able to keep from doing a jig in celebration of your freedom."

He laughs. "You are one of a kind, my lady. I cannot help but wonder if I have not gotten the wrong end of our wager after all."

"Whatever the case, I owe you a debt of gratitude for what you did for me all those many years ago. Thank you, my lord."

He bows graciously. What I see over his shoulder makes me wince. "Speaking of debts, my brothers have arrived. I do hope you will put them to work mucking out your stables to make them pay off their debts to you."

"Your wish is my command. Now that you mention it, I could use another groom or two." He chuckles and moves down the line.

His nephew, Lord Kinsworth, is next and bows elegantly over my hand, although his eyes flit eagerly in Maya's direction, so I mercifully pass him on to her. She greets him coolly, scarcely meeting his eyes. He tilts sideways to peer beneath her veil. "Would you be so good as to reserve the dinner dance for me? I should like to accompany you into dinner."

I miss her answer because Lord Ravencross stalks down the line looking as if he is about to draw swords with every gentleman in the room. He stops in front of Tess on my right, and bows curtly. "Would you like to ride in the morning?"

"I would." Tess curtsies prettily. "Please, do try to smile, my lord. You are frightening away the other girls' beaus."

"So long as I frighten any of yours, I'm satisfied."

"You might take a turn out in the garden to see how the wolves are doing. I daresay you are better suited to their company than in here."

His voice softens. "I will, if you'll meet me out there?"

She answers with a coy tilt of her head as she turns to greet our next guest.

His cheeks are still blotching pink as he bows to me and I feel for him. It cannot be easy being in love with Tess. It must be a little like trying to cage the wind.

Captain Grey is at Miss Stranje's side, serving as host. Lord Wyatt stands behind Georgie as if he's a footman or her fiancé, and refuses to leave. Earlier, I heard Georgie turn around and scold him. "Must you stand there like a sentinel? We are not engaged. It is not at all appropriate for you to hang over my shoulder."

"I don't care. Let them assume what they will. I refuse to abandon you to this riffraff."

"*Riffraff?* These people are not footpads and pickpockets. They're the *haut ton*, the cream of the *beau monde*—" The next guest in line, a young lieutenant, interrupts her argument.

Someone steals up behind me. Instinctively, I make certain my dagger is handy. It's Mr. Sinclair and he leans down over my shoulder. "How long must you stand in line?"

"Only a little longer, the line is beginning to slow."

"Don't forget the waltz belongs to me," he whispers, his words tickling my ear.

"I haven't forgotten." How can I when I'm counting every second until then?

"Good." He straightens and I miss his nearness. "I will be heartily glad when we return to Stranje House next week."

I'm as impatient to go home as he is. We are never alone here. Even though when we go back Mr. Sinclair will be residing at Captain Grey's cottage, it's bound to be better than here.

Mr. Peterson announces in a booming voice, "His Royal Majesty, Prince George."

A hush falls over the room. As one, everyone lowers into a curtsy or a bow, even Alexander. I half expect Lady Daneska to flounce in behind him. I wouldn't put it past her, except rumor has it she returned to France. No one is certain, we only know no one has seen her or Ghost since the explosion at Woolwich Naval Yards. According to Lady Castlereagh, Lady Daneska packed up and left town that afternoon. She sent a note to Prince George claiming Napoleon requested she return to Paris immediately.

My dance card is filled with the names of strangers. The evening whirls by in a flurry of dancing and polite conversation, and all the while I am wishing it was Alexander talking to me, Alexander pressing his palm against mine in the dance. Lord Harston stands up with me for a cotillion while Alexander broods on the sidelines. The last set before dinner is with Captain Maitland who thanks me for crying "bomb" at the unveiling.

As we circle one another, I ask him something that has bothered me ever since that day. "I've been told that it might have been more effective if I had cried out *hit the deck*."

"No." He turns to circle the corner lady. When he returns he assures me, "I doubt it would've changed the outcome. Having heard the command from a female rather than a seaman, the gentlemen would still have turned to see who was issuing the order."

Happily, I am also seated next to Alexander at dinner. Miss Stranje spared no expense. The table is spread with a meal worthy of a king. During the third course, Prince George rises to offer a toast. "To the brave young ladies of Stranje House. We are graced by your loveliness, charmed by your elegance, and most grateful you know when to shout a warning."

"Here! Here!" The Admiralty, Lord Castlereagh, and all the gentlemen that were on the platform that day, stand to honor us. All men who might have died. Alexander scoots back his chair and raises his glass along with theirs. "To the young ladies! To their health and long life!"

"Huzzah!"

When they finally sit, the Prince remains standing and lifts his cup again. "And to peace."

"To peace!" We all raise our glasses. This is no idle wish. No mere whim. All of my life we have been at war. England hungers for peace. Crippled and wounded soldiers haunt us on every street corner.

The clinking and cheering subsides, but still the Prince stands. "*Peace.*" He stares into the blood-colored wine in his cup. "We have been at war with Napoleon Bonaparte for eleven long years. Eleven years our men have given their lives. It is time to bring it to a close." He lifts his goblet. "I am pleased to tell you that I have agreed to meet with Napoleon in order to negotiate a settlement. In two weeks' time we may finally have the peace we have so desperately wanted."

Gasps ripple across the table.

Peace at what price?

Raised cups droop to half-mast. Only the Prince tosses back the remainder of his wine. A few naïve debutantes and their mothers follow suit. Suddenly the toast to our good health and long lives feels tainted, sullied by the shock of his willingness to meet with Napoleon.

Admiral Gambier sets down his cup and rises, wordlessly he bows to Miss Stranje and stomps out of the dining room. His wife jumps up from her chair hurriedly and rushes after him.

Lord Castlereagh, ever the diplomat, holds his cup steady. "To our prince."

There are murmurs of agreement, and cups raised out of obligation. His announcement dampens the mood. Forks resume working, lifting food to mouths, but at a much slower pace as if the roast beef has lost its savor. My appetite has disappeared entirely. I turn to Mr. Sinclair. "I doubt we shall be returning to Stranje House next week. It may be some time before we have that luxury."

He nods solemnly. "I shall remain here, too. No doubt, the Admiralty will be pleased to have my assistance for a few more weeks."

Our coming-out ball turns into mournful wake for England's future. Most of the guests understand the underlying menace beneath Prince George's announcement. Those that don't are left to wonder what the Prince intends to trade in exchange for a treaty with Emperor Napoleon. Everyone in England knows Napoleon will only be satisfied with complete power.

After dinner, Maya and Lord Kinsworth do their best to soothe our bruised spirits with a musical rendition of "Romeo and Juliet," a clever adaptation of Shakespeare's play as a ballad. From the very first note, their voices transport us into the hearts and minds of two innocent young lovers in Verona. We feel the joy of their first love. We swoon and sigh with the sweetness of their passion. But in the end, the song's anguished ending breaks our hearts and leaves us grieving even deeper.

Lady Jersey, *stalwart unmovable Lady Jersey*, breaks down in shoulder-shaking sobs. Lady de Lieven and dozens of other women sniff and blot their eyes with kerchiefs. During Maya and Lord Kinsworth's practices, we'd thought the song so perfect. *Divine. Magnificent.* A phenomenally moving piece. Now, following the Prince's announcement, it can only be judged a tragic mistake.

We enter the ballroom the way most people enter a funeral. All we need are black drapes and a dirge to complete the effect.

The musicians strike up a lively *Boulangère,* and I direct Mr. Sinclair's attention to Admiral Elphinstone's daughter. Poor lady has sat against the wall all evening. Mr. Sinclair invites her to join him in the set and I nod with approval. Lord Kinsworth partners me in the same dance. Every time I glance in Alexander's direction, he performs a proper leap. I know he is only doing it to be amusing and to cheer me up, but I can't help but notice he winces when he comes down on his broken toes.

The third dance is his favorite, a waltz. *Finally.* As we promenade, I can't help but detect a slight limp. "How are your broken toes?"

"Throbbing like the very devil. Thank you for asking."

"We ought to sit this one out. I don't want you to suffer."

"Some suffering is worth it."

"Be reasonable. It's only one waltz—"

"Take your position," he commands.

I sniff my annoyance at being ordered about and obediently poise my hand atop his shoulder. His gloved hand rests against my back, grazing the skin above my gown. Shivers race down my arms. I make a vain attempt to regain my composure along with my breath. "If you would prefer to not dance, I completely understand." The words come out much wispier than I intended.

"Not a chance. I wouldn't miss this for the world. After all, if Napoleon is coming to England this might be our last waltz."

I gather up my sternness. "Now you're just being maudlin. Your foot is injured. There are empty chairs along the wall." I urge him in that direction.

He holds me firmly in place. "Jane, I told you before I do not need a governess." He leans in menacingly close. "You are far too dangerous to be anyone's governess." He whispers this in so husky a tone, it sounds almost seductive. "Least of all mine."

"Alexander." I thump his shoulder. "The two-foot rule."

"You're blushing." He grins, pleased with himself, and sunlight bursts through the funereal fog. "See, I told you it was worth it."

I have the most scandalous desire to kiss him—right here on the ballroom floor, in front of the Prince of England, the Patronesses, and everyone else.

He stares down at me. "I know what that look means."

"W-what look?"

My uncivilized American whirls us into an efficient turn. "Your *kissing* look. Isn't that a balcony on the other side of those doors?"

"Why yes, Mr. Sinclair, I believe it is."

He waltzes us toward the balcony with tiny flecks of mischief doing a most improper jig in his eyes. Without breaking a step he twirls us out into the moonlight. I know what will happen next. It doesn't take a mastermind to guess.

Even so, I can barely breathe in anticipation. I don't have long to wait. The minute darkness cloaks us, his mouth covers mine. He kisses me and I forget all the other games in the world. I forget Napoleon, and Ghost, and Daneska. I even forget to worry about the future. When we're together like this, I believe anything is possible.

Believing is a lot like trusting.

And it is enough.

Afterword

Dear Reader,

I hope you had as much fun reading Lady Jane's story as I did writing it. Alexander Sinclair was a treat to write. Robert Fulton, the American inventor who developed the steamship, has always intrigued me. Including his fictional nephew, Mr. Sinclair, in the story provided an opportunity to showcase Fulton's phenomenal inventiveness. However, Alexander's quirky sense of humor came as a delightful surprise to me. Lady Jane mentions his prediction that newspapers would one day be printed using steam. December 1814, the London *Times* did indeed become the first newspaper printed via a steam-driven press.

While doing research for this story, I found the Lady Patronesses of Almack's also surprised me. It fascinated me to learn how enormously influential several of these beacons of society were in the political scene. The historical tidbits included in this story about their various backgrounds are all true. The only departure from fact is their friendship with Emma Stranje and my insinuation that Miss Stranje's father trained them in spy craft.

Throughout history, young women have served as spies. George Washington found young ladies extremely useful for information gathering during the Revolutionary War. The two most important spies in the American Civil War were young African American women, who transmitted crucial information to the North. This year a Danish researcher announced she has uncovered a spy ring consisting of more than seventy women active during the seventeenth century. Historically women have demonstrated an uncanny ability to influence the political landscape from behind the scenes.

The more research I do, the more I see that women have been discreetly altering history since the beginning of time, starting with Eve. Whether you realize it or not, you are changing the world around you, impacting the people in your life. You may not understand today the far-reaching effect you have. You may not even realize it in your lifetime. It might be revealed generations later, perhaps some researcher like me will notice that because you chose to do X, Y happened. But your family, friends, brothers, sisters, and children—they'll know. In fact, they feel the gift of your presence now. To some degree, so do we all.

Wishing you joy, peace, and love,

—Kathleen

Kathleen Baldwin loves hearing from readers. You can contact her through her website. You'll discover other goodies there: book-club guides, a Regency glossary, excerpts, and historical extras. www.KathleenBaldwin.com.

READING AND ACTIVITY GUIDE TO
REFUGE FOR MASTERMINDS
A Stranje House Novel

By Kathleen Baldwin
Ages 13-17; Grades 8-12

ABOUT THIS GUIDE

The Common Core State Standards–aligned questions and activities that follow are intended to enhance your reading of *Refuge for Masterminds*, the third title in the Stranje House series. Please feel free to adapt this content to suit the needs and interests of your students or reading group participants.

PRE-READING ACTIVITIES

1. *Refuge for Masterminds* can be read as a story about protecting a vital new technology from falling into the wrong hands. Make a brainstorm list of exciting technological innovations of the past 25 years. Invite each reader to write a short essay imagining what his or her life might be like without one of the technologies on the list. Or, write a 1–3 paragraph synopsis for a fictional story in which a real-life technology is put to frightening fictional misuse.

2. The novel is set in the Regency Era, the period during which Jane Austen, Percy Bysshe Shelley, Mary Shelley, E. T. A. Hoffmann, and Sir Walter Scott were writing. Consider this quotation from Jane Austen's 1815 novel *Emma*: "Seldom, very seldom, does complete truth belong to any human disclosure; seldom can it happen that something is not a little disguised or a little mistaken." Do readers agree or disagree with Austen's observation? Why or why not?

Supports Common Core State Standards: W.8.3, W.9-10.3, W.11-12.3; and SL.8.1, SL.9-10.1, SL.11-12.1

DEVELOPING READING & DISCUSSION SKILLS

1. Early in the novel, the narrator, Jane, admits to keeping a terrible secret. Before you discover the substance of the secret, how does this admission impact your sense of Jane's character? Despite her keeping a secret, what qualities make her seem trustworthy?

2. What are Jane's feelings toward Mr. Sinclair? Do you think it matters to Jane that he is American? How does the special invention in Mr. Sin-

clair's care affect the nature of his relationship to Jane? Describe the other romantic relationships depicted in the novel and the complexities they involve.

3. While discussing the task of protecting home, friends, and country, Maya counsels Jane, "These burdens are not yours alone to carry." (Chapter 3) Does Jane take Maya's advice? How is the question of whether to work in collaboration or in isolation a key motif in the novel? Cite examples from the story in your answer.

4. How is the England of this work of historical fiction in danger? Who are Lady Daneska, Ghost, and Napoleon, and how are they part of the threat to England? In Chapter 7, what dastardly act do the girls of Stranje House conclude Lady Daneska may attempt?

5. What relocation does Miss Stranje plan to enable her students to continue their work protecting the *Mary Isabella* and their country? How do Jane, Sera, Maya, Tess, and Georgie feel about her scheme?

6. In chapter 9, Jane observes that "The world is racing forward . . ." How might you explain the phrase in terms of the technology she seeks to protect, and in terms of the way Jane perceives the pace of events in her own life?

7. Who is Lord Harston? What threat does he pose to Jane? How does the author counterpoint Jane's personal vulnerability with the risks faced by her nation, particularly in scenes that play out in London society?

8. What is the "test" the girls must pass in Chapter 13? Who administers the test? What surprises Jane about the qualities of those assessing her and why does she believe she should fail their examination?

9. Midway through the novel, Jane wonders, "Can it be that all mothers possess the power to both break and mend the souls of their children?" (Chapter 13) What about her history makes her consider this question? How would you answer Jane? What comfort might you offer her?

10. Compare the characters and interrelationships of the Patronesses with those of the Stranje House students. Are Jane and her friends the successors to the Patronesses? Cite quotations from the novel in your answer.

11. Who is the traitor inside Stranje House? How do Miss Stranje and the girls treat her once they discover her identity? Do you agree with their strategy? Why or why not?

12. Why does Miss Stranje choose Haversmythe House for the girls' London

quarters? How does this choice attest to both her grit and her cleverness?

13. How do the Haversmythe House servants react to the arrival of the girls? How do Jane and the other girls react to being thrust into society?

14. Why does Jane feel especially connected to the runt of the wolf pup brood? In what ways do the puppies offer inspiration to Jane?

15. What terrifying dream wakens Tess in Chapter 26? What actions do her dreams cause the girls to take?

16. Who is Lady Castlereagh? How might you interpret her Chapter 27 statement "Sometimes . . . one must run with the foxes in order to keep the chickens safe" in terms of her own behavior, and in terms of the actions of others seeking to protect England? To which characters might this statement be most aptly applied?

17. Explain the series of events that take place on the docks. Does the girls' plan to thwart Daneska and Ghost go as planned? How and why is the plan altered? What is the result?

18. Though Jane criticizes her late parents and her brothers for gambling and disparages games of chance, might one look at her own behavior and lifestyle as one that involves a great deal of "gambling"? Explain your answer.

19. How has the relationship between Jane and Sinclair evolved by the end of the novel? What do you predict for their future? What do you hope for their future?

20. In the first chapter, Jane asks herself, ". . . what are we without trust?" How would you answer her question at the end of the novel?

Supports Common Core State Standards: RL.8.1-4, 9-10.1-5, 11-12.1-6; and SL.8.1, 3, 4; SL.9-10.1, 3, 4; SL.11-12.1, 3, 4.

DEVELOPING RESEARCH & WRITING SKILLS
Character

1. Throughout the novel, Jane struggles to understand how and why she is loved by her classmates, by Mr. Sinclair, and by Miss Stranje herself. From the perspective of Tess, Sera, Sinclair, Ms. Stranje, or another character, write a journal entry describing the qualities you appreciate in Jane and why you love her.

2. Jane has been ill-used by her late parents and her brothers. In the character of Lord Harston, write a letter to Jane releasing her from her en-

gagement and sharing your thoughts about the actions of her family members. Then, in the character of Jane, write a reply to Harston.

3. *Refuge for Masterminds* features several characters who seem socially limited due to their national origin (American, Sinclair) or their race (Indian, Maya). With friends or classmates, discuss whether such kinds of discrimination continue in our world today. Can contemporary readers glean any insight into ways to handle discriminatory treatment from the actions of the characters in the novel?

4. Discuss the term "mastermind" as it is used in the novel. What qualities do masterminds possess? Which characters in the story could be called masterminds? How is the term applied to both protagonists and antagonists? Can being a mastermind of grand schemes be detrimental when the same skills are applied to personal situations? Why or why not?

5. Many characters in the novel are "loners" in one way or another. In the character of Miss Stranje, Madame Cho, Lady Daneska, Mr. Sinclair, or another character of your choice, write a journal entry beginning with the words "I am lonely because . . ." or "I choose loneliness because . . ."

Genre and Setting

6. *Refuge for Masterminds* is an "alternate history," a work of fiction which combines real historical figures and events with fictional characters and plotlines. Create an "Alternate/History" timeline which shows the relationship between nineteenth-century European history, particularly dates related to Napoleon and Robert Fulton, and the events depicted in Kathleen Baldwin's version of the era.

7. This novel, perhaps more than previous books in this series, can also be identified as a Regency Romance. Go to the library or online to learn about the characteristics of this literary subgenre. Then, list at least four ways this story fits into this category.

8. Go to the library or online to learn more about the real history of Almack's Assembly Rooms and its Patronesses. Compile your findings in a short oral report to present to friends or classmates.

9. Go to the library or online to create a list of nineteenth-century inventions, such as the electric telegraph, the velocipede, the electromagnet, and Morse code. Create an informative poster describing your chosen invention, its inventor, and its impact on history.

Plot

10. In the opening chapter of the novel, Jane invokes the image of a "Gordian knot" as she ponders her troubles and responsibilities. Go to the library or online to find a definition of this term and its origins in mythology. Write a short essay explaining how this term is especially appropriate to the way Jane ultimately solves the problems with which she is presented.

11. At the novel's end, author Kathleen Baldwin has her fictional Prince George announce his intention to meet with Napoleon. Jane and the others wonder and worry what this will mean for England. How might the next novel in the series begin? What real and "altered" historical elements might you incorporate to move the series forward? What title would you give the next book? Write 2–3 paragraphs describing your ideas, followed by an outline of the first 5–10 chapters of the story.

Themes

12. In chapter 16, Jane observes the traitor Alice's deceptive behavior and observes that, "She won't change. People don't. My parents didn't. My brothers won't." Do you agree? Write a poem or song lyrics reflecting your own beliefs as to whether people are, or are not, capable of change.

13. Might this novel be read as an exploration of the questions: Why do we love? Why are we loved? What answers do characters in the story find for these questions? Do all human beings struggle to answer these questions in the context of their life and work? Write a new scene in which at least two characters from the novel ponder these questions.

14. In *Refuge for Masterminds*, Lady Jane Moore keeps it secret that she is from a family both noble and nearly bankrupt. These tensions within her identity are key thematic elements in the novel. Find a newspaper, magazine, or online article that offers an example of how socioeconomic differences contribute to local, national, or international conflict in the world today. Share selected articles with friends or classmates and make a list of possible strategies for ending such conflicts.

Supports Common Core State Standards: RL.8.4, RL.8.9; RL.9-10.4; RL.11-12.4; W.8.2-3, W.8.7-8; W.9-10.2-3, W.9-10.6-8; W.11-12.2-3, W.11-12.6-8; and SL.8.1, SL.8.4-5; SL.9-10.1-5 ; 11-12.1-5.